Catherine Cookson was born in East Jarrow and the place of her birth provides the background she so vividly creates in many of her novels. Although acclaimed as a regional writer – her novel THE ROUND TOWER won the Winifred Holtby Award for the best regional novel of 1968 – her readership spreads throughout the world. Her work has been translated into twelve languages and Corgi alone has 30,000,000 copies of her novels in print, including those written under the name of Catherine Marchant.

Mrs Cookson was born the illegitimate daughter of a poverty-stricken woman, Kate, whom she believed to be her older sister. Catherine began work in service but eventually moved south to Hastings where she met and married a local grammar school master. At the age of forty she began writing with great success about the lives of the working class people of the North-East with whom she had grown up, including her intriguing autobiography, OUR KATE. Her many bestselling novels have established her as one of the most popular of contemporary women novelists.

Mrs Cookson now lives in Northumberland.

Catherine Cookson

Feathers in the Fire

CORGI BOOKS

FEATHERS IN THE FIRE

A CORGI BOOK 0 552 09318 1

Originally published in Great Britain by
Macdonald & Co. (Publishers) Ltd.

PRINTING HISTORY
Macdonald edition published 1971
Corgi edition published 1973
Corgi edition reprinted 1974
Corgi edition reprinted 1975 (twice)
Corgi edition reprinted 1976 (twice)
Corgi edition reprinted 1977
Corgi edition reprinted 1978 (twice)
Corgi edition reprinted 1979
Corgi edition reprinted 1980
Corgi edition reissued 1980
Corgi edition reprinted 1981
Corgi edition reprinted 1983
Corgi edition reprinted 1984
Corgi edition reprinted 1985
Corgi edition reprinted 1986

This book is set in 10pt Plantin

Corgi Books are published by Transworld Publishers Ltd.,
61-63 Uxbridge Road, Ealing, London W5 5SA,
in Australia by Transworld Publishers (Aust.) Pty. Ltd.,
26 Harley Crescent, Condell Park, NSW 2200, and in New
Zealand by Transworld Publishers (N.Z.) Ltd., Cnr. Moselle
and Waipareira Avenues, Henderson, Auckland.

Made and printed in Great Britain by
Hunt Barnard Printing Ltd., Aylesbury, Bucks.

Contents

He born tethered to a byre
And he born upon silk,
Both suck the sap of milk;
Life above or below the sod
Viewed coldly by the Gods
Is but a feather in the fire.

Feathers in the Fire

Book One: 1881

One

'I tell you I know nothing about it. God in heaven! I've said it four times already, I didn't give it her.' Davie Armstrong turned on his father, crying, 'An' don't say again it couldn't get there on its own; bloody well I know it, it couldn't get there on its own.'

'All right, all right, lad.' It was his grandfather speaking and he came towards him and patted his arm and, his voice soothing, said, 'I believe you. We all believe you, lad.' He glanced fiercely at his daughter and his son-in-law; then, looking at his grandson again, whom he loved better than he'd ever loved his one and only offspring, he added quietly, 'But, you know, you'll be given the blame, for you were courtin' her.'

'Courtin'!' Davie glared at his grandfather now. 'I might have been knockin' on, but we weren't courtin'; except for a dance in the barn and taking her to the fair and a nudge on the quiet, that's all it's been. I tell you, she ran off from me when we were at the fair, an' I didn't see hilt or hair of her till I got back here, eight o'clock. It must have happened then; but I wasn't at t'other end of it, honest to God.' He now looked at his mother, who was standing at the far side of the trestle table that was laid for a meal. She had her hands on the lid of a black cooking pot set on a square of wood; her fingers were beating an unconscious tattoo on the handle, while her eyes, unblinking, were riveted on her son; and now she said, 'Come and sit up and have your meal, time is passin'.'

'I want no meal.'

Her hand lifted the lid and she banged it down on the table and, her voice harsh now, she said, 'You'll eat, we'll all eat. We've got to work, so we'll eat.' And at this she began ladling out thick mutton broth on to four plates. When they were filled

11

she cut large shives of crusty bread and stuck one in the middle of each plate, which she then placed at each side of the table.

Ned Armstrong sat down, and old Sep sat down, but Davie still stood. He had his back pressed to the dresser, his square chin was thrust out and stiff with the tightness of his jaw bones. His mother said to him quietly, 'You know I won't sit till you're sat, so how long do you intend to keep me standin'?'

His head drooped to his chest, his lips pushed against each other as he sucked them inwards; then, thrusting his body from its support, he came to the table and sat down, but not before banging the high rail-back wooden chair hard on the stone floor.

Winnie Armstrong now sat down and picked up a spoon, and they all began to eat, and only the munching and the slopping of the stew filled the silence until old Sep, putting his spoon down on the bare table and placing his hands one each side of his plate, leant across towards his son-in-law and said, 'You know summat, I smell a rat.'

'How?' asked Ned, gulping on a mouthful of food, his spoon held in mid air.

'Geary, that's how, Geary.' The old man's voice was low and he jerked his head back and slanted his gaze in the direction of the fireplace and the wall to the side of it, the wall that divided their cottage from the Gearys'. Then, casting a glance, first at his daughter Winnie, and then at his grandson, he brought his attention back to Ned and said softly, 'He finds their Molly has fallen an' what does he do? He goes to the master and demands that she be chastised . . . flayed! There's no woman been flayed on this farm since I was a lad sixty odd years gone, and then it was the master's grandfather what did it, and then he had to be roaring drunk afore he could tackle it. You mind, I've told you 'bout Nellie Cassidy pinching the gold retriever watch, and he gave her the option of goin' along the line or standin' a flaying. She took the flaying. But Geary there' – he again jerked his head back – 'who's got no feelin' for either God, man, or beast, but he doesn't lift a hand to her.' He now turned and looked at Davie and said, 'Lad, just think; imagine that house and Molly comin' in and sayin' she's fallen; what do you think he'd do?'

Davie looked at his grandfather, then answered slowly, 'Knock hell out of her.'

'Aye, you've said it, lad, knock hell out of her and take joy in doin' it. But he doesn't knock hell out of her, he goes to the master and asks him to do it for him . . . I tell you, I smell a rat.'

The three men looked at each other; then they turned their gaze on Winnie and she stared back at them for a moment before saying, 'Well, you've added up two and one, not two and two, you haven't reached four yet, so what do you make of it?'

Her eyes came to rest on her son, and Davie answered her, 'I don't know, but I mean to find out.'

'Do' – she nodded her grey head slowly at him – 'but go about things quietly. Remember, to all intents and purposes it's you who are named; never was it so silently done, but never so clearly.'

As she rose from the table she said to no one in particular, 'Now I must be goin'. Flood, storm, or tempest, the master will want to eat. But how I'm goin' to put up with that one flitting about me in the kitchen I just don't know. I've always said she was a flighty-cum-jaunting-Sunday. I told you' – she nodded towards her husband – 'didn't I, I told you I caught her dancin' in the sitting-room to the musical box when the mistress was out. Dancin', mind, in the mistress's sitting-room.'

'Aw, Ma.' Davie's chair scraped back over the stone floor as he got to his feet and, confronting his mother across the table, he said, 'Let's get things straight. There's no harm in a bit of dancing.'

'I'm not sayin' there is, but there's a time and a place for everything. And it's how you dance. There she was with her skirt held right above her knees like any quay trollop.'

'Quay trollop!' Sep looked up at his daughter and, his good humour returning, he slapped out at her thigh with his hand as he repeated, 'Quay trollop? You wouldn't know a quay trollop, me girl, if you saw one.'

'Wouldn't I, Pa?'

'No, you wouldn't; so go on and get about your business.'

'I'm goin'.' She nodded her head sharply at him. 'And you get about your business and see that you wash them plates up properly and don't leave them stuck with thick grease.' And on this she went out to her work.

The three men, left alone, said no word to each other, but Ned got up and, going to the mantelpiece, took from a rack two clay pipes and, picking out a long twist of brown baccy from a jar standing near, he cut two pieces off the end, then handed one of them together with a pipe to his father-in-law. When he sat down again, each worked the knot of tobacco loose by grinding it with the stub of his left hand into the palm of his right hand. When the tobacco was sufficiently shredded, almost simultaneously they filled their pipes and Ned lit them from the same spill.

While this was going on Davie had been standing looking out of the small window and along the mud-dried road that curved in front of the house to end abruptly, cut off by a railing that circled a dark mass of trees.

The Armstrongs' cottage was the end one of the three labourers' cottages farthest from the farmhouse, which was a hundred yards away. They had been built ninety years ago when the new additions had been made to the farm. There were no gardens at the front, but at the back of each was a piece of land as wide as the cottage, which was sixteen feet. It ran in a narrow strip for about seventy feet downhill to the brook which supplied water for all purposes. The ashes from their fires formed dry middens, the contents of which, together with that from the house, was collected once a week by a farmcart and dumped in the old workings of a lead mine half a mile away.

Davie had been born in this cottage, and up till this very day he had considered himself lucky to have been brought up on this particular farm, for the master, although strict in all ways, and narrow and churchy in his views, was a go-ahead progressive employer, as his efforts at modern sanitation proved – no stinking cesspools and middens near the house for him. He had once overheard him say, the excrement from animals was sweet compared to that of humans, and it was the badness in humans that made it as it was. Moreover the master had not allowed him to start work until he was six. No child on the farm started work until he was six, even at scarecrowing. And then, since the master took over, twenty years ago, every child on the farm attended Sunday School, and this was long afore school going was made compulsory. He had been very strict about them all going to Sunday School, and so they all learned their letters, those who could take them in. He himself had taken them in, sucked them in, he had lapped it all up. He still did; the older he got the more he knew there was to learn. He was proud of what knowledge he had; he could count, he could add and subtract, he could write a letter. However, he had never yet written a real letter to anyone, there was nobody to write to, but if it ever came to pass that he had to write a letter he would be capable of doing it. And he could read, oh aye, he could read.

He had got this far in book learning because he was interested. He wanted to learn something else besides milking cows and the other work on a farm, and Parson Hedley was out to learn anybody who wanted to learn. Not so Parson Wainwright; oh no, old-nose-in-the-air Wainwright only gave you his blessing when he knew how much money you were likely to leave to the church, or, to put it plainly, to him.

Parson Hedley had said only last week, 'I'm going to lend you a book by Mr Dickens, Davie; it is called *Great Expectations*. And you know, Davie,' he had added, 'that is a very good title, *Great Expectations*; it's based on hope, and hope is a mighty fine thing to carry you through. And by the way,' he had ended, 'bring Molly to the readings. She hasn't been for a long time and she was getting along fine.'

Bring Molly to the readings! She hasn't been for a long time. No, Molly had been otherwise occupied. Blast her! . . . But with who? Who? His granda was right about smelling a rat. There was a big stink here somewhere. Nothing escaped his granda.

He turned slowly and looked at him. He was puffing quietly at his pipe, his eyes were closed, his shoulders stooped; he looked old, worn out, yet mentally Davie knew he was much more alert, even at his age, than was his son-in-law.

He cared deeply for his grandfather and he always felt a pang of anxiety when he saw him sitting like this, his body sagging, his lids drooped, for then that vital spark of life which showed in his eyes was hidden. He said flatly, 'I'm off,' and at this his grandfather opened his eyes, his father lifted his head, and they both said, 'Aye,' and he went out of the front door on to the road.

He passed the Geary house, which was strangely quiet today. It wasn't very often he passed this door without hearing Cassy Geary bawling at one or the other. If it wasn't her husband it was the two lads, or Molly. It was worse before the three younger lasses went into service. The hardest worked part about Mrs Geary, he considered, was her mouth.

He passed the next house, which was always quiet, having only Will Curran in it. But even when Mrs Curran had been alive, and their grown-up son and daughter in the house, it had always been quiet; Will Curran was a domineering man who would be obeyed. He wanted to be a master did Will Curran, and he practised it hard under his own roof. His son had run off to sea and his daughter had done a moonlight flit with a fellow from across the valley.

15

He went on down the road and into the farmyard.

Everything here looked neat and spruce, especially since the mud was baked hard. There had been no rain to speak of for weeks, but it wouldn't be long before they had it for the clouds were breaking up. He passed the house lying back to the left of him, then turned at right angles into the long yard that lay between the byres and barn at one side and the stables and store sheds at the other. He stepped over the channel of water which ran down the middle of the yard. Fed by inlets from the byres, it took the main part of the slush and muck.

When he entered the byres Fred Geary was already at work, which was unusual so early in the afternoon session. The man turned his small thin body and looked towards him, but didn't speak, and Davie hesitated just within the doorway, wondering what he should do. His first impulse was to go up to him and say, 'Look here; you can think what you like, but I know nowt about it.' But he thought better of it; what had to be said he would let come from him first.

But when fifteen minutes had passed and Geary had said no word to him, good, bad, or indifferent, he covertly watched him as he clumped back and forth to the dairy. He still had the explosive look on his face that had been noticeable when they were all called into the barn to witness the chastisement . . .

The chastisement. He couldn't get over it. When the bell had rung he had dashed from the beet field thinking there was a fire, for the bell was only rung to gather them together for the march to church on a Sunday or in case of fire or Flood; it was also rung, merrily for a birth, slowly for a death. But this morning his granda had been pulling it at the rate he did on Sundays, and so he had cried at him, 'What's up?' His granda had merely pointed along to the barn.

When he had reached the barn it was to see the master and Molly standing up on the weighing platform, and below them the five Gearys, Will Curran, his own mother and father, and the mistress and Miss Jane. The master had looked down on Miss Jane and ordered, 'Go to the house and stay there,' and the girl had hesitated a moment before doing as he bade her. Then the master had said, 'There is trouble among us . . . Fred' – he had nodded towards Geary – 'Fred has come to me with bad news concerning his daugh– Molly here.' He had hesitated over his words, which was unusual for the master, but it was plain he had no stomach for what he was about to do. Then he continued, 'He tells me she's in trouble and will not name the man, and because of her stubbornness he has asked me to chastise her. I have no heart for this, but he demands it be done as was usual . . . ' It was at this point that his granda had cried out, 'But them days are past, Master!' and the master had replied, 'I have already pointed this out to Fred.' 'Then why do it, Master?' his granda had dared to question, and the master's reply was, 'If I don't he will take her in hand himself, and I think in this case I am the lesser of two evils.'

At this he had asked Molly again to name the man, but all she had done was to shake her head. And then he had told her to grab hold of the stanchion post and he had laid his horsewhip across her back. She had on a cotton blouse and although his hand was not heavy she jerked at each of the five lashes, especially the last, for the tail-end of the thong caught her on the bare neck.

When it was over Molly had walked away with her head down, she had not cried. He had stared after her helplessly. The whole thing had come upon him so suddenly he couldn't believe it had happened. Everybody seemed stunned, all except Geary, who showed no satisfaction in the outdated punishment he had demanded.

He had wondered at the time why Geary's big-mouthed, slovenly wife hadn't done something to prevent the whole business; but no, she had just stood there and watched her seventeen-year-old daughter being made a public spectacle.

When he came to look at the affair from a distance he couldn't make it out, because Cassy Geary was the one to spew mouthfuls of abuse on anybody who laid a finger on a member of her family, even when they were all bairns together and in a straight barnyard fight . . . As his granda said, there was a smelly rat here somewhere. But where?

When he had finished his work in the byres he went out and across the yard to the harness room. There, young Mickey Geary was sitting on a high bench with his back towards the wood-panelled walls, and he was almost entirely obliterated by a saddle arched across his knees. His face was bright and cheery. What he had witnessed happening to his sister this morning had apparently left no impression on him, for he said airily, 'Want me to come now, Davie?'

'You finished that?'

'All but.'

'You've been some time; you started it first thing.'

'Aye, but I've cleaned it bonny.'

Davie lifted the saddle away from the boy and examined it, then nodded and said, 'It'll do.'

'We goin' for the cows?'

'Aye.'

The child slipped agilely from the bench on to the floor, where his diminutive height and thinness questioned his eight years, but for all his smallness he was a bright little fellow and a favourite with Davie, or had been up till today. Now he hated the whole job lot of Gearys.

As Mickey trotted beside him he chatted. 'You goin' to make up some polish the night, we're nearly out, Davie?'

'We'll see.'

'Can I help you? Can I stir the wax, you said I could last time?'

'We'll see.'

'When is Primrose gona calf?'

'Soon.'

They went out of the farmyard into the road, through a gap in a dry-stone wall opposite, across a field and over a stile towards the steep hill they called The Ridge. The grass was slippery and Mickey measured his length once or twice, but Davie didn't stop until the small voice suddenly said, 'Ee bugger! I'm not 'alf hungry, me bloody belly thinks me throat's cut.'

Another time this would have brought a smothered laugh from Davie and he would have cuffed the boy's ear while admonishing him, but now he just admonished him sternly, saying, 'Let the master hear you an' that language an' he'll sort you out.' Then staring down into the small round face, he asked, 'Didn't you have no dinner?'

'No. Me ma never made none, she's in a hell of a sweat. Everybody is . . . you gona marry our Molly?'

Davie's face stretched; his whole body stretched, and before he could say anything the boy backed away a step, saying, 'Well, I only axed, 'cos our Johnnie said you had a shy on her.'

'Well, you can tell Johnnie to keep his mouth shut,' he bellowed at the lad, then turned away and closed his eyes for a moment before tramping sharply on again.

On the top of the ridge he waited for the boy to catch up. From where he stood he could see a great expanse of land beyond the boundary of the farm. To the right of him were hills, young mountains some of them; showing green, and brown, with here and there great black patches, telling scars of dead lead mines. To the left the land rolled into moorland flatness on its way to Haltwhistle and the South Tyne. In front of him, eight miles as the crow flew, twelve miles by the twisting road, lay Allendale in its nest of moors.

Even in the winter he always paused at this spot to breathe in the air, it seemed purer from up here. Today, a late hot summer day, it was thin and clean and scoured his ribs as he drew it inwards, it was almost as good he considered as the air you breathed from the top of Shale Tor.

Mickey, crawling to his side on all fours, straightened himself and gasped, 'Whew! I'm out of puff. It's all slack. When the rain comes I bet it'll be claggy,' and Davie, now looking down at him, half smiled and cuffed his ear gently, and the boy laughed and ran ahead of him down the slope and into the field where the cattle were grazing.

They did not bring the cattle back the way they had come, but by a narrow track that skirted the hill and finally led across the twenty-acre field and into the farm by the back road.

But before they came to the field they had to pass along a road so narrow that the cattle walked in single file. Lowing and ambling at their own pace, their bags almost touching the ground, swinging rhythmically from side to side, they went.

More out of habit than in any effort at persuasion, Davie ambled along behind the last stragglers, crying, 'Git up! Git up there! Move Daisy! You Bella, move! Move I say!' and when he stopped issuing his fruitless commands, Mickey took them up, 'Hie-up there! Hie-up there Daisy! Hie-up you Bella! Get along, Vicky, along you get.'

As Mickey's piping went on Davie happened to glance to his right beyond a low scrub hedge where the land fell away over what was termed the shale field. It was a large strip of land, almost on the north boundary of the farm and in most parts useless because of the outcrops of rock and shale shelves protruding from the ground. Grass did grow in the far corner of the field; contrarily a couple of acres gave luscious grass; perhaps it had something to do with its proximity to the old malt house.

The malt house was in ruins; it had been a ruin when Davie's grandfather was a boy. One section alone remained. This had been the habitation, but now the ground floor was used as a shelter for the horses in rough weather, when the mares and their foals were brought out here to grass. Halfway across the ground floor an open stairway led to a gallery, which had once, in turn, led to rooms which adjoined the malt house. But now all that remained of these was a wall of doors; the gallery itself was given over to storage of hay and bags of oats.

What had drawn his attention to the malt house was the figure running in that direction; although some distance away he recognised the slight form of Miss Jane. She was holding her skirt in both hands, and her legs were leaping over the ground; from this distance she put him in mind of a two-legged deer. He thought she was going to the mare and foal, the foal being at the pretty enticing stage of four weeks, but when he saw her pass them and make for the malt house he stopped. Mickey stopped too, and, his small face screwing up, he exclaimed, 'Yon's Miss Jane, an', aw look, she's fallin' bad!'

When seconds passed and the form on the ground made no move to get up Davie said quickly to the boy, 'Take them on, I'll go down and see what's wrong with her.'

He now hurried back down the narrow path to where the hedge was thinnest and, having pushed his way through, he ran quickly across the field; but before he had covered half the distance he saw his young mistress get to her feet and start running again, not so quickly now and slightly erratic.

When he reached the front of the house, which was paved with large flags of natural stone and was on the side facing away from the field, he paused for a moment before walking quietly to the doorless gap. The stanchion was rubbed smooth in one part by the horses' hides; the floor inside was of stone too but the flags were smaller and covered with horses' droppings. The atmosphere was hot and dim and the odour pungent.

He looked about him, then upwards to the railless gallery at the sound of stifled sobbing came from the hay. Quickly he ascended the open stairs to the floor above.

'Miss Jane!'

There was no answer.

'Miss Jane! Are you hurt? It's me, Davie. Are you hurt?'

He walked quietly and slowly towards the hay. She was lying deep in it, and after a moment she turned on her side and looked up at him. Her face was awash with tears, her mouth was wide and her tongue jerking on each sob.

'What is it? Have you hurt yourself?' He dropped on to his hunkers beside her, and she closed her eyes and shook her head.

20

'You fell, I saw you fall; I was takin' the cattle in. Are you all right, Miss Jane?'

She nodded her head while she gulped.

'You're sure you're not hurt?'

'No. No, Davie.' Her voice was a cracked whisper. Then she looked at her knees that were exposed by her rumpled skirt. One grey stocking was torn and showed scraped flesh oozing specks of blood, and as she eased the stocking off the skin she muttered, 'I'm not crying because I fell, but because Father . . . Father whipped Molly. He whipped her, Davie . . . you saw . . .'

He blinked his eyes and looked down and away from her, then said, 'The master told you to go to the house. Anyway, it's done, over, so forget about it.'

'I can't, Davie. I keep thinking, and just can't believe that Father . . .'

When she began to cry again, he said briskly, 'Now, now. Come on, dry your eyes and come away home. The mistress will be wondering, it's on your dinner-time.'

'No.' She shook her head. 'Father's gone into Hexham; he . . . he didn't want any dinner, nor . . . nor did Mother.'

'Well, that doesn't mean because they don't eat you've got to starve. Come on now, Miss Jane, up with you!'

He was about to rise from his hunkers, he had his hand extended towards her, when there came to them to unmistakable sound of horse's hooves on the stone paving. The sound in itself should not have caused any surprise for was there not a mare and her foal in the field, but this sound was of a single animal and it had a rider. When the order came for it to stop he recognised the voice. And he wasn't alone in his recognition; Jane was staring towards the glassless window at the end of the gallery. Then she quickly turned her head towards Davie, and he was on the point of saying, 'It's the master,' when a question flashed through his brain: why should the master, who was supposed to be in Hexham, which was in the opposite direction from this, be coming into the malt house?

He put his hand out and pressed Jane back into the hay with a warning to be quiet, and by moving his head just the slightest he could see, around the mound of hay and between the sacks, the figure of his master framed in the doorless aperture. He was standing with his back towards the room looking out.

The master was waiting for somebody but he was wearing his

town coat, three-quarter length, slightly flared; it had a velvet collar and was cut to his figure. His brown leather gaiters were shining like burnished copper, thanks to the elbow grease of young Mickey Geary. As the riding crop hit the leather the crack startled not only Miss Jane but also himself, and for a moment he almost lost his balance.

When a new sound broke the silence he put his fingers to his lips and warned his young mistress to silence. The sound was of light running steps. The steps turned the corner; then a small plump figure came flying straight into the arms of the waiting man.

The grim tautness of his body was broken by the smothered gasp from his side; the young mistress had moved. She was seeing what he was seeing; her mouth was dropping into a wide gape, and he knew within a second there would issue from it a cry, and then all hell would be let loose, for if he went down there God alone knew what he would do to either of them. But what was equally important, if they looked up and saw him here in the straw with the young mistress their mucky minds would be capable of putting two and two together. The young mistress was but twelve but that wouldn't matter when some people were looking for ways to defend themselves.

His hand gripped her jaw tightly and, staring down into her eyes, he moved his head twice. Then the voice from below brought his head round, for his master was speaking and using words of passion that a man should use only in the darkness of the night, and he finished them with 'Oh! Molly, Molly my love, forgive me. How could I! How could I! To beat your flesh like that! Oh! my sweetie, my sweetie.'

'Aw, don't you worry, Master, don't you worry your head. Each stroke was like a kiss 'cos it came from you.'

The girl's voice was as impassioned as the man's, and Davie now tried to press Jane back into the hay so that her eyes should not witness her father's actions, for the master had pulled down Molly Geary's blouse and was moving his lips over her flesh like a man demented. He closed his eyes against the red flick of the tongue as it washed the weals and to the girl's flung back head, her face filled with unholy ecstasy.

When he next looked at them the master was holding her tight, his hands were on her buttocks pressing her into him, while he talked rapidly: 'Your father, he came last night. He didn't come out in the open, he's too sly for that. "I've asked her to name the man," he said, "and she won't." Do you realise, Molly, he's known all along?'

'Aye, Master, I do now. But I didn't till this mornin' when I vomited and he came out with it, not naming you, but hinting at it. It's money he's after, an' a house . . . new built, separate.'

'He'll get both if he's sensible, give him to understand that. I won't be blackmailed, but I'll do anything, you know I will . . . '

There were more words, too low now for Davie to hear, but they caused Molly Geary to bury her face in the master's chest, then suddenly to fling her arms around his neck and cover his mouth with her own while her body moved on his like that of any whore on market day.

His own body was writhing with rage, and again he was only checked from jumping up and diving down the stairs by a movement from the wide-staring-eyed girl at his side. She had her own hand tightly across her mouth now, but she was no longer crying. He had always thought she had a fine pair of eyes, Miss Jane, the best feature of her face, and they would likely stand her in good stead later on if she grew up as plain as she was now. The look in her eyes had been like a picture mirroring the simplicity of her nature; now the look was gone, never, he guessed, to return. It was a known fact among them all that she worshipped the master. It was also a known fact that she was a disappointment to him for he had wanted a son; but he was never harsh with her, yet not tender, and up till now his unspoken wish had been her law. As he looked down into her face he likened the look in her eyes to that of a young fledgling being rent by a hawk.

And the master was a hawk, a buzzard, a vulture. God Almighty! and to think how he had always looked up to and respected him . . . His train of thought was punctured by his master's voice coming to him clearly now, saying, 'You'll have to come out in the open and name a man, for you must marry, the child must have a name. Whom do you choose?'

'Davie, Master.'

'Yes, I thought so.'

'Aw Master, Master, no need to look like that, none, for no matter whose name I take there'll only ever be you; always remember that, there'll only ever be you, Master.'

They were joined again, and the silence that settled on the ruined house was stupefying; the place was filled with heavy oppressive air like that which comes before a great storm. And

23

the storm might have broken at this point had not young Jane's hand come on his; and now there was a share of the horror and hurt in her eyes for him. They both turned their heads and gazed down on the locked couple below as the master said, 'I'll tell him tonight.'

'What if he won't, Master?' This was the first note of uncertainty she had expressed.

'He'll do as he's bid, leave it to me. Go now, I should be in Hexham, and I'm late, I must hurry. But – ' His voice changed and, his tone like that of a young ardent lover, he ended, 'how will I ever do without you, how will I manage, what will I do when you are at the beck and call of a husband?'

'Aw, don't worry your head, Master; leave it to me, I'll fix that.' Her reassurance could have come from a mature woman, not a girl of seventeen.

They embraced once more, then she went out, backing from him, buttoning her blouse as she did so.

Two minutes later, her master followed her.

When the sound of the horse's hooves going over the flagstones faded away he got to his feet; his whole body was trembling, his legs felt weak. He had never experienced such a feeling in him before. He wanted to hit out. But at what? He had a desire to kill that bitch . . . and the master an' all. They were a conniving pair of devils. Be told off to marry her, would he? By God! not as long as he had breath and legs.

'Davie!'

Although he had been looking at the girl he hadn't been conscious of her. Now, seeing her stricken face, he swallowed to clear the dryness from his throat and muttered thickly, 'Don't worry, Miss, don't worry.'

'But Father, and . . . and – ' when she shook her head desperately and bowed it, he put his hand out and, taking her arm, drew her upwards, saying, 'Get away back to the house; the mistress will be missin' you.'

'Oh Davie!'

Now she was holding her face with both hands and her mouth was pressed into a soft shapeless gap as she whimpered, 'Mother! If Mother gets to know. Oh! Davie . . . what must I do?'

'You know what to do, don't tell her, tell nobody.'

'Nobody?'

'No, nobody; least of all the mistress, for you know she's in a condition.'

Jane stared up at the young man whom she could remember since she first remembered anything. He was as familiar to her as were her parents, perhaps more familiar than her father because he had always been kind to her, jolly. He used to make her laugh. He had said that her mother was in a condition as if he was telling her something. She knew all about such conditions; conception and birth were natural to her, she had watched them both. It was something that God made happen to animals, but she hadn't, up to a few minutes ago, associated it with people. Even her mother's rising stomach hadn't caused her to liken 'the condition' to Betsy, Rene, Flo and Jessie, who were all in calf. It was a different condition, a condition as yet not probed. She had not begun her periods, and she had no companion of her own age with whom to discuss the secrets of the body. Her mother did not talk of such things or encourage her to probe. It was sufficient that her mother loved her, and she gave her great affection in return because she knew that the love her mother had for her was the same as she herself had for her father, and not to get a love returned was a very painful thing, so she was always extra affectionate to her mother no matter how she felt.

But now she was probing and had opened a deep well in her mind that smelt. She saw pictured in it the thing that happened between her mother and father, the private thing. But she also saw the same thing happening between her father and Molly.

She knew Molly as well as she knew Davie. Molly had been a kind of elder sister to her. Although there was only five years between them Molly had taken care of her when she was small, and had often washed and dressed her. But when she was seven years old her mother decreed that she should do these things for herself. She had also pointed out at that time too the difference in their stations. So Molly had been relegated to helping in the kitchen and doing the housework . . . and now Molly and her father . . . She turned and threw herself face downwards on the hay again. But almost immediately Davie's voice roused her, crying sharply, 'Come on! Come on now, none of that. An' I've got to be on me way. It's milkin' time, they'll be crying out for me. Come on now, get up.'

He pulled her none too gently to her feet and pressed her forward across the balcony and down the stairs, and when they were once more in the open he said, 'Go on over there and wash your face in the brook, then make your way home an' leave things as they are, they'll work out . . . Do you hear me?'

When she didn't speak he bent down to her and said gently, 'Miss Jane, did you hear what I said?'

She lifted her face to him but still she didn't speak; then turning, she walked from him over the grass and towards the brook. And he went up towards the track again, but he didn't run, nor even hurry, he was too stunned to do either. He felt like a dolt. She had made a monkey out of him. He had denied courting her for he hadn't been over fresh in his advances; she was saucy and so he had kept her guessing. But inside he had courted her; he had even seen them married and got as far as wondering if the master would build them a new cottage . . . The master! He spat vehemently on to the grass.

'I was right then.'

'Aye, you were right, Granda.'

'My God! I still can't believe it. But then, you know your ma's always said she was a scut. Your ma's never far out when she's judgin' people. Your ma's told us on the quiet that she was at it when she was little more than a bairn, not thirteen. She caught her on with young John Curran and she scattered the pair of them. It's a wonder to me she's not had your trousers down long afore now, lad.'

'Aw, Granda, what do you take me for?'

'A man, lad; that's all, just a man. But you're probably late in startin'. It's them books. I was sayin' to Ned only this dinner gone it's them books, an' Parson Hedley. But then the master's a read man an' all, but it hasn't stopped him. No begod! it hasn't stopped him. But then it's his time of life; turned forty, something happens to you, lad.' He nodded at his grandson and his eyes stretched in owl-like wisdom. 'You have the urge to plough another field. At least that's how the ordinary man feels. But then the master, I didn't take him for no ordinary man. I've followed him to church Sunday, year after year, sunshine and shadow, sleet and snow, not because I wanted to hear old Wainwright but because I was following the pattern of a good man, a man o' God. Aye, I always thought him an upright man o' God.'

'Upright man of God!' Davie was walking the kitchen floor: six strides from the door to the settle, around the table, four

26

strides back to the door; here his fingers lifted the latch, then dropped it again, click-click, click-click. After he had repeated the pattern four times he turned fiercely and cried at his grandfather, 'Man of God! and coolly planning to shove the blame on me, the both of them. If you could have heard them. How in the name of heaven I didn't show meself I'll never know.'

'It's a wonder they didn't spot you,' said Sep, ' 'cos by the sound of it that was their nest. An' very comfortable. An' who of us goes down there, except young Johnnie or Mickey to see to a mother and foal, and the cart once a week with the fodder. Stop prancing lad,' he said now; 'go on, go back to your work. Say nowt to nobody; we'll talk this over when your ma and da come in . . . he won't be back from Hexham afore seven and that'll give us time to think . . .'

By seven o'clock they had thought a great deal, but it hadn't got them very far, and the four of them were sitting in the kitchen now waiting for the summons to the house. For countless times in the last half-hour Winnie had exclaimed, 'I cannot believe it, the master, and him a God-fearing man.' And now it was not Davie but her father who turned on her harshly, crying, 'Aw, have sense, girl, have sense. God fearin'? Even God is no longer afeared when the body cries its needs.'

'Oh Da! stop talkin' such.'

'I'll stop talkin' such when the Almighty decides to change the pattern.'

Ned now spoke. He looked at his son from where he was sitting in the corner of the settle, his arms folded across his chest, and he said in a conciliatory tone, 'I would let him have his say, Davie, and whatever you answer, I mean when you tell him you're not for havin' it, do it quietly because we don't want no trouble. What I mean is . . .'

'What you mean is – ' Davie's voice was barking, but it was brought tones lower by wild gestures from his mother with her arms flung out towards the wall, indicating that it had ears, the ears of the Gearys. 'What you mean is that he could give us all the push, bonded or not bonded. Well, here's one that needs no push, Da, 'cos I'm goin'.' He got to his feet now, staring back into the three pairs of eyes riveted on him, and his mouth worked for a moment before he added, 'The world's wide, there's things out there I've never dreamed of, so . . . so I'm goin'.'

27

'Aw no. No.' Winnie came towards him, her two hands joined together as if in supplicating prayer. 'No, boy, no, don't go as far as that. Think, now think.' She tried to press him into a seat, but he pushed her away, then looked at her, half in apology, and, his voice toned down, he said, 'It'll be all right; he can't do anything to you if I go. He wouldn't, it would be cuttin' off his nose to spite his face. Where would he get another like you, cooking, cleaning, dairy, the lot? You do the work of two and a half women.'

Winnie now bowed her head to the side, and it was as if she were, by her gesture, indicating her husband and his rheumaticky twisted hands. Rheumatism had struck him early, whereas her father had reached the middle fifties before his joints had knotted. But Ned wasn't of the stamina of her father; he suffered greatly from his aches, and had done for the past ten years. And now at forty-three the winters presented a nightmare; wet sacks over his head and shoulders; feet often so swollen and painful that his boots had to be eased off them, had taken an early toll.

Four generations of the Armstrongs had worked on Cock Shield Farm. It was their home, their place, and now Davie was rocking the very foundations of their livelihood because, like herself, he did much more than his share, and between them they made up for any slackness on Ned's part and the fact that her father had to be cared for. True, the old 'un still did odd helpful jobs here and there about the place, in the summer that is, but in the winter he didn't earn the one and sixpence pension the master gave him. But the master made no complaint because most of the work he used to do Davie had taken on. Besides his own work as second cowman, Davie acted as coachman when the master and mistress went in style on their twice yearly visits to The Manor, he took a turn on the plough, he saw to the hunters; there wasn't a job on the place he didn't turn his hand to. He had done a fourteen-hour day for years and rarely grumbled, because he was young and strong and willing; but he was also stubborn, hot tempered, and had ideas in his head beyond those of his station, and all through Parson Hedley and his books.

Davie knew they were all looking at him, their thoughts hard on him, but he continued to stare out of the window until Johnnie, Fred Geary's eldest son, aged ten, came running down the road.

As he knocked on the door the boy called, 'Davie! Davie!'

Slowly Davie moved a few paces towards the door, lifted the latch and looked down at the boy.

'Master's back, Davie, and askin' for you. He says come to the office.'

When Davie didn't answer him, the boy repeated, 'He's askin' for you now, the master.'

'All right, all right.' His voice was tight and thick. 'I'll be along.' They nodded at each other; then Davie turned and looked at his people, all standing now.

His mother said tentatively, 'I'd put a clean smock on.'

At this he tore off his soiled smock, threw it on the floor, then swung round from them and went out, banging the door behind him.

As he walked down the dusty road in the direction of the farmyard his angry gaze lifted towards the house. He had always liked the farmhouse, the shape of it, the mellowness of it; it was the best of its kind for fifty miles in any direction you went. The old part of it dated back to 1699 and had three storeys. The lower floor was now the dining-room; it was a very large room. Above it the same space was divided into a bedroom and two small rooms, one used as the master's dressing-room and one as a night water closet. Above these there had been two attics, but the dividing wall had been pulled down to form a large store-room for all the odds and ends of the house.

The new part of the farmhouse, which was built in 1794, had only two storeys, and the bedrooms were on a lower level than that of the old part. Four steps led down from the old house into the new and on to a fine big landing, as big as a room, with six bedrooms going off it. The house had been built for a family, and at one time these rooms had held seven sons and three daughters. This was because they had been lucky enough to be born and reared between the bad plagues. On the ground floor there was a fine sitting-room, and at the end of a passage leading from the hall a room that had once been the breakfast-room – the house had been styled on those of its betters – but now was the master's office. The end of the passage gave access to the kitchen, and this room, like the old dining-room at the opposite end, was stone-flagged, and held everything that a kitchen should hold, from a pepper mill to a row of twelve graded pewter pots hanging above the long mantelshelf, seeming to form a bridge between the great copper pans that

29

gleamed, also in rotation of size, where they hung on wooden pegs down each side of the fireplace.

If Davie had ever had a wild dream it hadn't, up till now, been of sailing the seas and discovering new lands, as did the people he had read about, but of owning a house such as this with a kitchen where he could enter without scraping his feet, taking off his cap, or touching his forelock.

He now scraped the dust off his feet on the scraper and then on the roped mat outside the kitchen door.

He paused inside the door and there, at the long wooden trough sink, stood Molly Geary washing dishes. She turned her head quickly towards him, her hazel eyes narrowed, a faint smile on her face. 'Hello, Davie,' she said softly.

He glared at her, then walking slowly to the edge of the sink he bent his shoulders slightly forward and said in a low voice, 'You go to hell's flames, Molly Geary, and as far beyont; and you can take that' – he stabbed his finger down at her stomach – 'along with you.'

Her eyes stretching now, her mouth fell open and she turned her head quickly and looked towards the far door that led into the passage, as if she would run to it; but Davie was walking towards it. Before he went through he turned and looked at her again and, his voice still low and his words spaced, he said, 'The – master – wants – me,' and he laid strong emphasis on each word.

Her face showed him that she was in no doubt as to how much he knew of the truth of the situation. He went into the passage and towards the office door, and there he had to force himself to knock.

'Come in.'

Slowly he opened the door and entered the room, then stood with his hand on the door looking at the man seated behind the desk.

Angus McBain glanced upwards as he pushed a ledger to one side and rearranged some papers on the desk; then he said, 'Come in and close the door, Davie.'

Davie did as he was bidden, and slowly walked up the narrow room until he was standing in front of the desk looking down into the face of his master. The face looked all thin, nose, lips, eyebrows, yet the hair on his head was black and thick. It lay like a silk sheath and was as yet untouched with grey. Until this moment Davie hadn't realised how thin the master was in all ways. His body was tall and thin, his face was long and thin, even the grey of his eyes was a thin colour; and his voice was thin, clear, sharp and thin.

'Do you know why I've sent for you, Davie?'

Should he say 'Yes, Master', or 'No, Master'? He stared down into the flickering half-veiled gaze. The drooping lids suggested that they could close at any moment, and he said, 'I've got a good idea' – he paused a second before he added, 'Master.'

Angus McBain brought his attention once again to the papers on the desk and his Adam's apple made a rapid movement in his neck, stretching the skin in its passage. 'You have been courting Molly for some time . . . '

'I've never courted Molly, Master.'

Again they were looking at each other, and now McBain's eyes were wide and his voice stiff as he said, 'I have seen you myself walking the fields.'

'You can walk the fields, Master, without courtin'.'

Again there was a pause before McBain said, and thickly now, 'The girl is with child and she won't name the man.'

'Won't she, Master?'

McBain made no reply to this. At another time the young fellow's tone would have brought his tongue lashing at him for he allowed no servant, man or woman, young or old, to approach him as an equal. His forebears had always run the farm as gentlemen farmers, not like the ordinary trish-trash who worked neighbouring farms and allowed their people to pig in with them at a central table in the kitchen. Those he employed knew their place and gave him his. He was a good master to them and acted as their counsellor. He demanded respect and subservience as his right.

But there was neither respect nor subservience in young Armstrong's manner. Of course he was peaked at discovering Molly had fallen and he'd had no hand in it, it was natural he supposed, and, therefore, he must make allowances. Well, the thing to do was to get it over and quickly. He picked up a sheet of paper from the table, scrutinised it for a moment, then laying it down but his eyes still on it, he said, 'You will marry Molly.'

' . . . I'll not you know . . . Master.' Again there was the pause before 'Master'.

'What!' The thin face was thrust upwards now. 'Did I hear you aright?'

31

'Aye, you heard me aright.'

'You would defy my order, and, and leave her with an un-named child?'

'Aye, both, Master.'

McBain's eyes were wide now. There was more in the young fellow's attitude than frustrated virility; he felt a sense of uneasiness. Had Geary, because he had been thwarted in his attempt at blackmail, hinted something to the fellow? Surely the man would have more sense. Had he not a family to support? And did he not realise that the roads were crawling with farm workers begging for work? Nine shillings a week he was paying Geary and three shillings between his sons; that was a tidy sum, not counting the two shillings a week from Molly. Then there was his cottage, milk, potatoes, and two cords of wood a year, surely the man wouldn't jeopardise all that? No, for he was a cunning individual, was Geary. What he wanted for his knowledge was a rise in pay, a house, more perquisites . . . he would not jeopardise that. But why then young Davie's attitude?

The muscles of his face tightened as he looked into the brown eyes, almost black now with what he recognised as suppressed rage. He leant back in his chair and surveyed the young fellow as from a distance and it was as the master of destinies that he slowly spoke. 'If you disobey my wishes you know what it could mean?' He held up a finger as Davie was about to speak, and continued, 'Now think, think hard. I'm not a man to use empty threats. Those who do me service are repaid, well and truly repaid, as you and your family know. You have a good job; ask yourself, where in this county would you get seven shillings a week? What is more, there is a great deal of money going into your house from my pocket . . .'

'Aye, and you're gettin' a great deal of work for it, Master. Me ma and me both do two people's jobs each; me granda did the same for years till he was worn out.' He did not mention his father.

McBain was sitting upright now, stiff as a ramrod. His voice had a steel thread to it as he said, 'You are forgetting yourself entirely. Be careful, Armstrong, be careful.'

'No, Master, I'm not forgettin' meself. You sent for me, didn't you, to tell me I had to marry Molly? Well, I'm tellin' you I'm not goin' to, 'tis a free country.'

'You are a bonded man.'

'Bonded, or no bonded, I've only got a few months to go. I could leave at the end of the year and you could do nothing about it.'

McBain slowly drew himself up from the chair, stretching himself until he appeared to stand head and shoulders above Davie, although in fact with his six feet he could give him only two inches, and his words had an ominous ring. 'Yes. Yes,' he said, 'you could leave at the end of the year and I could do nothing about it. But I could do something about the cottage and your father . . . don't you want time to think, boy?'

'All I can think, Master, is you'll go a long way afore you'll get anybody to work for you like me ma does, an' me da an' all, they both do a twelve-hour day, more, never no less. And you won't find me da droppin' asleep on the job either. An' me, my hours never end, you see to that . . . an' you've no need to tell me the roads are crawling with families looking for situations, I know it, but what I also know is that Farmer Hetherington from over Hunstanworth would jump at me ma like a shot. His wife's been on her back for years an' he can't get anybody right for the house; he's asked me ma twice . . . that's news for you, Master . . .'

'*Stop!* Stop your insolence this minute!' As McBain came round the desk Davie did not retreat, and when his master stood within an arm's length of him he faced him unblinking. It was strange for him to realise that he had no fear of this man now, even in his wrath, for he had always stood slightly in awe of him, not only as a master, but as a man. Because he appeared a way above the ordinary mortal, his example was something to follow. But for three years now he had questioned the church-going and psalm singing; strangely it had been the books Parson Hedley himself had recommended that had brought the vague questioning doubts to the forefront of his mind; without his reading he doubted if he would ever have troubled to think about it.

> God was in His heaven,
> The cattle were in the field,
> Man ploughed and sowed
> And lived off the yield.

That was the pattern he could, like his folks, have lived and died by. Yet, his reasoning told him, even in this moment of stress, that it was this man, this enraged master towering before

33

him, who had allowed him to go to Parson Hedley's Sunday School. However, he questioned this man's progressiveness in the face of the prevailing parsimoniousness of thought and asked himself would he have been allowed such a privilege if the master hadn't been a friend of old Parson Wainwright, and Parson Wainwright hadn't been full cousin to Lord Powlett, and Lord Powlett's niece hadn't married Sir Alfred Tuppin, who lived in The Manor. The master had a taste for high company; it was known around the county he didn't live like any ordinary farmer, so the sending of him and the rest of the young 'uns on the farm to Sunday School he saw now as a means of impressing Sir Alfred and the rest of the gentry with his progressiveness.

He had a mental picture of his master reading the lesson; that was when his awe of him had first begun, for he did not seem like a farmer, or his master, but a man full of God . . . A man full of God! The words ran through his mind like an audible sneer. In this moment he had the desire to spit them into the face before him.

The master was speaking. His voice low and very thin now, he was saying, 'You have your choice, you'll marry Molly or you'll go.'

'You've had me answer, Master, and I'll add something to it.' His own voice was low and thick. 'I'd rather be crucified than give me name to her an' — there was a long pause before he ended — 'your fly-blow.'

He watched the colour drain away from the thin face, leaving the skin grey and muddy looking, except for two white spots on the cheeks where the bones showed through. He could not continue to look at the fall of a God as it were, so he moved to one side, then went towards the door, only to be checked by McBain saying, 'Wait!'

Again they were looking at each other, but Davie saw that the master had recovered quickly, and the tone of his voice bore this out as he said, 'I could horsewhip you, or take you to the justice for defiling my . . . my character. Do you know what you have said, accused me of?'

'Aye, Master.'

'Well, it's a lie, bred of your jealousy. This is final, you'll go, and if you spread this lie around I'll have you transpor . . . ' He had been about to say 'transported', but realised he was more than sixteen years too late for that; but Davie took it up.

'And Miss Jane along of me, Master?' he said.

There was a short silence before McBain muttered, 'What?'

'I said Miss Jane along of me, Master?' His voice was quiet. 'She was in the malt house s'afternoon, as I was meself. I was bringing the cows in and I saw her fall. She was running towards the malt house. When I got to her she was up in the straw, you know – ' he inclined his head forward – 'the straw that's in the gallery. She had cut her knee and was cryin'. She wasn't cryin' 'cos of her hurt, not that kind of hurt anyway, she was crying for . . . now who do you think she was crying for, Master? She was crying for Molly 'cos you had flayed her. And then she sees you, Master; we both see you comin' in and waiting. I don't need to tell you any more, do I? It isn't me you've got to worry about, Master, not me, it's Miss Jane.'

He walked from his master's presence without being given leave and he didn't bang the door.

Angus McBain put his hand behind him and gripped the edge of the desk, then took a step back and rested his buttocks against it. God above! What was this? His mind leapt back to what he had said to Molly in the malt house . . . and what he had done to her, kissing her flesh, fondling her . . . ah, dear Lord!

It was characteristic of him that he wasn't concerned so much over the impression his infidelity might have made on his daughter as by the fact that a member of his immediate family should be aware of his intrigue. That his employees should have knowledge of what was going on was, after all, of no great import; they would never dare voice, or even hint of any such thing to their mistress. They could, and would, talk among themselves, but what did that matter? He had after all only done what was commonplace all over the countryside, taken his pleasure with a serving maid . . . This might even add to the respect granted him in some quarters, and arouse it in others where it had been lacking – their knowledge of his peccadillo would have made him appear much more a man of the world. What was shaking him now with fear and foreboding was the possibility that through his daughter the facts might come to his wife's ears. But again his particular worry did not concern the effect it might have on her but on what she was carrying. She had carried for nearly seven months, the first time since Jane was born, and he had willed it to be a son, willed, and willed,

35

and willed it to be a son, until, deep within him there was the sure knowledge it would be a son. A few more weeks and he would never claim it.

Molly! Even the name coming into his mind made him feel weak. He had never had a desire for anyone like he had for her. Ignorant, untutored, it did not matter, her body was a delight to him. He liked young things, soft, rounded things. His first wife had been like Molly, all flesh. She had died and taken their first child with her, and that had been a son. Why then, with his inclination running to tender soft young things, had he picked on Delia to bear his children? Delia had been twenty and thin; pretty, yes, but thin, almost as thin as himself. She was still thin; she had got thinner with every miscarriage. Seven of his children she had dropped; he had grown weary of trying to bring permanent life out of her bony frame. Now for the first time in thirteen years she was holding his seed and nothing must cause her to drop it before it was due . . . Where was Jane? He must find her, explain to her; she was twelve years old, old enough to understand.

He seemed to be catapulted from the desk, out through the door along the passage and into the kitchen, only to find it empty. He went into the passage again, then on into the drawing-room, calling 'Delia! Delia!' and when his wife didn't answer, he went into the hallway and out through the front of the house. The garden was deserted. Delia, he saw, had been on the lounge chair, for her work bag was lying on the grass. He went through the house again and out into the side yard, and there called to young Mickey Geary, 'Have you seen your mistress, boy?'

'Aye, Master. Her and Molly are lookin' for Miss Jane; she didn't come home to no supper.'

He bit tight down on his lip before asking, 'Which way did they go?'

'I don't know, Master; they just went round 'n' round the place callin'.'

Swiftly he made his way out of the yard and into the road. Then he crossed the fields almost at a run, leapt over a low stone wall, and made for The Ridge. He slipped as he scrambled up the steep path and when he reached the top he was gasping.

The evening sun was in his eyes and he put his hand to his brow and peered around him. Then he saw them, two small

36

figures a good distance apart, his wife on the cow track above the malt house field, and further away the unmistakable figure of Molly running down towards the brook; he could not see his daughter. He left the top of the hill and took the curving path at a run, which he kept up across the fields. He could not remember running like this since he was a boy of fourteen.

Delia McBain had been looking for her daughter for the past hour and a half. She had started the search quietly. Rising from her outdoor couch, she had gone into the kitchen; she had asked Molly if she had seen Miss Jane and Molly had answered, 'No, Mistress, not since this mornin'.'

As Delia had gazed at Molly she had for a moment forgotten that she was looking for her daughter, and had, in spite of this girl's sinning, felt overcome with compassion for her. She herself had previously been quite unaware of the reason for ringing the bell; the sound of it had brought her swiftly from the dining-room and she had asked Angus as he was crossing the hall, 'What is the matter? What has happened? Why have you ordered the bell to be rung?' and he had spoken to her over his shoulder as he went out, saying, 'Come to the barn and you'll soon find out.'

And having found out she then understood her husband's reticence in speaking to her of the matter, for she knew him, in spite of her private knowledge of a certain facet of his character, to be a very moral man. But when she had seen him lift the whip to Molly something within her had become outraged. Those undercurrents in her apparently placid nature, which were known to no one but herself, swept up through her in a torrent and almost escaped her lips in protest. She reminded herself only just in time that any protest of hers would appear as if she were censuring her husband, and would present a bad example to his people. She always thought of the workers as his people, not her people, but Angus's people; she was no queen to his king, she had always been aware of her inferiority with regards to him, for Angus had a great mind, a cultured mind.

She herself came from a well-connected family. Her grandfather having once been a shipbuilder, that was before they brought the iron ships in, and if her father had not squandered his inheritance she would, no doubt, have never been allowed to marry a farmer, even such a one as Angus McBain. But penniless and living on the bounty of a cousin and having reached the age of twenty and no one having as yet asked to marry her, the widower, the young, lean, stern-faced widower had appeared to both her and her cousin's family like the answer to many prayers.

She had not loved Angus when she first married him, but in a very short time she had been consumed by her feelings for him, and it wasn't until the fifth year of their marriage that there began the long, slow, dying of her love. He blamed her for the loss of each child. The third month of pregnancy was agony to her; as the blood flowed from her carrying away yet another of his frenzied efforts to make her body bear his son, she died afresh.

As the years wore on, and she sat in church, Sunday after Sunday, and heard him read the lesson with as much or more feeling than either Parson Hedley or Wainwright put into their readings, she began to contrast him with the man of the night, the man who tore at her body like a hungry lion at a doe. Yet she knew she must suffer this, as it was the lot of all women; men's appetites must be satisfied. But the daring, probing part of her mind questioned God's handiwork in combining in her husband His adherent and the wild beast of the night.

So her love died. But not her respect for his superior knowledge. He was well read. His office walls showed lines of books you might find in a library, and Sir Alfred Tuppin always referred to the office as the library, and never failed to admire her husband's taste in literature when he called as he sometimes did after a meet. And what was more, both parsons respected his knowledge.

She found pleasure of an evening when Parson Hedley came to supper, and after the meal she sat with her handwork and listened to her husband and the minister discoursing on all subjects, lately about Disraeli, Parliament and the Queen. From their conversation she had visualised the Red Sea and the Mediterranean joined by a great canal. She had listened attentively to the discussion on a man called the Khedive. He was the ruler of Egypt and he had sold his shares in a canal called the Suez Canal to Mr Disraeli, at least Mr Disraeli had bought them for the Queen and the Empire. Of course neither her husband nor Parson Hedley agreed with all Mr Disraeli had done; they criticised him a great deal and were pleased when his Parliament fell. But they didn't seem much happier with Mr Gladstone, who was now Prime Minister. Undoubtedly he was

38

a moral man, a righteous man, but he was, they said, swaying the people, the working man, and not, they both agreed, in the right direction.

They were very enlightening and enlivening evenings when the parson came to supper. When they had supper alone her husband never talked to her except upon household matters, or visits that had to be made. And if such a visit were to be special and to occur some little time in the future, he would advise her to plan for it and would give her the money to buy the material for a new gown.

For this purpose she loved the trips into Hexham, and twice over the years she had been as far as Newcastle. The shops in Newcastle had beautiful material, such an assortment; foreign silks straight from the boats, beautiful velvets of the gentlest hues. Her husband was generous when he wanted her to appear well dressed, and of late he had been more generous. When she was safely past her three months' pregnancy he had given her twenty pounds and ordered Davie to drive her into Hexham, there to choose a material for a gown that she could wear during her last month. This she looked upon as a tender extravagance as it would have to be taken to pieces later and re-modelled.

She had never known such contentment as that which had filled her these past three months, all fear had dropped from her. She knew she would carry this child, and it was all due, she knew, to Mother Reckett. Why hadn't she gone to the old woman years ago? She knew why; it was foolish to ask herself this question. When, after her second miscarriage, she had said to Angus, 'There is an old woman called Mrs Reckett whom I understand makes up potions . . . ' he had silenced her before she had got any further. Mother Reckett was a heathen, a woman with the evil eye. He wasn't a superstitious man, he told her, but he knew that Mother Reckett possessed powers of evil; some people gave her credit for the power to cure animals, but she also had been given credit for bringing blight and disease to the land of many a man who had crossed her.

So for years she had resisted the temptation of consulting Mother Reckett, until desperation and a word from Mrs Swinterton, when taking tea with her at her house outside Halt-whistle, had supplied the courage. Mrs Swinterton was an old lady herself and had been a friend of the McBain family for years. She had expressed sorrow for her many miscarriages and suggested that, unknown to her husband, she sought help from Mother Reckett; and Mother Reckett had worked the miracle.

It was now eighteen months since she had taken her first bottle of medicine. It had been as clear as water and as bitter as gall, and she had drunk it as if it were nectar. Three doses a week she had taken for twelve months, and then the miracle had happened. For four years prior to this she hadn't even conceived. At times she had longed to conceive even though it would mean carrying the child for only three months, for following a miscarriage Angus always let her body rest for some weeks.

Once she had conceived again Mother Reckett had changed the medicine to a thick substance that had a sweet acrid taste and which had to be taken by the teaspoonful three times a day. And so periodically she went for a walk over the moor. Angus was used to her taking long solitary walks, when she might be absent for three hours at a time, and so he had not questioned her journeyings. From her last visit to Mother Reckett's cottage on the outskirts of Harper Town she had brought back enough medicine to last her until her time was up because her body was already heavy, and she was tiring very easily . . .

But here now was Molly, and she, too, was carrying a child, even if it was the product of sin, and this morning she had been whipped. She had the desire to go to her and comfort her. But Molly was apparently still suffering from the injustice of her treatment for she turned her head from her.

When she asked 'Have you seen Miss Jane, Molly?' Molly, still with her head down, muttered, 'No, Mistress, not since dinner-time, when she couldn't have nothin' to eat.'

'Oh, but she was here well after that. It's now close on seven. I'm worried; she seemed upset . . . ' She did not go on and say, 'The fact of you being whipped upset her; she did not do as her father bade her but witnessed the scene through the back of the barn,' but added, 'We'd better look for her. We'll take the cow path to the burn, she may be there. You can run down; she is often at the burn because the foal is near.'

Molly dried her hands, then turned from the sink and said, 'Master's back, Mistress.'

'Oh, I didn't hear him. Is he in his office?'

'Yes, Mistress, but Davie's with him.'

'Oh!' Delia looked at the girl and thought she understood. It would be Davie. Of course it would. She had seen them

40

together. But she was very disappointed in Davie; if he had come forward he could have saved this poor creature from being flayed; she had thought better of Winnie's son. She liked Winnie, she considered her a fine woman, in her place of course, and she had at times envied her her son, for she considered Davie an intelligent boy, worth perhaps something more than the position of second cowman. But she was sure that her husband recognised this and would bear it in mind for his future. She had said as much to Winnie. But now the boy had come out of this situation without any honour; he would get a severe rating from Angus, that was sure, and serve him right, but once they were settled, Angus, fair man that he was, would no doubt see to building them a cottage of their own. Some time ago he had talked of renovating the old malt house. The foundations and part of the structure were still good; it was a picturesque place and a shame that it should be given over to the occasional stabling of a mare and foal. He had seemed very keen on the idea. That was some time ago; he had not mentioned it for months past. But now it would likely come to his mind again. It would make a most superior dwelling, fit for a bailiff, or in his case foreman. And why not? If Davie behaved himself from now on he could in time rise to that position, for Angus had talked more than once of engaging an intelligent man to act as a kind of manager, so that he himself could have more time to devote to other things, which, she had thought indulgently, included hunting and fishing. Last year he had been invited by Sir Alfred Tuppin to his Scottish estate to indulge in the latter sport when the salmon season was on. It was at that time he had talked about employing a capable manager.

But now she was sure everything would work out both for Molly and Davie, and the household, for Molly, being trained under Winnie, would take over when Winnie was too old to carry on, and outside Davie, she was sure, in spite of his lapse, would run the farm in the interests of his master.

They went out, not together, Molly walking a foot or so behind her mistress, as was right, and Delia spoke to her over her shoulder. 'I'm seriously thinking of sending Miss Jane to Madame Lovell's private school in Hexham,' she said.

'Oh, aye, Mistress.' There was little interest in Molly's response.

'She is too old for the day school now, and it is not advanced

41

enough in its teaching. The master agrees that she should attend Madam Lovell's.'

Again Molly said, 'Oh, aye, Mistress.'

'She will learn French and music, although she is quite good at the pianoforte now.' She paused, then ended, 'I thought I might like her at home to help with the . . . the baby, but the master is arranging to have a nurse. She will attend me as long as is necessary.'

When Molly did not answer she turned her head slightly and looked at the girl. Her face was sweating; there were beads of perspiration running from her hair line and down over her plump cheeks. She wanted to reassure her and say, 'Don't worry, everything is all right, the master will see that you're cared for,' but instead she said, 'Run on ahead, Molly. Go down to the brook and see if she's there; I'll have to take my time. But you be careful too.' She smiled at the girl, but it brought no response for when she passed her she hung her head, and she noted that she kept it down as she ran along the lane. She watched her sit atop the dry stone wall that hemmed in the burn bank and kept the cattle from straying; she saw her swing her legs over one after the other; then she was lost from view.

She herself was very hot and feeling weary. Her step slowed. She hoped that Molly found Jane down there and also that she had got over her distress. She was a highly sensitive child, very young in some ways for her years, yet in others she was old beyond her years. She had a great fund of natural sympathy and affection, but she had one shortcoming in that she was given to wild fits of temper. This trait, she was sure, her daughter did not inherit from herself, for no matter what her own feelings, she was always able to conceal them. And she certainly did not inherit it from her father; Angus might get angry, but it was a controlled anger.

Sometimes she thought that the free life her daughter led might tend to make her become wilful; it was with the thought of erasing any possibility of this that she had suggested Madam Lovell's school to her husband. In making this suggestion, she had made a personal sacrifice, because up to now Jane was the only proof she had to show that she was capable of bearing a child. So, therefore, she loved her very much. And the child had always given her affection and comfort . . . but never, she knew, love . . . that she had kept for her father.

42

She started as she heard Jane's voice, high and shrill now, coming from the direction of the burn. It was as if she was crying, and in distress. She hurried along the lane to the spot where Molly had crossed the wall, but to make her descent she herself had to go much further along the winding path to where a gap gave way to natural slate steps down to the burn itself; and all the while she hurried she could hear her daughter's voice.

When she reached the gap she looked down the slope and the sight that met her eyes astounded her. Jane was actually fighting Molly, striking out at her with both hands and feet. She had never witnessed anything like it. Molly was protesting, but not loudly, just warding off the blows, saying, 'Aw, Miss give over, give over. For God's sake, Miss. Aw, for God's sake, Miss, be quiet, it'll cause trouble. Aw, Miss, Miss, come on away, come on up home.'

'Don't touch me, don't dare touch me, you're filthy, filthy. Molly Geary, you're filthy.'

Delia was about to call out, command her daughter to stop making such an unladylike spectacle of herself and demand to know the reason for the scene, when Jane's next words gave it to her without further questioning. 'I hate you, Molly Geary. You and father . . . I saw you both. I saw you in the malt house. You were horrible, and you let him whip you while all the time you knew it was him . . . YOU ARE HORRIBLE, HORRIBLE.'

Delia stood transfixed looking down on them. Her daughter was still gabbling and Molly still pushing off her hands and feet.

Like someone sleep-walking she slowly descended the shallow steps where they turned in a half moon towards the burn. Jane was now spluttering, 'Planning with Father to make Davie marry you, pretending it was him. You are horrible, dirty. I hate you, Molly Geary.'

'Jane!' Delia had not spoken loudly; she was amazed herself at the quiet tone that issued from her lips, for inside her head her thoughts were whirling and screaming.

They both turned towards her now, Jane staring up at her, her face dirty, tear-stained and, in this moment, ugly; but Molly, after one glance at her mistress, drooped her head on to her chest and stood limp, her arms hanging downwards away from her body as if she had no longer any control over them.

'What is this?' Delia was addressing her, and when the girl

43

did not lift her head she cried at her, her voice expressing her emotions now, 'Answer me, girl! What is this I hear?'

When Molly raised her head, startled as much by this new aspect of the mistress as by the fact that she was advancing on her, she could only stammer. 'Oh, Mistress, Mistress.'

Delia stopped within an arm's length of the girl, and now demanded, 'Tell me that my daughter is deranged and not speaking the truth.'

Molly now swung her head from side to side, gulped in her throat, opened her soft wet mouth wide, closed it again; then her head seemed to be jerked off her body by a blow first to one side of her face and then to the other. As she cowered down a voice thundered over them, crying, 'Delia!' and Delia turned and looked up the steps to where her husband was standing in the gap.

McBain had taken in the situation; he was too late. Well, what was done was done, and couldn't be undone; what he must do now was to calm her down, she mustn't get excited, not at this stage.

He came rapidly down the steps. He looked neither at his wife, nor yet at his daughter, but addressed Molly, whose eyes were on him, her manner now showing her confidence in his protection – the master, her love, whom she knew she could twist round her little finger, he would show the mistress, and the young one an' all what was what.

Her confidence was wiped away and her mouth brought again into its soft gape by the master addressing her as if someone of no account. 'Get back to the house, girl, and get on with your work.'

She paused a moment before obeying him. Even before that night when the master had come into the kitchen late on and found her with her skirts above her knees dozing in front of the fire, and she had woken to find his hand on her groin, even before that he had never spoken to her uncivil; it had always been, 'Molly girl, do this. Molly girl, do that.' But now he had spoken to her in the voice he used to gipsies and tramps on the road who came abeggin' and wanted food without offering to work for it.

As she sidled past she cast a quick glance up at him, but his face was stern; she didn't recognise the man, who only a few hours earlier had held her tightly and kissed her wounds. She

44

scurried up the steps and when she reached the road she burst out crying.

Now McBain looked at his daughter and he said, 'And you, Miss, get back to the house and to your room. I will talk with you later.'

Jane stared at her father, amazed that he was putting her in the wrong, it was as if she had committed the crime against her mother, and against herself, for in destroying his image he had destroyed the beauty of life for her. The rage that she had nurtured against Molly all afternoon, then had released on her, was now over like something that had never been. She felt weak, and spent, she did not seem to have the strength even to cry any more; she wished she could die like the foal last week, just lay her head sideways on the straw and die, or be frozen stiff in the snow like the young lambs; or at this moment, she would even thank someone to stick a knife in her neck as they did with the pigs. She had not known how the pigs died, and when her curiosity had been satisfied she was sick for days and wouldn't touch bacon for a long time.

She didn't want to live, and if it wasn't for her mother she wouldn't live. But her mother was going to need her. As if she were being given a glimpse into the future she knew she was the only one on whom her mother would be able to rely; she also knew that now all talk about her going to Madam Lovell's school in Hexham would cease. She would never go to that establishment and learn French and music and dancing.

A similar train of thought was passing through Delia's mind. The knowledge that had come to her in the last few minutes would alter life for all time. It wasn't just the fact that the man before her had had his way with a kitchen slut; she was no fool, there was hardly a household of any standing for miles around where the masters did not demand their pleasures from their female employees, and not only from girls not yet wedded; a working man's wife had to have a strong personality and indeed be virtuous if at least one of her many children did not show a marked resemblance to the man who employed her husband. And the husband might black his wife's eyes because he couldn't dole out that very medicine to the man on whom he relied for his bread.

No, it wasn't entirely the fact that her husband had been sporting with that skit of a girl while she herself was carrying his child, but what was indeed filling her with rage was that

45

this man, who was looked up to, whom she herself had been forced to respect even while she had stopped loving him, was nothing but a hypocrite, a sanctimonious mealy-mouthed hypocrite, daring to stand in the pulpit Sunday after Sunday and read the lesson, and sit smugly in their pew listening to old Parson Wainwright singing his praises after yet another donation towards the upkeep of the church: 'Our good Brother McBain has yet again come to our rescue . . . ' She could hear the thick fuddled voice of the minister who more often than not was still carrying the previous night's load of port when he ascended the pulpit. And then Sir Alfred Tuppin, she could hear his thick guttural voice saying, 'Your husband, Mrs McBain, is an upright man. There are so few left in this England of ours today. Good stock, good stock, the McBains.' Such praise had even silenced her cynical self, which at times would rise up and present her with a picture of McBain in the night; and she would recall the advice her cousin had given her before she married: 'There are two men in every husband,' she had said, 'a night man, and a day man. See that you satisfy the night man and you will be both master and mistress of the day man.' Yet even as she offered this sop to herself from time to time she knew it to be trite, untrue, except in very rare cases. There was no opportunity given a woman to satisfy a man; the animals and birds were more courteous to each other, more patient than a husband.

But still she could have forgiven all that, as she had done, accepting it as part of a woman's existence; but not his play acting, his lapping up of homage as due payment for his integrity: the head held high, the clear eyes, the tones of the sage, in all appearing like a reflection of God as it were.

'TAKE YOUR HANDS OFF ME!'

'Now Delia, you must listen to me . . . I, I want you to listen to me.'

'You may want, Mr McBain, you may want.'

'DELIA!'

'That, Mr McBain, is your "Thou shalt not" tone. Well, I may tell you that for sometime now it has ceased to fill me with awe. Yet I have respected you . . . but never no more.' They were glaring at each other when she asked grimly, 'Will you go to church on Sunday, Mr McBain, and read the lesson? Will you?' The last words were high piercing, and he answered coolly, 'Delia, I command you, be quiet, keep calm for your own good. You must not get excited; you must think of the child.'

'Which child? Whose child? Mine or hers?'

'Don't talk stupidly, Delia.' He again extended his hand towards her, saying briskly, 'Come.' But she stepped back from him, and she said again, 'I ask you, will you go to church on Sunday and read the lesson?'

His patience was running short now and he answered grimly, 'Very likely. I see no reason why I shouldn't.'

'Do, do that, Mr McBain, go to church and read the lesson. And you know what I shall do? I shall scream the truth to the rafters. Enter that church again and I shall scream the truth to the rafters. I could forgive you for sporting with a low scut if you had ever accepted that you were an ordinary man, but you sported with her while playing God. In two months' time they are unveiling the stained glass window. Do you remember why you donated the window to the church? In your own words you told Parson Wainwright it was because God had allowed your wife to carry your child. The window is to be unveiled the day your child . . . your SON is born; it wasn't to be another daughter, no, no, you had told the Almighty it had to be a son and . . .'

'QUIET, WOMAN. How dare you!'

McBain's thin pale face was almost purple with rage now but it was having no effect on his wife, for, looking at him, her eyes full of disdain, she said, 'I dare, Mr McBain, at last after thirteen years I dare.' And with this she passed him and walked with firm but heavy tread up the steps and on to the road.

McBain watched her, but he did not follow her; he stood now with closed eyes, his fists clenched tightly by his sides. There was running over his entire body a cold sweat. No one in his life before had dared to talk to him as his wife had done. No one, except himself, had seen the man beneath the skin; but now his wife had seen him. She had called him a hypocrite, and he supposed she was right, he was a hypocrite, not only since he had begun to ease himself on Molly, but in the man he presented to outsiders, for this man had no connection with the one his wife was acquainted with in their personal life. He had used her roughly for years. But then that was his nature; it was ravenous for something he couldn't attain. He would have respected her more if she had turned on him, refused to put up with his madness; but she had never protested, and so he had used her . . .

Yet all the while, underneath her apparent calmness, she had known him, known him for what he was, for what he knew himself to be, a man with an insatiable appetite that was like a disease, a two-faced man, a hypocrite.

He rubbed his hand hard around his face. What was he to do, he was in a cleft stick? If he stopped attending church, what excuse would he give? Illness? No. Dissent? No, he was a firm Protestant. The thought came to him that perhaps by Sunday he would have reasoned with her. He turned it aside. He had not been mistaken in his early suspicions of a self in her that he had no access to. He'd had glimpses of it when they first married, but he had soon subjected her to his wishes and, consequently, he had imagined, stifled all life out of the wayward self. But now he knew that that self had remained very much alive. There were two women in his wife as there were two men in himself.

But dominant self, or no dominant self, she must not be allowed to get the upper hand, yet at the same time he must tread very warily, even gently, with her, until the child was born; once that was accomplished she could show to him whatever self she liked and he would deal with it.

He turned now and followed her, hurrying to catch up with her so that they could enter the farm together. He must put a bold front on things, keep appearances normal, because he knew that the whole incident, like a nine-days' wonder, would blow over.

Two

McBain was more disturbed than he would admit to himself. The blowing over of the affair was going to take a stronger wind than he had anticipated. Something quite unprecedented had happened last night, Delia had refused him his bed; she had dared to refuse him his bed.

Sitting straight up against the pillows, a hand pressed tightly down on the bedclothes at each side of her, she had stared at him as she said, 'No more, Mr McBain. If you insist on getting in I shall get out and take up my room across the landing. And

48

I promise you I shan't do it quietly. But you can save your face by going into another room; you might even convince people it is out of consideration for my condition, at least you can order them to accept such an explanation, what they might think privately is a different matter altogether.'

McBain knew himself to be a passionate man but not a violent one, yet in that moment he had the urge to knock her flying out of the bed, more so to use the whip on her, for he considered that she had earned it much more than ever young Molly had done, even if he hadn't been the man responsible. Yet while his desires raged in him he had stood dumb before her knowing she had him in a cleft stick; excite her, upset her, and the child could be brought ahead of its time; like a cow in calf being chased by an unruly dog she would drop what was in her without it being fully fledged.

Only his deep-seated craving for a son, a legitimate son, gave him the strength to turn from her without uttering a word . . .

By morning he had decided that if she could see Molly married and apparently out of reach of his hands, this would calm her. There was only one eligible man on the farm and that was Will Curran. He was forty-two years old, the same age as himself, and he was certainly not the man he would have chosen for Molly. But what other course was open to him? He had no doubt but that Curran would be willing; he was a widower these past five years. About Molly's reactions to the man he gave no thought. She would do as he bade her.

He rose, as he always did, at seven o'clock in the morning and followed the same procedure as always. Leaving the bedroom, he went into the closet room. One side of the room was taken up with a long wooden seat with three holes in it; underneath stood three pails, and high up on the wall behind each hole, suspended from a hook, was a lavender bag. Flanking the wall opposite the row of pails was a long narrow table and on it, placed upside down in a neat row and ranging in size from an extra large one to a very small one, were ten spare chamber pots.

The first part of his ablutions over, he went into the dressing-room. Here the whole length of a wall was taken up with a long wardrobe, of which the frame was shining rosewood encasing three huge mirrors. Underneath the window at the end of the room stood a table and on this there were two wash basins, with jugs inside. Over one was draped a white towel, through which a thin film of steam was permeating. A couch, a chair, and a bow-fronted chest-of-drawers were the only other articles of furniture in the room. It took him fifteen minutes precisely to wash and shave and dress. His working clothes were simple, consisting of cord knee breeches and a short homespun coat over a fresh white cotton shirt. His feet were encased in black boots freshly dubbined, his legs in black gaiters equally so.

He did not even glance at the communicating door leading into his bedroom as he passed it, but went out and across the landing and down the steep oak stairs.

When he entered the kitchen Winnie alone was there. She did not look up from where she was cutting thick gammon rashers from a ham, but she said, as always, 'Mornin', Master,' and he replied, 'Good morning, Winnie.'

She now went to the stove and took from the hob a china teapot that was standing next to a homely brown one. She went to the end of the table where stood a tray holding a cup and saucer and a sugar basin, and having poured out a cup of tea that looked jet black she spooned four heaped teaspoonfuls of sugar into it; then she handed the cup and saucer to her master.

Now, the master should have walked to the kitchen door and stood looking out on to the farmyard, taking in in one sharp covering glance that everything was as it should be. Even in winter the procedure never altered. Sometimes she wished she could shout at him, as she would have to one of her own, 'For God's sake close that door, me legs are froze.' But this morning her master surprised her by walking towards the door through which he had entered only a few minutes previously, saying as he did so, 'Get Will Curran to me. If he has already gone to the fields send a boy for him. I'll be in my office.'

Winnie did not say, 'Yes, Master,' until the door had almost closed on him . . .

Will Curran, on the point of leading the horses out of the yard and to the plough, was given the message by young Mickey. 'Me?' he said. 'Just gone seven in the mornin', Master wants me in the office?'

'That's what Winnie says,' said young Mickey.

'You're not havin' me on, boy, Aa hope?'

'No, Will, no. Winnie . . . look, there she is.' The boy pointed, and Will Curran looked towards the kitchen door where Winnie was waving him forward.

Three minutes later, chaffing his hands together as if to rid them of dirt, then wiping them down the back of his breeches, he knocked on the office door and was bidden to enter.

McBain looked at his ploughman and he didn't like what he saw; he had never liked the man. Perhaps it was his appearance that put him off, red hair, red nose, nearly always with a permanent drop on the end. He was an ignorant man, dull-witted in one way, yet sharp and sly in another.

His voice curt, the words clipped, he said, 'I won't beat about the bush, Curran. Are you agreeable to take a wife again?'

'A wife! Me, Master? What wife?'

'Molly.'

He watched three drops in rapid succession leave the end of Curran's nose, two being caught by the man's chin, and one falling to the floor. It was odd, but a thing like this could make him feel sick; there were niceties in him that years of dealing with animal nature had not erased.

Curran was now rubbing the palms of his hands together in a circular movement, but his voice had a touch of genuine amazement as he said, 'Molly! Why she'd have no truck with me, Master; I'm a couple of years older than her dad.'

Ignoring this, McBain said, 'She wants a father for her child; no man has come forward. She will do as she is bid, if you are willing.'

Will Curran's head wobbled on his shoulders. A smile, sly, yet filled with amazement, spread over his face. 'I'm willin', Master. I'm as willin' as a tethered bull.'

'Very well. Get back about your work; I'll see you later.'

'Thanks, Master. Thank you, Master, thank you right kindly.' Will Curran was backing towards the door, touching his forelock, when McBain said to him, 'Tell Winnie to send Molly into me.'

'Aye, Master. Aye, Aa will, Master.'

McBain sat back in his chair, drooped his head on to his chest, and waited. The term 'lamb to the slaughter' came to his mind. But Molly was no lamb; she hadn't even been a virgin when he took her for the first time, and she wasn't sixteen then. Whoever had taken her virginity she hadn't said, not even hinted at it; but one thing seemed certain, it hadn't been young Davie. The name coming into his mind made him think he was going to find it hard to replace young Davie; but still, there was never a good but that there was a better. Even so, he didn't like new faces about the place, and he'd always had a personal

51

liking for the boy. But not for the man he had suddenly sprung into; it was no boy that had faced him across this desk yesterday. Still, it was a pity he had to go. But go he must; he could not allow himself to be thwarted by one of his work people.

When the tap came on the door he answered softly, 'Come in,' and Molly entered.

After closing the door behind her she rested her buttocks against it for a moment, then came slowly forward. She had her eyes tight on his face, and she hesitated at the side of the desk wondering whether to go round to him or stand with the desk between them as a servant should. Something in his face made her take the latter course and she took two further steps, then stopped and stared at him. What she saw disquietened her.

He wasn't the master of the malt house. He wasn't the man who tumbled her in the straw. There was no vestige now of the man who had told her to slip back from the fair to the malt house, nor of the man who had arranged there should be no one on the farm but old Sep Rummery, for he had taken the mistress and the young miss to Allendale visiting, and left them there while he supposedly went into Hexham on business. The business he had done was to take every stitch off her until she was as bare as the day she was born, and although she had experienced his love making before and been surprised by it, there were things had happened in that one hour that she was sure had never happened to anyone else on God's earth. And she had protested against not one of them, but joyed with him; oh aye, she had joyed with him, and would be willing to die for just one such hour again.

She said softly, 'You sent for me, Master?'

'Yes, Molly.' He did not even put his hand out towards her. 'I have something to tell you.'

She watched his thin lips wetting each other; then her eyes sprang wide at his next words.

'I've arranged you should marry Curran. He is willing.'

She pushed her head back on to her shoulders and her mouth widened; then she swallowed deeply before gabbling, 'No! no! Master, not Will Curran. I couldn't, not him; him with his runny' – she had almost said 'snotty' – 'him with his runny nose. And he's old, old . . . aw, Master, not him. Not Will Curran.'

He looked at her for a moment in pity while at the same time feeling gratified that she did not consider him to be old. 'The child must have a name, Molly,' he said quietly.

'But Master!' She was now leaning across the desk, her face only a foot from his. 'I don't mind, I don't mind havin' the bairn and him claimin' no name. I don't, I don't.' She moved her head slowly now and, her face full of pleading, she gazed at him. And he could have been softened by the look of her if it weren't for the fact that if she were to roam loose about the place she would be a thorn in Delia's flesh, an agitation; and he could not risk that agitation. He said firmly, 'You must be married, Molly. I want to hear no more.' He rose to his feet.

'Master!' She rushed round the desk now and caught at his hand. 'I'll plead with Davie, I'll beg him to take me. I can make him do it; just give me time.'

'Your time will be wasted; he was up in the gallery of the malt house when we met yesterday.'

She put her hand tightly over the lower part of her face, and he nodded slowly at her. 'He had seen Miss Jane in distress and had gone to fetch her.'

Slowly she took her hand from her mouth and her head drooped, and like this she whispered, 'Will I be able to see you again, Master, if, if I marry Will Curran?'

Tenderly now, he put his hand under her chin and raised her face upwards, and, his voice as low as hers, he answered, 'You'll see me again, Molly, when the time is ripe, never fear. Go now and do as you're bid and I'll always see that you are well looked after.'

She stared up into his eyes. She had been loved by this man, and she had known pride because of it; and power an' all, aye, power. She had defied her da because of the secret power her master's patronage had given her. But now she no longer felt she possessed any power. In spite of the master's promise he was different. She couldn't understand it. Why? She had imagined she had him in the hollow of her hand. Her head on her chest she walked out of the room.

McBain turned to his desk and seating himself he placed his hands palm downwards on the ordered pile of papers in front of him and stared ahead for a moment. This part of the business might not turn out so bad after all. If she had married young Davie there would not have been much hope of their continued intimacy, no matter how much she manoeuvred, for Davie was no fool. But with Curran, she could handle Curran, and things would go on as before, for now that he had been deprived of his wife's bed until the child should be born and for some time afterwards he must find release in whatever quarter was available. And he knew of none sweeter than Molly; neither of his wives had satisfied him as she had ...

Until eleven o'clock in the morning he saw to the business of the farm, visiting the dairy, the byres, inspecting the animals; his eyes ranged knowledgeably around the harness-room, and the coach house where Davie was getting the gig ready. He passed him without a word. But when, in the grain store, he gave a good morning to old Sep, who was setting the terrier on to a rat's nest, and received no verbal reply, only a curt motion of the head, he walked briskly out and across the yard and into the fields. He was annoyed. There had been disdain in the old man's look, and the movement of his head had been no answer to his morning greeting, rather it had been one of censure.

He walked right to the top of Shale Tor from where he could see his sheep, well outside the precincts of the farm, away up on the distant hills. And nearer, his herd of eight cows were grazing in the morning meadows. They were the best herd he had reared and he was proud of them. He was going into Hexham this morning to meet Parson Wainwright and the Hospital Board with a view to passing on to the hospital any milk which was surplus to that which he sold to the town. He was a member of the Hospital Board, also of the Board of Guardians. Parson Hedley had proposed that he should allocate the milk to the workhouse, but he was not for this at all, not good, full cream milk – he already made an allowance of skimmed milk to that establishment; he did not believe in pampering the poor and feckless – and Parson Wainwright seconded him strongly in this.

By eleven o'clock he had returned to the farm and was ready for his journey to town. Going into the kitchen, he said to Winnie, 'Where is the mistress?'

'In the sewin' room, Master, along o' Miss Jane. The seamstress has come from Allenheads.'

He noticed that Winnie had not stopped her work when he spoke to her, nor had she looked at him once today. He felt angry that she dare show her displeasure at the turn of events. Who were they, these Armstrongs? What were they? Chattels, depending entirely on him for their livelihood. They lived well; he was a good master to them; his private life was no concern of theirs and should have brought no response from them. He said curtly, 'Tell your mistress I shall be back in time for dinner,' and on this he went out.

Winnie looked towards the door that had banged closed, and she muttered under her breath, 'Aye, I'll tell her, but not that she'll care much what time you'll be back, not from the looks of her this mornin'.'

In this moment she loathed the master. She had always looked upon him as a good master, not too easy to get on with, but fair and honest in his dealings. But now that she knew him for what he was, she realised that she had never liked him, and she hated him now for being the cause of her losing her son, and she was going to lose Davie for he was bent on leaving. Any day now he would just walk out and tramp to Newcastle, that was what he was going to do, and there find a ship, a ship that would take him round the world so that he could see places. That's what he said. He was glad, he said, things had happened as they had done, or otherwise he would have been stuck here for life and never known what he was missing.

She stopped kneading the dough in the big brown earthenware dish and looked down at her hands half lost in the elastic mounds of paste. Her life would be empty without her lad. She had never imagined them parted. He would marry of course, oh aye, and have children, but she had imagined her life would start over again with his children. And now she was to be left with her father and her husband; her father, galloping rapidly towards the grave, and her husband a creaking door that might go on for ever, yet so eaten up with rheumatics that he had forgotten, even now, how to live. The prospect of life ahead was dull and empty because the days would pass and the weeks would pass, aye, and the years would pass, and she might never see her lad again.

McBain returned at a quarter to three in the afternoon. He was wet to the skin, for the weather, which had been unusually fine for the past two weeks, had suddenly changed and he had driven through heavy rain. He was highly irritated and not a little troubled. The meeting with the Hospital Governors should have been pleasant. Usually, the manner of individual members towards him conveying their respect, which he had come to look upon as his right, pleased him; but there had been something lacking in their attitude today. One, a farmer from

55

as far away as Haydon Bridge, had slyly prodded him with the words, 'Hear you had to do a little chastisin' of a female yesterday gone.'

He had stared at the man fixedly for a moment; he was a person for whom he had no feeling, a type of farmer who smelt strongly of the byres even in his best clothes. He had answered him, 'News travels fast,' and the man had come back with, 'As fast as the crow flies.'

The crow would have had to fly all of fifteen miles to get to this man's farm, and he gauged that if he knew about the incident then so did the others present.

During the remainder of his short stay in the Assembly Rooms he had searched one face after another, looking for some reaction to the news that he had flayed a maidservant, for, to a man, he would have expected them to say, 'Those days are gone, the time is past when you can flay a servant.' All except one, that is, old Parson Hetherington, the parson was for subjugation of the flesh.

When he entered the yard no one ran to take the horse's head, and he glared about him before he got down from the trap. Where was everyone, skulking away because of the wet?

It was his practice whenever embarking on or returning from a journey, however short, always to leave and enter the house by the front way, but as he crossed the yard he saw Winnie coming from the direction of the kitchen door. She had a ripped sugar bag over her head, the corner not standing straight up but weighed down with water, and the expression on her face and her wet condition brought from him, 'What is it? What's the matter?'

'The Mistress, Master, she left the house shortly after you was gone; to take a walk, she said, but now it's past four o'clock an' has been stormin' hard this two hours or more.'

'Where did she go?' As he spoke he glanced around as if about to dart off, and she said, 'It's no knowin', Master; I've sent them out in all directions. I was anxious afore it started to rain an' sent Mickey lookin'. And Miss Jane was along the road waiting for her long afore that. But there wasn't a sight of her, and so I took the liberty of tellin' my Davie to take Prince and ride over towards Harper Town.'

'Harper Town? She would never get as far as Harper Town.'

'The Mistress is a good walker, Master, and she had a hankerin' after that part, to look at the Castle over Feather-

56

stone, an' the river. On the other hand, she might have skirted it and gone straight over to Plenmeller Common.'

'Don't be a fool, woman.' He turned on her angrily now. The very thought of Delia walking as far as Plenmeller Common, let alone being on it in a storm such as this, filled him with anxiety for the mist coming down unheralded, as it was apt to do in these parts, could in a matter of seconds turn a warm atmosphere into an icy blast and blind one to direction; unless you knew the ground with the knowledge of a shepherd you could wander for hours.

'You have no idea of the direction she took?'

'None, Master.' Winnie's tone was stiff.

'Well then,' he cried at her, his voice still angry as if she alone was responsible for the situation, 'she could have gone over there . . . over there . . . or over there!' He pointed rapidly in three different directions 'to Whitfield Moor, or Slaggyford or she could even have reached Glen Dhu and gone over the waterfall, or to Nine Banks and taken up residence in the Peel.'

Winnie stared at him. He was being sarky, but that showed he was very troubled, and right he had to be troubled an' all.

He was stalking away from her when he turned and shouted, 'Why had you to give him Prince?' and forgetting for a moment that she was talking to her betters she bawled back at the top of her voice as she would have at one of her own men, ' 'Cos he was the fastest thing on the place if you want to know.'

Her manner checked him for a moment; but only for a moment, there would be time to deal with her later.

There was no one in the stables, no one in the harness-room. He grabbed up a saddle and hurried with it to the stable, passing the gig and the patient standing horse. He could have gone searching in that, but only on the main roads, and then they too would soon be quagmires. Anyway, of one thing he was sure, wherever Delia had gone it wouldn't be for a walk along the main roads. She had done this to spite him. If anything happened to his child, if this brought her on before her time he would . . . he paused, checking the thought that he would kill her with his own hands.

As he galloped out of the gate little Mickey Geary came plodding along the road towards him, and he pulled the horse up and shouted down at him, 'Well?'

'No sign of Mistress, Master. Bin up on Peel and as far away as the start of Whitfield.'

He urged the horse on and into a gallop and in the direction of Beltingham; this way he could take in Plenmeller Common from the east side.

The rain increased and when a distant roll of thunder came to his ears he gritted his teeth. God help her if she succeeded in thwarting him.

Two hours later, soaked to the skin, outwardly cold yet burning inside with a mixture of righteous indignation and fear, he entered the farmyard to hear sounds coming from the cow byres which told him the animals were in and had been milked. He barked at a figure crossing the yard half hidden by a sack. 'Here! take him,' and Fred Geary turned and came towards him.

Dismounting stiffly he said to the man, 'Your mistress, has she returned?'

'Aye, she's returned, Master.' Geary's tone gave him no information, it was just a statement.

He drew in a deep breath and hurried from him and into the house. Winnie was coming down the stairs. She paused halfway, then came on towards him.

'How is she? Where had she been? How long has she been in?'

She answered the three questions in their order. 'She's in some distress, Master. She lost her way on the Common in the rain. She's been back this half-hour.' Then she added, 'Miss Jane found her.' She prevented herself from going further and saying, 'The child was in as bad a state as her mother,' for she knew he wasn't concerned with his daughter's welfare, nor yet for that matter with his wife's – his main thought centred round what she was carrying. He was a single-minded man was the master, always had been, except for diversions now and again. Since yesterday she had called to mind a diversion he'd had some years ago. That had been with a girl hardly out of childhood an' all. A strange man was the master. She went on into the kitchen, he up the stairs, and without ceremony he entered the bedroom.

Delia was undressed and in bed. Her face looked colourless; her breathing was deep and inclined to gasping. He stood over her and stared at her, but she did not return his look. Her eyes were hooded, their gaze directed over the mound of her stomach towards her feet.

'What madness have you been up to?'

She remained silent while she imagined, as she had often before, that there was no measurement she knew of which could take the depth or width of his voice when he was angry or merely displeased, the tone was so thin it flattened the words until they had no substance, yet held and maintained some element that pierced like the point of a knife.

'You did this on purpose, didn't you? In retaliation.' He waited for some response before going on, 'All right, retaliate against me but save it until the child is born. You can spend the coming weeks working out ways and means to make me suffer for my lapse, but I warn you' – now his body was bent over hers, drips of water from the front of his hair actually dropping on to the breast of her nightgown – 'if you purposely harm that child, if you have harmed it by your escapade today, you will live to regret it. You know me, Delia. When I speak as now, I don't make idle threats.' Slowly he straightened his body, and again he waited, but still she made no response.

Not until he had left the room did she raise her eyes. Then she looked towards the door, and when she heard him shouting from the top of the stairs: 'Winnie! See that I have hot water for bathing in the closet room immediately,' she knew how far she had tested him, for he never shouted his orders around the house; always on his guard, always giving the good example; his tone might be icy, but he kept it controlled. Now, like any ordinary common farmer, he was bawling at his servants.

She lay staring up at the ceiling. She felt exhausted, slightly ill. She'd had no intention of hurting the child. What had happened today had come about purely by accident. She was on the Common and about to turn for home when the storm had overtaken her. At one period she had become frightened, at another resigned, and had thought, if I lie down and this rain continues all night I could be well on the way to death in the morning, and it with me. But she had not lain down, she had tried to find her way home. She had not known that she was only a short distance from the road until she heard Jane's voice crying, 'Mother! Mother! Are you there, Mother?' But for her daughter's timely coming she might have had to lie down through sheer exhaustion. That being the case he would have said it was deliberate, as he did now. But what matter? What matter anything? She was very tired and no longer cold, her body was burning, her heart was burning, scalded.

Three

'Don't talk of the morrow, lad.' Winnie, her shoulders stooped with weariness, gazed sadly at her son. 'Wait until I have time to get me breath an' talk to you, quiet like, and know what you're going to do. As it is I'm run off me legs over there and I'm droppin' for want of sleep. He says I've got to sit by her the night again. I wonder what he thinks I am, a machine that doesn't need rest? . . . So lad' – she put out her hand and touched Davie's shoulder – 'let it rest for a day or two. He hasn't actually told you to go, now has he? If you're determined to go, well you can pick your own time, but wait until the mistress is on her feet again?'

'But when will that be, Ma?'

'Soon as the fever goes down, a couple of days at the most I should say.'

'Is she goin' to lose it?' Sep leant forward in his chair. 'A fever such as this could bring it on.'

Winnie bit on her lip and turned her head to the side as she said, 'I hope to God she doesn't, there'll be hell to pay, he'll go mad. Yet I could bet ten to one she's havin' her pains though she doesn't say.'

'How could she keep quiet havin' pains?' Ned cast a disdainful glance at his wife.

'She could.' Her voice was harsh. 'She's got an inner stubbornness. It doesn't show, but it's there. I've 'tected it more than once. Still I hope to God I'm wrong; she's had enough to put up with in her life without this final blow. An' if he were to lose his son . . . '

'Son be damned!' Davie's voice cut her short. 'How does he know what it'll be, has he had a word on the side with God Almighty? I bet he thinks he has, the psalm-singing holy lecher.'

'That's enough!' His father's voice cut him short, but he turned on him, crying, 'It isn't enough, Da. An' don't try to shut me up here; if I can't speak me mind in me own home then I'd better clag me mouth up altogether, for I can't open it outside.' He paused and looked from one to the other, then ended, 'By God! things want changin' in this country; they've got us all so bloody nooled, we're no better than the niggers, it wants a Wilberforce here. Charity begins at home. An' they're pattin' themselves on the back for freeing the Boers from the Zulus, when it's us that wants freeing. As do the Irish; no wonder there's risin's there. If they can free the bloody Boers why can't they let the Irish rule their own country and not have them floodin' us an' takin' the bread out of our mouths. They hate Parnell; I say good luck to him.'

Mother, father and grandfather gaped at him. They had never heard of Parnell, nor yet of Wilberforce, not one of them could read. The bedroom in the roof held a conglomeration of old newspapers and three books, all passed on to him by Parson Hedley. He never discussed what he read but in this moment his garbled smattering of world events made him appear as a being apart, a creature of another species, older than themselves, very learned.

Winnie felt a warm pride flood her, a pride that brought a smarting of tears to the back of her eyes. This lad of hers would go places, he would become something; with a mind as knowledgeable and inquisitive as his nothing could stop him once he got away. No matter what her private feelings were she knew it was a good thing for him that he was leaving the farm.

To stop her tears from falling she applied herself to everyday necessities by saying, 'That's as it may be, but there's a meal to see to and I cannot get it; you'll have to fend for yourselves 'cos I'm away across again.' She went hastily towards the door, but there she turned and looked at Davie, and as their gazes linked and held she knew he would do as she had asked and not go yet awhile.

As she went out of the front door of the cottage Ned rose from his seat and went out the back way, down to the midden. He was distressed at the thought of his son going, but could not show it. But not so old Sep. The old man, looking at his grandson, said slowly, 'You're fixed in your mind then, lad?'

'Aye, Granda.'

'Well, I'm not blamin' you, no fraction of me is blamin' you, but I'll tell you one thing, things'll never be the same when you're gone . . . If you take to the sea how long do you reckon you'll be away?'

'Hard to tell, Granda. It could be a year, two maybe, or three.'

'Aye, that is what I was fearin'.' He nodded. 'Well, I only

hope I'll be here when you come back. Now' – he raised his hand – 'I'm not latherin' you with soft soap, I'll go when me time comes an' not afore. But I can tell you this much, if I was your age and livin' in this changing day – although I can neither read nor write I can tell the signs, you've only got to be half an hour in the town to see them – aye, things are changin' and changin' fast, an' as I said if I was in your shoes, lad, I'd be off the morrow and matchin' up to the times, for after all what is life but a feather in the fire. We're all feathers in the fire; time passes on us like a lick of flame, one minute we're there, the next we're gone, forgotten, as if we'd never been.'

'I wouldn't say that, Granda.'

'It's true, it's true, lad, and remember it. Kings and great men are forgotten, so why should the likes of us be remembered.'

'I'll never forget you, Granda, never fear.' Davie walked towards the old man and, bending, put his hand on his shoulder. It was an unusual gesture of affection, perhaps the first open expression of their love for each other since he had been a small boy. 'You're a wise man, Granda. I have always known you to be a wise man, and you'll not be forgotten, at least not by me. Anyway' – he punched the old man playfully in the chest – 'what you talkin' about? You'll likely be smokin' that stinking old pipe of yours when I'm pushin' the daisies up, or more likely chasing the mermaids at the bottom of the sea.'

Although old Sep laughed now, he said, 'Don't talk like that, lad. If you pray for anything, pray that you die on dry land and be settled to rest firmly in the ground.'

At this point the back door opened and Ned entered. Looking from one to the other he asked abruptly, 'Does nobody want to eat?' and at this they all three set about getting the evening meal, which was, as usual on a Friday, as on Thursday, Wednesday and Tuesday, mutton broth.

For the second night running Winnie sat by the mistress's side, and tonight there was more need for her presence. Although the mistress wouldn't admit it, Winnie was positive she was having pains; if not, then she must be suffering some sort of cramping seizure.

The truth was that Delia was having pains. Though her temperature was high and at times her head swam and was full of strange thoughts, she nevertheless knew she must not admit to the pains. She told herself to lie still, perfectly still, and everything inside her would settle. Anyway they were not true pains; the intervals between them, she considered, were too long to be true pains, and she mustn't have true pains. When she thought of true pains she saw McBain's face hanging over her. She heard his voice again saying, 'If you purposely harm that child, if you have harmed it by your escapade today, you will live to regret it. You know me, Delia. When I speak as now, I don't make idle threats.'

She was aware that he visited her frequently, but she never looked at him. Although her hidden strength had come to the surface and she dared now to defy him, there still remained in her a fear of him. The fear had been with her too long, and was too well founded on her private knowledge of him for her to erase it now, and she dreaded the consequences if she failed to carry his child to its time . . .

It was towards eleven o'clock at night that a pain attacked her which told her that the child was coming and nothing she could do would prevent it. She had been woken from a nightmarish dream by a grinding in her loins; it was a well remembered experience and couldn't be disregarded. As it forced the truth on her she gripped handfuls of the bed tick in an effort to stifle her moans and still her fear. Winnie was sitting by the bedside, her head was drooped in sleep, and she put out her hand towards her, but Winnie didn't move. The pain subsided, and she gave herself the ease of gasping.

She leaned on her side and stared towards the fire. It was bright and had recently been tended. The lamp too was burning steadily. Should she waken Winnie? No, no what was she thinking about? She'd run straight to her master. Anyway, she was tired, worn out, let her sleep. She lay back and looked at her servant, and wished from the bottom of her heart that she could change places with her. She was the centre of a close family, the pivot around which father, husband and son revolved. She envied her her life.

Winnie opened her eyes and blinked; then bending forward, said quickly, 'You all right, Mistress?'

'Yes, Winnie.'

Winnie put out her hand and touched the deep brow. 'Ah, that's better, you're cooler.'

'Am I, Winnie?'

63

'Yes, Mistress.'

'Winnie.'

'Yes, Mistress.'

'Hold my hand.'

Slowly Winnie put out her square, broken-nailed hand and clasped the slender white one held towards her, and after a moment she asked softly, 'Are you sure you're all right, Mistress?'

Delia didn't answer, she just nodded, and at this point Winnie, who was never given to tears, had for the second time in two days a strong inclination to cry . . .

At seven o'clock the next morning when she handed McBain his tea in the kitchen she answered his question. 'She's better in that the fever's gone down.'

As he took the cup from her he said shortly, 'Well, is there anything else?'

'I can't say, Master, only that she seems tired.'

'Rest will cure that. There's . . . there's no sign of the child coming?'

'She doesn't say, Master.'

'Say or not' – his voice had risen – 'you'd be able to tell.'

And now, also for the second time in two days, her voice rose to answer his. 'How can I tell when she gives no sign? I am no doctor.'

He gritted his teeth while he stared at her; then forcing himself to calmness, he added, 'Well, you don't think the fever has had any effect?'

She turned her head to the side and shook it as she answered, 'Not that I can say at the moment, Master. Yet the mistress is not herself.'

He turned away and walked to the door. He was well aware that she was not herself, but her emotional condition didn't trouble him; as long as she held on to what was in her and gave it a chance of life, that was all that he was concerned about at the moment.

So much did this matter take up his mind that Molly, coming out of the far door of the dairy, caused no ripple to pass through him. She was carrying two large pails of skim, and she dropped them with a clatter on a small platform ready for Johnnie to pick up and take to the pigs, and when she hitched up her full breasts with the cushions of her thumbs there was no tightening of his loins, no deep drawing in of breath.

64

He finished his tea and turned from the door and, coming back into the kitchen, said, 'You think she necessitates the doctor?'

Again Winnie turned her head to the side and shook it before saying, 'That's up to you, Master. That's up to you.'

Yes, that was up to him, but the last person he wanted to talk with Delia at this moment was old Cargill. He was a fusspot, a gossiping, probing fusspot. By now, like all those in Hexham, he would have heard of the flaying and were he to call, he would, with a question here, a nudge there, as he sauntered around the farm, come to the truth quicker than any judge, after which he himself would be in for a long rigmarolling admonition. No, he didn't want Cargill here just to attend her in a fever. But if he thought there was the slightest suspicion that the child was affected then he would gallop into the town himself and fetch him.

He glanced at Winnie again. She'd know. She was a knowledgeable woman, a sensible woman, and she had an affection for her mistress, so therefore her perception would be keener.

Winnie brought his attention to her again as she said, 'Who's to stay when you're all at church, Master? I think it should be somebody who could use his legs just in case; me da's not much use in that way.'

He was walking towards the door again as he said briefly, 'I'll be here.'

Although Delia in her present state could not carry out her threat of denouncing him in church, he thought that her indisposition would not only supply an excuse for his absence today but also for the coming Sundays ahead until the child was born. After that he would meet events as they came. One thing he was certain of, once the boy was born he'd put her in her place again.

The pain that now rent her body seemed to split it in two. It had attacked her quite suddenly, waking her from a half-dazed sleep. To save herself crying out against it she bit tight down on the side of her hand, and when it had passed she lay gasping.

The sound of her heavy breathing should have brought Molly from the dressing-room, but it didn't. When the sweat had cleared from her eyes she looked towards the open door where, reflected through the mirror of the wardrobe in the light of the lamp, she could see the girl, her head lolling to the side as she slept in an upright chair.

She had said to Winnie, who was very tired, 'Go and rest, I'll be all right,' but Winnie wouldn't listen until McBain commanded, 'Go to bed woman, the girl will take your place,' then she herself had been forced to protest and had cried at him, 'I do not need a watchdog. Anyway, Jane can sit with me.'

To this he had replied calmly, 'Jane has been on her feet all day, she is worn out. Anyway, you need a night-attendant, a nurse, and tomorrow morning I'm sending into Hexham for one, and the doctor too. You have been too long in this state for your health.'

She had lifted her hand and dismissed Winnie from the room. Then looking at him fully for the first time in days, she had muttered from deep in her throat, 'I will not have the girl in this room. Nor will I have her in the house once I am about.' And he had turned his back on her as he gave her his reply, 'She will sit in the dressing-room within call. As for your whims, we will deal with them when the time comes.'

Winnie had come up before going home at nine o'clock and said soothingly, 'I will just take a few hours, Mistress. In the meantime, if you should feel you want me call to her and she will come and fetch me.'

She had almost put her hand out and said, 'Sleep here, Winnie,' but had she done so it would have shown her alarm, and so she had allowed them to install the girl in the dressing-room, and for well into the night she had lain and watched her. Twice she had disappeared from view and gone into the closet-room. At this, she had wanted to shout, 'Come away from that room, girl. How dare you! Go out to your midden, that is your place, the midden.'

Yet as she berated the girl in her mind she knew the situation wasn't of her making; although she had become a party to it she would never, in the first place, have dared to approach McBain.

As another pain seized her she wondered why she was trying to hide the fact that the child was about to be born. What would it avail her now? She brought up her knees to her chest and groaned; then she cried aloud as the whole of her inside slipped into a flaming hell of pain, and now with her eyes screwed up tight, she groaned, 'Girl! Girl!'

When the spasm eased for a second and she opened her eyes there was no one by her side. She could not see the girl through the mirror now because her vision was blurred with sweat. Again her body was shot into pain, so excruciating this time that she lost consciousness. When she came to herself she was lying on her back, her legs wide apart, and the child's head had thrust itself into life. When the shoulders followed she screamed a thin, high piercing scream, and to her own voice was joined another, and she knew the girl was with her. She heard her yelling, 'Master! Master!' There followed another pain . . . and then another . . . and then great ease.

Her eyes closed, everything was quiet. She felt that she herself had stopped breathing. In the peace she lifted her lids and saw McBain standing halfway down the bed. He had on his long nightshirt and he was staring downwards, as was the girl standing by his side. Slowly she allowed her limbs to relax, and now she lifted her head slightly and looked down along her deflated body, and there, lying between her legs on the blood-stained sheet and still attached to her, was her child – or part of her child. There was something wrong with it, something missing. She looked upwards to her husband's face, and God in His wrath could never have looked like this. She took refuge against it in unconsciousness . . .

The turmoil in McBain's brain was something beyond even his own understanding, for the feelings of revulsion, anger and disappointment were so deep, so desolate that they combined to a torture, and when he looked back he knew that for a space of time his brain had been turned, and that, like any madman, he might have committed a crime, except that Molly had torn his hands from his wife's neck, then had dragged him into the dressing-room, pleading with him while she repeated just one word, 'Master! Master!'

Not until she had managed to thrust him down into the chair, saying, 'Stay, stay, Master, for God's sake, while I get Winnie,' did a little of his sanity return, and he checked her with his hand gripping her arm. Then he wiped the sweat from his face while he gulped air into his lungs, and he continued to hold her until he had the power to speak, when he said, 'Take . . . take it out and bury it.'

'MASTER!'

'Do as I bid you.'

'B . . . but, Master.'

'Go on, do what I say. And quickly.'

She backed from him and slowly went into the bedroom, and

as if approaching a lion's cage she went towards the bed. And there she separated the mother and child. The cutting of the umbilical cord was not new to her, she had helped her mother on several occasions. And she knew what to do with a newborn child; if it didn't yell straight away you took it by the legs and held it upside down.

Frantically she looked about her for something to put round the child. Her eyes alighting on the mistress's cashmere shawl, she grabbed it and put it over the infant, then rolled it on to its face so that she could lift it up without touching it. As she straightened her back it gave a thin cry, and at this her eyes and mouth sprang wide and her terrified glance went towards the dressing-room door, then returned to the wrinkled face peeping out from the fold of the shawl, and she muttered, 'Oh, God Almighty!' Placing the child on the day couch at the foot of the bed, she ran into the dressing-room and, standing before McBain, she spluttered, 'I, I can't. I c . . . can't, Master, 'tis alive, breathin'.'

McBain had been sitting with his head deep on his chest, almost as if he was asleep; and now his whole body jerked upwards and he grasped her again, by both arms this time, and slowly he said, 'Listen to me, girl. It's for the best. You have seen it; imagine if it were allowed to live. Each time I looked on it I would see it as God's hand on me in retribution . . . you understand?' He stared into her red sweating face. He knew she was a simple girl and here he was asking her to understand something he was only dimly comprehending himself. It was all bound up with the saying that God is not mocked. Delia had been right, but he felt the retribution wasn't because he had lusted with this young girl so much as that he had done it while praising God. Jesus Christ's one abhorrence was a hypocrite, and the thing in there was God's answer to hypocrisy . . . and in this moment he hated God for it.

'No, Master, no.' She was whimpering like a hurt animal.

'Molly, you love me?'

'Aye, Master.'

'Then do as I bid you. Look.' He got to his feet, still holding her. 'Take it to the copse and drop it into the pool, the bog part.'

Her head was back on her shoulders wagging in desperation. 'But what'll you say, Master, what'll you tell them? Dead or alive, Winnie and Miss Jane, they'll expect to see it.'

He shook her impatiently now, then whispered, 'It came away in bits. Tell them that, it came away in bits and you put it in the muck cart. When you come back you can take the afterbirth and dump it there. Go now, go on.'

He thrust her towards the bedroom door, and like someone drunk she staggered into the room again. Stopping for a moment she looked over the foot of the bed at the inert, distorted, unsightly figure of her mistress; then she grabbed the small bundle in the shawl and crept out of the room.

When she reached the bottom of the stairs and heard a door above her open with a squeak, she knew that Miss Jane had woken up, and at this she took to her heels and flew through the kitchen, out into the yard, and along the road towards the copse.

Davie sat on the side of his bed looking out of the low attic window. The rain had stopped, the moon was shining and seeming to be wafted from one scud of clouds to another by the high wind that was blowing. There were only the clouds and the noise in the chimney breast behind him to indicate the strength of the wind; as far as he could see the land was treeless and fell, to rise again sharply to the hills beyond. His vision did not take in the copse that lay to the right of him, for his head was resting against the wooden shutter that barred the window from the inside and kept out the weather in the winter.

This was to be the last night he would sleep in this room for a long time to come. He didn't know how long, years perhaps, or never again. He felt sad, depressed, yet at the same time he was experiencing an odd kind of elation, for whatever lay before him he knew would be strange and exciting. He gave no thought to a hungry belly, or hardship, he was young and strong, and, as he told himself, he had his wits about him; what was more, he had advantage over the majority of his kind for he could read and write and, if it was required of him, talk with the best of them, at least so he told himself. But nevertheless, he was sad, deeply sad. He was going to miss his mother, and he would even miss his father; but most of all, aye most of all, he'd miss his granda.

It was odd, he thought, but if the events of yesterday had not taken place he might in the end, in fact he knew he would, have married Molly Geary and remained for the rest of his life on this farm, in this hollow in the hills, and might never have got even as far as Alnwick. He had promised himself for the last two or three years that one day he would go to Alnwick and see the castle, the stronghold of the Percys. Parson Hedley had told him quite a bit about the Percys, great fighting men the Percys, men it was an honour to serve. He wished now he could go back down the centuries and ride by young Hotspur's side, even if he was but a lad of twelve, and with him retake Berwick and kill every damn Scot in it, his master included, for it was McBain's boast that his forebears went back to the fourteenth century. He had a sword hanging in the hall that he was forever pointing out was used at Duns when the Scots routed the English, but he said nought about the defeat of 50,000 of the hairy-legged galoots being beaten by half their number at Neville's Cross. Why, when he came to think of it, what was McBain compared with men like the Percy's? Midden muck, that's all, midden muck.

Two days ago he wouldn't have thought of the comparison, but now it seemed apt, not because he had found out about the master whoring, nor that he hid his escapades under a cloak of piety. No, his animosity was derived from the personal insult McBain had directed towards his manhood. 'Marry Molly,' he said, 'and cover up for my fly-blow.' Like hell he would. If he was to father a child he would know the beginnings of it as well as the end. Oh aye . . . By, she was a rampant cow, that Molly. You found them here and there among the stock; not for them, waiting for their turn, right at the front they were, almost putting the bull to shame . . .

As if his thoughts had conjured up their substance into form he saw her. She came running into a patch of moonlight opposite Curran's back gate. She was on the grass bank raised above the lane and was carrying something in her arms. He bent forward, his face close to a small pane. What was she up to at this time of night, or mornin' as it was? Where could she be making for running along the bank? It was a dead end, the railing shut off the copse.

A cloud distorted her shape for a moment. The wind was lifting her skirt into a half circle behind her legs, and she looked as if she were flying.

He stood up but still stooped and moved his head to the other side of the window. He saw that she had reached the railings, and he watched her drop the bundle on to the ground, climb over; and then she was lost in the low scrub, all except her hands that came out and pulled the bundle under the bottom rail.

He stepped three paces back from the window to where the ceiling allowed him to stand straight and he looked from one corner of the little room to the other as if he would find the answer to his thoughts. What was she taking into the copse at this time of night? It was dangerous in there in the day time; there was bog all round the water hole. Whatever she had with her was meant for the water hole. But what?

He did not wait any longer for an answer but pulled open the door and ran down the stairs; and as he rushed out of the back door he heard his mother's voice crying, 'Is that you, Davie, you awake?' Within seconds he had reached the railing and was over it and into the copse. He paused for a moment and listened; but the wind covered all sound but its own thrashing. There were two narrow paths not more than twenty feet apart and both leading to the water hole. They had been made many years ago before the springs had started to divert and make the place a danger to man and cattle.

Before he reached the end of the path he had taken he saw her. She was standing on the edge of the bog looking down at the thing she was holding in her hands. The moon was full on her and she was rigid, but she was evidently going to throw whatever she was carrying into the pool, and once in there it would be lost for ever – it was said to be bottomless. He had never tried to prove this; even his adventurous boyish spirit hadn't been brave enough to test the depth of this awesome place, not after he had seen a cow sink like a stone in the mud at its edge.

'What you up to?' He thought for a moment she was going to fall backwards into the bog and he rushed forward and gripped her arms, that were in turn gripping the bundle to her.

'What you up to? What's this?' He had to hold on to her to keep her steady for her whole body was now shaking like a cart going over a rutted road. He took one hand from her arm and touched the top of the bundle; then he pulled the blanket back and gazed downwards.

'Aw, my God! YOU! YOU! YOU WICKED HUSSY YOU!'

'No, no, Davie, no, no, I wouldn't, I couldn't have.'

'What did you come in here for then?'

'The master. But . . . but I couldn't.'

'You would if I hadn't stopped you, an' it breathing an' all.'

71

He pulled the shawl farther away from the face; then he said in a deep tone that might have been used by Pastor Wainwright, 'If there's a hell you'll go to it for this.'

'Davie! Davie!' She was crying now and loudly. 'I wouldn't, I wouldn't.'

'Shut up! an' get back.' He gripped her by the shoulders and pushed her forward, and she tried to turn to him as she spluttered, 'You don't know, you don't know, Davie.'

'Go on, out of it.' He thrust her along the path until they reached the railings, and there he let go of her and she pushed the bundle under the bottom rail, and when she tried to climb over she almost fell on to the other side. She did not stoop immediately and pick up the bundle, but stood leaning against the rails gasping as she looked up at him. The tears were raining from her eyes, her mouth was wide; she tried to speak but the words were choked in her throat.

He bent down to her.

'Get!' He pointed, and at this she stooped and picked up the child again. And once more he was pushing her forward and towards the figure that was standing in the road outside the front door.

Winnie, a coat over her calico nightgown, came towards them, saying under her breath, 'What in the name of God is it? What's happened?'

'Get inside.'

Her eyes flashed from him to Molly; then she hurried back into the cottage and he followed her, still thrusting Molly before him.

Although there was a candle burning on the kitchen table the light in the cottage was dim compared with that outside. Davie peered towards the stairs, where his father was descending with his granda behind him. His granda was saying, 'What's up? What's up, lad?'

For answer he turned to Molly saying, 'You tell them.'

Molly now placed the bundle on the table and leaned over it, her shoulders shaking, her sobbing uncontrolled, and Winnie, going to her, said, 'What is it, girl, what is it?'

But all Molly could say was, 'I wouldn't have, I couldn't, I couldn't.'

Winnie put her hand out tentatively towards the bundle, asking now, 'What have you in there?' and before Molly could answer Davie cried, 'Go on, tell her. Tell her what you've got in

72

there, an' what you were aimin' to do with it.'

They were all surprised at Molly's next reaction for, turning from the table and gulping on each word, she bawled at him, 'You! You! God you are, aren't you! God. Well, I wouldn't have, no matter what you think, I wouldn't have. I couldn't, I was just wonderin' what to do. Even though the master bade me.'

Taken aback for a moment Davie remained silent, as they all were, and then he said, 'He told you to drown a bairn? the missus's bairn . . . couldn't be anybody else's.'

'Aye, aye, he did. An' 'cos why, cleversides. Look, look.' She swung round to the table and tore the blanket first one way and then the other from the tiny form.

They all stared down at the little creature. It had a head and two arms and a body, but no legs. There were two fleshy protusions where the legs should have been and from these hung two pieces of distorted flesh, what might have been termed, with a stretch of imagination, a pair of feet.

'God save us this night.' It was a faint whisper from Winnie, but it was echoed in the eyes of the three men.

There followed a long silence, which wasn't broken until Winnie went to a table in a corner of the room on which stood a bucket and bowl, and took from its drawer a square of rough linen, and having dipped it into the bucket of water she came back to the table and gently wiped the slime from around the child's eyes; then she passed the cloth over its face, and as she did so it cried out loud for the first time in its life.

It was Ned who spoke first. Quietly he said, 'I can understand why he wanted to get rid of it, it's natural.'

'Natural! God! Da! You say it's natural, a child livin' and breathin'. And then he hadn't the guts to do his dirty work himself. Natural!'

'It hasn't happened to you, lad. You're born but you're not buried yet.' His father's voice was harsh, and Davie cried back at him, 'Well, if it did happen to me, I'd put up with the consequences. Any road, I'd do me own murderin'.'

Sep put in quietly now, 'There's bairns been born without legs afore the day and lived to be old men, good old men at that. You remember the Millburns over near Newbiggin, well they had a lad who hadn't a leg to stand on so to speak, and he was a potter, one of the finest in the country, and died worth a bit. An' he married at that.'

'Aye, well, when you're on remembering' – Ned nodded his head vigorously at his father-in-law now – 'also reckon-on Harry Watt's daughter, one stump of an arm and no legs and her head the size of two . . . And then not five years since there was a child they tell us born over near Beltingham not an arm to him, everything got to be done for him. There's somethin' to be said after all for makin' a quick end to such.'

As Davie turned away from the table, Winnie said, 'What's to be done?'

'He'll have to be taken back, lass,' her father answered, and at this Molly cried, 'No, no. Eeh! no. The master wouldn't have it, he wants a son, a real son.'

'Then you'll have to give him one, won't you?' There was a deep bitterness in Davie's voice, and Molly again faced him, but all she could say this time was, 'You! You!'

'Look, lass.' Sep touched her arm gently. 'He's got a son, a bit short in the limbs perhaps, but you never know. God works in strange ways, he might turn out to be a comfort to him.'

Molly's head swung from side to side as she muttered, 'I can't, I can't take him back.'

'All right, lass, I'll take him.'

The girl looked up into Winnie's face and whimpered, 'He won't have him, Winnie, he won't.'

'We'll see about that. Come on, Ma.' They all looked at Davie now. He was standing with the open door in his hand and when his father said, 'You stay out of this, it's none of your business,' he jerked his head towards him. 'No, none of my business. I've saved its life, haven't I? Another minute and it would have been at the bottom of the water hole. She can say what she likes but that's what would have happened to it, so I take it, it is me business . . . Anyway, in a few hours I'll be left this place an' I want to do him one last service. Come on, Ma.'

Winnie heaved a deep sigh, lifted the child from the table and followed her son out, and Molly, after glancing from Ned to Sep in a desperate fashion, went after them.

No one spoke until they were crossing the farmyard; then Winnie turned and whispered to Molly, 'The mistress, how did she take it?' And Molly muttered through her crying, 'Bad, she passed away in a faint.'

'Why didn't you come for me earlier?' They were nearing the kitchen door now and Molly, hanging back, said, 'I didn't know, I dozed; an' then I heard her cry out, an' there it was on the

bed.' She stood still before she added, 'I'm not comin' in, I'm
... I'm afeared.'

'Don't be silly, girl!' Winnie's voice was low and harsh.
'Somebody's got to see to the child, I'll have to attend the
mistress. Here, take him.'

Backing from Winnie, Molly shook her head and muttered,
'I daresn't, I daresn't, Winnie, I daresn't.'

'Give him here.' Davie's voice was quiet, even calm sounding, so much so that his mother looked at him in inquiry; then
after a moment's hesitation she handed him the child, saying,
'He'll have to be kept on the side for a time, away from both of
them.'

'You mean you're not goin' to tell him it's back?'

His tone was as it had been before, and she answered with
equal sharpness, 'Of course he'll have to be told; but let him
get his breath ... Molly' – she turned to where Molly had been
standing, but Molly was no longer there. There was no sight of
her in the yard, and again Winnie heaved a deep sigh, then said,
'Keep it warm; I'll rouse Miss Jane.'

The sound of a loud wail coming from up above startled
them both. When it rose to a scream Winnie rushed out of the
room. After a moment Davie went towards the fire, pulling a
cracket after him. Seated on it, he looked down at the baby on
his lap. The face was wrinkled, the eyes in the lowered light
from the oil lamp looked dark, black; the hair on the head was
fair. He never considered babies to be as attractive as young
calves, at least not until they started to gurgle and move about a
bit, but there was something about this one's face that kept his
eyes riveted on it. Somehow it didn't look like a baby's face at
all; not that it was marred, it wasn't. He supposed many would
consider it bonny for a new-born babe, but there was a look of
age about it that wasn't suggested by the wrinkles.

He started again as he heard another high scream from the
room above. The missis was taking it badly. There came the
sound of a door banging loudly, and then the screaming died
away.

He never heard McBain enter the room; the door from the
passage was open. McBain was wearing slippers, but he had
no sooner stepped over the threshold than Davie became aware
of his presence, and he turned slowly and looked at him. But his
master did not return his glance for his gaze was concentrated
on the bundle Davie was holding on his knee.

75

As McBain came towards the middle of the room Davie rose from the cracket and went towards the table, and there they stood, one on each side.

McBain's face was ashen. He no longer looked at the child but straight into Davie's eyes, and if it had been possible to strike him dead at this moment he would have done so; if there had been a knife in his hand he would have used it; the rage in him was like molten steel, white hot, fusing all his emotions into a bar of hate.

'You mustn't blame Molly, Master,' Davie's voice was low and cool sounding. 'She did her best to carry out your instructions, I just managed to stop her in time.'

'Get out! Get out of my sight, off my land.' McBain's voice was choked with his passion, and Davie, dropping his quiet pose now, cried back at him, 'Aye, I'll get out of your sight an' off your land. I'll leave at dawn and not afore, because I don't want to wake up Parson Wainwright and Parson Hedley afore the sun is up, because I'm going to give them a message, I'm goin' to tell them that your son's been born and you want either one of them to come over and christen him proper like, because you don't know what might happen to him. I'll make it me business to tell them both 'cos if I was only givin' me message to old Wainwright it's my belief it wouldn't take much for him to finish off what Molly started so you'll keep his hand greased. But not Parson Hedley, no. So I'll see that they both know that your son has been born. I'll tell them he's without legs, but, as me granda says, he's likely been given something else to make up for them. They say God's ways are strange.'

A gasp from the doorway brought his lightning glance to Jane. She was standing with one hand on the side of her face. How long she had been there he didn't know, but he dared to call to her and say, 'Come here, Miss Jane, and take your brother, he needs care.'

There was a wooden mallet lying at the end of the table – Winnie used it for tenderising the meat – and when like a flash McBain's hand went out to it and gripped the handle, Jane sprang towards him, crying, 'Father! Father!'

It was not her puny strength that stopped him but the fact of her presence, and as she hung on to his arm she cried at Davie, 'Go on, get out! Get away, go on!' and he went.

Slowly he walked out of the kitchen and across the farmyard and up the road into the cottage. He had burned his boats.

In the kitchen his father and granda were sitting by the rekindled fire. 'What happened?' asked Ned anxiously, and he told them, ending, 'He would have brained me, yet if I had lifted me hand he would have had me jailed. There's somethin' wrong with the laws of this land when a working man's life is held so cheaply.'

Ned looked at him, then said quietly, 'I'm sorry to say it, lad, but if he had hit you you'd only have got what you asked for. You tried him too far; a man, good or bad, can only stand so much.'

'Whose side are you on, Da?' Davie's tone was hurt and harsh.

'I'm on nobody's side. Only this I'll say, an' I don't want to, and at this time. You'll be gone in a matter of hours, an' we're left here, an' he's still our master. You're young, lad, and have your furrows to sow, but you should give a thought to others.' And on this he rose and went heavily up the stairs.

Davie stood looking hangdog for a moment. Some part of him knew his father was right, yet his youth protested against the injustice as he saw it, and he turned to his grandfather and said, 'Well, what d'you think of that? Nice partin' gift. There's something I'm gona tell you, Granda. I'm never going to let any man master me like they have him. As I said, an' I'll say again, lives are held too cheap, not worth a farthin' candle, they're not.'

'All life is cheap and brief, lad,' said Sep sadly. 'We're blown into it, then we're nipped out, king and commoner, all the same. But what I say is, God help the little life that was born the night, for his comin' will bring changes. Aye, it will that. This farm, this happy farm, for it's been that, say what you will, will never be the same again, nor anybody in it.'

Book Two: 1884

One

It was a week since the snow had disappeared but it was still only March and there would likely be more flurries, if not a deep fall, before spring really settled on the hills, but the bright hard sunshine was giving the impression that it had already come to stay and was agitating the restlessness in all life. It was working strongly in Jane, now bordering on sixteen years of age, but she didn't recognise it except as a desire to get out and walk; walk the hills, the moors, walk towards Allendale and climb the crags or lie on a high fell and watch the water racing down in froth-tipped leaps over stubborn stones to the river.

It seemed a simple desire, one so easy of fulfilment, for she was surrounded by the means of bringing her wish to life. But nearer at hand, within two arm-lengths of her, was the reason why she could not just walk out and over the hills. Amos McBain, three years and six months old, was seated in a chair, the seat of which was nine inches from the ground. The boy's body was sturdy. The arms were rounded and filled the sleeves of his dress. His face had a squarish look; the mouth was wide, the nose thin, but it was the eyes that caught the attention. They were almond-shaped and gave him a curious appearance. His hair, very fair, clustered in unruly curls about his head. Altogether it wasn't a face, you could say, that typified those bred in the northern dales. The colouring and shape of the head might have suggested Scandinavian blood, but the eyes, dominating the whole face, brought one firmly to the conviction that somewhere along the lines of either the McBains or the Lawsons there had been oriental blood. This conviction would have been entirely misleading, for both families had been firmly entrenched in the north of Britain, the McBains going no further north than Edinburgh, and the Lawsons south to Yorkshire.

The overall impression given out by the seated child was one of strange fascination; that was until, thrusting himself forward, he attempted to walk, then embarrassment and a slight revulsion, which could not overwhelm pity, would have been the first reaction of any visitor. But then this contingency never occurred, for there were no strange visitors to the attic in the old part of the house, the only people who had ever entered the room, and who made up Amos McBain's world, were Winnie, Molly, Parson Hedley and Jane.

But Winnie and Molly, and even the parson, were as visitors in his life, only Jane was permanent in his narrow world, the world that was like an egg shell about him and out of which he was now aiming to break through and be born.

'I want to, Jan,' he said; 'I want to.'

'Not today, dear; some ... some other time.'

'When? When, Jan?'

Jane turned from making the low bed set at right angles to the fireplace and looked at him where he was sitting beside the window gazing down on to the farmyard. In her look was love and pity and concern, deep concern. She knew that the child could not be kept here for ever, no matter what her father said. He would one day soon be able to fight his way out, and what then? He was extraordinarily strong already for his age, his arms could thrust her off; she was amazed at his strength, as she was by his mind. She herself could not remember being able to read before she was five, and she had been nearly seven before she could recite her ten times tables. She didn't know at what age she had begun to write but it was certainly not at three and a half years old, and yesterday Amos had written his name. True, the letters were unwieldy and only discernible to herself, but nevertheless he had written Amos, and he could go through the alphabet in the primer.

It astonished her how quickly he grasped things. He could remember small details of a story she had told him weeks previously. Should the telling of a story divert from its original theme he would quickly call her attention to it. This brightness confused her, and she had to be on the alert against it.

When she looked into the future she became apprehensive. What lay before him? She had put this question to Parson Hedley and he had, in his own inimitable kind way, reassured her, saying, 'Don't worry, his head will carry him through. God has strange ways of dealing out compensation. He will, if I'm not mistaken, have a thirst for knowledge which may lead him to make his mark in the world.'

Jane wondered what she would have done over the past three and a half years if it hadn't been for Parson Hedley. He was thirty years old, but he laughed and acted like someone of her own age, and he always succeeded in brightening the dullest day for her. Moreover, he was so kind to everyone, even to her father after he found out what he had tried to do to the child.

On the morning of that dreadful day when he had come to christen the child – because Davie Armstrong had kept his word and on his way to the sea had called at the vicarage – Molly had had hysterics in the kitchen. She had gone on to her knees before him and begged him to ask God to forgive her, and into his astonished ears she had poured her confession, her intrigue with the master, her being the cause of the mistress's coming on before her time, and then in her spluttering and crying she had brought out the fact that she had been ordered to drown the child. But she had insisted that she wouldn't have done it, no matter what Davie Armstrong said.

He had lifted her up and held her and given her no word of censure, but Jane knew that if Parson Wainwright had been the one to listen to her confession he would have damned her to hell's flames and branded her over the countryside, more so than she was already.

And knowing all this, Parson Hedley never failed to visit her father at least once a week; even her father's changed ways did not deter him, not even when he cursed God, as he sometimes did now because he had become a slave to drink, strong drink. Scarcely a night went by when he didn't indulge himself; although in the daytime he still carried out his duties as a farmer he was no longer the master he had been. Where once he had inspired awe through respect he now inspired hate from some quarters, and disdain and condescending pity from others.

It was the disdain, Jane guessed, that disturbed him most, for the disdain came from the townspeople. True, they said, he had been dealt a blow by his wife bearing him a bit of a monstrosity, but why hadn't he taken it like a man? And there were the rumours concerning him: some said he was for cutting the child up and throwing him into the cesspool, others said that, not having the guts to kill the child himself, he had sent out the young trollop, who was really the cause of all the trouble, and told her to bury it alive. Well, whatever the rights or wrongs of it were, it was well known that he had banished the child to a fortress at the top of the house and had never looked upon it from the morning it was born. Nor, it was said, and this in stern condemnation, had he spoken a word to his wife, and she was almost as great a prisoner as the thing she had given birth to, for she was confined to her bed most of the time.

The townsfolk of Hexham still saw him once a week, but he no longer graced the boardrooms of either the Workhouse Guardians or the Hospital Governors, nor yet was he seen at the Agricultural Show at Stanhope, nor that of Allendale. Either Fred Geary or Will Curran took the cattle to the shows, but they brought back no prizes, not even a third.

In the gossip in the markets and at the fairs they said Cock Shield Farm was finished; some said, God is not mocked, others said, the sins of the fathers are surely visited on the children; but it was only the women who said pointedly that all this tragedy was the result of him carrying on with the scut under his wife's nose, the men did not voice this opinion for few had room to speak.

Jane was fully aware that her father and mother were not the only people whose lives were changed with the coming of the child. She knew she had been prematurely thrust into womanhood the morning she had stood in the doorway and watched her father and Davie Armstrong facing each other across the kitchen table, the bundle between them. It was when she had picked up the child that she had ceased to love her father, and her heart and emotions had become centred on the legless infant. Strangely, too, about this time her brief hate of Molly disappeared. When the child was but four days old and already ensconced in the attic room that was to become its world for years ahead, she had found Molly bending over it, the tears raining down her face. The girl had looked at her and, heartbrokenly, said, 'Will you believe me, Miss, I would never have done it, an' that's the truth. I'm wicked, very wicked, I know I am, but I hope God strikes me down dead this minute if I'm tellin' a lie; I wouldn't have done it, I was for turning and coming back when Davie collared me. But you couldn't make him believe that 'cos he loathes me hide; he'd have me strung up if he had his way. I'm sorry, Miss, I'm sorry for all I've done to the mistress; I'd never, never in me life do such a thing again, never, never. An' I'm not gona marry Will Curran, Miss I'm not, I'm not. What's in me' – she had touched her stomach gently – 'I'll care for on me own, work for it, but I'll not marry Will Curran, not if the master was to beat me black and blue, I'll not.'

Jane had been surprised, too, at her own reactions, for she had gone to Molly and put her arms around her and like two young girls they had clung together and both cried.

Afterwards when she thought about the incident, she knew she shouldn't have embraced Molly, for by doing so she was condoning her sin, the grave sin Molly had committed with her father. Yet, nevertheless, something in her was glad that she had forgiven Molly.

In those terrible early days, she had only known that she must look after the child and that for the rest of her life he'd be her care, her responsibility. Winnie could see to her mother, but she must see to the child, for no one wanted him or would ever want him. But as the years went on she'd had to reconsider this last statement, because there was something appealing about the child; it wasn't his handicap, it was something in his face, and nature, the way he had of looking at you . . . except, that is, when he was in a rage, and then she had to admit he became fiendish. His spasms were not just bouts of childish temper, but extraordinary rages, when she could not control him, when he twisted his body like an eel in her arms and flayed at her with his hands until she was bruised.

It was with the dread of such a rage coming upon him now that she went to him and, coiling herself on the floor in front of his chair, took his hand and said, 'Only be patient, Amos. Soon, soon you'll be able to go out; I promise you.'

He stared back into her eyes before asking flatly, 'When soon?'

Her lids fluttered, her head moved in small jerks.

'I want to see that little girl.' He pointed to the far corner of the yard where Molly's daughter, Biddy, was running towards the road. 'I want to see her.'

'You will soon, darling.' She went to pat his hand, but he pulled it away from her.

'Always you say soon. I want to go now. If you don't take me I'll ask Molly. Molly is her mother.' He looked down into the yard again, then asked slowly. 'Why has she got legs?'

She hadn't been waiting for this question, she had wondered why it hadn't come before and now she was dumb. There was no strength in her hands to stop him when he pulled up his dress, then his calico petticoat and his two flannel ones, and exposed to her gaze and his own two firm stumps of about six inches in length from which protruded a pair of distorted feet.

'Everyone there has legs.' He nodded his head towards the window now. 'Why have I not legs?'

She kept her tears from brimming over, but they were in her voice as she said, 'Well, you see, darling, you . . . you had an accident.'

'An acc . . . cid . . . ent? Did a giant chop them off, like in the story with the bad man's head?'

'No, no, Amos. The accident was to your mama.'

'My mama?' He stared at her. 'Why does my mama not come and see me?'

'I've told you, I've told you several times, she is sick in bed.'

'You could take me to see her.'

'She's . . . she's too sick to see anyone at present.'

'My papa is not sick. There's my papa. Isn't that my papa?'

Jane looked down into the yard. Her father was going towards the stables. Being Tuesday he'd be riding into Hexham, he'd be gone for at least four hours.

The idea coming into her mind was interrupted by the child saying again, 'You said that was my papa?'

'Yes, dear, that is your papa.'

'Then why doesn't he come up to see me?'

'He is very busy, there is a lot to do on the farm.'

'Parson Hedley comes to see me.'

'Yes, dear, but Parson Hedley hasn't a big farm to run.'

'I like Parson Hedley.'

'So do I.'

They stared at each other for a moment, then with one of his impetuous gestures that brought joy to her heart he brought himself forward and flung his arms around her neck, and with a heave of his body landed on her knee. But the way she was sitting forced her to lose her balance and they rolled over together on the floor, and she laughed now with him as if she herself, too, were a child.

Winnie, coming into the room at this moment, stopped and exclaimed, 'Well! Did you ever! What are you two up to?'

Still laughing, Jane got to her feet, and the child, with an expert twist of its body, turned on to its hands and using the stumps as another child would its knees went towards Winnie at a remarkable speed, then, dragging at her skirts, he pulled himself upwards and, standing on his stumps, dropped his head back on his shoulders and said, 'Jan, she says I am going down soon, I am going down into the yard to the people, I am, I am.'

As she patted the boy's head Winnie looked at Jane, and Jane made a slight movement with her shoulders.

The boy now shook Winnie's skirt vigorously and cried loudly, 'I said I am going down.'

'I heard you, I heard you, Master Amos.' She tapped his cheek, then said, 'Now leave go of me, leave go of me afore I slap your backside.' She bent down and playfully tapped him on the buttocks, and at this he let go of her, dropped on to all fours and in a crab-like fashion, his middle body swaying, he scurried to the window.

Winnie now went to the other side of the bed where Jane was spreading the quilt and once more they exchanged glances, and Winnie murmured under her breath, 'It's got to come, Miss Jane. One of these days he'll be out of that door afore either of us can stop him, and like a dog off a leash he'll be down the stairs. You should speak to the master.'

'I . . . I can't, Winnie, not again. You know what happened when I broached the subject before, he didn't open his mouth to me for weeks.'

'Well, you can see for yourself, Miss, somethin'll happen sooner or later, an' then the master'll have to face up to it. It isn't as if' – she jerked her head backwards – 'he's an idiot. Never in me life have I seen one so bright. If the master would only bring himself to look at the child, or even the mistress for that matter. But then, I think there's less likelihood in that quarter than in t'other. Aw, it's a nice kettle of fish. Look' – she came round to Jane's side, her voice a whisper now – 'the master's gone into town, left as I was comin' up; now why don't you take him down, there'll be no chance of him seeing anybody that matters. The mistress hasn't been out of her room for three months. An' there's another thing' – she now stabbed her finger into Jane's shoulder – 'you're gettin' as pale and peaked lookin' as a lady in decline. You've got to get yourself out, an' you've got to take the chance as it comes. Look, why not take him down this minute? Take him round the farm. An' think of the good it'll do yourself. Now, what about it?'

'Oh, Winnie, do you think I dare?'

'If you never dare now, Miss, you'll never dare at all. It's a bonny day. The wind's fresh, spring's in the offing, and that child has got to get out of his room sometime or other else he'll break out . . . Come on, come on, it's now or never.'

There was a flutter in Jane's heart as she ran to the cupboard and took out a shawl. The child had no outdoor clothes, there had been no necessity to buy any, and when she went towards him holding the shawl out before her, he anticipated the excitement in the air for, leaving the support of his low table, his body seemed to fold up like a concertina before he sprang it upwards and into her arms.

'There now, there now, don't get excited.'

'I'm goin' down, Winnie! I'm goin' down!'

'Darling. Listen.' Jane shook him, bringing his attention to her. 'Listen. You must be quiet until we get out of doors, understand? Your mama is not well. Don't talk until you're in the open, you understand?'

His face now soft, his mouth closed, he nodded at her, and to show her that he was falling in with her wishes he pressed his lips tightly together. But when the door was opened and closed behind them and he did not hear the sound of the key turning in the lock he looked down into her face; then as they went along the passage his mouth fell into a childish gape, and on descending the stairs his head turned from one side to the other in wonder.

'Go down the back way, Miss Jane,' Winnie whispered from behind her.

Jane didn't answer but nodded her head once, and when they came on to the floor below she turned sharply to the left and went down the four steps on to the next landing, past the doors of her father's bedroom and of the room that had once been her own and still was, although she slept with the child in the attic. Then passing the head of the main stairway they turned left again, and went through a door and down the back stairs that dropped into a passage way. This in turn gave on to the side yard.

The yard was paved for only half its length, the rest being covered with turf, which continued round to the back of the house, inlaid here and there with flower beds. The paved half terminated at the corner of the house and was shut off from the main yard by a thick wall, part of which had a dubious claim to Roman structure, but the archway leading into the farmyard proper, although deep and ruggedly built, was of modern design.

It was as Jane entered the arch from the side of the house that her father also entered it from the main yard.

Which of the two was the more affected was hard to tell. Jane thought for a moment that she would drop the child, so weak did her fear make her.

The boy could have put his hands out and touched his father, but the touch would have scorched him for McBain was full of a body-burning rage. His livid glance touched on the child for but a second or two and its pale flat face and almond-shaped eyes hooded by the shawl only emphasised the impression of the monstrosity he always carried in his mind.

'TAKE . . . IT . . . BACK.' The words were sieved through his teeth, which were clenched, the lips straining away from them.

'No . . . No, Father, I can't. He must . . . he must have air.'

'TAKE IT BACK.'

She stepped away from him while shaking her head as she defied him, saying, 'I can't. He's a human being, I can't.'

'You are my papa.'

If a pig had walked on its hind legs and spoken these words McBain could not have been more surprised, they were so clear, so firm, so normal sounding. The thing had said, 'You are my papa.' The shawl had dropped from around its head and he saw the mass of fair curls. But they could have been a crop of horns he was looking at. No male McBain had ever been fair, all had been raven black; the fairness he was looking upon was no ordinary fairness, it was a weird, strange silvery fairness. Yet the voice was ordinary, normal. But no, there was even something weird about that too, for it wasn't the voice of a child. The thing did not look like a child, and it showed no fear of him.

When it said in the same clear ringing tones, 'Are you going to ride your horse?' he brought his shoulders up round his chin as if to protect himself against some hideous attack and, turning about, almost ran from them and disappeared into the main yard.

Jane now leant against the wall, the child clutched to her. Then she turned her head slowly and looked to where Winnie was standing some little distance away, and Winnie, as if coming out of a trance, now darted towards her. 'Give him here. It's all right, give him here.'

The weight of the child taken from her, Jane felt the strength returning to her body; but the sweat was running down her face and, looking at Winnie, she whispered, 'What now, what shall I do now?'

'Take him out as you intended. It's well it happened, it's over, you've won.'

'I have?' She was like a young dazed child herself asking the question.

'Aye, lass. Or at least he has. He's proved that he's no oddity, not up top anyway. "You are my papa," he said. Didn't you, lad?' She hugged the boy to her. 'Come on, come on back into the kitchen and I'll make a cup of tea. There's no need to hurry any more; that over, you'll go out into the open whenever you like from now on an' take him with you.'

'Oh, Winnie! Winnie!'

'There you are, Miss, there you are.' She put one hand around Jane's shoulder and as she led her back towards the door she said, 'Don't frash yourself, lass, don't frash yourself. You did splendidly. By! you did that. Things should go plain sailin' after this.'

Two

Jane was to remember Amos's fifth birthday and look back on it as a day of happenings, happenings that were the beginning of events which would shape her life . . . and Amos's.

The first happening took place at nine o'clock in the morning. She had risen before six and, leaving the boy sleeping peacefully, she had gone out, locking the door as usual, which was more necessary now than ever. Then she had gone downstairs and prepared their breakfasts; but before bringing it up she returned to her room on the first floor and gathered together his birthday presents, one of which was a coat that would serve him in the winter. She had sent into Hexham for the material and had the seamstress make it up to her design, with a cap to match. Both were of a soft brown colour which, she knew, would suit the boy's fairness. Also, there was an engine that ran on wheels and had what appeared to be smoke coming from its funnel when a string was pulled. She herself thought this very ingenious as the smoke was supplied by flour, or any other powder you had a mind to put in the box beneath the funnel. She had been told that the engine was an exact replica of the one that ran between Newcastle and Hexham. Also, she had a bag of coloured marbles for him, as he loved to play marbles.

But, this birthday, there was a very special present for him, and not from herself, but from old Sep. Sep had made a pair of crutches which, he had told her, would serve the boy as good as legs, with a little practice. The arm supports were padded with blue velvet. She had supplied the material and Winnie had done the padding. She was as excited about the crutches as if she were going to use them herself.

It was half-an-hour later when she woke him up. She had sat on the floor gazing at him for some time before doing so. She often sat watching him while he slept, but this morning she looked longer and deeper; today he was five years old. In years he was still a child, yet in some strange way he had leapt beyond childhood; in fact, on looking back, she could hardly remember him being a baby, he seemed to have been born with age on him. His head seemed full of all kinds of things that shouldn't occur to a child. At times she became afraid for him. Being so forward now what would he be like when he was, say, ten years old? Would his brightness emphasise his handicap? Would he be hurt by it more because he possessed an awareness more keen than others? Suffer more? Still, that was all in the future. There was today and this was his birthday.

'Amos.' She shook him gently. 'Amos, wake up. Look what I've got for you.'

Slowly he opened his eyes and stared at her. His face was soft and warm and beautiful.

'Happy birthday, Amos.' She bent and kissed him, and immediately his arms were around her neck and he was kissing her in return and crying. 'I'm five. I'm five. Have you my presents?'

'Yes, here they are.'

He tore the paper from the first parcel she handed to him and revealed the coat and cap, and within seconds he had them both on, tugging the arms over the sleeves of his nightshirt. When he put on the cap Jane laughed out loud, and running to the dressing table near her bed she brought back a hand mirror, and when she held it before him he glanced at her, his mouth wide, and said, 'I am pretty,' then lay back on the bed and laughed.

Next she gave him the marbles, and he juggled with them expertly for they had played chucks together for years.

When, next, she lifted the unwieldy parcel on to the bed, he paused before opening it and asked, 'What is it?'

'Look and see.'

When he saw the crutches he sat straight staring at them. His whole manner was changed, all the gaiety gone. This often happened when his deformity was brought to the fore.

Last year Ned and Sep had contrived between them a go-cart for him, so constructed that, sitting in it, he could guide himself wherever he wished, except up steps. They had gone to a lot of trouble with the cart, especially with regards to the wheels, concerning which they had consulted the wheelwright over near Ninebanks. He was an old man, as old as Sep, and finished with his trade, but he had been kind enough to construct four broad-rimmed wooden wheels each with a fancy hub. Yet when they had presented the boy with the cart his face had flushed to a deep red, scarlet in fact, which was usually the prelude to a burst of temper; but she had been swift to lift him into it and put his hands on the front wheels and propel him forward. As he felt the movement the hot colour in his face had subsided and the light had come back into his eyes, and as if he had been used to propelling it every day of his life he whirled it round the yard, scattering the hens and ducks, causing the dogs to bark and the bull to roar and making everyone laugh.

This had happened on a Tuesday. Of course, they had picked the day to present him with it when the master was in the town.

And now the crutches were having the same effect on him. The laughter had died from his face, his mouth was tight, his colour was rising, there was that look in his eyes that even now brought a thin thread of fear into her. As with the cart so now she again acted quickly. Lifting him out of the bed, she swiftly tucked a crutch under each arm. Their sizes were exact; they touched the floor at the same level as his distorted feet.

'Like this,' she said excitedly. 'Your feet on the ground, so, then put your weight on your oxters, like this . . . That's it. That's it.' When he almost overbalanced she put her hand gently at his back; the next minute he was away from her. Wobbling, the crutches sprawling out away from him, he went

90

up and down the long room. Twice he fell but pushed her hands off, when she went to help him up. Soon he had the feel of them and swung into a rhythm.

She stood and watched him, her hands held tight together under her chin, and when at last he stopped in front of her, his shoulders hunched, each hand gripping the middle bar of the crutch, she dropped on to her hunkers and took his face between her hands and shook his head from side to side. And as the tears flowed from her eyes, she whispered, 'You can walk. You can walk now.'

'I can walk.'

They looked at each other. Then, his voice holding a tone like that of an adult, a man, he said, 'I won't have to wait for anyone any more, I can walk on my own. I won't have to wait for anyone . . . '

She rubbed the tears from each side of her cheeks and on a breaking laugh said, 'I hope you'll always wait for me, Amos.'

As the brightness slowly seeped from his face so it did from her own, and again in a voice like that of a man he said, 'Oh yes; I'll always wait for you, Jan.' Then he brought his head forward until it touched her arm, and she held him, and her tears flowed fast . . .

For the next few hours he became totally engrossed with the crutches; the distance he covered in the room must have amounted to miles. She felt dizzy with him going round and round. She had to make him stop in order to tell Winnie to thank her husband and father for their wonderful gift.

Winnie, staring at the boy careering round the room, said, 'Why didn't we think of it afore, Miss, I mean giving him crutches? He could have been on them since he was three. They should have got the crutches instead of the cart in the first place. Didn't you ever think of them, Miss?'

Jane nodded her head as she said, 'Yes, but . . . but for the future, somehow I couldn't see him balancing.'

'Why not?' said Winnie. 'He balances on his stumps.'

Jane nipped slightly on her lower lip. It always did something to her to hear his short appendages referred to as stumps.

As they stood watching him Winnie voiced a fear that was already growing in Jane's mind. 'The job now,' she said, 'will be to keep him put. You knew where you had him afore, but now he'll be as free as the rest; and you can't go on forever locking the door . . . '

'No, don't lock the door again.' They both started. The boy had stopped and was staring at them. His face was straight, it was wearing the set look of determination they both recognised. They were amazed that he should have heard their low pitched conversation. It came to them in different ways that he must have heard all that they had ever said in that room, be their voices ever so low.

Jane moved slowly towards him and, dropping on to her hunkers again, she said, 'I must lock the door, darling.'

'NO.'

'Yes, yes, I must. You see, your mama is not at all well.' It was strange but she herself had never called her mother 'mama' or her father 'papa', but in placating the child when answering his first questions about his parents, which incidentally came after she had explained that Molly was the mother of the little girl he often saw down in the yard, she had used the terms mama and papa because they seemed softer, warmer somehow, making up for the lack of physical presence of what they represented.

'If I saw my mama I would be good, I would not make a noise.'

She glanced back at Winnie, and Winnie said softly, 'Your moth . . . your mama has to be kept very quiet, and can't have visitors. That's what the doctor says.'

'Does no one see my mama?'

'Only the doctor and . . . and Parson Hedley.' Winnie nodded down at him, and he stared back at her for a moment, then turned from them both and began once more circling the room on the crutches.

Winnie turned towards the door, saying, 'Well, I'd better be gettin' a move on, Miss, but I'll just slip across the way first and see if my lot have eaten, and tell them about' – she nodded towards the boy – 'and that they are fine, just fine.'

'Thank you, Winnie.' Jane went to the door with her. 'Tell Sep and Ned I'm so grateful, and we'll be over later. He'll' – she jerked her head backwards – 'he'll thank them himself.'

'They'd like that.'

When the door had closed on Winnie, Amos came towards Jane, walking slowly now, the crutches making a clip-clop, clip-clopping sound, and he said, 'I want to go down and show Biddy.'

'As soon as I've tidied up and you're washed; you must be

washed and dressed, you can't go out like that, can you? You can wear your blue velvet dress today.'

The boy looked down towards his feet, at the hornlike big toe sticking out from beneath his nightshirt, and he said, 'When can I wear trousers?'

'Oh!' She was nonplussed. 'Later. Later, you can wear trousers.'

'When?'

'Well, when I get them made for you.'

'Soon?'

'Yes, soon.'

'I should wear trousers, I am a boy. I'm not like Biddy; Biddy has to sit on the ground to pee.'

'Oh my God!' She actually muttered the words aloud. Not only were his observations distressing to her, but more so was the fact that he had a very keen interest in Biddy. One day he would have to be told of their relationship, for his attraction to their half-sister – because that was what Molly's daughter was – was troubling her even at this stage. It would have solved the problem if Molly had left the farm years ago. But where could she have gone except into the workhouse, because employers didn't take on young mothers with suckling babies, a suckling baby deprived a mother of some of her strength . . .

It was half-an-hour later that she went out of the door and turned the key in the lock and was immediately startled by a loud hammering on the door from the inside and the child screaming, 'No! No! Jan. Don't lock it. No! No! Don't lock me in. I can walk, Jan. I can walk.'

When she quickly unlocked the door and thrust it open she pushed him on to his back, and he lay there looking up at her with a crutch in one hand.

'Oh, Amos, Amos.' She brought him upright. 'Oh, I'm sorry, are you hurt? But I've got to lock the door, I must.'

'No!' He shook his head slowly. 'No, Jan, not any more. Please, please, Jan, I'll be good. But if you lock it I'll scream, I will, and batter, yes, with the crutch, I will all the time.'

She lowered her head on to her hand and closed her eyes; and after a moment she looked at him and said softly, 'Well now, listen. If . . . if I don't lock the door will you promise not to leave the room until I come back?'

He stared into her eyes for a moment, then drooped his head, and she passed her hand over his curls and murmured, 'That's a good boy. Now I won't be more than five minutes. Play with your toys, and when I come back we'll go out. We'll go and see Sep and Ned and you'll thank them for their present, eh?'

He nodded his head but did not look at her, and so she backed from him, then turned slowly and went out and closed the door. On the landing she stood looking at it, at the lock, and only resisted the temptation to turn it by hurrying away and running down the stairs.

At the bottom of the stairs she paused and glanced across the landing towards her mother's door. It was time for her morning visit but she must go to her own room first, there to attend to her personal needs which she had never been able to perform in front of the child.

Delia heard her daughter come down the stairs, she heard her hesitate before going to the lower landing and to her room. There was no movement that her daughter or the child made that she did not hear. Sometimes she might only be dimly aware of the activities in the room above her, especially after she had taken the strong medicine that Doctor Cargill prescribed from time to time, yet some part of her mind was always conscious of the activity in the attic room. She knew when they went to bed, and when they awoke in the morning. She heard the child cry, and scream, and laugh, and at times she heard her daughter laugh with him. This, strangely, hurt her most of all.

In the past eighteen months she had been only twice out of the room. Prior to that, except during the first six months after the child's birth when she was prostrate and often not in her right mind, she had periodically made an effort to get back into life. It might be once in two months, or three. She would dress and go downstairs into the sitting-room, but she never went outside, her legs didn't seem strong enough to come in contact with the hard earth, nor her face the sharp air. But for the past nine months she had not even moved out of the bed.

No one spoke to her of the child, his name was never mentioned. But then she saw so few people. Only four in fact: Winnie, the doctor, Parson Hedley, and, of course Jane.

She wondered time and again why she was not dead. She had no strength in her body, and seemingly very little left in her mind; what she had she used in the wish to die. She knew she was dying, but the process was slow, a fading away.

From early this morning she had listened to the strange sounds above her. They were not the usual sounds and they had gone on for hours, a hard clip-clop, clip-clopping all over the ceiling.

Years ago she had wanted to leave this room, fly from it and never see it again, but were she to move to the other landing she'd be near her husband, and that situation would be more unbearable than this, because never one word had they exchanged from the night he had stood over her and cursed her for bringing a monstrosity into the world. When she had come to herself the thing she had given birth to was gone; but he was there, and there had been murder in his eyes, and he had said things to her that could never be forgotten.

Sometimes she had seen him from her window striding about the farm. Only twice had she encountered him. Even then they had not looked at each other; she had passed on into the sitting-room and he across the hall as if both were blind ghosts. Yet even if he didn't look at her, or speak to her, from time to time she heard his voice; although his office was not below her room, the one below being the dining-room, its chimney flue connected with the same main flue as her bedroom's, and through this funnel she heard his distant gruntings when he was in drink.

The fact that he had taken to drink was, even in her dim and half aware state, surprising. Only when there were visitors at dinner had he indulged in wine, and then in moderation; he would pour it out generously for Parson Hedley or Parson Wainwright, oh very generously for Parson Wainwright, but he himself drank very little. But now, not infrequently of an evening, and more towards midnight when the house had settled, she would hear his mutterings, and although unintelligible she gauged the ferocity of his mood by the inflexion of his voice as it was sucked up the funnels of the chimneys.

Beneath the laudanum-dulled layers of her mind there was an activity, a threshing process that winnowed all the sounds in the house and brought the residue near enough to the opiate to bring her some awareness.

The stamping on the floor above had stopped, just before Jane had come down the stairs; but now it had started again, only the rhythm was different. There was a longer time between each clip-clop, and each thud seemed to be lighter, such as the difference between walking and tip-toeing. The sound turned into a tap-tap. It was now no longer above her head but on the landing. Then there came a soft bump, bump, bump, followed by a succession of bangs. The child was coming down the stairs, and seemed to be dragging something with him. But how?

She knew when he had reached the bottom. She made an effort and pulled herself up further on to her pillows. She could see over the rail of the bed now, and to the door opposite. The sound had returned to what it was when above her head, a clip-clop, clip-clop, clip-clopping sound.

She felt she was drawing her last breath as she watched the door handle slowly turn and with a sharp thrust the door was pushed back wide, and there came into the room, and towards the bed, her son. The nearer he came towards her the less she saw of him, until he reached the side of the bed and two movements of his crutches brought him within a yard of her pillow.

She was unable to breathe, the constriction in her throat was choking her. She stared at the curly head, into the face with the almond-shaped eyes.

'Are you my mama?'

The voice was as surprising as the rest of him. It brought her face stretching and her breath fighting for escape from her throat.

'Can't you talk?'

No, she couldn't talk, she could not utter one word to this son of hers.

'Are you sick?'

She wanted to make a motion with her head, but it refused to obey her. What was more, she wanted to do something else, every fibre in her wasted body urged her to lift up her arms and stretch them outwards and grasp this child, this child who spoke so clearly, who looked so bright and intelligent. It might have only half a body but he was a child, not a monstrosity . . . What had she done lying here for five years listening, while up above was this child, her child, someone who could have brought her comfort? An agony filled her body as she realised she had rejected comfort, and that was what she needed most, comfort.

She lifted her hand and slowly moved it towards him, and as slowly he moved back from it, and what he said to her was, 'I don't like you,' and on this he swung his body round and stumped out of the room. But he had no sooner passed out of the door when he was grabbed and lifted bodily upwards, and when the crutches fell to the ground, these, too, were lifted, and

96

Molly's voice hissed in his ear, 'Oh, you bad lad you, you bad lad!'

'I'm not. I'm not.'

'Ssh! Be quiet! Wait till Miss Jane finds out.'

'Put me down, I can walk.' He was beating at her with his fists, and she hissed at him, 'Give over, Master Amos, 'cos I'm not puttin' you down; you're goin' back upstairs.'

She had to make a detour round the main landing to reach the back stairs again because she couldn't pass the mistress's open door, for she knew the mistress couldn't stand the sight of her, she was a thorn in her flesh.

As she turned on to the main landing the boy struggled so much that she was forced to put him to the ground, and as she did so she exclaimed under her breath, 'Oh, you are an imp, you are that! Here.' She pushed the crutches at him. 'No, not that way, back up the stairs.'

'I won't! I won't!'

Neither of them was aware of the door opening until McBain's shadow fell over them, and then they both looked up. Molly's was just a fleeting glance before her eyes dropped away from the master's face; but not so the child's. His face now red with anger and indignation at Molly's rough handling, he glared up at the man, the man who passed him at a distance without turning his head in his direction, the man who was his papa but who would not speak to him. His next words linked up with those he had said in the bedroom as if he were just finishing a sentence. 'And I hate you, too, I do,' he said.

In no way intimidated by the rage-filled countenance high above him, he continued to stare up into McBain's face for some seconds before he turned his back on him and stumped away, not upstairs towards the prison that had been his since birth, with only rare escapes to the yard below mostly on a Tuesday, but down the main staircase, stumbling once and nearly going headlong to the bottom, through the hall and across the farmyard, passing gaping faces, and in the direction of the Armstrongs' cottage.

One thing had been made clear to Jane, the child could no longer be kept a prisoner in the attic; and this fact had got through to every occupant on the farm, including its master.

After the encounter on the landing McBain went back into his room and there he paced the floor trying to face the fact

97

that this half-being could no longer be concealed.

He still looked upon the child as a monstrosity; even the fact that it might be intelligent did not veer his thoughts from the ignominy of having produced such an object. He thought of the child as 'it'. He spoke of it, when he spoke of it at all, by that term. To him the boy was an object, a threefold curse, emphasising first his lack of judgement in taking a wife such as Delia; second, forcing the question that his own ancestry might be at fault; thirdly, and most important of all, he looked upon the boy as an act of God, a punishment to expiate his lust, the lust that had eaten him up for years, the lust that could only be satisfied by the very young. And now this same lust had turned sour on him; Molly who had excited him as no other had, at least at the time he was most in need of her, had repulsed him, not once, but twice, and yet a third time. He was a proud man, he would not beg, so on a Tuesday he went into Hexham, and sometimes as far away as Newcastle, and when his business was done he paid for the release of his passions. But it was never the same as of yore.

Nothing was the same as of yore. He did not command the respect as he had, at one time, in the town. He sometimes wondered whether, if he had accepted his tribulation, taking it into the open, and drawing pity to himself for it, life would have been better, easier.

At one time, on his own land he had been looked up to as a god. He had felt as a god. Now he was as a fallen angel. And the only succour he received was from the brain-dulling effect of whisky.

Concerning the present situation he asked himself what was to be done. He could not have 'it' running about the place where he would encounter it at any time of the day. He could send it away, put it in a home, or a school – there were places for such as he . . . But, there was a question here. Were he to do that, what would be the effect on Jane? He could not risk alienating her. Jane, the child, had loved him at one time; he doubted if Jane, the young woman, still loved him. But, strangely, he loved her. She was the only thing left in his life that he could love, and he knew that whatever he did to the child in an adverse way would affect their relationship. They might not have much to say to each other now, but she was the only human being in the house to whom he could talk. What was more, her understanding was deep. She could accept his ignoring of the child, but he knew that she would never forgive him were he to dispose of his son in some institution.

There seemed nothing for it but that he must face this situation as best he could. But one thing he would never allow, he would not allow 'it' to eat at his table, ever.

As if this decision had in some way made his position bearable he straightened his shoulders, stretched his neck with a chin-wagging movement up out of his loose cravat, then marched from the room.

When Molly informed Jane of what had happened she ran and almost dragged Amos from old Sep and back to the house, and all the way he had protested as he had never done before; not crying like a child of five might do, but arguing and questioning with a reasoning that startled her. Why must he stay up in his room if he could walk? Why wasn't he allowed to go round the farm on his own? Had his papa said he must not go round the farm? Was it because he had no legs?

It was after the three o'clock dinner that Molly, coming upstairs to clear the dishes, said in an aside, 'It's done this, the ice is broken, so why don't you let him go out by himself? Or better still, the day being fine, take him up on the Tor; by! that would be an eye-opener for him.'

Jane looked at Molly, and as if Molly read her thoughts she said, 'I can look out the landin' window and see whether he's about . . . the master. An' you can slip out the back way. 'Bout time you did get out an' about, 'cos you're still peaked lookin'.'

Yes, she knew she was peaked looking. White, thin, and shapeless, that's how she saw herself, whereas Molly, who worked fourteen hours a day and saw to her child as well, remained plump and rosy-faced and bonny.

Molly was a woman of nearly twenty-two. She was almost, Jane considered, past marrying age yet she seemed to grow prettier every year. But she was no longer flighty; her manner in fact was inclined to staidness, much more so than her own; but this, Jane considered, befitted her years. She wondered sometimes about Molly, she wondered why she didn't marry. Was she still attached to her father? She doubted this. Perhaps she was waiting for Davie Armstrong to come back. But she doubted very much whether Davie Armstrong would ever come back, for there had been only two letters from him in five years, one from London, and one all the way from Barcelona, and this second one had come some eighteen months ago. She had read them both to Winnie, and Winnie had told the men what they contained. They were quite interesting letters, but the spelling wasn't good and the writing left a lot to be desired. No, she thought that Molly would have a long wait if she waited for Davie Armstrong coming back.

Again and again Jane had asked herself over the years how it was she had turned completely about face in her attitude towards Molly, because at first she had held Molly responsible for the ill fate that had come upon her mother . . . But on reflection, she owned up to the fact that her mother would have given birth to Amos as he was even if she had carried him for the full time.

Perhaps, she thought, she liked Molly because she was the only person near her own age on the farm, or for miles around for that matter; no one visited them now except the parsons and the doctor, and they, in turn, visited no one. Sometimes she was filled with envy when, on her rare walks to the top of the Tor, she saw in the distance the Reed girls cutting across the bottom field with the hunt. You could always tell the Reed girls. The three of them had red hair and they dressed flamboyantly. Their names were bandied about quite a lot. Even the youngest, Agnes, who was just on sixteen and almost two years younger than herself, was allowed to go to balls. She understood that the sisters were the belles of every ball they went to, and it was said that men came to fisticuffs over them. There was no possibility of men coming to fisticuffs over herself. Well, it didn't matter, as long as she had Amos to look after and he was happy; that was all she cared about.

Although she no longer went to church, she felt that God had given her an allotted task in life: He had put Amos into her care. But Amos, more often than not, disclaimed any connection with his heavenly Father, and did not live up to his name at all, the name that Parson Hedley had given him on the first day of his life. As no one had been forthcoming with a name, Parson Hedley had said, 'Well, we'll call him Amos, for Amos was a farmer who eventually did great deeds and was good in God's sight, as this child will be.' And she knew he would be, for Parson Hedley was always right.

She said to Molly, 'I'll do that, it's a lovely day.'

'There's heather in plenty on the Tor, you could gather some on your way back. He'd like that.'

100

'Oh yes. Yes, I'm sure he would.'

They both turned and looked at the boy. He was staring at them. He had heard all their conversation and he said bluntly, 'Shall we go now?' and Jane and Molly looked at each other and suppressed their laughter with tight-pressed lips, and Jane said, 'Yes, we'll go now . . . '

The sky was endless, seemingly without horizons. The bracken on the right of the Tor was shoulder high, some already tinged yellow, forerunner of the reds and purple that would turn the fells and hills into a warm flame. At the foot of the Tor were clusters of bilberry bushes, their fruit standing out like black and purple stains, and she pointed this out to the boy. But he didn't seem interested, for his gaze was directed upwards.

The easiest way was through the bracken, but the child would be enveloped in it and the fronds would impede him and they could so easily cut, so she led the way along the narrow road that skirted the foot of the Tor on the north side and where it was mostly shale, giving place to rough rock. Starting from the road was a path, cut diagonally and slowly mounting its way to the summit, and she took this. Picking Amos up in her arms with the order for him to hang on to his crutches and not to get excited in case he overbalanced them both, she began the ascent. The end of the path was out of sight of the east side of the Tor and away from the road, and when she finally reached it she dropped the boy to the ground, then sat down on a rock and, panting and laughing, said, 'Well, here we are.'

The child was now standing, supporting himself on his crutches. She stared at his face; it was wearing the most strange expression. He was gazing towards Whitfield Moor and the hills beyond. She watched him look from one side to the other, taking in the great range of space; then his head went slowly back on his shoulder and he stared up into the sky.

'Isn't it beautiful?' She put out her arm and encircled his waist, and he turned and looked at her and smiled. And he was beautiful too. This fact often made her sad, but not today; it was as if she also, like him, was seeing the world outside the farm for the first time. She gripped him to her and he dropped his crutches, and as she had been wont to do since she was a small child, until she was twelve years old, she rolled on the grass, but now with him pressed tightly to her. When she stopped they lay, their faces close together, laughing; then like an eel he was away from her, scrambling over the grass on all

101

fours, his body from his waist to his hips wobbling from side to side. When he reached his crutches he began to run wildly here and there like someone demented, and she chased him, laughing as she called, 'Amos! Amos! Stop! Keep away from the edge! Be careful. Be careful!' Every time her hands went to grasp him he ducked or slithered from her hold.

The agility on his new-found legs amazed her; it was as if he had used the crutches from birth. It seemed that Parson Hedley was right, he was going to be very adaptable. Parson Hedley said he was the brightest child he had ever come across. For a moment a cloud passed over the bright day as she thought, if only her father could see him as Parson Hedley saw him; or for that matter, if her mother had viewed him as a human being; if only one of them had taken him to their hearts. Anyway, he had her, he would always have her.

She lifted up her skirts and raced towards him, for now he was some distance away and nearing the edge of the Tor where it dropped almost sheer to the road below. This part was strewn with loose rocks and boulders and as he went twisting in and out of them she had a job to outmanoeuvre him. When at last she caught him she sat down with her back to a boulder and laughed as she rocked him. Then suddenly she said, 'Listen,' and they both became still and listened to the sound of a pony trap below them. It was coming around the bend of the road below them. Jumping to her feet and pulling the boy with her, she raised her hand and shouted, 'Parson Hedley! Parson Hedley!'

The man in the trap stopped and looked about him, then lifted his head. She waved down to him again, and at this he waved back, then he lowered his hand and stared at the small figure by her side, and she knew that he was very surprised at what he was seeing. She put her hand to her mouth and shouted, 'We'll come down,' and at this he called back, 'No, stay there, I'll come up; just let me fasten Toby.'

She watched him drive the trap to where the ground levelled off sufficiently for him to take it off the road and where there was grass for the pony to nibble; then she followed his movements as he made his way up the winding narrow path, and when he was below them she laughed down at him. Then with Amos stumping by her side she ran back towards where the path came out on the summit. They reached the spot simultaneously and their greetings were high and pleasurable as if

102

they hadn't met for some long time, instead of twenty-four hours previously.

The parson was a man of medium build. He had flat rather blunt features, none of which had any claim to good looks, except perhaps his eyes; even these were nondescript in colour, being a flecked grey. But it was the eyes that gave interest to the face; perhaps it was the kindliness and understanding in their depths, and a certain sharp keenness in their glance, which rarely held censure, that made them attractive.

He gazed down at the boy who had become a deep interest in his life, as also had his sister, but whereas he could express his feelings on the former, he had to hide them on the latter; for all her capabilities, he still considered Jane a child, and, even if she hadn't been, there remained circumstances which prevented him from presenting himself as anything but a friend, pastor and tutor. But with the child it was different, and now he exclaimed loudly, 'Well! Well! A day of miracles. What is this?' He stood back and surveyed the boy standing erect, shoulders hunched, on the small crutches; and when Amos, in his forthright manner, stated, 'I've got legs,' he had to pause before answering, 'Indeed, indeed you have, Amos. Now why didn't we think of this before, eh, Jane?'

Jane smiled widely at him. 'I did, but I didn't think he could manage them.'

'I can manage them, look, look,' Amos interrupted while he demonstrated, going round in small circles, and she laughed as she caught him, crying. 'We can see. Yes, darling, we can see. But you'll make yourself dizzy. Come along, sit down.'

When they were seated on the grass Arnold Hedley gazed before him for a moment in silence, then said, 'It's years since I was up here; I'd forgotten how magnificent was the view.' Then glancing at the boy who was sitting to the side of Jane he said low, under his breath, 'It was good for him to see the world for the first time from this spot. It was like you to think of bringing him up.'

'It wasn't my idea, Parson, it was Molly who suggested it.'

He looked into her face. She was so honest, she would not even take a little credit to herself when it rightly belonged to someone else. Her face to him was beautiful for it held the beauty of honesty, the beauty of an unselfish nature and a kindly heart. True, she was given to bouts of temper, but then she was but human; and she was young, so young, too young to have the responsibility of mothering this boy and running that dis-embowelled tortured household. He was often amazed at the gaiety she managed to maintain. But then her charge, although terribly handicapped, was a lively, intelligent little fellow, too intelligent, he considered at times, for his age. But he supposed God in His wisdom had given him the gift of memory and keen perception to make up for his lack.

He was bending forward towards Jane to make a further comment when he was pushed aside by Amos roughly forcing himself between them from behind. The force levelled by the child's arm into his ribs was of a strength one would associate with a boy of ten or twelve. He held back his head and surveyed the child as Jane admonished him, saying, 'That's naughty, Amos. You mustn't push like that. That's very naughty.'

Amos was now sitting upright between them. There was a slight smile on his face, and with a lightning movement he turned to the parson, raised his hand and viciously nipped the lobe of his ear.

When Arnold Hedley actually cried out with equal amounts of surprise and pain Jane, snatching the boy's hands, slapped them hard as she cried, 'That's very wicked, Amos, very wicked. How dare you!'

Amos stared wide-eyed up at her, and, his smile sliding into a grin now, he said, 'He pulls my ear.'

She exchanged a glance over his head with Arnold; then she swallowed and said, 'Parson does it playfully, he never hurts you. There is a difference between pulling and nipping. If you ever do that again you'll get a sound smacking, a real smacking.'

The smile slid from the boy's face, his eyes clouded, his lips fell firmly one on the other. In a child of similar years this might have been a prelude to tears, but he showed no signs of crying; instead he threw himself forward on to his hands and knees, crawled swiftly to where his crutches were, stood up on them and, looking from one to the other, said firmly, 'I'm going down to the farmyard.'

'You will wait a moment.' Jane put out her hand to stop him, but he was gone, and when she rose and ran after him Arnold Hedley got to his feet. His ear was still stinging, the boy's nails had almost pierced the skin. He felt the lobe gently as he looked to where Jane was struggling to hold the child from going towards the path, and now he went swiftly to them, saying, 'Let's go down; I've got lots of calls to make before evening.

Here, you take the crutches and I'll carry him.'

When he stooped and lifted the boy up, Amos smiled into his face, and he smiled back at him; and he said as Molly often did, 'You're an imp, young fellow, you're an imp.'

'Can I ride in your trap?'

'Yes, of course you may.'

'I'm going to have a trap and a horse.'

Arnold turned and glanced enquiringly at Jane. When she shook her head, the motion did not go unnoticed by the boy for he twisted round and cried at her, 'I am! I am, Jan. I'm going to have a horse and trap. And I'm going into the town, I'm going to race papa into the town.'

Neither of them gave any answer to this. In single file they made their way down the sloping path of the Tor, and along the road to the pony and trap. There was a quietness on them now, a restraint, and Jane was acutely aware of it; she was to remember this day for as long as she lived, the day when Amos had nipped Arnold's ear.

Three

The sun was going down as Davie Armstrong came up the south side of the Tor, walked over the top and stood on the summit, almost in the same place where Jane and Parson Hedley had sat a few hours earlier. A feeling, long starved of expression, rose from the depths of him and escaped on a long, long breath. He sighed before muttering aloud, 'The bonny hills. Aye, the bonny hills.' There was a softness in his tone and a moisture in his eyes as if he was being reunited with a loved one.

He hitched the canvas bag further on to his shoulder as he looked to the left of him where he could see the smoke rising straight up from the farmhouse chimneys and, a short distance away, three spirals in a row from the cottage chimneys. His gaze moved over the fields into the far distance to the ridge on which he used to pause for a moment before going down to the meadows to collect the cows. It was a fine view from the ridge, but up here was finer, more wide, grander. In his remembering it had been from this point he had viewed his land, and when he compared it with the places he had seen over the last five years he had always found them wanting.

He had landed in Newcastle last night, and for the past week he had been telling himself that was as far as he was going to go into Northumberland. Although he was longing to see his folks, he knew that, once back, the sickness would start up in him again, the sickness for the hills, for the wide sky, wider it seemed than any he had viewed on the oceans that he had crossed. There, you couldn't tell which was sky and which was water, but here the sky was an endless canopy of clear light. And up here you knew it went on for ever and ever.

'Aw well, enough of this.' He spoke aloud, then stepped over the edge of the Tor on to the winding path and went down on to the narrow road, along it and on to the main road, and slowly with steady step and a slight swaying to his carriage he came back to the farm.

Mickey Geary was the first to see him. Mickey was coming along the road with a dog by his side. The dog barked and ran from him and towards the oncoming stranger, and as it stood yapping the boy stopped and, his jaw dropping and his face spreading into a wide grin, he exclaimed, 'Why! Why it's you, Davie. Eeh! you've come back. Why, man? Eeh! we never thought to see you again.'

Davie came up to the small boy, for Mickey at thirteen was still undersized, but his face as always was round and bright. He put his hand on the boy's head and ruffled his hair, saying kindly, 'By, lad! Mickey, how you've grown. I wouldn't have known you,' although he was thinking that the boy had hardly changed in five years. 'Well, well! an' how is everybody?'

'Oh, you know.' Mickey jerked his head. 'Things've changed a lot since you left, Davie. Eeh! your ma'll be over the moon.'

'Granda all right?' He asked this question tentatively; it had been a fear in him for a long time that he wouldn't see his granda again.

'Aye, oh aye, like a linty. Me ma says he'll never die, they'll have to take him to the slaughter house.'

Davie laughed and jerked his head, then said, 'Well, I'll be seeing you again, Mickey. So long for the minute.'

As he walked away the boy called, 'You home for good, Davie?'

'No, no, lad, no farm life for me, not after being on the

briny.' He saluted from the peak of his cap, and the boy stood watching him in admiration as he stepped off the main road, crossed over the wide grass verge and on to the narrow path fronting the cottages.

Just before he opened the door he dropped his bag from his shoulder and took off his cap; then thrusting the door back with a flourish, but still holding the knob, he bent forward, his hat held like a quoit in his hand, ready to throw, as he cried, 'Do I have to chuck it in to test me welcome?'

'Oh my God!' Winnie muttered the words, but she didn't immediately rise from her chair or put down the pair of mole-skin trousers she was patching, nor did Ned take the tacks from his mouth or lift the last from his knee on which was a boot he had been soling. It was Sep who first rose to his feet. The clay pipe had dropped from his hand on to the mat, and he made no effort to retrieve it, but came slowly across the room. Yet before he had reached Davie, both Ned and Winnie were by his side. Then on a gabble of high exclamations they all stood en-twined, and it was Winnie who held on to him to the last. The tears raining down her face, she kept saying, 'Oh lad! Oh lad! what a shock,' until he pressed her from him and, holding her at arm's length, cried, 'Well, if that's the way it's gona be I'd better make me stay short, eh?'

'Sit down, sit down, and let's look at you.'

'You'll get a better view standing up.' He posed before her, spreading his arms wide and turning round. And she laughed, they all laughed; and then, still looking at him, still crying, she said, 'Eeh! I'd better put the kettle on. Are you hungry, lad, have you had anything to eat? Why didn't you let's know you were comin'? Where've you been? I mean where've you come from?'

'Hold your hand, woman.' Ned pushed her in the shoulder. 'Give him time to get his breath; it'll take him a week to answer that lot. Come and sit down, lad. Come and sit down.' His voice was soft and breaking and he stood aside and watched his son take his own seat by the fire.

Davie looked at his father, and Ned said quietly, 'It's good to see you, lad.'

'You, too, Da.' He felt warmth towards his father that was new. He had expected to find him much older looking, more crippled with the rheumatics, but it was as if he had left him only yesterday; and his grandfather, five years added to his sixty-seven had done little to alter him outwardly, except to bleach his hair to a silvery white and turn the stubble round his face to a dirty grey. It was his mother who was altered. Her hair had been touched with grey, now it was all grey, not a brown streak to be seen; and her face was thinner; she was thinner all over. He leaned forward and caught her hand as she stood with her back to the table gazing at him, and she came to his side and with a quick movement pressed his head against her breast before pushing it from her again and turning away to busy herself with making the tea.

'I can't believe it, lad.' Sep was shaking his head now. 'Out of the blue, just like that. When did you get in?'

'Last night, Granda.'

'Where've you been?'

'Where haven't I been!' He pulled his brows down and moved his head slowly.

'Well, wherever you've been it's broadened you.' His father's eyes were looking over him, from his brown hair that seemed lighter now, over his tanned features, over his shoulders filling his melton-cloth coat, down to his stout boots, and he ended, 'You've put on some weight I'd say.'

'Aye, Da; but mind' – he pointed – 'it isn't from the good grub they feed us, by! no.'

'Bad?' Sep poked his head forward, and Davie nodded at him. 'Rotten would be a better word, Granda; terrible on some boats. You mightn't believe it – ' again he was pointing his finger – 'there was many a day during the first year I was away I envied the pigs their swill. By, lad! when I think what I used to give those pigs, and what we got on that boat.'

'You've been on more than one boat?' Winnie turned from the table, and he looked towards her and said, 'Aye, Ma. This one now is me second; I've been with her nearly four years. It's a good ship, that is if you can say any of them are good.'

She turned her attention fully on him now and stared at him in silence for a moment before saying softly, 'You don't like it, I mean the sea?'

'Well, Ma – ' he leaned back in the chair, stretched his legs out, then flung his arms wide and said, 'That's a question that's going to take me three full days to answer, for sometimes I do, an' sometimes I don't. When I'm on it I hate it, when I'm off it and on dry land I'm longing for it. Tell you truthfully, I don't know me own mind. Yet there's one thing I do know.' He

108

nodded first at his father, then at his grandfather before he continued, 'It's a damn sight better than working on the land, I mean the prospects. Don't you notice anything about me?' Now he was grinning at them, sweeping them with a merry glance; and they looked him over again and shook their heads while they laughed back at him, and he said, 'Oh well, a prophet in his own country. That's what I'm always saying.' The phrase was not applicable to the situation but it sounded fine, learned, but one thing he had said was accurate, that he was always quoting it was true, 'You're not looking on any ordinary donkey room pony you know.'

'No!' Old Sep's mouth was wide, his face one great beam.

'No, Granda, no; you see before you a second mate.' He now sat up and preened himself, and his chest swelled naturally when they murmured. 'Second mate on a ship!'

'Well, the *Arcadia* is not a fish barrel, although mind, I have to confess she's had to stoop low sometimes when she's been short of a cargo out there and fill her hold with whale carcasses.'

'How in the name of God did you come into that, lad?' His grandfather's face was screwed up with an inquiry. 'I thought you had to sit for your ticket for that kind of thing.'

'Well, he can read and write can't he? He could have sat for his ticket . . . did you?' Winnie was looking at him.

'Not exactly, Ma, not in the ordinary way. You see when you're out there plying between one port an' another, scrounging cargoes, you're likely to get half-eaten up by the thousand and one different kinds of flies that they breed, and some folks' blood objects to them like, those beggars polished off two second mates within nine months, so when nobody seemed to want the job, 'cos there was the idea that them flies made a bee line, so to speak, for second mates, though how they picked them out beats me, not being able to read. Well, as I said to the captain, there's one born every minute so I'll take the job, thank you very much. An' that's how it came about.'

At this there was a gale of laughter, and Winnie wiped the mixed tears from her face as she handed him a mug of tea. Then after he had drunk more than half of it at one gulp he said in a more serious tone, 'That was how it happened in a way. But as me ma said, it was because I could read an' write, and I wasn't slow to pick up things.' He smiled quietly now and looked from his father to his grandfather and added kindly, 'You must have given me something atween you; or did I get it from me ma?'

109

He was laughing again and he reached out his hand and slapped Winnie's buttocks, and she turned round quickly, her face a bright red as she exclaimed, 'Well I never! you've never done that in your life afore. By! it would seem you have learned more than sailing a ship since you've been away.'

He grinned at her now as he said, 'Could be, Ma, could be.' And they laughed again.

They laughed while the meal was being prepared. They laughed during the eating of it. They laughed until Winnie, rising from the table said, 'Eeh! I've forgotten all about it, I should be over the road; the missus will think I've forgotten her.'

'Nine o'clock!' Davie looked up at her. 'You go over there at nine o'clock at night?'

'I've got to settle her for the night.'

'Why?'

'Oh, it's a long story. She's hardly been out of bed since . . . Well, you know, since that night.'

He looked from one to the other. He hadn't asked about the concerns of the house, about the master, or the legless baby, yet it wasn't because they hadn't been in his mind; he had thought he'd let the topic come naturally. But nobody had mentioned the house until this minute, perhaps because up till now he having had all the say. He looked at his mother now and said, 'Well, don't be long then,' and she smiled back at him as she answered mischievously, 'I won't. I'll be back in time to put you to bed.'

'Go on with you.' As he slapped her buttocks again his mind leaped back to the days when, as a small child, well under five, he had refused to go to bed unless she was there, and she would say to him, 'Now sit still an' don't wander, an' I'll be back afore you know it and put you to bed.'

When she had gone and they were sitting before the fire he asked a question. 'How are things round about?' he asked, and they told him, Sep doing most of the talking, while Ned added points that sounded pessimistic, even beyond his chequered outlook on life, such as when, speaking enthusiastically about Amos, Sep said, 'Eeh! he's a marler. You've no idea. And as bright as a button. You should hear him talk, talk about a sea lawyer. Just you wait till you hear him. And you should see him on his new legs. Ned here made him a pair of crutches; you'd think he'd been on them since he was born an' he just got them the day. Aw, he's going to be a bright spark than 'un.' It was at this point that Ned put in, 'Aye, but he's got a cruel streak in him, I think.'

'What d'you mean, cruel streak? He's no less of a lad 'cos he hasn't got any pins. You mean 'cos of what happened with Biddy the day?'

'Aye,' said Ned. 'But that isn't the first time that he's swiped her, nor taken her glass alleys.'

'Aw, that's bairn's playin'; Miss Jane always brings them back.' Sep now turned to Davie, explaining, 'He plays marbles with Biddy. You want to see them both at it; she's nearly as good as him, but he always manages to win her best blood alley. He's even beat Mickey at it. Oh, he's a great one with the plonkers.'

'Who's Biddy?'

Sep was about to speak, but his breath caught in his throat, and he coughed, then, rubbing the tip of his nose with his first finger, he mumbled, 'Molly's bairn.'

There was a short silence while the three of them looked at each other, and then Davie, his eyebrows rising, his lips pursed, repeated, 'Molly's bairn?'

'She's a nice child.' It was Ned speaking.

'No doubt.'

So the master's son and Molly's child played marbles together. Well, well.

'What's past is past,' said Sep quietly. 'Molly's turned out a hard workin' lass, an' sensible at that. It's five years you know, lad, since you left, an' she's worked every day of that time, from mornin' till night she has, an' she's bringing the child up decent. Dresses it well, spends most of her wages on it; that's after she pays that old skin-flint Cassy for minding it.'

'She didn't marry . . . she didn't marry Curran then?'

'No, no; she refused flatly. She did that.'

'What! After her lord and master giving her her orders?'

'Aw now, now' – Sep wagged his head – 'that's all over. As I said, five years is a long time, and she was little more than a bairn herself.'

'By! lad –' Davie grinned sardonically now, looked first at his grandfather, then at his father, then back to his grandfather again before he said, 'We've changed our tune, haven't we?'

'Speak as you find.' Ned's voice was quiet. 'Whatever harm she did she's payin' for it in the only way she knows how. She's devoted to Miss Jane an' works like a nigger to ease her plight.'

'What plight? What's happened to Miss Jane?'

'Nothing's happened to her except that she's had to give every hour of her time, not only wakin' but sleepin', to the child. She's brought him up, and for the first three years of his life she lived in the attic with him an' hardly left it.'

Davie slowly moved his body forward and repeated, 'The first three years she lived in the attic with him? Why in the attic?'

Now Ned and Sep exchanged fleeting glances, and it was Ned who in his terse way gave a rough description of the circumstances under which the child had been brought up, and when he had finished Davie sat straight in his chair and stared at his father. Then he said softly, 'And you mean to say that neither of them, him nor her, ever speak to the child? You mean that all these years they've kept it up?'

'Well' – Ned reached out his hand and knocked the dottle from his pipe against the hob – 'the mistress, she's been more or less bedridden. It's said she could slip away any time. Winnie believes that some mornin' she'll go in an' find her gone. As for the master's attitude, well, you know as much about the cause of that as any of us. He's a changed man an' I never thought I'd be able to say I pity him, but I do! In his eyes, he has neither wife nor child while havin' both.'

'Aren't there any young heifers left round about?'

Ned lowered his head at this and remained silent, leaving it to Sep to say quietly, 'As your da says, lad, the master's a changed man. He's got nowt left, not even God. Parson Hedley comes twice a week to tutor the boy, and has a word with him. But it's got no effect, the only one that he has any use for is Miss Jane. The whole household seems to hang on the lass an' I wonder meself how long her thin shoulders'll be able to bear it. But now that the young master can get out and about things should be better for her.'

'What'll happen if she wants to get married, what'll they do then?'

'Oh! married?' said Sep. 'I can't see Miss Jane marryin', her whole life's taken up with the child. You'd really think it was hers. An' he won't let her out of his sight. She's mother, father, nurse, the lot to him. No, I can't ever see Miss Jane marryin'.'

'Well, well.' Davie again pursed his lips. 'What a prospect for a young lass. What does she look like?'

'Oh' – Sep put his head on one side as he smiled – 'still plain some would say, an' no figure to speak of, but she's got somethin'. Hard to tell, hard to put a finger on, but she's good for a crack, she'll listen to you, she seems to want to listen to folks. If she hadn't been handicapped with the child I think she might've blossomed into somethin' fine. What I mean is, if she'd been able to mix with them of her own age, 'cos she's got a sort of gaiety about her. It's quiet, under the skin like, but she's not without spirit. Oh no, she can take a firm hand with Master Amos. Sometimes when I've looked at her I've thought she's just missed being bonny; but there, she's a sensible young woman.'

Davie got to his feet and placed his pipe on the mantelpiece; then punching his grandfather gently on the side of the head he said, 'God save me from sensible young women, Granda.'

As he went slowly towards the door Sep asked quietly, 'What kind of women have you seen, lad?' There was more to the question than the actual words conveyed, and he turned and laughed at them over his shoulder as he said, 'I've three days afore I go back, I'll give one of them up entirely to tellin' you all about that, an' likely at the end you'll get the parson to me, aye. By the way, how are they? Has old Wainwright kicked the bucket yet?'

'No, lad.' Sep laughed. 'But Peter Skillet was past here t'other day an' he said the old codger can hardly stand on his pins. He said, when he was takin' Alice Knowles's burial service he wanted to say "Go careful, parson, else you'll be lyin' on top of her, then it'll be a toss up whether to cover you up or pull you out." '

Davie chuckled, then asked, 'An' Parson Hedley?'

'Oh, he's all right. Good man, Parson Hedley. But I'll tell you something. You remember Clarke, Sam Clarke?'

'Sam Clarke, the verger? Of course.'

'Aye, cast-thy-bread-upon-the-water-Clarke, an' the size of the bread he'd cast wouldn't choke a sparrow. Well, an uncle in Australia died an' left him a fortune.'

'Go on.'

'He did, it's a fact. Ten thousand pounds they say.'

'Whew!' As Davie shook his head his father put in quietly,

113

'He cast his bread an' got a bakehouse back, full o' dough.'

Davie had never heard his father crack a joke in his life, and this was a real good one. He lay against the door, his head back, his mouth wide, and bellowed, and they joined him.

It was good to be back.

After he had wiped his eyes he said to his father, 'Don't think I've heard better, Da, since I've been away,' which compliment brought a slight flush to Ned's face.

He now opened the door and stood looking out on to the roadway. The twilight was deepening rapidly, and a missel thrush, making a late journey up the road towards the copse, shrilled petulantly as it passed him. There came the sound of a single moo from the direction of the farm, and somewhere in the near hills a fox barked.

For five years he had dreamed of these sights and sounds, now they were his again, but for only three days. If things had been different and he had left this place in ordinary circumstances he would have gone this very minute to the master and said, 'Have you a place for me, it doesn't matter what?'

The feeling in him to remain was like pain, he longed to rest in the folds of the fells and to be invigorated in turn by climbing the hills; he wanted to struggle against the keen winds, and breathe in the same air that he had taken with his first breath, to come back in fact to where he belonged. But this he knew was an utter impossibility, so he would make the best of the time he had. He would put a face on things; he would preen himself in his new position, which wasn't so bad after all was said and done for a raw farm lad to have achieved.

As he stood he saw a figure coming out of the farmyard gateway and into the road. He did not recognise it until it reached the bend of Will Curran's cottage, and then it slowed and he saw the mass of auburn hair topping the woman now, not the girl. He watched her walk slowly towards her own door. Her eyes were on him, and his on her, but neither of them smiled at the other, and neither of them spoke. But she paused a moment before she disappeared from his sight, and in that moment he thought he saw what his grandfather meant by the change in her. But ah! he told himself, she'd still be the same Molly underneath, as he was still the same Davie. Leopards didn't change their spots, and human beings didn't change their natures, only their coverings.

He walked out of the door, crossed the road and jumped

up on to the high grass verge, and so on to the fells, with the wish strong in him now that he had resisted the urge to come back. It had been a mistake, and one he would likely pay for in the months ahead.

Four

'You must keep it out of my way, Jane.'

'But, Father, that is impossible. And . . . and he isn't an IT, Father, he's a child. And . . . and don't you realise, won't you realise, he's a very intelligent child. Parson Hed . . .'

'JANE!' He turned from her, his hand on his brow, his eyes closed. 'I'm not going to go through this again. Do you want to make me angry, really angry?' He swung around and faced her. There were two high spots of colour on his thin cheekbones and his grey eyes held a light that glowed under their dullness, like the setting sun reflecting on ice on a dirty pond, and he growled at her under his breath, 'If you persist in letting him get under my feet' – the anomaly didn't apparently strike him – 'I will have him sent away; yes, yes, I warn you . . .'

Jane stared up into the distressed face. She understood his attitude, she was full of pity for him, but nevertheless his words had made her turn pale, and as she often did when afraid she now showed courage, for she said, 'Father, if you were to do that I would leave with him. I would take up a position of some sort as near to him as possible, and not even mother's predicament would keep me here, nor the fact that I'm still under your jurisdiction. Only by force, Father, would you keep me if you sent him away.'

She did not know what reaction her words would evoke but she did not expect him to sit down suddenly in his chair and drop his head into his hands.

His acceptance of defeat brought the tears to her eyes and she went swiftly to him and put her hand gently on his shoulder, saying softly, 'I, I will do my best to curb him, I promise you. But . . . but if only you could bear to tolerate him, just speak a word to him now and again, you would, I am sure, get to . . .'

He raised his head and looked into her face and said quietly,

115

'Too late, Jane, five years too late. I grant you he's intelligent, intelligent enough to know that I have rejected him, and still reject him, for I cannot do otherwise, so put out of your mind any idea of a reconciliation.'

Her heart was sore for him. Slowly she bent her head and kissed his cheek. It was the first time she had done this since she was a small child; and she was saddened further when the close proximity to him brought to her the strong smell of whisky. It was but eleven o'clock in the morning and he had begun already. She had thought he kept his drinking solely for the late hours.

She went out and up the stairs to her room. It wasn't often she could sit alone, but now she gave herself a few minutes' respite. Amos was in good hands at the moment; Winnie had taken him across to the cottage to see Davie. Davie had come home. She had never seen Winnie so happy for years. She must go across and give him a welcome, but for the moment she would just sit here; she felt tired, weary, not only in her mind but in her body. She'd already had a tussle with Amos before eight o'clock this morning.

She had overslept and had woken to see him going through the door dressed for outside. When she tried to prevent him from going down the stairs he had fought her like a young wild animal. But though she managed to keep him quiet until she was dressed, once outside he had raced about the yard like a dog off a chain.

When he would not return upstairs to have his meal but wanted it in the kitchen, it was then she made the mistake of saying, 'We don't eat in the kitchen, we eat in the dining-room.'

Oh! then he would have his meal in the dining-room.

There had been more explaining, more argument. His powers of reasoning were, in a way, beginning to frighten her. He could detect subterfuge better than an adult; moreover, she had known long before yesterday, when he had nipped Parson Hedley's ear, that he could be loving one moment and vicious the next. The latter trait she put down to frustration, for, with his temperament, restriction must be a form of torment.

Sadly, wistfully, she thought again that if only her father would countenance the child's presence in the house life would be so much simpler, in fact it would be wonderful. It did not

116

matter so much her mother ignoring his presence for they need never meet.

The thought of her mother reminded her that she had been without Winnie for the past half hour, so she must go and visit her. She rose slowly and went out and across the wide landing to her mother's door and knocked, as always, before she entered the room. To her great surprise she found that Delia was out of bed, actually sitting in a chair by the window and she ran to her, crying, 'Oh! Mother. You feel so much better?'

'Yes, dear. I, I thought that . . . that before the winter comes I may get downstairs and go out in the fresh air.'

Jane stared down into the faded blue eyes, the thin worn face, and she said softly, 'That would be wonderful, wonderful. Shall I help you dress now?'

'No, dear, not today, I will just sit here. I . . . I can see the gate from here. I saw Winnie; she . . . she had the child with her.' Delia turned and looked at her daughter and, putting out her hand, that was like a bony claw now, she clutched Jane's and with a break in her voice said, 'I . . . I have made a grave error in . . . in shutting him out. It was wrong of me, very wrong. I . . . I must try to make amends.'

'Oh! Mother, Mother.' The tears slid slowly down Jane's face; she gathered the two hands to her, and holding them tightly against her breast she said, 'Oh, that's wonderful, wonderful. He's so bright, clever, he could grow up to be anything he chose. Parson Hedley says that he has great hopes for him.' And now she bent forward and kissed her mother on the cheek, and she had not done this, either, for many years . . .

For a moment, Delia stroked her hair, then, her attention drawn to the window, she looked out and towards a small figure toddling across the yard below, and she said quite calmly, 'Molly's child is quite pretty, don't you think?'

Jane gave no answer to this, she was too overcome at the turn of events, she just watched Biddy toddling in the direction of the cow shed. Before she reached it, however, her father emerged. The child looked up at him, but he paid no attention to her, he ignored her as he would have done Amos.

Jane looked at her mother. She was staring down into the yard following her husband's progress. Her gaze still on him, she said quietly, 'He's getting old.'

There was such a deep note of satisfaction in the remark that again hope and joy was dimmed in Jane; whatever reconciliation would take place between her mother and the child there could never be any hope of such happening between her parents. Beneath her mother's fragile exterior she sensed an ever-growing hatred of her husband. She turned away and went out without saying anything further . . .

Down in the kitchen, Molly was busy cooking the dinner. Besides the housework and the dairy she now did most of the cooking, but the long hours and hard work seemed to have little effect on her, she was strong and straight-backed. She turned from the table where she was dressing a bird, saying, 'Eeh! Miss Jane, I think you're goin' to find these partridges as tough as your boots. This lot must've dodged the gun for the last ten years, they'll be stringy. Still, there's some saddle o' mutton left, an' I've made a plum puddin', you can fill up with that.'

She drew the inside out of the bird as she said, 'You could do with a bit of fish, we've never had any for over a week. Our Johnny's goin' eeling the night. Now if he gets any I'll collar one and that will be a bit of a change for the morrow, start the first course off . . . '

'Yes, that will be nice, Molly.' For a moment she stood watching her larding the birds, then she said, 'I've often wanted to cook. Perhaps now Master Amos can get about on his own I'll have more time; you'll have to show me.'

'No, not me, Miss, you'll have to get Winnie to do that. Winnie's a grand cook; given the time she can turn out anythin'.'

'Yes, given the time,' she repeated sadly; then on a brighter note she asked, 'By the way, you know that Davie's back?'

Molly did not look up from what she was doing, and she did not speak immediately, and when she did her tone was non-committal. 'Yes, Miss,' she said; 'yes, I know he's back.'

Jane went out thinking that perhaps she shouldn't have mentioned the fact that Davie Armstrong had returned. Yet why not, it wasn't a thing you could hide. It was a pity though he had gone away in the first place, for in spite of everything he and Molly would likely have been married by now.

Again she commented to herself how strange it was that her feelings towards Molly were utterly devoid of animosity; she would like very much to see her happy with a man who could be a father to Biddy, a real father.

It was rarely she thought of the relationship between Molly's

118

child and herself, and when she did she could not take in the fact that they were half-sisters.

She walked out of the gate and down the road towards the Armstrongs' cottage, and long before she reached it she heard Amos's high squeals of glee.

The cottage door was open and she stood unobserved for a few minutes watching the blue clad sailor, whom she hardly recognised, holding Amos up by one hand towards the beam that spanned the width of the stairs about a foot below the ceiling. There was a similar beam at the head of the stairs in the farmhouse; each acted as a span between the stout oak pillars to which the balustrade was attached. A fox's skin was nailed across the beam in the house. She stood breathless now as she saw Amos swinging from the beam without any support.

Davie Armstrong had withdrawn his hand and with his head back he was laughing up at the child, crying, 'Go on, move along it, hand over hand like I showed you.' And Amos followed his instructions. Six times he moved one hand in front of the other and swung himself along the beam. Then she put her hands swiftly to her mouth when, pulling himself upwards with the strength of his arms alone, he squeezed between the beam and the ceiling and, his head hanging over the side, he laughed down at them, until Winnie said, 'Come on, come on, that's enough.'

'No, no, I am not coming down.'

'Time's up, lower away.' She watched Davie Armstrong put up his hands towards the boy, but Amos just laughed at him and defied him.

She was about to enter the room when Davie ran up the stairs, then turned and stepped on to the banister. One hand outstretched supporting himself against the staircase wall, he leaned forward and gripped the back of Amos's coat and with a swift tug he pulled him from the beam and held him dangling in mid-air; then jumping down on to the stairs he hoisted him on to his shoulder. When he came to the foot of the stairs he stopped as he saw Jane standing in the doorway.

Amos also catching sight of her shouted, 'Jane! Jane! Look. See what I can do. Push me up again.' He bent forward and looked into Davie's face, and Davie saying, 'Enough is enough, young man,' lowered him to the floor.

'Hello, Davie. I'm glad to see you back home.'

He took her outstretched hand and shook it twice before he

119

said, 'Thank you, Miss Jane; I'm glad to be back. I'm only sorry me stay will be short.'

They looked at each other smiling, and she thought, 'He's changed so, bigger, broader, and he's very self-assured.' The second cowman was gone, there was no remnant left of the young man who had comforted her in the straw of the malt house, then put his hand over her mouth to stop her crying aloud at what she was seeing and hearing; nor yet of the young man white with anger who, in the dead of night, had put Amos into her care. She noted that he wasn't dressed like the common seamen. She knew how these dressed, she had picture books of them, and Winnie had already told her of his promotion, and more to follow. First mate he'd be soon, she had said, and then, who knew, captain. And she didn't doubt that Winnie was right. Davie Armstrong had grown into a man, a determined looking man.

'How are you, Miss Jane?'

'Very well, thank you, Davie.'

He considered she had a nice voice, not la-di-da or anything like that, and it had a lilt to it. He remembered that she had always spoken nicely, due to Parson Hedley's coaching no doubt; and her face – his granda had said she was plain, well he wouldn't have said that, not really, not when she smiled, she had a right bonny pair of eyes on her; she was on the thin side, but then she was young, she would fill out. She hadn't changed all that much; he could like Miss Jane, the young lady, as much as he had liked Miss Jane, the young girl.

'You've got a handful here.' He nodded down at the boy, who was now standing between them looking up first at one and then the other.

'Yes, I'm afraid so, Davie.'

'He's a bright spark.'

'He's a naughty boy at times.' She looked down in mock sternness on the boy where he was now supporting himself by gripping Davie's thigh, and Amos, his head back gazing up at Davie, said, 'Will you stay here? I want you to stay here.'

'Well now.' Davie nodded at Jane. 'Tell me, is that an order or merely a request from the captain? Oh, I'm forgettin', captains never make requests, they just give orders. But I'm afraid, Captain' – he saluted the boy now – 'I'll have to disobey your command. It's mutiny I know, farmhouse mutiny on the high fells, but it's off to sea I'm going the day after the morrow.'

Sep laughed, and Winnie laughed, and Jane laughed, but the boy didn't; what he said was, 'You're making fun of me.'

Davie looked down at the boy, who was a small child one minute, allowing himself to be hoisted up to the ceiling, but the next refusing to be treated as such. He was disconcerting. That word fitted here, he thought. It was his captain's nickname; Disconcertin' Surtees, they called him, for the only response that disaster, from minor to mortal, provoked in him was the term, 'It's bloody disconcerting.' And so was this youngster's attitude. He was an old child, and it was odd when he came to think about it but whatever he turned out to be, he, in a way, would be responsible for it. In himself he was still convinced that had he not appeared on the scene Molly would have done the job she had been ordered to do.

'Come along now, Amos; you mustn't be a nuisance.' Jane caught hold of the boy's hand but he thrust her aside and clung on to Davie's leg as he looked up and pleaded, 'Will you play with me?'

Davie stared down into the long narrow eyes and, assuming a stance, he said, 'Well now, let's see; when does this watch finish?' He looked round at his mother, 'Twelve o'clock dinner, is it?' And when, laughing, she nodded at him, he returned his gaze towards the boy, demanding, 'What time do you have your dinner?'

'Three o'clock.'

'Then at two o'clock meet me at the burn and we'll have a swim. What about it?' The last words were addressed to Jane; and now she blinked and stammered slightly as she said, 'He ... he has never been in the water.'

'Well, then it's about time he made a start. All right, young master' – he pointed his finger down at him – 'two o'clock sharp. Not a minute afore, nor a minute after. Meet me on the cow path.'

The boy stared at him for a moment longer, his face alight; then swiftly he took his arms from about Davie's legs, scrambled on all fours to where his crutches were leaning against a chair, tucked them one under each arm, and was out of the door, all within a matter of seconds, and his voice came to them as he cried loudly, 'Biddy! Biddy! I'm going to the burn. I'm going with the sailor to the burn.'

121

'Oh dear me.' Jane was turning hastily to the door when Winnie put her hand on her arm, saying, 'He'll be all right, Miss Jane; just let him go his own road. It's got to be like that, he's doin' no harm. Remember he's a lad an' he's got to run his energy off.'

'But . . . but I promised Fa . . . ' she stopped, aware that Davie Armstrong's eyes were on her, and aware too that there was still one thing left of the second cowman, his hate of her father, and her father's hate of him. She ended haltingly, 'You won't let him stay in too long, he may catch cold not being used to it?'

'He won't catch cold; there's no chill on the water, I was in this mornin'.'

'Oh!' She stared at him, until a flush came to her face, then she turned quickly away and went out of the door. Slowly he followed her and watched her walking to where the boy was standing leaning on his crutches looking down on a little girl who was sitting on the grass verge cuddling a wooden doll, and he thought, it's a damn shame.

He carried the boy pick-a-back down from the cow path to the burn. It was a strange feeling because there were no legs around which to entwine his arms. He carried the crutches under his arm and did not hold on to the boy's hands clasped round his neck for he was clinging like a monkey and his arms seemed as strong as any man's.

He did not stop at the bottom of the steps but walked along the bank until he came to the shelf of rock from which he had dived since he was a small boy. He couldn't remember having learned to swim, only that he had once fallen in and after that it was easy. The water above the shelf of rock ran two feet deep but he had never yet touched the bottom beyond the shelf, although he had tried many times.

He sat down on the grassy bank and let the boy slide from his back. 'There, get them all off.' When the boy hesitated he cried at him, 'Come on then, off with your gansey first.' He laughed as he watched the boy struggling with the tight neck of the jersey, and he helped to ease it over his head, saying, 'Don't start by chokin' yourself.'

In a matter of minutes they were both naked.

'Come on.' Davie held out his hand, but the boy didn't rise from the grass, he was staring up at the firm, thick-set bare

122

body. His eyes moved up and down it two or three times, and then he turned his gaze on to his stumps with the protrusions, which should have been feet, and his face crumpled as if he was about to cry. Whether or not he would have cried he didn't know, for the next minute he was jerked from the ground and Davie was saying, 'No, not on all fours, stand up straight, you can walk on them. Use them like feet; come on, let's see you. Hang on to my hand. That's it, come on. Toss your body from side to side like this' – he demonstrated – 'an' you'll get it. Come on now have a shot . . . Aye, aye, that's it.'

When they reached the water's edge he said, 'There now, you keep that up and you won't need those crutches half the time; and your muscles will harden and be as good as any feet.'

Amos looked up steadily into his face and Davie nodded down at him, saying, 'I'm tellin' you, it's true. Try standin' straight, try walkin' straight. Keep off your benders; that's no way to get about, on all fours it isn't. Come on now.'

When the water rose above his stumps and touched his loins Amos shuddered, then gurgled, then laughed aloud, and when it reached his chest he closed his eyes for a moment as if experiencing ecstasy.

'There now, let yourself go, I've got a hold of you. Just let yourself go, you'll float on the water. Move your arms . . . Aw no, not like that, not up and down like the dogs. Look, stand there a minute and watch me.' He now lowered himself from the shelf of rock into the deep water and swam back and forth for a short way, calling as he did so, 'Like this, see. Like this. Use your arms and your shoulders.'

When he got back on to the shelf he laughed out loud when the boy fell fearlessly on to his face in the shallow water and began to imitate him.

'That's it, that's it. Well I never! You're like a duck.'

Amos righted himself and stood up, and still with the ecstatic look on his face he began to move his hands over his naked body as if he were feeling contact with it for the first time. Then of a sudden he seemed to go mad. He jumped and waved his arms about and shouted. He did not shout words, just sounds, but the sounds indicated glee, pure unadulterated glee. When, the water supporting him, he began to prance like a mythological horse, Davie cautioned, 'Steady on, steady on'; but Amos had found that by jumping up he went further down into the water and hit the rock bottom, which sent him up again.

123

It happened so quickly that Davie didn't realise that it had taken place until he saw the body sinking into the depths; and then he dived. Head first he went through the water that appeared like a silver curtain. His mouth was closed tight but he knew that he was bawling out inside, 'God Almighty! God Almighty!' For a moment he couldn't see the child; then there he was. His hand darting out, he grabbed him by the hair and in the filtered sunlight he saw the boy's face and it had not a vestige of fear on it. So calm was the countenance that for a moment his mind cried at him, 'God! he's dead. He's dead.'

When he broke the surface again he held the boy up under the armpits and he pushed him on to the ledge and scrambled after him. Then stooping quickly, he carried him up out of the water and on to the bank, and there, putting him on to his face, he began to pump him. When, after a few minutes, he realised he was breathing he turned him round and on to his back, and the boy gazed up at him, his eyes wide. Then swiftly the child thrust his arms around his neck and pulling himself up to him pressed himself close while a deep gurgle came from his throat before he exploded on a high piercing note, 'I can swim! I can swim!'

'Swim!' Davie gazed into the face so close to his. His own body was trembling; he'd never had a shock like that in years. It would be odd that, having once saved his life, he had now to go and drown him. By! he was a little marler; he was going to be a handful all right. He didn't envy Miss Jane, or anybody else who had to look after him. By God! he had got a shock. What he could do with was a drink; he was shaking like a leaf. 'Come on,' he said, loosening the arms from around his neck; 'it's time to dry off and get into your togs; enough for once.'

'No! No!' Amos now threw himself on the grass and began to gambol about on all fours; then lying down, he rubbed his body backwards and forwards like a dog rolling in excrement, and with much the same delight on his face.

'Here, come on, stop your antrimartins and get into your togs.'

As he went to pull the boy upright he let out a high cry of pain, for with a lightning movement Amos had plucked a long black hair from his groin. 'God Almighty! you young devil you. Now why had you to go and do that, eh? For two pins I'd lather you.'

They stared at each other now intently, so intently that they

124

did not see the small figure, until Davie, catching sight of Biddy out of the corner of his eye, again exclaimed, 'God Almighty!' He dropped on to his face and reached out for his shirt and pulled it roughly about him. Knotting the sleeves at the back, he now looked at the little girl who was surveying them both; but before he had time to give her any greeting Amos had risen on to his stumps and was shouting at her, 'Go away you! Go away. He's my sailor.'

'I don't want your sailor; I was just lookin'.'

'You mustn't look. Go on, go away.'

'I'll not.'

The blow from Amos's flat hand knocked the child on to her back; the next second he himself was swung round and knew what it was like to be really struck for the first time in his life. The blow across his ear was not forceful but it was hard enough to knock him too on to his seat and make him gasp, as much in surprise, as in pain.

Biddy was crying now and Davie, attempting to maintain the shirt in its precarious position, lifted her to her feet with one hand, saying soothingly. 'There now, there now, you're all right. Go on away with you to your ma. Go on now.' He turned her about and tapped her bottom gently; then he returned to the boy and said sharply, 'Let that be a lesson to you. By the looks of you you've had too much your own way, young man. Get into your clothes, and sharp.'

'Jane helps me.' The voice was sulky now.

'Well Jane's not here to help you now, and you're big enough to dress yourself. If you're big enough to belt little girls you're big enough to get into your togs, so the quicker you start the quicker you'll finish.'

Davie got dressed and waited patiently for the boy to get into his clothes. He knew as he slyly watched him that he was purposely lengthening the process. By! he was a strange youngster. Loving you one minute, not like a lad might but like a little lass would do, then pulling the hairs out of you wholesale the next. His granda had been right, there was a vicious streak in him, and if it wasn't curbed somebody was going to suffer, and by what he was learning of this young gentleman it wouldn't be himself.

'I'm going to tell Jane that you slapped me.'

Davie jerked his head round and looked sternly into the face looking up into his, and he said, 'Do that. You do that, and you can tell her that I'll do it again if I catch you at the same trick. Come on, up with you, get on to your crutches.'

'Aren't you going to carry me?'

'No. You're a big fella, at least to yourself, so you walk up those steps. Get goin'.'

And casting speculative glances at the sailor, Amos got going . . .

It wasn't until Jane was putting him to bed that night that he said to her, 'The sailor struck me.'

'What! you mean, Davie?'

'Yes, Davie, the sailor. He boxed my ears like Mr Geary does the boys!'

'He never did!'

'He did.'

'But . . . but why?'

He blinked at her, then grinned, saying, 'I slapped Biddy, I knocked her down. She wouldn't go away when we were bathing. I told her he was my sailor and she had to go away and she wouldn't, so I slapped her; and he slapped me. But I still like him, he's still my sailor.'

Jane ignored this last, she felt highly indignant. How dare Davie Armstrong slap the child, even if he had first of all slapped Biddy; children often slapped each other. She would have a word with him about it, indeed she would. He would have no right to do such a thing even if the boy had been an ordinary boy. Had he no feelings for his handicap? She was surprised at Davie Armstrong, especially as the child had taken to him and had openly shown affection for him.

She couldn't really believe it; perhaps the child was romancing. Anyway, she would find out tomorrow, she would ask him outright. And if Amos had been speaking the truth, well then – she paused in her thinking. How did one chastise a man like Davie Armstrong had turned out to be? He had been a headstrong youth before he had left the farm, even Winnie admitted that, but now he was a man who sailed the seas and he had gained a certain position. Whether this had given him his authoritative attitude she didn't know; what she was aware of was that he wasn't a person one could chastise. Still, if he had struck the child it was her duty to do something; after all, he was but a labouring man . . . Oh really! Some part of her flounced at her priggishness, but she defended herself by muttering aloud, 'Well, you just can't let a thing like that happen and do nothing about it.'

Before she went to sleep she definitely decided to have a private word with Davie Armstrong in the morning. But before nine o'clock the following morning she was standing in the dining-room defending him . . .

'Why,' said McBain angrily, 'did you not tell me that Armstrong was back?'

'It . . . it never crossed my mind, Father.'

'It never crossed your mind!' He brought his closed fist down on the dining-room table. 'You are no child, so don't act like one. You're bound to know that the very sight of that man will make me want to use a gun on him.'

What she did know at this moment was that five years ago the enraged man before her would not have thought of using such an expression, no matter what his feelings were. She had always been aware that he had despised the more ordinary farmers roundabout, but now his own manner of living and speaking wasn't much removed from theirs, and this unfortunately was reflected in the farm.

There was no real outward sign that the standard of the farm had depreciated, but she was aware that it had. The hand that had once held the reins of the business had been a sober hand, sober, strict and knowledgeable, and this made for good husbandry, but now his knowledge wasn't used because he woke each morning to a mind fuddled from the excess of the night before.

The name of Davie Armstrong had never been mentioned from that awful night they had faced each other across the newborn child in the kitchen, but instinctively now she realised that Winnie's son had been growing like a canker in her father's breast, because but for Davie's interference Molly, he felt, would have carried out his orders and there would not have been gambolling round the place like a child he looked upon as a monstrosity.

She said quietly, 'You cannot stop him visiting his parents.'

'Can't I? I can turn the whole damn lot of them out.'

The muscles of her face tightened, her mouth set against the unreasonable injustice of this threat; and now, her voice rising, she dared to say, 'You'd be hard put to it to find anyone like Winnie; you don't appreciate what she does. Have you ever thought what it's like looking after mother seven days a week?'

127

'Be quiet, girl!' His face had a bleached look, even the mottled pattern of blood veins on his cheekbones had paled.

She remained quiet for a moment while they stared at each other and then in a controlled but stiff voice, she said, 'He'll be gone tomorrow and if you're wise, Father, you'll say nothing against him to Winnie, for things are not so bad over the countryside that she wouldn't be snapped up; there's still Farmer Hetherington, and his wife is still alive. And I must remind you, Father, that I cannot take on any more, my hands are full from morning till night, I'm . . .'

Her words faded away as she watched his head droop heavily forward and his shoulders hunch as he lowered himself down into the chair, and with his fists pressed together on the desk he brought out in a voice like a groan, 'Don't . . . don't keep on, Jane.'

When, after a moment, he raised his head and looked at her she was so swamped with pity she wanted to put her arms about him and press his head to her, for she had never seen such need for comfort in any human being; his need she felt was greater than her mother's, or the child's . . . or her own . . . What was her need? She refused to go into it now; this was something that one wrestled with when unable to sleep. And anyway, it was only a part of life, for as the Bible said, the body was not one member but many. The Bible also said, 'Though I speak with the tongues of men and of angels, and have no charity, I am become as sounding brass, or a tinkling cymbal.'

The thought urged her to carry out her desire and comfort her father, but as she made towards him he turned his head from her as if in shame, then rose from the table and went out of the room. The moment was lost never to return, and she knew this and was saddened to the depths of her . . .

When she went to collect Amos from the kitchen, where she had left him, Molly turned from the stove and said, 'It's no use, Miss; might as well try to tether a streak of lightnin'. He scooted out of the door afore I could stop him.'

'Oh dear! Molly; why didn't you hold him?'

'Hold him, Miss? I tell you I'd just as soon try to hold on to the bull. But don't worry' – she gave a thin smile – 'he'll come to no harm, he's gone down to the Armstrongs.'

'Dear, dear! He'll make a nuisance of himself.'

'I don't think so, Miss.' Molly lifted the black stock pot from the stove and brought it to the table.

Jane noticed that Molly had made no further reference to the visitor in the Armstrong household, so she herself did not bring his name up. Under the circumstances it would, she felt, have been indelicate.

Molly now said, 'Would you like a blackberry pie made, Miss? The bushes at the back are laden.'

'Yes, that would be nice. Could I gather them for you when I get the child?'

'No, no, Miss; you'll get all messed up and you've got your new print on. I like that one.' She nodded at the mauve print dress that Jane was wearing which had a thin gold stripe running through the material; the skirt was full and the bodice fitted her narrow waist. 'It suits you; mauvy tones suit you.'

Jane flushed slightly as she passed her fingers over the front of the skirt; she was feeling a deep embarrassment as if she were being paid a compliment by a man, for it was the first time anyone had ever remarked about her clothes, or her appearance. She thought again that Molly, in spite of everything, was a kind creature.

Molly watched her young mistress go hurriedly from the kitchen, then she went to the window and watched her progress across the yard. She was running like a young girl should. She watched her pick up her skirts away from the slime as she jumped the drain down the centre of the yard, and aloud she muttered three words, 'God help her.' She was as sorry for Miss Jane at times as she was for herself. In a way they were both in the same boat. Miss Jane had as much prospect of getting married as a bitch in a brothel; and then there was herself; she'd had two offers in the past year, not counting Will Curran, who watched her like a chained dog. Both the offers would have given her a better life than she had here, so why hadn't she taken them, why? In the past she had refused to answer this question; now as she returned to the table she cried at herself, 'Stop damn well askin' the road you know.'

He was along there, a few hundred yards from her, Lord Davie Armstrong . . . God Almighty Armstrong, and he had never opened his mouth to her. She thought she would have dropped down dead when she saw him through the dusk two nights ago, and she had tossed and turned half the night as she lay with the child at her side, knowing that there were only two layers of brick atween them.

The dawn had come before she closed her eyes, for she had

129

faced up to the fact that she had been a bloody young fool. Yet she wasn't going to take all the blame, she wasn't going to pour more guilt on herself than she had already done; she had enough to carry; she looked back on the episode with the master as a sort of summer lunacy. Her Grannie Talbot used to tell her about such happenings when she was a girl, things that happened after the Harvest Supper; things that had made her put her hand across her mouth and giggle and say, 'Eeh! Grannie, you're spinnin' 'em.' Now she knew her grannie hadn't been spinning them; the master had taken her and, let her face it, she had enjoyed it. When John Curran had first taken her there had been no joy in that. She hadn't wanted it, but he had forced her and she had been frightened. But John Curran was a babe in arms, in fact an unborn child compared to the master, and yet what had taken place between them had not frightened her. Looking back on it though, over the distance, the mere thought of it now sickened her; it was as if she had been mesmerised and changed into another being.

If she had at that time taken any of Mother Reckett's medicine she would have blamed it on that, for Mother Reckett's doses had been known to do funny things to people; she had known that the mistress had visited Mother Reckett for she had found the hiding place where she put the bottles. She had never let on to anyone about that, not even to Winnie, and certainly not her ma, though her ma knew all about Mother Reckett. The old woman had got rid of three of them for her ma, although each time it had made her feel bad, and she had never been right since the last do, tired all the time. Anyway she couldn't blame Mother Reckett for what had happened between herself and the master, she only knew that her whole attitude towards him changed when she had stood on the side of the bog with the child in her arms. She had known then that the master was the kind of man who would sell God to the devil if it suited him; and it was strange that what rankled in her mind most was that she had allowed herself to be flayed by him. She did not think of it as a piece of utter hypocrisy, she just thought that no real decent man would have put her up to it, then done it himself. But the bitterest pill of all she was constantly swallowing was the knowledge that through her madness she had thrown away the chance of getting a decent man. And not only that; she had a feeling for Davie Armstrong, not the same kind of feeling she'd had for the master, it was different, deeper, going right back to the days when she first began to follow him into the fields when he was crow scaring. He had never pushed her off when she pestered him, and as she grew up she had thought of him as her property. She was fourteen when she had slapped their Lena's face for saying that she, too, liked him. She had wanted to tell him about John Curran, but she didn't dare for she felt he would have bashed his face in for him, and she knew it was very important that everybody should get along with everybody on the farm.

But from the night the master had gripped her thigh she seemed to have lost her senses, gone stark staring mad. Strange, she had thought no less of Davie, but the master's passion and attention had drugged her almost to death. It was as if she had chewed foxgloves and raw poppies.

The whole thing now appeared to her like a bad dream, something that could not have happened in reality. But she had only to look at the master, watch his thin legs in the cords and polished gaiters hanging each side of a horse; it was at such times that she knew it wasn't a nightmare for she had seen those legs, hairy and bare, prancing and dancing like a dervish.

What madness got into people! She couldn't understand it. She couldn't understand why, when Davie Armstrong wouldn't look the side she was on, when his contempt for her was deep in his eyes, that the feeling inside her for him should grow, and keep her lying alone when her body ached for lack of use.

She picked up her basket and went out of the kitchen by a side door, through the arch into the paved court, and through a gate into a lane that led to a copse where grew the low blackberry bushes.

There was a tangle of undergrowth behind the bushes and she hadn't put out her hand half-a-dozen times to pluck the berries when Davie walked round from behind the bushes.

Although he had been in her mind up to that very minute, nevertheless the sight of him made her start. Determined not to speak first she went on picking until he said, 'Why hello, Molly Geary' – it could have been that they had just met after a long time, except that his tone was weighed with mockery – 'Fancy running across you. I would have thought you would have been up and gone to the big city years ago.' And then she turned on him saying, 'Think you're funny, don't you?'

'Me funny? I never thought I was funny in me life . . . me funny?'

'You're born but you're not buried yet.'

'Tut! tut!' He made a clicking sound with his tongue. 'Where've I heard that afore. Aye, me da; it's a favourite sayin' of his. And it's a daft saying when you come to analyse it. Of course we're born, and some of us get the chance to live . . . ' He paused and their gaze held before he finished, 'Long enough to know that they'll be buried some day.'

'You still don't believe me, do you?' Her voice was quiet now, full of pain. 'You'll go down to your grave not believin' me; nothing will ever make you think other than I meant to do it, isn't that true?'

'Aye, that's true.'

'Well' – she gulped in her throat. Then her voice rose. 'You're wrong then, you're blasted well wrong. You think as you do 'cos you wanted to think the worst of me. It gave you something else to pin on me . . . t'other wasn't enough.'

It was a few moments before he said, 'T'other was enough, but you went a long way with the bairn afore you changed your mind, didn't you?'

'Aye, I did; right to the very brink. But I did change it. I'd changed it afore you came on the scene and played God . . . You're good at playin' God, aren't you?'

'Sailor! Sailor!'

They both turned sharply and looked down the road, where Amos was hobbling towards them on his crutches, followed by Biddy. Both children were panting when they came up to them and Amos cried, 'I've been looking all over for you. Do you know I've been looking all over for you? Where have you been?'

'Up to London to see the Queen.'

Amos didn't follow this, but Biddy did. On a high clear laugh she looked up at Davie and chanted, 'Pussy cat, pussy cat what did you there?' And laughing, Davie finished with her, 'I – chased – a – big – mouse – from – under – her – chair.'

'Good, good!' As Davie looked kindly down on the child, the while ignoring her mother, Amos put in sulkily, 'I don't like that.'

'You don't?' Davie turned to him. 'Then you don't know a good rhyme.'

'I know 'nother one, Mister.' Biddy was smiling up at him, and without more ado she repeated:

132

What's your name?
Mary Jane.
Where do you live?
Up the lane.
What do you keep?
A little shop.
What do you sell?
Gingerpop.

Amos was supporting himself now on one crutch, the other was lifted breast high, the point end thrust towards Biddy, when Davie cried, 'A-ah! you do young fellow, you do. Remember yesterday?'

Their eyes held, the boy's and the man's; the crutch was lowered and tucked under his arm, and then he said, 'She shouldn't say lines to you.'

'And why not, boy?'

'Because I don't want her to.'

'Oh! Well, let me tell you somethin', young man.' Davie went down on his hunkers before them both. 'What you want, and what you're going to get out of life, are two different things, and the quicker you learn this the better. Now off you both go on to the green there and play.'

'I want you to come.'

'I'll come in a minute; go on with you.' He gave the boy a push that almost overbalanced him, then stood watching him hobbling off, sulking, following Biddy this time. When he turned towards Molly she was staring at him, and he returned her glance for a full minute before saying, 'There's not much resemblance atween them, is there? None at all I should say. But it should show somewhere, don't you think?'

Her lips were quivering, and the muscles of her face worked before she said from deep in her throat, 'You're a cruel bugger, Davie Armstrong! That's what you are, a cruel bugger . . .'

Jane did not have her private word with Davie until about an hour before his departure the following day. Her determination to reprimand him with regard to his treatment of Amos had faded, but even if it hadn't she doubted if she would have been able to carry it through.

Thinking of what to say to Davie Armstrong when out of his presence was a simple matter, to say it in his presence was a different matter altogether. Although his manner was pleasant, even jocular, he had an air of authority about him which she had noticed from the beginning. Nevertheless, they talked of Amos, and in the boy's presence.

Davie stood at one side of the hearth in his mother's kitchen with Amos clinging to his leg while Jane stood at the other side. She watched him put his hand on the boy's head and ruffle his curls, curls that had taken her quite some time to comb into place; and he looked down on the child while he addressed himself to her, saying, 'He wants a firm hand; as I said yesterday the bit wants tightenin'.' And when he added with a glance at her, 'Though it's none of my business, Miss Jane,' she prevented herself from answering, 'You're right, it isn't.'

She remained silent looking into his face, while she thought, I'm glad he's going away, he'd be a disturbing influence here. And then he brought the colour flooding to her face with his next words. 'I went over to the vicarage last night,' he said. 'I had a long talk with Parson Hedley. Fine man, Parson Hedley. An' he thinks highly of you, Miss. Talked at length about you, he did. Lonely life for a man stuck in the big barrack along o' that old hypocrite. Real old face-both-ways is Parson Wainwright. I said to Parson Hedley he should get himself married 'cos he looked more lonely than a sailor in a dead calm. You should be thinking along those lines yourself, Miss Jane. Coming up to eighteen, aren't you?'

The heat rushed down her body to her very feet. He was talking to her as if she were a child, or a girl of the farm. She managed to say with some dignity, 'Really!' And then her colour went a tone deeper when he burst out laughing. 'Aw now, Miss Jane; don't come the fine lady, you're too nice for that. An' I meant no impitence, I was just thinkin' about your future, 'cos somehow I don't think you'll bother much about it yourself. You won't get much chance will you, not with this?' He again ruffled Amos's curls while the child stared up at him, his mouth slightly apart as if he was sucking in every word.

Her lips tight, her expression prim, like that of a maiden lady of twenty-seven not a girl of seventeen, she lowered her eyes from his, then held out her hand towards Amos, saying, 'Come along.' But Amos answered her quickly with, 'No! Not yet. I'm going to see old Sep; he's in bed bad.'

Jane turned her head to the side with impatience, not only at his disobeying her, but at the term 'he's in bed bad'. She'd have this to contend with too. The more the child went about the farm the more of the jargon, the bad grammar, was he likely to pick up. She covered her annoyance by asking, 'Is old Sep really ill?'

'No.' Davie's left eyelid drooped. 'But he thinks that if he puts on his rheumatics it'll keep me here another day or so. He won't believe that cargoes, like the time and tide, wait for no man. To hear him talkin' you'd think I was second-in-command to the admiral.'

'I want to see Sep. Carry me to see Sep.'

'Aw well, come on then; there'll be no peace till you get your way.' He hoisted the boy up into his arms. 'Young devil you are . . . Isn't he?' He addressed the question to Jane as he passed her, and his left eyelid flickered again.

She watched him mounting the stairs, talking all the while to the boy who had his arms clasped tightly around his neck. He had winked at her twice within the last few minutes. Davie Armstrong had winked at her. She did not have to remind herself that this Davie Armstrong was not the Davie Armstrong that she remembered. Really! She was glad he was leaving, otherwise the situation would become most embarrassing. He didn't seem to realise that she was Miss Jane in charge of the household, which she ran very efficiently. And what was more important she was in charge of the child. She realised that her position with regards to Amos would become untenable were he to remain here, for he treated her as little more than a girl, a very young girl at best . . . Yet he had suggested that she was old enough to marry, and had even put a name to the man, Parson Hedley. Really! He was outrageous. Parson Hedley was almost thirty years old.

Davie stood on the top of the Tor on the same spot on which he had stood three days before.

The sailor's bag rested against his leg. It was much lighter than it had been on his arrival, but it had in it something more valuable than baccy, whisky, and trinkets, for it held three large crusty loaves of bread, the like of which he wouldn't taste again not for many a year. •

There was in him a new sadness; he knew that he was unlikely to see his grandfather again. Moreover, over the past three days the sea had fallen away from him and the soil had seeped back into his being. But he was already empty with the

135

loss of it, even while it weighed him down; these hills, these mountains, the fells and the valleys, how could a man tear his roots from them? They said the mandrake cried when it was pulled from the earth; he was crying at this minute, his body was sweating his tears, only his eyes were dry.

He looked towards the farm for the last time and when he saw the dim outline of a figure come out of the gate and walk along the road towards the cottages he thought, but for her I'd be down there still. A cruel bugger, she had called him, and she had been on the point of crying as she said it. He was glad he could hurt her. He stooped down and swung the bag on to his shoulder and, turning abruptly, he walked over the Tor to where it sloped into a bracken-covered hillside, and he went through this until he dropped on to the fells and then on to the main road.

He had been walking on the road for only a matter of fifteen minutes when he heard the familiar sound of a trotting horse. It was approaching round the bend from which he had just come. He walked on to the grass verge, turning every now and again to watch its approach. It could be a carter or some friendly soul who would give him a lift into Hexham, from where he would take the train to Newcastle.

When the trap came into view and he recognised its driver he turned abruptly and walked smartly forward, his gaze directed ahead. The trotting came nearer, and it was just behind him when McBain's voice cried, 'Get up there!' There was the crack of a whip, then the trap was abreast of him. When the whip cracked for the second time and the tip of it came over his kit bag, whipped his hat off his head and struck its thong against his left temple, he staggered and almost fell into the ditch. Recovering his balance, he threw down his kit bag and, running into the middle of the road, he bawled, 'You bloody cowardly swine you! That's all you are, a bloody cowardly swine!'

He stood staring after the racing trap; then he put his hand up to his face and looked at his fingers. There was no blood on them, but he could feel the swelling rising from his cheekbone to his temple. He picked up his cap and thrust it on his head and hoisted his bag once more on to his shoulder.

He walked slowly, hesitantly, along the road for he had the desire to go back and set the whole farm on fire, do something to get even with that smarmy hypocrite.

He had congratulated himself that he had kept out of the

man's way during the past three days, and then this to happen at the last minute. Well, it was five years since he had been here, it had better be ten before he came back again. It would take that long for his temper to cool. But five, ten, or fifteen, one day he'd get even with that swine, by God he would!

Book Three: 1896

One

Up till a few years ago Cock Shield Farm had been pointed out as an example of how a farm should be run. The example extended back to McBain's great-grandfather and the pattern appeared so set it seemed impossible of alteration either for the better or the worse. But for some time now McBain's neighbours, both immediate and those not so, had taken great satisfaction in watching the example disintegrate.

McBain, it was said, was rarely sober now. He was no longer in command of his own business. There was slackness on the farm, and it was not only hearsay, you had just to pass the gate and there you saw evidence of it; more evidence still in the cattle he sent into market; and his milk yield had gone down, so much so that he had stopped the supply of milk to the hospitals.

Not that some of the more kindly neighbours didn't pity him, for his son, 'McBain's bit' as he was cruelly nicknamed, was a handful. He might be without legs but he caused more uproar than a human centipede. Not quite sixteen yet and throwing his weight about like any man; but then he had looked like a man for years. To see him sitting in the trap you'd swear you were looking at a man in his twenties. And his trap was something too, made up from an old one and mostly by himself they said, with a set of portable steps at the back up which he could hop; a seat for himself on one side higher than that for the passengers at the other, so that generally his head would be above theirs; except when he drove young Biddy Geary into Hexham, and she topped him.

That was a nice state of affairs, the people of Hexham said, when at the age of fourteen he had first driven her into the town. It was noted that from the time the boy drove into Hexham

McBain ceased to attend the market. Fred Geary went in his place; and everyone knew that Geary was as bottle conscious as his master. And it was Geary who, when well oiled, gave the avid listeners details of the happenings at Cock Shield. He never tired of repeating the fact that father and son had uttered not one word to each other; except that is but once when the youngster had hobbled into the dining-room and seated himself at the table. He was ten years old at the time and McBain had cried at him, 'Out! Out!' and when the boy hadn't moved he had picked up a carving knife. What might have happened if Miss Jane had not thrown herself between them was anybody's guess, so Fred Geary said. But mind, Geary always added, not that he would want Master Amos sitting across the board from himself, for did you ever see such eyes as he had in his head, long and narrow but so sharp looking they could pick winkles. And that fair hair of his that grew thicker than wool on a sheep's back, it made his head look twice its size. Even then it didn't do anything to diminish his shoulders. Did you ever see such shoulders and arms on an ordinary man? Mind, he would say this, given a pair of legs he'd have been a remarkable specimen, six foot at least when fully grown he guessed, and as broad as a bull with it. But having no legs didn't stop him prankin'. The things that lad got up to, even from when he was a mite, was something nobody'd believe. Teased the life out of the lads he did, and the cattle an' all. He wasn't seven when he lashed one of the cats to Rover's tail, then hung a kitten around his neck. Old Rover was as quiet as a lamb, but that day, God, he nearly tore the place apart, they thought they'd have to put him down after.

Bossy, he was an' all. Everything had to be his. He sort of claimed people; Miss Jane, well, she hadn't a life of her own. As far as he could see she'd never marry Parson Hedley although there'd been an understanding 'twixt them for years. She had her hands right full had Miss Jane. He was dead sorry for her. What with bringing that young 'un up and then the master, and the mistress. Never put a foot out of bed had the mistress from the day the young rip bashed her across the ankles with his crutch, and that was some years ago. It was the very day after Davie Armstrong had gone back to sea. He remembered it as if it was yesterday . . . and so on and so on . . .

It was in the late autumn of '94 that something disastrous happened at Cock Shield, but Fred Geary was unable to relate it. Typhoid struck the farm, and not only the farm but most of the county. The epidemic brought forth indignation as well as horror, indignation because it was thought that typhoid had been overcome. Hadn't all the corporations been ordered to see to their drainage, to pull down slums where congestion led to filth, and filth to disease? Parts of Shields, Jarrow and Newcastle had been breeding spots, but much had been done to eliminate them. Hexham had done her part too. The huge rubbish dumps lying on the banks of Skinner's Burn had disappeared and everything had been done that was possible to eradicate the fever, so how had it reached this part?

It had reached the farm through a carrier, a man named Peter Hanratty. He had brought Jane some packages from Newcastle that she had ordered by letter, and for Winnie he had brought two pieces of leather for soling and heeling the boots. There was a stall from where he picked up pieces cheap, so cheap that he could afford to add coppers to their price and still leave the leather at half the price Winnie would have paid for it in the shop.

Strangely Winnie didn't get the fever, nor yet did Jane. The first one to go down with it was Delia. She died within four days. Ned was next, he went quickly like the snuff of a candle. The following week Fred and Cassy Geary died within a few hours of each other. One by one the other occupants of the farm waited for death.

With the exception of the doctor and Parson Hedley no one came to the farm and no one left it, they weren't allowed to.

And no outsiders came to the funeral of any of the four who died. The farm itself seemed near its final end. Even the cattle made sounds like echoes of the death throes.

Yet when the epidemic finally passed and they could throw off the fear of catching the fever, each individual acted as if he had been given a new lease of life. First, Johnnie Geary went to the master and told him he wanted to be married, and could he have the malt house, he'd do up the big room and make it habitable.

McBain's prompt answer to this was, no; he couldn't have the malt house. He had other uses for the malt house. If he wished to marry he could bring his wife to the cottage that he shared with his sister. It was big enough, hadn't his mother and father reared seven in it?

Johnnie Geary had to be content with this.

Mickey, too, went to the master. But he posed a very odd question. Who was his master? he asked. Who had he to take orders from, himself, or Master Amos? Mickey pointed out that he just wanted to know where he stood.

McBain's answer to this was to say grimly, 'Where you've always stood. You know that without asking.'

It was after Mickey's visit to him that McBain, too, seemed to change. He reverted back to a shadow of his former self. It was noticed that there was no smell of liquor from him in the morning now; he moved more briskly around and he gave orders so that all could hear. Moreover he brought in two day labourers to help out the three men who were left. Two further surprising things. First, he began riding again, and then, six months after Delia died and, for no apparent reason, he engaged builders to renovate the malt house . . .

The first indication Jane had of her father's intention with regards to the malt house was when she was walking along the cow path. Looking down over the scree-studded field she saw men at work on the roof and others unloading a wagon full of bricks. She did not go down to investigate but returned quickly to the house in search of her father.

McBain was not to be found on the farm. She asked here and there, everyone in fact except Amos – she never mentioned her father to Amos. It was Will Curran who informed her that the master had gone down to the bottom pasture to see what the animals might be picking up, as three cows had dropped their calves during the past month.

She did not give way to her feelings and run down to the lower cow pasture; she was nearing her twenty-eighth birthday and her running and scampering days were over, but she hurried almost on the point of a run.

The ten years that had passed had not altered Jane very much. She was a little taller, a little less thin, but she was still neither pretty nor yet plain. Often, in a matron of twenty-seven, you could add the word comely but not to Jane, there was nothing comely about her. If she had ever thought of dressing up like a boy she could have passed for one. She would have been shocked at the suggestion for within herself she was utterly feminine, and being so her emotions tended to guide her tastes. She liked a good story with a love interest in it. She was a devotee of the Brontë sisters; on the other hand she didn't care much for Mr Dickens, whose writings smacked too much of caricature, and caricature, she thought, was cruel; and all the pictures in Mr Dickens's books tended to show queer creatures. In music her taste was towards Strauss and did not go beyond Mozart. She thought that it was because her tastes were so plebeian that nothing satisfied her. In spite of being betrothed to Arnold she felt lost. Amos no longer needed her, even when he persisted that she keep him company. It was only her father, and of course Arnold, to whom she could act as a staff. Yet Arnold, as dear as he was, had for twenty-five of his forty years taken care of himself. His only need of her, she felt, was as a loving companion. Well, what more did she want at her age?

She lifted the top bar of the gate from the hook attached to the low stone wall, closed it after her, then went across the field to where she saw her father standing breaking up a tuft of grass with his foot.

'Father.'

He turned showing slight surprise, he hadn't heard her coming. 'What is it?'

'I've . . . I've just passed the malt house. There are men there, workmen.' She watched his eyes flicker to the side. It was an evasive action; she knew it of old when he was reluctant to discuss the matter in hand. 'What are they doing, Father?'

'Well what do you imagine builders do when they go into an old house, they restore it. I'm having it restored.'

'The malt house?'

'You've just said you've seen them there. Yes, the malt house.'

'Have you changed your mind? Is it for Johnnie?'

His eyes flickered away again, and his lips went into a hard line; then he brought his head sharply upwards and looked at her, saying, 'No, it is not for Johnnie, it . . . it is for you . . . and . . .'

'Me! Father?'

He did not immediately answer her startled exclamation but dusted a straw from his breeches before saying, 'It will be your home when I remarry.'

She thought she was going to sink into the ground; she actually recoiled as if from a blow. It was her expression that brought his head up and his body straight as he said rapidly, 'I am not an old man, I am but fifty-six, I have lived an isolated life long enough. Anyway, this should be good news for you for,

143

from when I take a wife, you will be free to marry. I have been a hindrance; you might never have married with me at this end, and old Wainwright at the other.'

Her body slumped slightly; the shock was leaving her, being replaced by a certain tenderness. He wasn't remarrying out of purely selfish motives, he had been thinking of her. It was true what he said. With him holding her here and Parson Wainwright refusing to allow a married woman to share his home, they had been handicapped, for Arnold's stipend wasn't sufficient to provide for himself and a wife. And this state of affairs might have gone on until they were too old to care, but her father had thought of this. She blinked her eyes and said softly, 'I . . . I understand, but . . . but what about Amos?' The eyes flickered away again. 'He'll go with you of course; that will be one of the crosses you'll have to bear in your married life.'

She would have liked to say, 'Oh, Amos won't be any cross, Father,' yet she knew that he would be, for he was of a jealous nature. He did not even like to see Arnold touch her hand. They had to be very circumspect in his presence. But that didn't matter; that contingency would be met in the future. As Arnold would quote, 'Sufficient unto the day is the evil thereof.' She gazed at her father tenderly now. Perhaps things were taking a turn for the better at last. Perhaps the woman he was marrying – although at the moment she couldn't think of anyone he might have chosen – perhaps she was motherly and she would grow to love her.

Then it was as if a mighty hand passed over her, sweeping her generous thoughts away into the wide sky and filling her body with anger and resentment, for her father was saying, 'I want you to prepare a dinner for a week come Wednesday. I will be bringing the Reeds over. They are aware of my intentions; I will be settling the matter with them at the weekend. I am in little doubt but that Agnes is willing.'

AGNES REED! The name came spiralling upwards and seemed to dive out of the top of her head like a startled lark, the echo of the name filled the sky. 'You can't mean AGNES REED, Father!'

His colour changed; the nose that had at one time been thin, but was now bulbous, turned purple, and the tinge spread up over his eyes and brow into the bald dome at the front of his head until it became lost in the black and grey streaked hair sprouting above his ears.

'She's younger than me!' she was yelling at him. 'You can't. You can't, Father, not Agnes Reed. She's flighty, common, the talk of the countryside, she's . . .'

'Be quiet! I command you, hold your tongue. She's a fine young woman of proper' – he had almost said proportions, but quickly altered it to principles. 'Because a young woman rides a horse as good as a man, why should she be slandered?'

Her indignation was burning her up. As she glared at him she saw him as he really was, as he had always been, a man who favoured young girls. She had a picture of him as he held Molly to him; she saw his lips like wet slugs sucking her breasts. And Molly hadn't been the first. No, her mother in her delirium had mentioned a name, that of another girl, a very young girl, who was now a married woman but who had always looked at her strangely when they met in Hexham . . . And his jaunts into Newcastle on a Tuesday, what did he do there? He had no business in Newcastle. Oh, she knew what he did there.

But Agnes Reed; that silly addle-headed girl. She hadn't met her more than half-a-dozen times but once would have been enough to know the type she was. And now she was to be turned out of her home, the home that she loved, that she had helped to tend and care for over the years, the home where she had thought she and Arnold would be spending the rest of their lives . . . when they married. It was no use her reason telling her that if her father had chosen an older woman she would still have been turned out of the house, for she would have countered this with, the house would not have been closed to her as it would be if Agnes Reed became its mistress. She shouted at him now, 'You can't do this, Father, you can't! It's indecent . . . Arnold won't marry you; he wouldn't, he wouldn't countenance it.'

'Arnold shan't be asked to countenance it, I shall be married in Hexham.'

They stood glaring at each other now. The wind had loosened her hair and a strand had fallen over her eyes. She pushed it to one side and with it the first tears, but so full was she of anger that they ran slow. But not so her legs when she turned from him and, picking up her skirts, raced through the fields.

When she entered the farmyard she looked like someone demented. Amos was coming out of the stables and he called to her, 'What's the matter, Jane? Jane! Stop a minute. What is it?' But she took no heed. Nor of Molly in the kitchen who came from the sink, saying, 'Good God, Miss, what's happened to you?' She ran past her and up the stairs to her room, and there she stood gasping for a minute before throwing herself on to the bed.

It was only seconds later when Molly entered the room and, putting her hands on her shoulders, said gently, 'Tell us, Miss, what is it? What's upset you?'

'Nothing, nothing.' She shook her head from side to side.

'Aw, Miss! now come on, you don't get in a state like this, not you for nothin' you don't.'

'What is it?' Amos came hobbling into the room and, thrusting Molly aside, he dropped his crutches on the floor and hoisted himself on to the side of the bed and, pulling Jane round to him, gazed tenderly down into her tear-swamped face, saying, 'Tell me, tell me what's happened. Someone done something?'

She gulped in her throat, then drew her fingers across her eyes, groped for a handkerchief, wiped it round her face, and looking at him, gulped quietly, 'Father . . . Father's going to marry again.'

The expression on Amos's face remained as it had been a moment before, full of concern, kindly; then as the seconds passed it slowly took on a look of utter blankness.

She glanced from him to Molly, who was standing near the door now. Somehow she felt it was right that Molly should hear the news first hand. 'But . . . but Amos' – she moved her head from shoulder to shoulder – 'I wouldn't mind him . . . I wouldn't mind him remarrying, but . . . but it's who he's going to marry.'

'Who is he going to marry?' Amos's inquiry was quiet.

'Agnes Reed.'

'Reed? Agnes Reed, the twin girl?'

She nodded her head. 'She's two years younger than me, it's indecent. And, and Amos, it's not fair' – the tears were still raining from her eyes as she gazed into his face – 'is it? Is it?'

He did not answer her, nor did his expression give her any indication of what he was thinking, or if he was thinking at all. But he was thinking; his mind was galloping ahead into the future.

Sitting taut, his body straight, and in this position he could have been taken for a tall, hefty young man sitting on the side of a bed, his feet on the ground, and speaking figuratively his

146

feet were on the ground, so much so that he knew exactly what to expect from life, but also what he meant to demand from it by way of compensation . . . Going by age his father was not really an old man, but in the jargon of the farmyard, which he used more often than the stilted form of speech taught him by the parson, he considered his father was not long for the top – frustration and drink had played havoc with him over the years – and it was not a thought brought up from his deep subconscious when he wished his father dead, but an ever present desire in the forefront of his mind.

The hate for his father had increased with the years. He had hated him before he learned, through eavesdropping on Will Curran talking to Johnnie Geary in the harness-room, about his father giving orders to drown him, and how Molly Geary was said to have hesitated, and the question still remaining open whether she would have or not if Davie Armstrong hadn't appeared on the scene. He had heard vague reference to the episode of his father whipping Molly Geary because she had fallen, and he knew that his mother had taken to her bed, not only because of his birth, but because his father had had a woman on the side. He hadn't as yet learnt the name of the woman but it wasn't of any interest to him anyway. He was also aware that there was sniggering in certain quarters with regards to his friendship with Biddy, but he put this down to her being Molly's flyblow and himself McBain's son, which in one way was correct.

He gathered a great deal of information through his quiet approach. There were rubber cups on the ends of his crutches, and he wore hand-made soft leather shoes on the appendages referred to as his feet; he came upon people so suddenly that he startled them. He had discovered this trick early in life and had always used it to advantage, sometimes to scare an unsuspecting worker almost out of his wits, or to creep up on a conversation.

He had worked out for some time past what he was going to do with the farm when it became his. He would sell all the lower land lying towards the river. Sir Alfred had been after it for years, not only in order to extend his own land but with the idea of building a house for his son, for from the rye field there was one of the finest views in the county. The Manor had nothing to compare with it; all the manor lands lay too low, whereas this particular part of the farm took in the source of the burn; it sprang from high up in a rock wall as out of a gorgon's mouth; it was a silver spray in the summer and a roaring cascade in the winter. But who saw it unless they made the rough journey to it. No, that part could easily be done without, and it would bring in a pretty penny. He would enclose the farm, bringing it down to workable size so that they needn't employ outside labour. What had to be done would be done by Will Curran and the two Gearys. What the farm wanted was reorganisation; less land would need less scattered labour on walls and ditches and hedges. And he'd get rid of the hunters; they ate money, hunters. Look at what was spent on them and look at what was doled out to himself. On the first of every month Jane gave him a pound . . . the allowance his father made him – a pound! He wanted to spit at the thought. At one time it had been only five shillings and he had been forced to supplement it with his winnings from the marbles and chucks. Even as a child he could beat the men at their own game. A ha'penny a game he would play. They had thought it funny at first, until, losing as much as threepence a week, they called a halt to his monetary gains.

Lately he'd had a craving for money. He had designed a new trap, a spanking affair, something different from the makeshift he used now. It was to have a removable hood and a soft leather seat shaped like a tub armchair from which he could drive. He imagined himself galloping into Hexham or even as far as Newcastle in the rig-out. In it he would feel the eyes on him, women's eyes, in fascinated admiration. God, what he would have done to them if he'd had legs! But he wanted to rivet their attention on to what he had become without legs, a smart dashing figure in a spanking rig-out.

With money he'd have a tailor who'd make clothes to suit his bulk. And trousers. He had even designed a pair of false legs made of light wood strapped to his waist by leather . . . And the picture these last presented to the forefront of his mind was of him walking up the aisle of the church with Biddy on his arm.

Apart from her being the only one who was likely to have him, he loved her, craved for her. He hadn't seen her bare body since she was ten. She'd got shy and proper after that, but every time he looked at her he stripped the clothes off her. It made not an atom of difference that she was old Geary's granddaughter and that she didn't know who her father was. What the hell did that matter?

148

And the idea of marrying Biddy had an added attraction, for it would cause a stink roundabout. One thing he was sorry for, his father wouldn't be here to see it because all this could not happen until he died.

. . . Now Jane was saying he was going to marry again, and to Agnes Reed, which would mean he would start a family, for the woman was a frustrated breeder by all accounts. Goodbye to the farm; good-bye to dreams; good-bye to compensation; where would he end his days? up in the attic? The bogey man to the litter that would fill the house. As if he had asked the question aloud Jane said, 'He's . . . he's having the malt house renovated for us.'

'The malt house?' He gaped at her, then brought his head down towards her and repeated, 'The malt house?' She nodded silently. 'Well, well, that is kind of him. It's quite a way to the malt house from the farm, we'll be nicely tucked out of his sight.' He now put his hand on to her shoulder and, gripping it, said, 'Don't worry; he hasn't done it yet . . . he could have a stroke.'

For a moment, she looked horrified; then hastily wiping her face she muttered, 'Oh, Amos, don't say things like that.'

'I was just hoping.'

'Oh Amos!'

He brought his joined hands together and pressed them down into the coverlet between the stumps of his legs. Then he turned his head and looked at Molly, who was still standing by the door, and as if he too considered her one of the family he asked, 'And what do you make of it?'

'I'm not all that surprised,' Molly answered, then turned and walked out, down the stairs and through the kitchen and into the dairy, where Winnie was scouring milk pans, and without any lead up she said, 'He's gona marry again.'

Winnie turned her head, her face wrinkled in perplexity, then she repeated, 'He?'

'Aye, the master.'

'No!'

'Aye, it's true. An' who do you think it is? That Miss Reed, the horsey one, the one that got her name up two or three years back and went away for a long holiday abroad they said, you remember?'

'No, never! She's younger than Miss Jane.'

Molly now folded her arms and patted her bare flesh as she

149

said, 'Well, here's one who won't stay and welcome the bride.'

'Where will you go, lass?'

'I don't rightly know as yet, Winnie, but I think it's time I was making a move, for more reasons than one, don't you?'

They looked at each other in silence now. The reason was speaking from both their eyes and Winnie, turning to her work again, said, 'Well, perhaps you're right, lass; in fact I know you are. Pity you didn't tell her years ago.'

'Aye, it is. But then there are some things that are hard to get out.'

Two

The dawn was breaking when Amos slipped out of the house the following morning. Molly was not yet in the kitchen, or Biddy in the dairy. Their time for arriving was half-past five, half-an-hour earlier than in the winter, but winter and summer now Winnie did not begin work until half-past six, it was a concession to her age.

There was a ground mist over the land and his head just came above it; as he bobbed along on his crutches, he appeared to be swimming in it. He was careful when going along the Tor path for there was a drop on the off side, not over steep but enough to keep you rolling until you reached the valley bottom should you step off the road at certain points.

He left the ground mist behind when he took the Tor path, and when he reached the top the sky had a warm glow to it, although as yet he couldn't see the sun.

It wasn't the first time he had been on the Tor at dawn; since his first visit the Tor had held a fascination for him. But when up here he liked to be alone, even Jane's company irked him. He seldom dreamt when in bed but he always dreamt up here. The Tor soothed him, brought him peace, and gave him a sense of power. He knew it had a power all its own. And this seemed proved to him one day when, the rain pouring down on the hills around, the sun still shone on to the top of the Tor and it remained dry. And there were days when it matched his black moods, when the rest of the surrounding country was bathed in light, but dark clouds remained station-ary shadowing the Tor rocks, tinting their hue to the despair in his mind.

He knew the history of the hills: the mud-rocks, beaten by time into slate; these would take grass and wear it like a cloak, whereas the slates born of volcanic lava were as cold and hard to the buttocks as steel. But his tor, like a human being, was a mixture. The north side above the path was made up in part of loose scree; yellow or grey or black according to the light; put a wrong foot on it and away you went tumbling down into the road. But on the top, like a soft mantle studded here and there with rock gems, were great stretches of turf, moss and lichen, which sloped down south-west to a wooded area.

But he wasn't interested this morning in the softer aspects of the Tor. What took his attention was a cluster of boulders, eight in all, situated about twelve feet from where the land dropped at its steepest to the road below. As a child he had played in and out of these boulders, chasing Jane and being chased by her. There was one he could rock back and forward. When he was seven years he stood as high as it; now he could support himself by leaning his arm on it, and he often did while rocking it gently.

There had, in the past three years, been two rock falls from the Tor, both occurring after prolonged periods of rain. The last fall had blocked the road to a height of ten feet and some of the fall had spilled down into the valley below. A good job, everyone said, it had happened during the night, for someone might have been coming round the bend, and then it would have been a bad look out for them.

He walked on his crutches to within two feet of the edge of the rock and above the point at which the road below began its curve around the base of the Tor. The rock, shale here, was slack in parts. There was a deep split, a two-inch crevasse, not more than a foot from the edge. A few boulders placed on the outer part could bring it down . . . but perhaps at the wrong time. They would have to be placed just this side of the crevasse. But how to get them this far.

He went back to the boulders and rocked his favourite stone, but try as he might he couldn't budge it. Yet when he tried the same manoeuvre on the one to the side he was greatly surprised when he found he could move it with comparative ease.

Within a short space of time he had moved four boulders to

within four feet of the edge of the rock, and then he sat back and surveyed his handiwork. If the combined weight of them didn't cause a slide, one of them alone, toppled at the right moment, could send a pony and trap, or a horse and rider, skiting down into the valley below.

Now on all fours, he scrambled to the very edge and peered over, and as he stared down he had a vivid picture of his father looking up at him that split second before the boulder hit him, and he anticipated the feeling the picture would give him when it took on reality.

The feeling that he had for his father, which was bred of hate, would at times take on a raging feeling of lust for revenge. Apparently small things could awaken this feeling, such as the sight of Winnie carrying in the cover dishes to the dining-room, or his father throwing a leg over a horse.

He had known before he left Jane last night what he intended to do; the only question now was when – it was all a matter of time. There was only one snag that he could see. His father didn't always take the Tor road; but if he was going to the Reeds he'd surely come this way for it was the nearest road to the village, and the Reeds lived beyond the village.

He shambled back, picked up his crutches and stood looking at the boulders. If Jane should come up here before he could carry out his intentions, then he would suggest that it was the work of some of the village lads, they had been up to their pranks. It was well known that they came poaching. But he wasn't worried about Jane, he could always convince Jane of anything he wished.

It was Thursday night, his father had been out twice and had not used the Tor road, neither going nor coming. He had waited through the long twilight last night, even until it was dark. Jane had questioned him as to where he had been, and he had snapped at her, 'Let go my halter,' and had felt little contrition when he saw the tears coming into her eyes.

His father had returned at nine o'clock this evening from wherever he had been, and was now in the sitting-room drinking; and he would be there until midnight. Or perhaps not. He recollected that over the past few nights he had come upstairs to bed a little earlier; perhaps, he thought, he didn't need so much drink now he had comfort in anticipating the pleasures of a young wife. What a pity he didn't get drunk enough to fall downstairs and break his neck . . .

The thought brought his body slowly upright where he sat in the leather chair before the low toilet table that held a standing mirror. In the candlelight he looked at his reflection. His eyes were slowly widening, his lower jaw drooping. He leaned forward and stared at his face. It was a habit with him. He had spent a great deal of time over the years looking at his face. He knew it was an extraordinary face, very uncommon, beautiful in a way. His mouth was full-lipped and looked tender, his nose was straight, his cheekbones flat, and his eyes, his eyes were really extraordinary. He knew he resembled neither of his parents, nor yet any of his forebears. Jane had introduced him to the two albums of forebears when he was very young. 'That is your grandmother McBain; and that is your grandfather McBain. That is your great-grandfather McBain and that is your great-grandmother McBain. And that is your grandmother Lawson and that is your grandfather Lawson.' On and on. She had always stressed his claim to his forebears to make up to him for the lack of his parents, who had been as dead to him from the day he was born.

He had, over the years, worked out for himself the comforting thought that perhaps he was a changeling, a being from some other existence, another world where no one had legs, just short appendages thrusting out from the hips. The feeling of difference from those around him was emphasised when he was visited by strange and weird ideas, ideas more fearsome than those in the stories of Mr Edgar Allan Poe, ideas that would have horrified Parson Hedley had he voiced them, for Mr Poe had never thought up ideas so macabre as the ones his mind prescribed for his father.

And now his thinking had offered him a solution, not a very original one he admitted, but it could, like the landslide from the Tor, be set down as an accident. He wondered why he hadn't thought of it in the first place.

He slid down from the chair and, going to the door, opened it slightly and listened. He did not expect to hear any sounds. Jane had gone to bed early with toothache; Winnie had given her some herb tea and a dose of laudanum, she would be fast asleep by now.

He turned and peered through the candlelight at the clock on the mantelpiece. It said ten to eleven. Swiftly now he sat down and pulled off his soft leather shapeless boots. He was about to take off his coat when he changed his mind, thinking, no, he might have to lie there for some time and it would act as a pad against the wood.

As silently as a cat, and not unlike some huge animal, he went along the passage and down the stairs, across the landing and down the other four steps on to the main landing. When he reached Jane's door he stood for a moment and listened; then he went on to the top of the stairhead.

There was a table to the left-hand side on which stood a lamp. Its wick, only half turned up, gave a dim glow to the head of the stairs. He turned it down lower still. At the right-hand side against the open balustrade, that gave to part of the landing the effect of a miniature gallery, stood a heavy wooden monk's chair. Gently, he eased it a foot further until the stout back was within a few inches from the square upright post that ran from the ground floor up past the head of the stairs to the ceiling above and acted as a support for the lintel beam placed about two feet from the ceiling.

Pulling himself on to the chair, he stood peering up at the lintel. It was a replica, or more correctly the mother and father of the one in Winnie's cottage. Since the sailor had first introduced him to it, it had become a practice that whenever he was in the cottage one or the other of them would lift him up and he would swing from the beam. Often, as he had on that first day, refusing to come down, he would lie, his head hanging over the side, laughing at them. But he had stopped swinging from the beam when he was nine or ten because he had become too heavy for them to lift.

This beam was more than twice the width of the one in Winnie's cottage and he had no doubt that once up he would rest comfortably on it. But it was the getting up; he had only his arms to rely on.

The back of the monk's chair was about six inches higher than the top of the balustrade. It was made of black bog oak and the top horizontal rail was flat, but he knew that even if this supported him there would be more than four feet to go before he could reach the beam. He himself stood exactly four feet from the end of his stumps to the top of his head. His arms extended, measuring from the top of his head to his wrist, would give him another foot or so. But the point was he wouldn't be able to extend his arms, his arms would have to act

154

as legs and grip the post while supporting his weight, and his body would then be concertinaed. He could grip tight with his stumps if he could get the object between them, but this post was too wide for that. Once he left the support of the chair he'd have a perilous foot to traverse, he could hang and swing from a bough like a monkey and slide down a tree, but he had never attempted to climb up one, fearing that the feat would end in defeat, and he couldn't contenance defeat.

He heard a movement somewhere in the distance below him, and it acted like a starting pistol. He flung his arms upwards and to the side, and as he gripped the post his body swung into mid-air. When he felt himself beginning to slide he spread his stumps as wide as it was possible for them to go, and when each one pressed tight against a corner of the wood the pressure was like a hot iron searing his flesh, but it checked his descent. Drawing in a deep gulp of air, he moved his arms upwards once, twice; and then he thrust out a hand and clutched the top of the lintel. He had made it, he was safe. Letting go the other hand, he encircled the beam with his arms, then slowly drew himself up on to the top of it, and there he lay breathing heavily, one cheek pressed tight against the wood.

After a moment he moved cautiously, easing his body into a more comfortable position for the wait, however long it be . . .

It was longer than he anticipated, long enough to make him realise that he wouldn't be able to swing forward from this beam, for it was too wide for him to grip with a single hand; he'd have to join his hands over the top of it if he wanted to put force into his body. He also realised that his movements must be swift; he must not expose himself until his father reached at least the fourth step from the top. Then he would swing sideways and catch him on the third or the second step.

By the time the clock in the hall struck half-past eleven his body was becoming cramped, and he knew that he could not lie like this much longer. Nor could he ease his position on the beam, for his previous movements had brought him in contact with nails. The lintel, he discovered, was a fake as to its width. Below it appeared like one massive piece of wood but he had found it was made up of two beams nailed and bolted together in parts. Moreover it was thick with dust; twice he had to pinch his nose to stop himself from sneezing.

As the clock struck a quarter to twelve he heard a door open, then close, and footsteps coming across the hall. He did not see his father until he was actually mounting the stairs, for McBain had stopped to turn out the lamp in the hall. His body stiffened; he raised it slightly upwards and watched the oncoming figure.

McBain had his head down, looking at each stair as if deep in thought. His step was steady, for his drinking had been moderate. He left the sixth step and it was on the fifth that something caused him to raise his head and look up, and the cry escaped him when he lifted his foot and put it on the fourth stair. But it was throttled in his throat as the stumps of his son's legs caught him under the chin and lifted him into the air and sent him tumbling to the foot of the stairs.

Jane was awakened by a scream and someone shouting. Or had she been dreaming? She'd had a nightmare. The pain from her toothache was gone but her head was very fuzzy. What was it? She lifted her legs slowly out of the bed and sat on the side of it. She was sure she'd heard someone call out. Had something happened to Amos? But what could happen to Amos?

She stumbled across the room, not bothering to put on her dressing-gown, and opened the door and looked out on to the landing. The light was still burning but it was dim and she couldn't see very far. She glanced towards the stairs that led from the landing to the next floor; then she turned her head slowly and looked towards the head of the main staircase. Could it have been her father calling?

At the top of the stairhead she stood peering down. Then she was crying aloud as she raced down the stairs. 'Oh Father! Father!' She had her joined hands tight against her mouth as she stared down at the contorted figure at the foot.

McBain was lying half on his side, half on his back. One leg was twisted underneath him, the other was across the bottom stair. His arms looked at strange angles; his face was deadly white, his eyes were closed. There was no sign of blood on him. She cupped his head in her hands as she moaned, 'Oh dear! Oh dear!' She looked wildly about her into the dark hall. Then laying his head back, she raced up the stairs again, across the landing, calling all the while, 'Amos! Amos!' She burst open his door. 'Amos! Amos!'

There was no light. She groped her way to the bed and shook him. 'Amos, wake up! Amos!'

He grunted, saying, 'Wh-at is it? What's the matter?'

'Father . . . Father, he's fallen downstairs. Get up, get up and go for Winnie. Go for the boys. Quick! quick!'

'How . . . how did he . . . ?'

'I don't know, I don't know, only get up.'

'Is . . . is he dead?'

'I don't know, I think so. Amos! Amos! please, don't ask questions, just get up and go for Winnie and get the boys, he'll have to be moved. Hurry, he's all twisted up . . . Come on.'

She went out of the room, and he allowed a short time to elapse, time enough for her to imagine he was getting into his clothes, before he went out and down the stairs. Without an upward glance he passed under the beam, and when he reached the foot of the stairs, he rested on his crutches and looked at the figure lying there and felt not the smallest spark of contrition.

Before he stepped over his father he asked again of her, 'Is he dead?' and she answered, 'His heart is still beating, but faintly. Amos, please, will you hurry!'

He hobbled away on his crutches, and as he was going out of the door she shouted at him, 'Please, Amos.'

He did not hurry as he crossed the yard, nor as he went up the road to the cottage. He decided to go to Winnie's first and was surprised when he passed the window to see a light through the shutter, and as he knocked on the door his surprise mounted at the sound of voices and laughter coming from within.

The door was opened by old Sep, who gaped at him, asking, 'What's it, Master Amos, what's it?'

'Father, he's hurt, he fell down the stairs. Jane says to call the boys.' He looked beyond Sep and into the room. In the reflection of the lamplight and bright firelight he saw Winnie standing by the chair in which the sailor was seated.

He would have recognised the sailor by his clothes if not by his face. It was more than ten years since he had seen him, but the memory of him had always remained fresh in his mind; twice the sailor had given him life, and through water; first saving him from Molly and the pool, and then rescuing him from the burn. He lifted his crutches over the threshold and stared towards the man who was staring at him, and he said, 'You've come home again then?'

'Yes, I've come home again.' The voice was deep, thick, and rich, and it was as if he had heard it only yesterday.

Winnie interrupted now, saying, 'The master's hurt, badly?' She did not wait for an answer but grabbed up her shawl, adding, 'Oh my God! this is awful. Come on, come on.'

157

'I'll come along with you.'

Winnie turned on her father crying, 'You'll do no such thing, you'll stay put.'

'Jane said to call the boys,' Amos said again. His voice was flat and unemotional and she answered, 'Aye, yes, that's who we must get, the boys. Come on then.' She put her hand on his back and went to turn him around, but he shrugged away from her and, looking towards the sailor again, said, 'How long are you going to stay?'

'I don't rightly know, a week, perhaps two.'

'I'll be seeing you then?'

'You'll be seeing me.'

When he stepped outside Winnie was hammering on the Gearys' door, shouting, 'You there, Johnnie, Mickey, you there! Get up! do you hear?'

When the upper window was opened it was Molly who put her head out, asking, 'What is it?'

'Get them up; something's happened to the master.'

Amos stood peering up through the darkness waiting for some word from Molly, but she didn't speak and it was almost a minute before she moved.

Winnie was now rapping on Will Curran's door, but Will was already up, the commotion having roused him; hanging out of the window, he cried, 'Fire? Is it a fire?'

'No, Will. The master's fallen downstairs. You may be needed, you'd better come along.' At this she hurried away and Amos followed behind, but slowly, taking his time.

At the entrance to the farm gate he stopped. There was the sound of activity coming from the cottages, doors slamming, voices calling, feet running. He looked towards the house across the yard; there was a light gleaming now from the fanlight above the front door. He brought his gaze in the direction of the byres and the stables from where were coming faint comforting rustlings.

For years he had hungered for possession of the farm and all it would mean to him, the feeling in him now was like one of glorious surprise, as if he had woken up and found that he had legs.

He moved on as the running footsteps of the men came nearer, his men. A rush of pleasure and power mounted in him until he reached the hall and there saw his father still lying on the floor, but straight now, Winnie on one side, Jane on the other. His eyes were open and he was staring at Jane while he tried to speak, but although his mouth opened and his lips formed words, they made no sound. The feeling of power seeped from him and he felt sick.

During the next few minutes he stood to one side and watched Johnnie, Mickey and Will Curran lift his father and carry him up the stairs while Jane admonished them: 'Be careful. Don't . . . don't hurt him. Be careful, he'll be in pain.'

Some short time later he was sitting in the kitchen. When Molly rushed in and, whipping up a kettle from the hob, was on the point of going out again, he said, 'Is, is he dead?'

She turned on him. 'No, no, he's not dead. It looks to me he's had a stroke, an' he could weather that.'

She went out of the kitchen, and he was left alone, and for the first time in his life he experienced fear. If he could have picked a death for his father it would have been slow and very painful, but not under the present circumstances, for if he were to speak now anything could happen. They could put him away. He wanted to vomit.

He knew it would be no use pleading that his father had treated him like an animal for years, even less than an animal, for animals now and again were given pats and kind words, whereas all he had received from the man who had fathered him was looks of abhorrence and disgust.

What must he do now? He'd have to think. He took up his crutches and went towards the drawing-room, the room in which he'd never been allowed to sit. But at the door he paused, then walked further on and opened the dining-room door. It was dark inside. He could see nothing but he knew where everything was, every stick of furniture in the room where he had never been allowed to eat was engraved on his mind, and such was his mind that, even in the state it was now, full of fear, he hobbled into the room, groped for the armchair at the head of the table, and hoisted himself into it, as if he were already master.

Three

'He keeps trying to say something all the time, Winnie, a word. Look, his lips come together, like this.' Jane imitated the movement of McBain's mouth. Then looking down at him again, she said, 'W . . . w . . . w . . . wound? work? worry? No?' She shook her head as she gazed into the eyes that were staring up into hers, their colour paler than ever now, yet their expression keen, even piercing, 'Will . . . Will Curran?' She glanced quickly at Winnie. Her father's eyelid had flickered, then stopped. She said softly, 'Will Curran?'

The lids closed and remained closed.

It was Winnie who said on a high note of excitement, 'Will . . . you know, his will. That's what it is. Master' – she was bending over him – 'your will?'

Now the eyelids blinked slowly and definitely, and Winnie raised her head and looked at Jane and stated excitedly, 'That's it, his will!'

Jane's voice too was excited. 'You want your will, Father? Don't worry, I'll get it, I'll find it.'

Hurrying out, she ran down the stairs, across the hall, and burst into the office, then stopped dead within the doorway at the sight of Amos sitting in her father's chair behind the desk.

'What are you doing?' There was an abruptness in her manner.

'What does it look like?' he answered coolly. 'I'm looking through the bills and things, somebody's got to keep things going. Or' – he pushed his shoulders back – 'do you think it would be better if I went upstairs and locked myself in the attic?'

'Don't be silly, Amos. And at a time like this. But you know that's Father's desk and . . . '

'And' – he mimicked her – 'I was never allowed in here. You don't have to remind me. And I'm going to ask you something. Do you think he'll ever use this desk and chair again? He's paralysed, and no matter what kind of a monstrosity he considered me, I'm his son and I'll take over when he's gone.'

'Amos, you talk as if he were already dead, it's dreadful.'

'Jane. Jane.' He screwed himself backwards into the chair,

then bent his body forward over the desk. 'It's dreadful you say. Because I'm honest you say it's dreadful. You don't say that his treatment of me over all these years was dreadful, inhuman . . . that's the word, inhuman. And you know something? He's made me almost inhuman, because if they got him out of that bed now and hung him on a cross it would not arouse one spark of pity in me. And that is dreadful, don't you think, Jane? That is really dreadful. Don't you realise that if it hadn't been for you I might have been a real "thing" . . . a real IT left crawling around that attic. He would have had the windows blocked up; he would have made me into an imbecile . . . '

'Amos! Amos!' She was covering her face. 'He wouldn't, he would never have done such a thing. He's not like that at all. He's . . . ' She stopped, then sank on to a chair, her face still covered, for even as she defended her father, denying all Amos said he was capable of, there was some part of her that recognised that what her brother said might have taken place if she herself hadn't been at hand was true. Human beings were capable of the most hideous things. It had been a hard lesson to learn but she had learnt it. She shook her head wearily, then her gaze focused intently on Amos. Somebody's got to keep things going, he had said. It came to her with an unpleasant shock that he was already running things in his mind; the farm was already his. She felt a shudder of apprehension. Strangely, she did not want Amos to be in control of the farm. True, he was his father's son and sons inherited without question, but her father would not have wanted Amos to have the farm; no, never . . .

The will. She must find the will. She rose and went towards the desk, saying, 'Have you come across the will?'

'The will?' He shook his head.

'Well, it must be here somewhere.'

She began to search, and he, too. They pulled out drawers, they looked through papers, until, stopping abruptly, she said, 'What am I thinking about? It'll be in the wall safe.'

She went over to the fireplace and, lifting down the picture from the wall above the mantelshelf, she exposed a door. It was an old-fashioned wall safe, having a keyhole to the side. She went back to the desk and, picking up a bunch of keys, said, 'It's one of these.' After trying a number of keys she found the right one and when the door was opened she took out a bundle of papers, some yellow with age, their seared edges curling. When she placed them on the table Amos grabbed half of them towards him and began looking swiftly through them. After a time he said, 'These are all deeds, old deeds, of the house and land.'

'Most of these, too.' She spread her fingers over the papers and bank receipts, then looked about her. 'It must be somewhere.'

Amos remained seated and quiet. He watched her going round the room, searching the cupboards and drawers. She hadn't as yet come to the old-fashioned desk standing in the corner to the right of the window. The desk was of a warm brown veneer; it had a four-inch flat top from where dropped a curved lid hinged in the middle which folded back. The writing flap pulled out in slots, and the inner panel could be raised up at an angle for ease of working. There were three doors down one side of the desk and cupboard space at the other. He knew all about this type of desk, he was interested in furniture, at least in wood, and it was through this interest that he had read books on period furniture. There was nearly always in such pieces a secret drawer. He wondered if Jane knew about it. He watched her lifting up the lid, pulling out the writing flap, and opening the little drawers above it. When she spoke to herself, saying, 'It couldn't be in here at any rate, it would be too large,' he made no comment. He watched her pull out the drawers at the side of the desk, and again he made no comment when she said, 'These are full of old bills dating back' – she paused as she scrutinised the sheaf of papers in her hand, then ended, 'Dear, dear; a seed bill from 1822.'

Her examination of the cupboards at the other side revealed only further bundles of bills and when she straightened her back and asked, 'Where can it be?' he answered, 'If you don't know how should I?'

She stood biting her lip for a moment, then said, 'I'd better get back; he may be able to give me some indication.'

He watched her go out of the room. Then slipping down from the chair and moving on all fours to the desk, he pulled himself up. Having raised the lid he drew out one of the small drawers above the writing flap and gently moved his fingers along the roof of the drawer and, as he expected, came upon a knob, and when he pressed this gently the whole top of the desk rose slowly and exposed a long narrow shelf with a similar drawer beneath, and on the shelf lay what Jane was looking for.

Without examining it he thrust it inside his coat. Then reaching out he pressed the top of the desk down into place again, closed the flap, crawled back into his crutches, and went out and up the stairs to his room.

The door closed, and having no fear of interruption, he sat down near the window and unfolded the long piece of parchment, to find it held a similar piece inside. He held them up and looked from one to the other; then he read the outer one first. It began in legal terms:

'I, Angus Forrester McBain, of Cock Shield Farm in the County of Northumberland, revoke all wills and testamentary dispositions heretofore made by me and declare this to be my last will.

I appoint my wife Delia Florence McBain, to be the sole executor of this my will, but if she shall predecease me, or die without having proved this my will, I appoint my daughter Jane Mary Alexander McBain, to be the sole executor.

Should my daughter have predeceased me I appoint my only brother, James Francis McBain of 8 The Knole, Birkside, Edinburgh, to be the sole executor. In the case that he has predeceased me my estate to be divided among his children.

I state here that I hope the above contingency does not arise as I have not seen or associated with my brother or any member of his family for twenty years.'

There was more, but he stopped here. This had been written before he was born; it was meaningless. He looked at the other parchment. It was dated 10th day of September 1889 and was not in the beautiful script of the other paper but written in a thin spidery handwriting; nor was the wording so official as in the other, yet there was a legal turn to the phrasing of the one paragraph which stated:

'I, Angus Forrester McBain, hereby revoke all my former wills and declare this to be my wish and last will. I leave my estate and all it entails completely to my daughter Jane Mary Alexandria McBain. I do this unconditionally. Signed Angus Forrester McBain and witnessed by . . .'

Underneath was the almost unintelligible signature of the Reverend John William Wainwright and underneath that the signature of the Reverend Arnold Hedley.

He held both parchments out before him. His jaws were tightly clenched. No word of him, not even a reference that Jane should provide for him. This last will was written when he

163

was ten years old, the day following his birthday, the very day his father had turned him out of the dining-room. Would anyone believe that a man could disown his own in such a way, even if his own had grown to be an idiot.

If there had been a spark of remorse in him for what he had done two nights ago it would have fled at this moment; this deed vindicated his action. His gaze dropped to the papers again. The last one had not been drawn up by a solicitor, but it would be held valid, the signatures of two such witnesses would be enough for that. And where would it leave him? At the mercy of Jane's generosity. Oh, she would be generous, she would look after him until he died.

He slipped from the chair and stood upright on his stumps. From now on there was no one going to dictate to him, not even Jane. He would rule, he would be master of this house or die in the attempt. It was either him or his father.

This last will taken care of, there remained only the other one, the legal one, which left everything to his mother; and his mother was dead, and he was his mother's son. Nobody could get over that, could they? And should the parsons remember that they signed a will in 1889, what could they do if it couldn't be found . . . what?

He went swiftly to the table near his bed and, taking up a box of matches, he lit a candle, and when it was well alight he held over it the piece of paper that would have robbed him of the recompense he considered his due. When it was burnt two-thirds through he moved on his stumps in a body-twisting motion and dropped the paper into the empty grate and watched it curl into black ash. Then he picked up the other will and, putting it in his pocket, he went to find Jane to tell her that she needn't worry any more, he had found what she was looking for.

Four

'What is it?' Winnie looked at Molly as she came slowly into the kitchen. 'Is he worse?'

'Aye, I should think so. He's agitated, got somethin' on his mind.'

'Well, that's natural,' said Winnie. 'It's likely that Miss Reed. Did Miss Jane tell him she'd called?'

'Not when I was in she didn't.'

'I'll take this broth up.' Winnie went to pick up a tray from the table, adding, 'Then I'll slip along the road for half-an-hour and get them something. Davie says he can manage, an' I dare say he could with a galley concoction.'

'Well, leave it down, I'll see to it. I've got to go up again anyway.'

'You sure, lass?'

'Yes, yes. Get yourself away. An' you needn't rush, 'cos the dinner here's all ready. Not that anybody'll eat it.'

'I know one will.' Winnie's voice was low, and when Molly didn't answer but stood gazing down at the steam rising from the broth, she went on, 'I know he hasn't been treated fair but he's struttin' around like a stumped peacock, as if he was already the master . . . ' Winnie stopped and, looking closely at Molly now, asked under her breath, 'What is it, lass?' But as soon as she had put the question she thought it was a stupid thing to say for there were three things at least that could bring Molly low at the present moment. There was the master near death, and if there had been nothing between them for years, there had at one time, and the evidence of it was in the dairy at this minute. Then there was the fact of her Davie coming back. Fifteen years was a long time, time enough to forget a man and marry, but she hadn't married. Then there was a third thing that was always worrying her, Master Amos and his constant chasing of Biddy, and his acting at times like a normal man who owned her. Yes, she had a lot on her plate had Molly, and she was sorry for her. She had grown to like her over the years, and that was odd because at one time she had thought her fast and brash, but at that time she had been fearful of her hooking Davie, and she had wanted someone better for her lad. She still did, but there was no fear of Davie falling again. Davie the man was a different kettle of fish from Davie the youth, or even the young sailor who had turned up five years ago in much the same way as he had come in the other night.

She watched Molly now pick up the tray as she said, 'Oh, I'm like the lot of us, just tired,' and smile weakly as she added, 'Go on an' get them something, an' as I said don't hurry back, Biddy'll help me here. There'll only be one for the dinin'-room, Miss Jane will have hers upstairs.'

'Thanks, lass.' They nodded at each other, then Molly went out with the tray and as she crossed the hall she looked towards the dining-room and she repeated to herself, 'Only one for the dinin'-room.' That maimed skit would be lording it in the master's chair when he should be in . . . She gulped and gripped the tray tighter. She'd have to tell somebody and the only one she could talk to was Winnie. But then Winnie might let on to Miss Jane, Winnie wasn't all that cautious. And what would happen then? Miss Jane had had nothing out of life but worry and frustration. Courting the parson for years, a walk across the fields on a Sunday or up to the Tor. There hadn't even been the comfort of a roll in the hay. No, Miss Jane mustn't know; but she must tell somebody about that devil or bust.

She had always known he was bad; she had tried to make Biddy see he was bad, but Biddy was sorry for him. Biddy said she understood him. And well she might.

When the master died he would take over completely; then God help them all . . . God help Biddy. Eeh! she'd have to talk to somebody. Parson Hedley? No. No, he was too near to Miss Jane. If he were to expose Master Amos as a murderer then how would Miss Jane take it?

When she entered the room Jane turned from the bed and, coming towards her, whispered, 'He's so exhausted. He seems to be sleeping, I wouldn't give it to him yet. And while you're here, Molly, I'll slip to my room, I must change my clothes.'

'Do that, Miss. And don't worry, I'll call you if there's any change. Have a wash and it'll freshen you up.'

Jane nodded at her, then went towards the bed again and looked down at the still grey face for a moment before turning away and saying under her breath, 'I'll leave the door open so you can call if you want me. I'll leave mine open too.'

'Do that, Miss. Yes, do that.' Molly nodded at her, then took her place in the chair at the head of the bed.

As she sat staring at the still form lying there she did not see the man who had once showed her ways of loving that had been as enchanting as witchcraft . . . at the time. Reality had faded with the years until now she imagined she had dreamed most of what they had experienced together. Even at night when her body ached for comfort and love her mind by-passed that early episode as if, like leprosy, it would contaminate her present existence; yet the thought was ever present in her mind that her life would have been different if his hand on her thigh hadn't awakened her from sleep on that night.

When his eyes opened and looked at her she bent quickly forward and said, 'Would you like a drop of broth, Master?' She watched his nostrils dilating, his breath coming in short laboured gasps, and when she saw his tongue come out and pass over his lips she took a square of lint that was floating in a bowl of water on the side table and gently drew it around his mouth. She asked again, 'Would you like a drop of soup, Master?' and when his eyelids closed once, she knew he did not want any. As she watched his tongue move over his lips again she said, 'A drink of water?'

His eyes remained open, and she nodded at him and smiled. 'I'll get you a nice cold one, there's a jug fresh from the well. I won't be a minute.' She nodded at him and hurried round the bed and into the dressing-room.

The glass was full in her hand when she heard the stifled cry. It was like the death rattle of a calf, a strangled whining sound. It froze her for a moment, and she almost dropped the jug from her hand and the glass with it. The water spilled from the glass as she ran towards the door. Just within it, she stopped. The master had moved. His head was up and he was choking, and there, standing between the door and the bed, was Master Amos.

'Get out, you! Get out, you!' She was bawling at him at the top of her voice. But he didn't move. His eyes flickered towards her, then returned towards the bed and to his father.

Thrusting the glass on to the mantelpiece, she rushed at him, hissing, 'Get yourself away! Get out of here!'

'Take your hands off me!'

She took her hands off him and stepped back. Her eyes darted from the door to the bed. Then she ran first to the door and yelled, 'Miss Jane! Miss Jane!' before rushing back to the bed. She slipped her arm under McBain's shoulders and tried to hold his heaving body, and she cried again at the hunched figure standing immobile on his crutches, his stare fixed as if he too, had suffered paralysis. 'Get out! Do you hear? Get out! You're determined to finish him, aren't you?'

'Amos! Amos!' Jane came rushing into the room. 'Oh Amos, how could you! Go away. Please, go away.'

But he did not obey her immediately, not until she had rushed to the bed and had taken her father from Molly's arms and the bobbing head had fallen to the side and become still. Then he turned and hobbled out, and Jane slowly laid McBain back on the bed.

Standing side by side, Jane looked down on her father and Molly on her one-time lover, and they bowed their heads and slowly they began to cry.

Five

'No, Ma. Now don't keep on asking me, for I'm no hypocrite. I stopped followin' him years ago, so I'm not going to start again on his last ride; nor am I going to say I'm sorry he's gone.'

Winnie closed her eyes tightly and shook her head as she said, 'Oh, don't be like that, Davie, it upsets me. Bad enough with that one across there. Dear God, there's going to be changes on this farm, if I know anything. Fancy' – she now looked at old Sep where he sat in his chair by the side of the fire – 'have you ever heard of such a thing, not goin' to have plumed horses and wantin' to cut the carriages down to two! Miss Jane had to have a stand-up fight with him. Eeh! that lass is upset. There's somethin' funny somewhere; the master would never have left things so that that young devil could take over. If he cared for anybody it was for Miss Jane. And then' – she turned to Davie now – 'Parson Hedley remembers signing a will just a few years back, and he told Master Amos straight. I never heard him talk like that afore. He's quiet like, you know he is, but not this time, oh no, he was fighting for Miss Jane's rights. When the house was clear yesterday she turned the office inside out. She's upset, she is that.'

'But there'd be a copy wouldn't there, there's always copies of wills? They've got a solicitor.'

'Aye, of course, an' as far as I can make out he's got a copy of the old one but not of the one Parson Hedley's on about.'

'Winnie, I'd like to go.' They both turned and looked to where Sep had risen from his chair, and Winnie cried at him, 'Now, Da, don't be silly.'

'Silly be damned, woman! I said I'd like to go an' I'm goin'. You get me suit out. It'll likely hang like a sack on me, but what matter!' Old Sep now looked at Davie and said firmly, 'Speak as you find, lad. He was always decent to me an' he give me one an' six a week when he had no need.'

'Speak as you find, Granda.' Davie nodded back at him, smiling quietly. 'Always speak as you find. You go if you want to.'

'My God! what a pair.' Winnie went towards the door, shaking her head. 'The one who could go won't, and the one who shouldn't go out the door will.'

When she had gone they both looked at each other and laughed quietly; then Davie said, 'I'm goin' to stretch me legs, Granda.'

'Aye, lad,' said Sep, sitting down again. Then he asked quietly, 'Getting restless?'

'Restless? No, Granda. I could do with a lot of this.'

'Then why go back, lad?'

'Well' – Davie pursed his lips – 'what else is there for me? And who knows' – he grinned now – 'the first mate might drop down dead and I'll get his place. That's the worst of likin' your captain an' mate and staying with a boat too long, you get into a rut, or I should say trough, shouldn't I?'

'If you sign on again how many years will it be this time?'

'God knows, Granda, God knows. Still, don't worry, old 'un, I've found that God doesn't want me to die by drownin'; He's tested me twice, as I've told you.'

'The third time might be catchy time, lad.'

'That's what they say, Granda, third time catchy time. But I'll have to chance that, won't I? Now don't you worry, just think of how you're going to stop slipping through your good suit.' Again they both laughed; and now Davie took his hat from a nail by the door, pulled it firmly on to his head, and went out.

He paused in the road, taking in deep gulps of air, and after

169

looking first to the right and then to the left of him he decided to take a walk towards the burn and to follow it down to the river.

He went along the road and past the farm gate, and saw, coming around the corner of the barn, which backed on to the road, young Biddy. She was a bonny piece, fresh looking, well made with no resemblance to Molly at her age, for her features were thin, like him that was responsible for her. But there was a soft delicateness in the thinness. He had seen her before in the distance but hadn't as yet spoken to her. He stopped in front of her and said, 'Why, hello there! You're Biddy.'

'Hello,' she said. 'An' I know who you are, I can even remember you.'

'You can? It's almost ten years.'

'I know, but I can, faintly, sort of. You were down by the river an' you were swimmin' with Amos.'

He was quick to note that she didn't say Master Amos. 'Well! well!' He shook his head at her. 'You have a long memory. I remember that day an' all. That young devil nearly drowned himself.'

She smiled as she said, 'He's always been grateful to you, learning him to swim. He's like a fish in the water now.'

He noted also the word, now. She must watch him swimming. He asked her, 'Do you like farm work?'

Her shoulders moved up in a shrug before she replied, 'Sometimes; yes and no. I'm taken more with the house than the dairy.'

'You still go to school?'

'No.' She flapped her hand at him now in a familiar way, then laughed. 'I'm fifteen, goin' on sixteen. But I still read. I like readin', when I get the chance.'

'What kind of reading?'

'Oh, all kinds, that Amos lends me. Some of the books are . . .'

'Biddy! you Biddy!' They both turned and looked towards Molly where she was standing by the farm gate. Then the girl looked at him and said, 'Seein' you.' And he nodded at her and answered, 'Aye, seein' you.'

He did not turn away immediately but stared along the road towards the woman standing in the sunlight, and he wanted to laugh loudly and shout at her, 'What you afraid of, like mother like daughter?' but he turned away wondering why it was that every time he set eyes on her he wanted to flay her with words, stir up the past, the dead past, for it had all happened so long ago, fifteen years ago. She was now what? Thirty-two. Why had she not married? Perhaps she had no need to, she could get what she wanted on the side. And she would want it, after the practice she'd had in her early days. By! she had been a young cow if ever there was one. 'Now, now!' he chided himself, and grinned as he came back with, 'Don't insult the animals.'

Ten minutes later he was on the point of dropping down the steep path towards the burn when he heard her voice calling his name; and it startled him, he thought he was imagining things. He turned fully round, and there she was running along the path that led from the back of the house to the garden. About two yards from him she stopped. She was panting and her full breasts were lifting from her print dress up and down.

Well! Well! He gave a short laugh but his face was straight as he waited for her to say, 'Don't you talk to my Biddy.' It would be just like her to think he would try to get his own back through the young lass. What was nineteen years anyway? Captain Surtees had married a lass twenty years younger than himself; it was done all the time.

'Can I talk to you?'

He was slightly taken back. He raised his eyebrows and jerked his head to one side. What was this? Her voice was quiet, soft, it even had a tremor in it. 'Talk to me?' he said. 'What do you want to talk to me about?'

'The young master.' She gulped, cleared her throat, then went on rapidly, 'I've got to tell somebody an' I can't tell anybody back there in case they tell Miss Jane.'

As he stood looking at her with narrowing gaze she stared back at him, deep into his eyes, and the secret part of her whimpered, 'Oh God, I was a fool.' Then she brought out in a low rush, 'He . . . the young one, he killed the master.'

'What!' His whole face was screwed up now.

'It's a fact.' She moved a short step nearer to him. 'You know the beam at the top of the stairs, like in our houses? Winnie said Ned used to lift him up on to it, and he used to swing from it. Well, he swung from the one at the top of the stairs an' . . . an' on purpose. I . . . I found the chair had been moved, the monk's chair. It's heavy and I always put it back in the same place, but there it was against the post. It was that that made me look up, an' I saw the piece of rag hanging from the beam. We only go up there when it's spring-cleanin', it's always dusty; so I got the step ladder, an' found that most of the dust had been wiped off. I mean on top of the beam. An' there was this piece of cloth caught on a nail. Then I went to his wardrobe and there was his coat. It was from the inside of the facing.'

'But . . . but you can't believe that, that he . . . ' He shook his head.

'I do. I know he did it. Mind, I won't say he hasn't had cause; the master's never looked the side he was on, an' he's never had a penny in his pocket, only what Miss Jane gave him. If it hadn't been for her God knows what might have happened to him earlier on, he mayn't have lived . . . ' She now bowed her head and, her tone changing into thin bitterness, she said, 'That was the wrong thing to say, but . . . ' Once more she was looking at him. 'I swear to you again I would never have done it. I was beside myself. He made me take it, but I'd never have done it.' She was shaking her head widely now.

She had stopped speaking, but he didn't break the silence for some time, and then he asked, 'Why did you tell me, what can I do?'

She put her hand to her cheek and pressed it tightly, while looking to the side. 'I don't know. But I just had to tell somebody, it seemed too big to carry meself. The right thing to do would be to tell Miss Jane, but . . . but I don't want to be the one to bring trouble on her. She's been good to me, more than good, and she has no life, no more than' – she stopped herself from adding, 'me'. She brought her painted defiant gaze on to him again, and after a moment she said, 'There's one thing I know, he's dangerous. He's but a lad, just on sixteen, but he's sixty in his head an' his ideas. And he's got a cruel streak in him, vindictive. I don't think Miss Jane can see it. She's always making excuses for him, and that's natural enough 'cos she's been mother, father and sister to him . . . everything. She lived in that room with him night and day until he was ten. How she stood it, God knows.'

He made no comment, and she went on, more slowly now, as if she were repeating old news, 'She should have married the parson years ago, but the master wouldn't have him here. And old Wainwright wouldn't have them there. And then the master going to marry that Miss Reed nearly finished her. That's what made the other one do it, I'm sure of it.' She nodded her head at him. 'It would have put his nose out. And he always wanted to boss. He's a weird creature, frightenin' . . . ' She looked up at

172

him for a moment without speaking, then asked, 'What am I to do?'

He rubbed his ear with his hand, then brought it over his stubbly chin and to the other side of his face before he said, 'I can't see what you can do except keep quiet if you don't want to hurt Miss Jane and cause a stir for miles. Not that, from what you say and what me ma's told me, there won't be a lot of sympathy with the lad. And you can understand him being a bit weird, handicapped as he is.'

'He doesn't see it as a handicap.' There was bitterness in her tone now. 'He can do most things, too many for that matter.'

He looked at her inquiringly, but she took the subject no further, instead she said, 'Well, I'd better be gettin' back. But I had to talk to somebody . . . you don't mind?'

'No, I don't mind.' His voice was non-committal and she half smiled at him, until he said, 'Though I don't know who it's going to aid, you telling me, 'cos I'll be on me way shortly.'

She stared at him for a moment longer before turning away and walking quickly up the path. He continued down towards the burn and stopped opposite the spot where he had taken Amos, the child, in and taught him to swim, and by way of thanks had a hair pulled from his groin.

She had said the boy was dangerous. Yes, he could say he would be if he was thwarted and didn't get what he wanted.

He had a sudden desire to be away from this place, yet all the while knowing that this was where his heart lay. He would go into Newcastle tomorrow and see how they were getting on with her bottom; a fortnight or three weeks at least they had said. Still, it could be sooner if the captain had got round them . . . Let's hope he had.

The following morning early he went by the carrier cart into Hexham, and from there took the train into Newcastle. Here, he mounted a horse-bus that eventually brought him into Jarrow and the dry dock.

The *Arcadia*, out of the water, looked enormous but she appeared old and battered. She did not arouse love in him as she did in the captain, perhaps because his quarters on board had never been as comfortable as the captain's, nor the first-mate's for that matter, his had just been a couple of short steps above the deck hands'.

On inquiry he was told the work would take another ten days

to a fortnight for it had been discovered that one of the boilers would have to be renewed. He saw no one he knew belonging to the ship. The captain, they said, had been over yesterday from Hull, where he lived. The first mate lived nearby in Shields, but he was spending most of his time in Edinburgh, where his parents were.

He left Jarrow and returned to Newcastle. The city did not attract him. It was like any other city, and made him feel like a fish out of water. As he wandered about the streets, glancing in the shops, he knew he was wasting his time. He had a longing to get away from it, away beyond Hexham and into the hills.

He went through the Cloth Market and the Bigg Market towards Grainger Street, deciding that on his way to the station he'd drop into a pub and have a drink. Unlike most sailors, he could take drink or leave it, but he felt in need of one today.

It was as he turned the corner into Grainger Street that he bumped into her. He went to side-step, saying, 'Pardon, Ma'am,' when he exclaimed on a high note, 'Oh w . . . why! Miss Jane!'

'Well!' Jane shook her head. 'Of all the places to meet.'

'It's right what they say after all; it's a small world.'

'Yes, yes.' She laughed gently. 'As you say it's a small world. I . . . I was just making my way back to the train.'

'Well, so was I, Miss.'

'Oh!' She remained still, her face slightly flushed. She felt embarrassed. If she had met Johnnie or Mickey or Will Curran, or anyone else from the farm, she would have walked with them down to the train and thought nothing of it, but this man, this sailor, was not of the farm, not any more, and his dress denied all connection with the country; he was very well set up, quite spruce; he had grown into a fine man had Winnie's Davie, but she found him a little disconcerting. She had spoken to him twice since his return and each time she had been made uneasy by his presence. It was as if he forced himself on her notice. But that wasn't true, because his manner was most correct.

'Shall I take those for you?' He was lifting the packages from her arms, and she said, 'Oh. Oh, thank you, Davie.' It did not feel natural to call him Davie, it was as if she was taking a liberty, but what else could she call him, not Mr Armstrong.

When, her four parcels held in one arm, he took her elbow and, turning sideways, shouldered his way through the crowd so that she could remain on the pavement and not be pushed into

174

the muddy road, she thought he had quite good manners. She had understood that most sailors were gauche and cumbersome owing to their being deprived of society for such long intervals, but then, country people too were considered gauche.

His courtesy surprised her further when, as they approached the station, he asked her would she care for some refreshment. She thanked him kindly and told him that she had just eaten, which was not true, and she could have done with a cup of tea, in fact she had intended to go and have a light meal before catching the train. She didn't know why she hadn't made this clear to him.

They were fortunate in only having to wait ten minutes for the train and as they stood on the platform he said to her, 'I don't know whether we'll be able to travel together, Miss Jane, I've only a third-class ticket.'

'We'll be able to travel together.' She nodded slowly. 'I have a third-class ticket too.' They smiled at each other, then laughed gently.

As he looked at her he thought, her skin's as white as milk; black suits her. Funny how she's escaped being beautiful. She could have been that; she's just missed it somehow. Now if her expression was different, more happy like. There's something missing. How old is she? Twenty-six. No, twenty-seven. She looks older, thirty if a day. She carries herself well; she's straight, a bit too straight perhaps. Pity she hadn't a bit of what Molly has up top. Well, not quite up top – he smiled inwardly – say just above amidships.

'Are you looking forward to returning to sea?'

'Well, yes and no. All the time I've been away I've dreamed of the farm and the country around, you know, and now when I'm back I feel at a loose end. I suppose it's not having anything to do. If I was working it would be different.'

'You wouldn't like to return to the land?'

'Ah, that's a difficult one, for what is there for a man in my position on the land these days?'

'Yes, things are difficult.'

The train came in and they took their seats, sitting side by side, and the silence that now fell between them caused little embarrassment because of the other occupants in the carriage and the rattling of the train itself.

It wasn't until they reached Hexham and were making their way to the stables to collect the horse and trap that they began talking again. Their conversation now took the form of question and answer, and strangely it was Jane who asked the questions: What did his work entail? What did he do in his spare time? Did he still read? To this last he answered with some pride, 'Oh yes, Miss Jane, everything I can get me hands on. I stock up well afore a trip. But what's more, I've teached others their letters. Afore I became second mate the fo'c'sle was like a schoolroom.' He laughed. 'You wouldn't believe, Miss, what it means to a man when he can write his own name; gives him a sort of dignity. In some boats there's not much difference atween the rats in the holds and the humans below decks, because they're not tret any better than you would treat vermin; an' there was many such in our boat. But you know, Miss, once those fellows could spell cat, dog, rat and fat, an' write their name, why, it was like a miracle, what it did for them. But mind, I'm not saying it acted in all cases for some of them had nothing in their noddles, and a belaying-pin wouldn't have knocked it in.'

'How wonderful!' she said; 'what a thoughtful thing to do, to teach men their letters.' And she did think so. Although his grammar left a lot to be desired she recognised in him an intelligence above the average, and the fact that he wished to impart his little learning to others gave him a prestige in her eyes.

At the stables she said, 'Will you take the reins, Davie?' and he answered, 'I'd like nothin' better, Miss.' And so in the growing twilight they drove home together, and laughed and chatted all the way.

Later, they both remarked to themselves in private that it was strange but they had not spoken of her father, or of Amos, or of Parson Hedley.

It was the following morning that Amos made his way to the cottage to see Davie. He'd had no real conversation with him since he had returned, but this was not to say that he hadn't thought about him, Davie had been in his mind constantly.

The feeling that he'd had for the sailor when he himself was a child still remained, he liked him. In his company, he felt a man, a whole man, they were men together. He would like him for a friend. Yes, and the balance of possession would weigh heavily towards himself, for the relationship would give him both a friend and a servant, a double advantage.

He knew Winnie was about her duties in the house, and he

hoped old Sep was still abed. And this he found when he knocked on the door and it was opened by Davie who stood aside to let him hobble into the empty kitchen.

Going straight towards a chair he hoisted himself expertly on to it, laid his crutches to the side, then, a hand on each arm of the chair, he leant back and said, 'Now then.'

Davie stood at the end of the mantelpiece and looked at the massive upper body of the boy, his width exaggerated still further by the grotesquely short stumps and feet. He had spoken to him as a master might speak to his man: 'Now then, let's get on with it.' He reached out and took his clay pipe from the rack above the mantelshelf, bent down and knocked the dead dottle out against the bars, then peered down into the empty bowl before opening a pen-knife and scraping it.

'Eeh! Oh! that puts my teeth on edge; why don't you smoke a wooden one?'

'This does me.'

Amos looked at him through narrowed lids. He sensed a lack of friendliness in his tone, definitely a lack of deference. Still, he wasn't his master . . . yet. 'Winnie tells me you went to see your ship yesterday.'

'Yes. I did that.'

'How did you find her?'

'Oh' – Davie allowed himself to grin – 'with her backside bare; she wasn't a nice sight.'

Amos's high fresh laugh brought Davie's eyes tight on him, and in this moment he was doubting Molly's tale; the laughing face looked good, incapable of such destruction as killing, and the victim of his own father, be he what he may. Yet put himself in the lad's place, ignored for years, treated like an animal, what would he have done? Very likely have tried to have a go at the old man long before this. You couldn't judge such things, a man could stand only so much. And what was more, this was no lad, no boy; although his years were few he was a man. Funny, his mother had said the same thing last night when they were talking. 'He was born a man,' she said, 'in his mind, that is.'

'Are you anxious to get back to sea?'

Davie was shredding a plug of baccy in the palm of his hand and he contemplated it before answering, 'Yes and no.'

'What do you mean by that?'

177

'Just yes and no. It's my job, but I'd be happier if my ship could sail around these hills.'

Again Amos laughed; then, his face settling into its sombre pattern, he watched Davie filling his pipe. He watched him light it with a spill before he said, 'You needn't go back, you could stay here and work for me.'

Slowly Davie turned his head to the side and looked at the figure sitting in the chair, the big head held up, the neck stretching away from the shoulders, the back straight. For a moment he was reminded of a figurehead such as one or two of the old ships still carried. He had said, 'You can work for me,' not, 'You can come back and I'll find you a job on the farm,' but 'You can work for me.' It was as his mother said, he was playing the master all right. He now threw his own head back and laughed, a deep short laugh, and, as if he was dealing with a child and a joke, he said, 'Oh yes, work for you. And what would you offer me?'

'Fifteen shillings a week.'

He took the pipe from his mouth, puffed out a thin stream of smoke, then raised his eyebrows, pursed his lips and repeated, 'Fifteen shillings a week.'

He would pay fifteen shillings, well! well! And in these days when a farm labourer who received ten shillings together with his cottage and perks would consider himself damn lucky. He was only picking up twelve shillings himself and sometimes the food turned his stomach, biscuits that walked towards you drawn by weevils, and meat that heralded its approach with a whiff that would knock you down. Fifteen shillings, well! well! His mouth moved into a twisted smile as he said, 'And what would you be expecting of me for fifteen shillings, because, you must remember, I haven't been on a farm for this many a long year, I've almost forgotten where the milk comes from. A fellow I once knew thought it came by pumping the beast's tail, I'm not much better. Fifteen shillings. You'd want something for your fifteen shillings, now wouldn't you? And would you mind telling me what it is?'

'A gaffer, manager, someone to see to the others; there's a lot of time-wasters about. Mickey's all right, but Johnnie's a dodger, and Will wants stirring.'

'And I would have to stir?'

'You would have to stir.'

'Well!' He let out a long breath, then drew on his pipe again

178

before saying, 'You won't remember it but there was a time when it took nine men going at it hard to run this place. Well, perhaps I shouldn't say they were all men because the two Gearys were young, but they worked hard, as did Curran's two, they were doing a man's work at ten, and now with only three left to do the work, you want me to hustle them.'

'The place isn't run as it was years ago, and you already know that, if you've walked round; there's walls down, gates hanging off. Anyway, I intend to cut the land.'

'Cut the land?' Davie's face was screwed up in inquiry.

'Yes. Sir Alfred's been after that bottom stretch for years. It's not productive, only pretty, and we can do without that.'

'That'll mean letting the burn and the malt house go.' There was indignation in Davie's voice but Amos did not seem to notice it, for he went on, 'The burn will go, yes, but I'm keeping the malt house; that'll be for Jane and the parson when I marry.'

Davie felt the muscles of his face sagging. He just stopped his jaw from drooping and from repeating the word marry.

When this young fellow here talked you could forget he hadn't legs, there was a virility in his voice, certainly a virility in his torso. The way he had of sitting straight, without movement, gave the impression of power. But when he spoke of marriage as if it was a certainty, you remembered he hadn't legs . . . Still – his shoulders made a slight movement – what of it, he had the necessary to make a marriage work, in one direction that was. But who would take him on? Which lass would be willing to go to bed with that? Oh – again there was a movement of his shoulders as he answered himself – some would. When they got past twenty there were those who'd hook up with a blind beggar, so desperate they became. There were others, who he thought were in the majority, who'd become sick at the thought, that is unless they cared for him. That was the word, cared. Not so much loving, but caring. There was a big difference here. He had learned that from watching his mother and father. He doubted if his mother had ever loved his father; but she had cared for him, and they'd been happy together . . . Yes, if the lad found somebody who cared, somebody of the type of Miss Jane who was all heart and sacrifice, he would marry. But there were few Miss Janes about.

'Well, what do you say?'

'Aw, you're not serious?'

'Serious? Of course, I'm serious.'

Davie stiffened at the tone, and his own matched it now when he replied, 'It's a thing that'll need considerin', a lot of thinkin' about. I could say no right away for I don't know whether I'd like working for you any more than I did your father . . .'

His words were cut off by Amos letting out a high laugh, and he looked at him in surprise, for the master was gone and the boy was back as he said, 'You know that's what I like about you, Davie; you're different, you're not afraid to say what you think. I remember, all those years back, you clouted me, didn't you? Any other one on the farm wouldn't have dared, but you did.' He reached for his crutches and slid from the chair, and looking up at Davie, he said, 'Think hard on it, I'd be obliged if you'd stay.' He paused, then ended, 'I need you, someone like you to balance things. And remember, it would make your mother happy.'

Davie made no answer to this, but watched him going towards the door. He hadn't rushed to open it for him but had left him to manoeuvre it himself. Not until he had gone through the door and was some way down the road did he go towards it and close it. Then he returned to the fireplace and, bending down, leaned his forearms on the mantelshelf and laid his brow on his hands and looked down at the fire . . .

A short while later, when he went upstairs, old Sep said, 'Did I hear the young master down below?'

'Aye, Granda, you heard him.'

'What's he after?'

'He's offered me a job, manager of the farm, sort of.'

'What!' Sep pulled himself up in bed with startling agility seeing that he could hardly move with rheumatics. 'Name of God! he didn't!'

'He did. Fifteen bob a week.'

'Name of God!' The exclamation was higher this time. 'Fifteen bob a week! Aw, lad. Well, I always knew you'd make it one day.'

'Now, Granda, now, now. You lay yourself down; this needs thinking about.'

The old man, now gripping his hand, looked up at him and whispered, 'Stay, Davie, stay.'

'We'll see, we'll see. As I said, it needs thinking about.'

But as he went down the stairs he knew he had already thought about it, he was manager of the farm.

Six

Jane stood before the desk in the office and looked down on Amos. Her face was tight and there was anger in her voice as she said, 'Please don't send for me as if I were a servant, Amos. And if you wish to talk to me I prefer that you do not sit in father's chair and behind his desk.'

He stared at her, his face equally tight and his voice grim as he said, 'And you forget that times have changed, Jane. This is no longer father's chair and desk, it is mine.'

Their glances held for a moment; then he quickly tossed his head from side to side and, his voice and manner changing completely, said, 'Aw, Jane, don't let's quarrel. Look, I'm sorry. I just asked Winnie to tell you I'd like a word with you.' He leaned across the desk and put his hand out and caught at hers, saying softly, 'Please, come on, sit down.'

She remained straight and stiff for a moment longer; then slowly she turned about and pulled a chair forward and, seating herself, looked at him, once her beloved child, her charge.

For sixteen years she had spent her energies and her love on him, and although her life had been hard, tiresome and dull at times, it had been without fear. But since her father died she had been full of fear; of what she didn't rightly know for she wouldn't admit to herself that it was fear of him.

In two short weeks the whole atmosphere of the place had changed. Everyone was on edge. The only good thing he had done was to persuade Davie Armstrong to become a working manager. Yet this hadn't found favour with the others. Will Curran was openly opposed to it, as also was Johnnie. Mickey was the only one who welcomed the new innovation, at least among the men. Winnie, she knew, was over the moon. And Molly – one couldn't tell what Molly was thinking. But Molly wasn't acting like herself these days either, so perhaps she, too, was disturbed by the new arrangement.

Arnold thought it was a very sensible move on the part of Amos, but then he had always been very fond of Davie, although he had pointed out that a sixteen year gap was a long time to be away from farm work, for things on the land had changed a lot. Davie's job wouldn't be easy if he wanted the place to pay its way.

This was another thing; she had discovered that the farm, far from paying its way, had been losing money; there was a heavy mortgage on the house. She had found out a great number of things when she went to Newcastle to see the solicitor . . . She had gone to him purposely because she couldn't believe that her father had made no provision for her.

Knowing the strength of her father's feelings concerning his son she was convinced that Amos had no right to be sitting in that chair, it was she who should be in charge of the farm. She was sure that her father would not have been so negligent as to omit leaving a document that would ensure that Amos would not inherit. In fact the thought was adamant in her mind that he would have ignored Amos's requirements, as he had always done, and left his future in her hands.

The solicitor had been of the same mind, but as he said, if there were a later will, they must stand by the present one until such times as it might be found. He suggested that she search the house, particularly the office. This she had done over and over again, but with no success.

Amos startled her by saying, 'I've ordered them to finish the malt house.'

'The malt house! But why? it won't be necessary.'

He leant over the desk and although she was out of his reach he extended his hands towards her, laying them palms down on the papers. 'You want to get married, don't you? You've waited long enough.'

'Yes.' Her chin was slightly to the side. 'Yes, I've waited long enough. But – oh' – she smiled now – 'I see.' She nodded towards him. 'You don't want to live with us, you want a place of your own. I can understand, and it's thoughtful . . . '

'No, no' – he was shaking his head vigorously – 'you've got it wrong. Turn it round. It's for you . . . and Arnold.'

'You mean . . . ?' She got to her feet, 'You mean I'm ... we're to go to the malt house?'

'Well' – he pulled his arms sharply back across the desk – 'I'm going to marry some day, and before long I hope, and two mistresses under the one roof wouldn't work.'

'You're going to . . . ?' She stopped. She had never thought about him marrying, not even that the idea would ever enter his head. Who would . . . ?

'DON'T LOOK LIKE THAT.' He was bawling at her now. 'My God! underneath you're like the rest of them. I'm not a man am I? just a thing!'

For the moment the malt house was forgotten as she tried to reassure him, saying, 'Don't be silly, Amos. And that's most unfair, you know it is. It's only that you're so young and . . .'

'And I'm odd. Who would want to take me on? That's what you're thinking, isn't it? That's what they all think. Well, I won't have far to go to find someone willing. I might as well tell you now I'm going to marry Biddy.'

She felt the blood draining from her face, from her arms; she had the sensation that there was a tap in the soles of her feet letting it flow away. She felt for the moment that she was going to faint. She knew now that Arnold had been right when he had advised her to tell the boy when he was no more than eight years old. He had again brought the subject up when Amos was ten, and then twelve, but she couldn't risk embittering him further against his father and taking from him the only young companionship he had. Anyway, she had foreseen the problem solved by Molly sending Biddy away into service, when she became twelve, with either Lena or Katie. Both of them had married, but remained in service. From time to time Molly had spoken of Lena, saying she could get Biddy into her household, but nothing had come of it. Molly, she knew, was loath to part with her daughter, for she was the only thing she had.

He was yelling at her again. 'Oh, for Christ's sake! don't come over all class conscious. Anyway, who cares? We're in the backwoods here, we might as well be on an island for all the visitors we get. And that's how I want it, I want it to be an island, I'm going to turn it into an island. I've written to old Tuppin about the bottom land. I'm having the walls and fences done, gates put up. I'll make it an island where we can . . .'

'QUIET! Do you hear, be quiet!'

'Jane!' His voice was deep in his throat and, without looking behind him, he groped for his crutches and, drawing them forward, tucked them under his arms and came round the desk to stand in front of her. And with his head just slightly back, he looked at her and said slowly, 'Gone are the days when you could tell me to be quiet.'

She moved one step back from him; then two. When she bumped into the chair she turned round and pushed it out of her way, then took another step in the direction of the door.

He stood watching her for a moment before he demanded, 'What's the matter with you? Why are you looking like that? You've always liked Biddy, and she's tractable and not ignorant; she can read and write as well as the next.'

'A . . . mos!' His name was strangled in her throat. She gulped spittle into her dry mouth, then breathed deeply three times before she said, 'You cannot have Biddy, ever . . . ever; it's . . . it's impossible.'

'I cannot have Biddy? What do you mean?'

'I . . . I should have told you before now, years ago, but I thought it . . . it would make you dislike Father more. And I didn't think you would . . . I never thought about marriage. It's impossible. Biddy . . . Biddy is your . . . our half-sister.'

For a full minute he did not seem to comprehend the meaning of her statement. His face screwed up, the almond eyes became long, narrow slits, his whole body was still; then in a lightning movement he came to life and she sprang back towards the door and screamed, 'Don't! Don't Amos. Don't!' as a crutch came spinning through the air like a boomerang at her. It struck her shoulder and she cried out again and ran into the hall.

Molly, coming from the dining-room, inquired urgently but quietly, 'What is it? What is it, Miss?' and Jane rushed towards her and clung to her for a moment; then grabbing her hand, almost dragged her up the stairs and into the bedroom.

'In the name of God, Miss Jane, what is it? What's he done?'

Again Jane was clinging to her. 'I . . . I had to tell him about Biddy; he . . . he said he was going to marry her.'

'God Almighty!' Molly's response to this was so quiet that it had a calming effect on Jane, and she dropped on to the side of the bed and joined her hands tightly on her knees and asked, 'What are we going to do?'

Molly didn't answer her directly but said, 'I've . . . I've been half expecting it, Miss. It made me write to our Katie and Lena some weeks back. The place has been filled in Lena's but they're looking for a stillroom maid in Katie's. But . . . but I didn't want to let her go that far; it's right down in the south of the country, back of beyond near a place called Teignmouth. Beautiful, Lena says, but lonely. Worse than this. I . . . I didn't want to send her to the back of beyont 'cos she's young. Yet she was for going when I mentioned it. I wish to God I'd let her now.

184

'Don't shake so, Miss Jane.' She came slowly to the bed and, sitting down on the edge of it, she put her arm around her and held her close, and Jane said, 'Oh Molly, Molly, what have things come to?' and Molly turning her gaze to the wall said flatly, 'Parson Hedley would say it's the sins of the fathers and of the mothers.'

'Oh, I wasn't meaning that, Molly.'

'I know, Miss, I know, but I can't help thinking that it's right; I carry a weight about with me all the time.'

'Oh, Molly!' Jane leant her head against her and in this moment they could have been the half-sisters.

After a time Molly rose to her feet, saying, 'You stay here quiet for a while, Miss Jane, till things settle down, but we'll have to put our thinkin' caps on, something must be done.'

On her way to the door she glanced out of the window, then stopped and exclaimed on a high note, 'Oh my God! there he goes into the dairy.' And with that she turned and ran from the room and down the stairs and out of the house . . .

As if Amos knew that Molly would come, he had immediately dropped the bar over the door when he entered the dairy from the yard, and now he stood with his back to it and looked towards Biddy, where she had turned from the marble slab on which she had been patting up butter and stared at him. It was she who spoke first. 'What is it?' she asked. 'What's the matter? What you barrin' the door for?'

He did not answer her, only continued to stare, and she turned from him and picked up a cloth and wiped her hands before looking at him again and repeating, 'What's the matter? You bad or somethin'?'

His face was colourless but running with sweat, as were his hands gripping the bars of the crutches. He leaned back against the door as he asked, 'Do you like me?'

'Like you?' She twisted her face at him. 'What's up with you?' The question was high.

'I said do you like me?'

'Well' – she wagged her head – 'I suppose so. Aye, yes, I like you.' She looked him up and down. She never thought about him having no legs; she was so used to him that way, and so she had never been sorry for him because of his disability.

'Would you marry me?'

'WHAT! What did you say . . . marry you?' Her dark brows

had moved into points. Then she gave a little laugh as she said, 'Don't talk daft.'

'BIDDY!' He bawled her name as she went to turn from him, and at the same time it was shouted from beyond the door. 'Biddy! Biddy! open this door. Do you hear me?'

Biddy stared at the door above his head, then down at him. 'That's me ma,' she said. 'Open the door.'

'Answer me first, will you marry me?'

As the glinting light of his eyes held her gaze she almost said, 'Marry you, are you mad? Who would marry you?' but she had some of her mother in her and so her answer was, 'Now look, don't act so daft; I'm not marryin' anybody, nobody.'

'Biddy! D'you hear me? Open this door. Push him out of the way an' open this door.'

'You'd better get by,' she said quietly, 'else I'll have to push you.' If she pushed him he'd overbalance, and she was quite capable of pushing him. Over the years he had sparred with her she had learned to defend herself the hard way; although he had always got the better of her once they were on the ground together. And so he made no effort to stop her when she moved close to him to swing the bar back into its socket.

When the door burst open it almost knocked them on to their backs. Standing in the opening, red in the face and enraged, Molly looked from one to the other before addressing her daughter. 'What's he done? What's he said?' she demanded.

'Nothin', Ma, nothin'. What you yellin' for?'

'Nothin' you say? Why did he bar the door then?' She turned her glance swiftly on Amos, who was glaring at her with a look of deep hatred on his face, and it came over in his voice as he said slowly, 'I asked her to marry me.'

'You dirty . . . '

'Don't say it. Don't say it, Molly.' As his head went down his eyes moved upwards under his lids, giving him a demoniacal look.

'I will say it.' She now turned to Biddy. 'You get out. Get out of here, go on up home.'

'What? Why?'

'Do as I bid you, girl. Go on up home.'

Biddy went slowly out, and Molly, banging the door closed again, leaned against it as she growled, 'Knowin' what you know, you asked her that?'

'Yes, I asked her that. And it makes no difference.'

'You mean you would . . . ?' Her lips moved away from her teeth and he finished for her, 'Yes, yes, I would. And she would an' all if you left her alone.'

'Never! Never in this world! An' when I tell her, that'll be the finish.'

He moved slowly towards her and stopped only a few feet from her before he said thickly, 'If you make it the finish it'll be the finish of you too; I'll send you packing quicker than a rocket.'

'You will, will you?' Her head was jerking in small movements. 'That's what you think.'

His expression showed he was surprised by her defiant attitude. But he spat at her, 'And you won't get a reference other than I'd give to a whore.'

Her lips became tight, her rounded chin knobbled. It was some moments before she spoke and then she said, 'I'm no whore, never was. Compared to you, your father was a gentleman. An' that's what you'll never be, not even half a one.' She flicked her eyes down towards his lower limbs. But in spite of her brave front, she became fearful for a moment by the look on his face. Even so she went on, 'I'll leave this farm when I feel so inclined an' not afore, and you can't do a damned thing about it, Mas . . . ter Amos.' She watched his lids blinking, his brow moving to a furrow of thought. 'That's set you thinkin', hasn't it? An' I'll tell you something' more. I've got it in me power to put you along the line any minute I choose . . . You killed your father; you swung from that beam an' you killed him. An' I've got the evidence of it. Not only have I got the torn piece from your coat but I've got the coat an' all. You made the mistake of givin' it to our Johnnie when you were rigging yourself out with your new finery . . . Now don't, I'm warning you' – her arm went straight out, her finger pointing at him – 'don't think you'll wallop me with that crutch an' get off with it; I'm not Miss Jane, I've got no niceties about me. You lay a finger on me, whether it's by hand or wooden leg, an' by God! you'll live to regret it.'

They glared at each other for a moment longer. Then she turned to open the door. Her hand on the bar, she cast her glance back at him and said softly, 'An' don't try to concoct a way of gettin' rid of me 'cos if anything happens to me you'll be for it surely, 'cos I'm not the only one who knows, I've seen to that. You see I know you, Master Amos; I've known you for a long time. Long afore others twigged what was in you I knew you.'

She held his gaze before turning away. Her legs were trembling under her long skirt and the sweat was running from her oxters. She made herself walk steady because she knew he was watching her . . .

A few minutes later in the kitchen of her cottage she stood looking at Biddy, who was crying loudly while she muttered, 'You should have told me, Ma. You should have told me.'

'Aye, I know I should. It's my fault, but . . . but I thought you'd be gone years ago to your Auntie Lena's or Katie's.'

'You, you can't blame him for carryin' on, you can't, 'cos he must have got a shock an' all, he must, Ma.'

'Of course he got a shock, I'm not denyin' it, but in spite of gettin' a shock he went an' put that to you. Marry him, he said. If he had been an ordinary being it would have been bad enough, not right, against God like, but him as he is, offerin' you a double handicap. Now stop cryin', do. Dry your eyes. Come on, dry your eyes.'

'I feel all of a dither, Ma.'

'Aye, lass, I understand. You're bound to. Look, I'll make a sup tea an' then I'll have to get back. But you stay here. Mind, I'm tellin' you, you stay put until I get things arranged.'

As Molly went to the hob and lifted the kettle Biddy said quietly, 'I can't take it in, the master being me da . . . father. He never looked at me, or spoke to me, no more than he did to Amos.' There was a pause before she ended, 'Funny him being me father. I'm not just nobody then. I used to wonder. But I'm not just nobody am I?'

Molly set the kettle into the heart of the fire, then she turned and looked at her daughter. It was odd that she should lay stock on who she came from. Yet not so odd when you came to think of it; she must have wondered many a time.

And Biddy confirmed this now by saying, 'You know, Ma, I used to think it was' – she thumbed towards the wall – 'Mr Armstrong . . . Davie. I used to think he was me da, an' that's why he went away.'

Molly turned again to the fire, saying grimly, 'Well, you thought wrong then, didn't you?'

'But Ma, why . . . why haven't we heard afore, either him, I mean Amos, or me? It's a wonder nobody let it out, isn't it? Me Uncle Johnnie or Mickey, or Will Curran, or them at the

Sunday School. It's a wonder they didn't pelt me with it, 'cos I was called a bastard more than once.'

As Molly measured the tea into the earthenware pot she said quietly, 'In Sunday School they were from well around, the places are spread out, they wouldn't know. An' anyway, they were just bairns like yourself.'

'Jim Doolin, or Frank Pearce, they're not bairns. Jim Doolin is after me proper; he waits for me market day.'

'Well, it's not likely that they would say anything even if they knew, is it? An' if they knew the master had been your da, it might have been a feather in your cap.'

'I don't know.' Biddy considered. 'Men are funny about such things. I know Frank Pearce's mam and dad wouldn't have liked it, they're stiff chapel.'

'Well, you won't have to worry about what any of them think; you'll meet a different class with your Aunt Katie. Down there there's butlers, an' footmen, an' proper coachmen, an' everything she says.' She leaned forward now and touched her daughter's cheek. 'You're a bonny lass, you'll likely make a good match.'

'I'll miss you, Ma.'

'And I'll miss you, lass.'

They put their arms around each other and remained quiet for a time until Molly said, as if she had been reconsidering the matter, 'It's no good, you've got to get out of here an' as quick as possible.' She moved briskly away now, saying, 'I'm goin' across to see Miss Jane. She's in a state an' all, poor soul. My! if anybody's had the rotten end of the stick, she has. Make yourself some tea, an' no more cryin'. You've got life afore you, an' it could be wonderful.' She smiled weakly; they both smiled weakly; then she went hurriedly out.

On entering the house she immediately heard the shouting coming from upstairs, and going swiftly through the kitchen, she found Winnie standing at the foot of the stairs. There were high spots of scarlet colour on her cheeks, the rest of her face was white. 'He's like a devil,' she whispered. 'He went for Miss Jane like a madman. Look.' She pointed to the corner where a vase lay broken on the floor. 'He swiped that off with his crutch. I thought he was going to hit her, I did . . . Where's Biddy?'

'Over in the house. I've got to get her away to Katie's as quick as possible.'

'Aye, the sooner the better. But how will she go? It's the other end of the country, she's never been farther than Hexham in her life.'

'I'll take her meself.'

'Right away, down there?'

'Aye, right away down there.'

'You'll come back?'

'Oh aye, Winnie; I'll come back.'

They both looked at each other; and they both knew why she would come back.

Molly asked quickly now, 'What time's Davie goin' in for the stores?' and Winnie answered, 'Around twelve I should say.'

'He would take us into the train, wouldn't he? He could pick us up along the road on the quiet.'

'Aye. Aye, he could do that.'

'I'll go an' ask him.'

They both hurried away as a door banged overhead, and in the kitchen Molly asked, 'Will you look after the lads for me the time I'm gone, Winnie?'

'That's the least of your worries, lass,' Winnie answered. 'Go on now, and arrange it with Davie.'

She found Davie in the grain store where the rats had been playing havoc, and without any preamble she said, 'You goin' into Hexham the day?' and he nodded as he replied, 'Aye, I'm going into Hexham the day.'

'Around twelve your mother says.'

'Yes, that's right, around twelve.' It was an aggravating habit of his to repeat everything she said.

'Will . . . will you give us a lift, Biddy an' me? I'm taking her away.' Now she had his attention.

'Why? What's happened?'

She looked down for a moment; then moved one lip over the other. 'He . . . he wants to marry her.'

'No! You mean?'

She still had her head down as she nodded. 'He's playin' hell, goin' mad. Even when he knew how they stood to each other he still went and asked her. I'm . . . I'm takin' her down to our Katie's. It's a long way an' I can't let her go on her own.'

'No, no, of course not. Where will I pick you up?'

'Round the bend of the Tor.'

'Good enough . . . How . . . how are you off for money?' His voice was gruff.

'Oh, I can manage, I've got a bit put by.'

'Enough to take you there and back? You're coming back?'

She looked up at him, a gleam of hope in her eyes. 'Yes, I'm coming back.'

'What if he won't let you?'

She nodded her head now as she said, 'Oh, he'll let me all right, he can't do anythin' else; I told him what I know about . . . about what he did.'

'You told him that?' He asked the question in a thin whisper.

'Aye, I had to. He was giving me the shove an' . . . an' this is me home, it's the only place I've got. An' what's more I like working along of Miss Jane.' As she lowered her gaze again he asked quietly, 'Do you think it's wise to come back? You could get a job anywhere.'

'I know that, but as I said this is me home, I was born and bred here.'

'Aren't you afraid of what he might try an' do to you?'

'I put a stop to that an' all; I told him I'm not the only one who knows.'

He stared hard at her before he asked, 'Did you tell him it was me?'

'Oh no, no, of course not; he might try and do us both in. I wouldn't put it past him.'

'He might at that.'

She heaved a sigh, then said dully, 'Don't let on about where she's going, will you? I mean not to Will Curran, 'cos he'd sell his soul for a penny bun. I'll have to tell the lads, but he won't get it out of them.'

'Don't worry,' he said; 'he certainly won't get it out of me. Be along there around twelve.'

'Ta,' she said, then she went out; and he picked up a handful of grain and ran it through his fingers. There was going to be trouble when he found Biddy gone, for she must have been his one solid hope of fulfilling himself as a man. He remembered the lad used to act as if he owned her when they were small children together. That feeling must have increased rapidly with the years. In this moment he experienced a strong sense of pity for the boy; but the very pity created a stronger sense of foreboding.

Of a sudden he had a longing to be back at sea.

Seven

'Where's she gone? Where's she gone I'm asking you, woman?'

'Take your hands off!' Jane slapped out at him. 'Take your hands off me. I tell you I don't know. Amos, stop it!' When she fell back on to the foot of the stairs she let out a high cry as her elbow struck the wood and the pain of it for a moment blotted everything from sight; but she was conscious of steps running from the kitchen and Winnie shouting, 'Give over! Master Amos, for God's sake, give over!'

But she wasn't aware of Davie's presence until Amos was lifted bodily from her; then she saw Amos scrambling on all fours towards the wall where he grabbed at one of his crutches and hurled it at Davie's legs. She closed her eyes tightly when the other crutch went hurtling after the first one. And then Davie's voice, seeming to shudder the roof, yelled, 'Don't you come any of that with me, Mister, for you've picked the wrong one!'

'Come away. Come away out of it.' Winnie was pulling her to her feet, and she groaned with the pain in her elbow. She glanced fearfully to where Amos and Davie were confronting each other, both strangely of a like breath, the only difference being in height; yet Amos's lack of legs did not seem to handicap him, for of the two at this moment he looked the more ferocious.

She was passing through the door when she heard Amos speak and she went to turn back, but Winnie pulled her on into the kitchen and banged the door behind them.

What Amos had said was, 'You'll find it better, Armstrong, if you mind your own business.'

'I take it as my business to stop you beltin' into your sister ... What's up with you anyway? What's come over you?'

'You're not stupid, so why do you ask? You know what's come over me? And you know where she's gone, don't you? You know where that bitch has taken her. They didn't walk to Hexham, you must have given her a lift on the cart.'

'That's right, I gave them a lift on the cart. But I don't know where they've gone. An' if I did I wouldn't tell you.'

He lied so convincingly that Amos believed him, and like the draining of a barrel the anger and the rage slowly seeped out of him, and he was left with a great sense of frustration and the futility of going on; for the moment the farm and his new power were as nothing to him.

Slowly he turned away, and as Davie had taught him to do years ago he shambled towards the stairs by throwing his body from side to side. When he reached them he sat down on the bottom stair and, gripping the oak post, he laid his head against it, and there welled up in him the torrent of emotion that had been dammed for years, and for the first time in his life he began to cry, great, tearing, shoulder-shuddering sobs. But when Davie's hand came gently on to his shoulder he turned fiercely on him. The water spurting from his eyes and nose and spluttering from his mouth in bubbles, he gasped, 'Somebody will pay for this, they will! they will! God Almighty! they will. I'll see they will.'

And they did.

Book Four: 1898

One

'Now, my dearest Jane, don't worry; nothing can happen. A week from today we will be together . . . for ever, for ever and ever; living or dead, we'll be together.'

Arnold Hedley held her thin hands tightly to his breast; his nondescript features glowed with love and happiness. He had waited so long for his superior to die and for Jane to throw off the chains that bound her to Amos, but now everything at last had come about, everything was arranged. Seven days hence she would leave the farm for good and all, and come here to the Vicarage to make it a home. And he so wanted a home, he had never known a home. His parents having died young, he had been brought up in the care of an uncle who had rid himself of him as soon as possible by sending him to boarding school; from there he had gone into the seminary, and from the seminary he had come to this house, this house that had been dominated by John William Wainwright, a man whom he knew in his inner heart was not really of God, for he had been a selfish, vain, self-seeking man. But he must not think harshly of him any more, for he was where God willed him to be these past three months, since which time the bishop had confirmed him in the living and so made his way clear at last to make Jane his wife.

Yet although he had said to her that nothing could go wrong, there was an uneasiness in him and he knew he wouldn't feel that all was right until Jane was safely installed in this house and away from the farm . . . or rather, Amos. Never had he been so mistaken in judging human nature as he had in that boy. Through all his early days he had prophesied great things for him. With such an active mind he could have become a writer, a profession he could have followed without exposure to the public. But what had he done? Used his powers to become a gambler. As a child he had been adroit at the game of marbles. He himself had been amused by his prowess in this direction. Now he was horrified at where the simple game had led him. The farm faced utter disaster if some check was not put on his activities. But who could check such a one as Amos had become? And then there was not only the gambling; oh no, there was the scandal of his trips into Hexham, trips that kept him there two and three nights at a time. His jaunts on this business would take him as far away as Newcastle. He could be away for as long as four days to a week. Only one good thing resulted from his absences; the inhabitants of the farm during such times knew a little peace.

He recalled the time when he first came to this parish. There were eighteen souls all told at Cock Shield, now there were but seven. In the last twelve months two more had gone from the place: Johnnie Geary had married and taken his young wife with him to another farm, and Winnie, that hard-working faithful servant, had gone to her long rest but two months ago. It was strange that old Sep should have outlived his daughter and her husband, and also weathered the epidemic that took four of them in a week. He supposed there was a purpose in it; God's ways were strange. He was thankful for one thing, that the Lord in His wisdom had seen fit to bring Davie Armstrong back, for without him he dreaded to think what might have come to the place. He had not been wrong in his summing up of Davie. A fine man was Davie in spite of his lack of faith and hot-headedness and sharpness of tongue at times, but nevertheless a fine, honest man. He was very fond of Davie; as was Jane.

He led her now across the brown-painted, dismal hall and into the brown-painted, brown-furnished, dismal sitting-room, and, pressing her into a chair, he said, 'Now sit there quietly, my dear, and I'll go and tell Mrs Spense you've come, and she will make you a hot cup of tea.'

'Yes, Arnold, that would be nice,' Jane said dutifully, knowing at the same time that Mrs Spense was well aware that she had arrived and that if she made her a cup of tea it would be with reluctance. Mrs Spense was not looking forward to having a mistress in the house.

She looked slowly around the room. How would she ever be able to think of this place as home? Would she even succeed in making it homelike? Would she ever be able to erase Parson Wainwright's presence from that great leather chair, the indentations, which even now gave the impression that he was sitting in it, smiling at her while he fought her off with unctuous charm? She looked at the heavy black sideboard taking up almost one wall of the room; the high glass cabinet of stuffed birds dominating another wall; the curtains of an indefinable colour hanging limply at each side of the narrow, deep stone window and which she guessed had never been washed for fear of disintegration.

If she'd had some money of her own and had been able to strip the whole place and refurnish it, she would have been happy, at least it would have given her an interest in her future, but she had no money. She would come to Arnold with only her clothes and her books, and a little jewellery which, under the present state of affairs, she had no right to. She had handled no money for almost two years now; since Amos had taken over he had seen to all the bills. Amos had treated her shamefully, and she didn't deserve it. No, she didn't deserve it, not from him, for she had given him her life.

He had blamed her for helping to spirit Biddy away. For months after that dreadful night when he had smashed nearly all the furniture in the sitting-room, he had refused to speak to her, treating her much in the same way as her father had treated him. Their normal relationship had never really been restored until three months ago when Parson Wainwright had died and she told him that she was going to marry Arnold and make her home in the Vicarage. She had been surprised at his first reaction to her news for he had appeared again like the young Amos who had demanded her whole attention. 'No, you can't,' he had said, 'Oh Jane, you can't. You wouldn't leave me here on my own.' But she had replied that he had little need of her now.

'That isn't true,' he had said, 'I do need you, I need you all the time. You're the only thing I have left. No matter what I do or how I act, you know you're the only thing I have to call my own.'

Although this had touched her, she had remained quietly adamant. She was going to marry Arnold, she said; it was settled, finally settled.

Shortly after this Amos had compromised. 'All right then,' he had said, 'all right, but come and live here. I can't be left

197

alone, Jane, I can't.' But even against this entreaty she had remained firm, saying she was sorry but the place of a parson's wife was in the Vicarage.

The place of a parson's wife was in the Vicarage. She now looked into the black iron grate where a low, dull fire was burning. She hated this house, she had always hated it, but it was her only refuge, that, and Arnold. Dear Arnold; so kind, so thoughtful, so loving; she wasn't worthy of him. If he could see into her heart he would be astounded for he would find nothing there but a thirty-year-old shrivelled case. How long ago was it since she had given the core of herself away? She didn't know, for at the time she hadn't realised she had parted with it. It was only these two past years that the knowledge had come to her, the shocking knowledge that she loved a man who, even in her reduced circumstances, was beneath her. Davie might be managing the farm, what was left of it, but he was still remembered as McBain's cowman.

Arnold came hurrying back into the room. He was smiling. He closed the door behind him – it was a precise action – then came towards her, his hand extended.

'There you are, that's settled. The kettle is on, ten minutes and we'll have a cup of tea.' It was as if he had achieved some extraordinary feat of diplomacy.

When he drew his chair up to hers she put her hand on his and said, 'There was no need to trouble Mrs Spense, Arnold; it's not long since I had dinner.'

'You've walked all this way and I'm not going to allow you to walk all the way back without some refreshment.' He now leaned nearer to her and, his voice dropping, he said, 'I have a nice surprise for you, I have acquired the third book in the trilogy by the Reverend Ingraham, *The Prince of the House of David*, and two of Mrs Henry Wood's books. Ah-ha!' He wagged his finger at her. 'I am not going to tell you the titles of those, I am keeping them as part of our recreation. I have it all planned out. One evening you shall read to me, the next I to you; when we're . . . ' Only just in time he checked himself from making use of the embarrassing terms 'in bed', and substituted, 'resting'.

Jane looked at him with a deep tolerant warmth in her eyes. She had a vivid picture in her mind of them both sitting up in bed, one reading, the other listening, and although the picture didn't bring her any joy she appreciated the gesture he had made in buying the latter two books, for his taste did not incline towards Mrs Henry Wood, but to much deeper subjects, slightly controversial subjects, such as science. He talked a great deal about Mr Huxley; he admired him yet could not countenance his attitude to religion. Mr Huxley, she understood, had brought into being a new word with regard to irreligious people, they were called agnostics.

Arnold was now moving his fingers gently around her wrist. Back and forward, back and forward they went, as if forming a bracelet. She couldn't stand it; she had never been able to stand this affectionate gesture of his. She wanted to jump to her feet, but she forced herself to rise slowly, saying, 'I must be getting back, I have so much to do.'

'But, but what about the tea?'

'Oh, thank Mrs Spense and apologise for my going.'

'Yes, yes, my dear.' His voice was hesitant; then he added, 'I feel guilty at not being able to accompany you, but I have the meeting with . . .'

'Arnold, Arnold,' she chided him gently, 'how often have I walked those two miles on my own, don't be silly.'

'You might have, my dear, but I still want to accompany you. And let us say, in place of guilt I feel a sense of loss in being denied your company.'

They stood under the porch of the Vicarage looking at each other; then he bent forward and kissed her gently, as a father might, and she went from him down the grass-grown gravel drive to the gate and out into the road, telling herself all the while not to be silly, she mustn't be foolish, she must not cry.

She was deeply fond of Arnold, he was the best man in the world, and she reminded herself she was near thirty and this would be her last chance of marriage . . . and she wanted marriage, she wanted a child. Oh yes, once she had a child everything would fall into place; her body would no longer torment her once she had a child.

She had entered the farm land and was within five minutes' walk of the house when she saw Davie. He was at some distance, but she knew it was he and that he was attending an animal. She cut across the fields in his direction, and before she came up to him she heard her approach and turned towards her, but it was she who spoke first. 'Is anything wrong?' she asked.

'Flo here, Miss Jane, if I'm not mistaken she's going to drop her calf an' all. If that happens it'll be the fourth in three weeks.

Something should be done.' He stared at her, and she turned her eyes from his and looked sideways down on to the grass.

'I've told him it's the lack of something. It's understandable one dropping now and again, but this'll be the seventh this year. He should get advice. An' you can you know, Miss; they're looking into these things now. There's a place where you can send. I've got the name and . . .'

He stopped talking when she looked up at him and said quietly, 'You've tried it, Davie, and I've tried it; we know it's no use.' She turned away, and he turned with her, saying abruptly, 'It's a thankless job. I'm telling you, Miss Jane, if it wasn't for me granda I'd be gone the morrow.'

'No, no! Davie.' She had stopped abruptly, and again they were looking at each other. 'If you desert him, well . . . well the place' – she shook her head, then slowly looked about her and, as if to herself, she finished, 'Twenty years ago it was the most thriving farm in these parts, no other could touch it.'

They were walking on again when Davie said quietly, 'I hear he's for selling the land beyond the Tor.'

'That's what he says, Davie.'

It was noticeable that neither of them referred to Amos as Master, or Master Amos, he was HE, as he had at one time been IT.

'I was worrying about losing Mickey but if this goes on it won't matter, it'll soon be a one-man plot. All that'll remain will be a smallholding left us by the grace of Sir Alfred . . . God Almighty! it's terrible when you think of it . . . Aw, I'm sorry, Miss.'

'It's all right, Davie. I say it too. God Almighty! it's terrible when you think of it.' She did not ask herself what Arnold would have said to her using such an expression, but added, 'I didn't know Mickey was thinking of going.' And he answered, 'Well, you can't blame him.' He didn't look towards her as he added, 'There's one good thing, you'll be finished with it all next week.'

Slowly they turned their heads towards each other, but they kept walking. 'The weight of it will still be on me wherever I go, Davie, and . . . and I feel as if I am deserting, like leaving a sinking ship.'

'Don't feel like that.' His voice was quiet and deep. 'If anybody in this world deserves a little peace it's you . . . Miss.'

She kept her head down as she said, 'Thank you, Davie.'

They walked in silence into the farmyard; then she went towards the kitchen where Molly was standing at the door, and he went towards the cow byres. But he passed them and let himself into the harness-room.

When he had closed the door behind him he stood looking about him from one article to another, from the table that held spoke, and water-brushes, bit and dandy-brushes and leathers all jumbled up together. He had ceased ordering Mickey to arrange everything neatly; there was no time for it, there was only time for keeping the gig spanking – for His Lordship. With the exception of one, the saddles on the walls had all gone dry, for the boiler was rarely put on now and the room was cold.

He moved slowly to the wooden block near the bench and sat down and dropped his head into his hands for a moment. Supporting it with his thumbs, his fingers moved across his brow, and not for the first time he muttered aloud, 'I must have been up the pole, bloody well up the pole to take this on.' If he had gone when he should have he'd be free now on the seas, not working for a young snot whose head he wanted to bash every time he looked at him. Not that he wasn't civil to him, himself; oh, butter wouldn't melt in his mouth at times; but ask him to lay out a penny on the cattle or the place and what did you get? Just that blank closed look that you couldn't get through.

He had spoken only half the truth the day he'd found Biddy gone, when he had cried and said he'd make somebody pay for it, because he'd made everybody pay for it. But her most of all.

His fingers now stopped moving on his brow and pressed tight against his temple bones. She didn't want to go through with it, he was sure of it . . . Well, say she didn't, where did that leave him? Aw, why in the name of God hadn't he gone when the going was good? Why? because he had gone barmy. You couldn't want two women at once; or could you? What was he on about? He didn't want two women; never in his life would he take Molly Geary, although she was hanging like a ripe plum just waiting to fall into his hand. Throwing herself at him she was. Never by a word, no, no, but he could tell, he could read the hungry look in her eyes. Well, she could throw herself from now until she was toothless and she would still bounce off him. But the other, Jane – he did not add the prefix Miss in his mind – how did she affect him? He was puzzled with regards to his feelings towards her. All he knew was that they had grown out of pity; he had been sorry for Miss Jane, a

201

young woman who had been used by her people since she was a child, until she was left with only one refuge, to marry the parson. He had nothing against Parson Hedley, oh no; if he respected anybody it was the parson, but not as a husband for her, a man to love her. No, he couldn't see the parson filling those roles. And Jane needed both, for she was warm and loving. But she was lost. For months past now every time he had looked at her he had wanted to take her into his arms. Just to comfort her, nothing more, just to comfort her. At least it had been nothing more at the beginning.

It was, he told himself, a hell of a situation, for there were the nights when, lying in his bed, he was as conscious of that one beyond the wall as if she was tucked in to his side. At times he felt she was willing herself into his bed. There had been one night not long ago when he'd had the urge to get up and hammer on the wall and yell, 'Stop it! Stop it! You're wasting your time. Once bitten, twice shy.' He fought with her cease-lessly during the night yet in the daytime he was civil to her. He called her by her name, and spoke the time of day, and at times talked of this and that. He also thanked her frequently for what she did for the old 'un; but then in this case there was likely more method in her madness than generosity. Aw, no! he had to give her her due there, she was kind. By nature she was kind, and it was in her favour too that she'd always been kind and loyal to Jane. But she'd been kind to Jane's father an' all, hadn't she?

He rose abruptly from the log and went outside. He had better see what Will Curran was up to. If he wasn't an old man he'd send him packin', lazy beggar that he was.

'Jane.' Amos stretched his hand along the dining-room table towards her. The gesture and his voice both held supplication, and his large fair face was soft with it.

It was a long time since she had seen him like this, but she remained untouched by it. Sitting straight in her chair, she looked at him as he said, 'I'm speaking for your own good as well as mine. Oh, I know I'm pleading for myself but . . . but on the other hand I know your heart isn't in this. Look, it's not too late to call it off. And I promise you, I swear on it, Jane, I'll take a pull at myself. I won't sell the bottom land, I'll get another hand in. I'll see to things myself, I'll take over . . .'

'You couldn't do better than Davie does.'

He drew his hand a few inches backwards and stared at her before he said, 'No, I know I couldn't. I'm not saying I could. I'll always need Davie. But . . . but there's things I could do to . . . Oh! Oh!' He now waved his hand in front of his face. 'I know I should have done them before, but Jan' – he used his old pet name for her – 'don't marry old Hedley, don't leave me, please.' On the last words his voice had dropped to a thin whisper.

Two years ago, even a year ago, if he had made such a plea she would have flown down the table and put her arms about him and held his head to her and said, 'As long as you need me, Amos, I'll never leave you.' But she knew now, and with a deep certainty that were she to comply with his selfish demand, he would, in a very short while, forget his promise to reform and argue and defend his right to do so. Oh, she knew Amos; to her cost she knew Amos. Never had she imagined that there would come a time when she would look at him coolly and see him as he really was, a bitter, totally selfish man; for, only eighteen years old, he was already a man in looks and mind . . . and in one particular, which was certainly not affected by his handicap.

As she walked from the table she said, 'I am marrying Arnold next week, Amos, and nothing you can say will change my mind. It's too late.' She was, she imagined, passing beyond arm's length of him when, with the agility that always surprised her, he leaned sideways, stretched out one arm, while hanging on to the table with the other hand and, grabbing hold of her skirt tugged her fiercely towards him.

When her hip hit the table she cried out, 'Amos! stop it. Have you gone mad?'

'No, I haven't gone mad . . . I am. Remember? You have told me on several occasions over the past two years that I am mad; everything I do comes under the heading of madness to you. Now, before I show you how really mad I can get, I ask you again not to leave me.' There was no plea in his voice now, and although he had said, 'I ask you,' it was more in the nature of a command.

'Leave go of my skirt.'

'I will when I'm ready. You're going to listen to me. What do you expect to get out of a marriage with old Hedley . . . now don't tell me he's only forty. I know his age. But add twenty years on to that and you've got the real man. Why, you'd get

203

more out of Will Curran than you would out of him. He's never seen a bare backside in his life, not even a child's. Do you think he'd want to look at yours . . . ?'

The force of her blow sent his head bumping against the back of the chair. If she had attacked him like a dog and bitten him he couldn't have been more surprised by her reaction. She stood back from him. Her face was not flushed with indignation but drained like a piece of bleached calico. The pumping of her heart was heaving her small breasts and pulsing in her neck. Her words, when she spoke, spurted out in jerks as if each one had to surmount an obstacle. 'F . . . father was right. He . . . he was right all along with regards to you. I've . . . I've heard said you were a devil, and . . . and you are, a . . . a wicked-minded devil.'

She ran out of the room, while he remained seated at the table, his hands spread out before him as if taking his weight. Her attack had surprised him in more ways than one. What had he said to make her so mad? That old Hedley wouldn't want to see her backside? He had said worse things than that in her presence. He had never seen her so wild, not even on the day he aimed at smashing up the whole house and she had literally fought with him, braving flying vases and bric-à-brac. Did she care for old Hedley all that much? No, she couldn't; she was just keeping to an agreement made years ago.

He lifted one hand now and felt his cheek. She had struck him, and no light blow; but he wouldn't hold that against her. It was a wonder she hadn't done it years ago; he knew he had tried her patience beyond endurance at times. But didn't she understand that you always tried the patience of those you loved? Didn't she understand that he loved her, in spite of everything he had done to her, he loved her? Anyway, she was all he'd had to love since they took Biddy away. And now Biddy was going to be married. Her mother had made a point of telling Will Curran within his own hearing. By God! he'd like to slit that one's throat. If there was anyone on this earth he hated it was Molly Geary, and he would have given her short shrift before now if it wasn't for the fact that she had him nobbled. It was true he had only her word for it, but he had to take it just in case. And now it looked as if he was going to be left with her. She would order things pretty much her own way once Jane was gone . . .

There were so many reasons why Jane shouldn't go, so many.

What would it be like at night in the winter when the snow was on the ground for weeks on end and he couldn't get into the town to ease his body's needs? He had been like a caged lion last winter, but a lion with a gentle keeper, a keeper he knew he could devour, metaphorically speaking, any time he chose. Now this keeper was leaving him, and there was the winter ahead.

But there wasn't only the winter to worry about, there were the nights in the near future when, because his bank balance was almost nil, he would be unable to enjoy the one thing that gave him real pleasure.

He had over the past eighteen months become a respected patron in Rafferty's Rooms; a seat was kept especially for him, he was a man among men. There, no one treated him as a youth; he knew that some of them were afraid of him. For the first six months his luck had been just average, then there was a time when everything he touched came up for him. During this period he had never gone to the tables more than twice in the same coat and waistcoat; what was more, Rafferty's niece had been very attentive to him. She was a bit long in the tooth, but after all, he had to face it, his choice outside the brothels was limited.

But it was those long winter nights ahead of him that were really worrying him, when with Jane gone he'd be deprived both mentally and physically. No one to talk with; he no longer found even slight amusement talking to those about the farm. What had he in common with Will Curran, Mickey, or even Davie Armstrong for that matter? It was strange about Davie. He would have been more than willing to listen to his yarns of the sea if they had been forthcoming, but the man was reticent. There was an aloofness about him that did not fit his position. True, he would discuss any point concerning the farm, but beyond that it was as if he had drawn a line. At one time he had wondered if it was he who was Molly's confidant, but had discarded the suggestion, going on what Will Curran had said that she was as much cow splatter to Davie, and he treated her as such, stepping out of her way whenever possible.

But in spite of Davie's manner, which irritated him at times because of its entire lack of subservience, he still retained for him the feeling the man had engendered years ago – he liked the sailor, in fact when he came to consider it he liked the sailor better than anyone else he knew, except, of course, Jane.

Jane . . . Jane. He touched his cheek again. Next week, and

for the rest of her life she'd be in the Vicarage with old Hedley. Apart from everything else it wasn't right; she might be thirty, and past the marrying age, but in a strange way she still remained a girl, a very young girl. It didn't seem right that she should be broken in by old Hedley.

He sat quite still for almost fifteen minutes; his face had taken on a look of deep concentration. When at last he slid off the chair and got on to his crutches he hobbled slowly from the room, went out through the front door, across the farmyard, and over the fell towards Shale Tor.

Two

'Is that you, Davie lad?'

'Aye, Granda, I'll be up in a minute.' Davie took the brown teapot to the hob and mashed the tea from the black spurting kettle. Then putting out his hand he went to pull a chair up to the fire to sit for a few minutes while the tea brewed, and to give himself a breathing space before going upstairs to talk and listen to the old 'un, but his action was halted by old Sep's voice, high now, calling, 'Davie! Davie! come up a minute. Here, quick!'

Thinking there was something wrong, he bounded up the stairs and burst into the small low-ceilinged bedroom to see his grandfather leaning towards the window, peering out into the deepening twilight.

'Come here a tick.'

'What's up with you, old 'un?'

'Nowt, nowt. Just get on your hunkers and follow me finger.'

Leaning over the bed, Davie looked in the direction in which the horny finger was pointing, and after screwing up his eyes he studied the far landscape for a moment. 'What you hoping to see?' he asked. 'There's nothin' out there.'

'Hold your horses, an' keep your eyes on this side of the Tor, above the road. Now, what do you see?'

Again Davie paused, then said, 'It could be a sheep going up the path. No, too big for that. Well, a wild pony strayed in.'

'It's no sheep an' no wild pony.' The old man's voice was low.

'Four nights running he's gone up there and around, on dark ... yon's Master Amos.'

'Master Amos! Don't be silly, old 'un; you can't make out what that is from this distance, man or beast, not in this light you can't.'

'Can't I, lad? Well, there's one thing I've kept, an' that's me keen sight, together with me mind; I'm neither blind nor in me dotage. No matter what's gone wrong with me limbs, those two faculties are much as they always were, an' that thing you see movin' over yonder is Master Amos. I tell you he's skited across those fields like a devil in a gale of wind these past few nights, an' always on dark ... now why, I ask you, why?'

'Perhaps he's got some piece from the village he meets up there. Some of them's not particular.'

Sep shook his head. 'Why should he go up there for his sport when he can get it in Rafferty's back room? Anyway, it would be a bit uncomfortable. Blow the hairs off your chin up there. No, you know what, lad? I smell a rat.'

Davie turned his head and looked at the old man, and like an echo rising from the past the words conjured up the scene in the kitchen all those years ago when his granda had said, 'I smell a rat,' and the rat had turned out to be the master. His granda was good at smelling rats although he couldn't unearth them. And now he smelt a rat with regard to Master Amos.

What was that legless giant doing up on the Tor at this hour? Tomorrow morning, first thing, he'd make it his business to take a walk up there. It was some long time since he had been up there himself, for with one thing and another he had more than his hands full down here, but tomorrow morning as soon as it was light he'd take a dander to Shale Tor, and maybe he'd unearth the rat.

At about the time Sep had called down to Davie, Jane was helping Arnold to pack the last of her possessions into the old Vicarage trap. And it was an old trap. It was old when Arnold had first taken up his position at the Vicarage, and since then its shafts had only known two ponies; the present one, Betty by name, was eighteen years old. She was sweet natured and patient, as a pony who pulled a parson should be. She had never taken fright or bolted; she was known far and wide and was loved by old and young alike, and her middle was inclined to thickness because of the fruit and tit-bits she received.

Jane went to her head now and patted her while Arnold lit the side lamps, remarking as he did so, 'The glass has cracked in both panels of this one. You wouldn't think a candle would generate so much heat, would you?'

'No, Arnold, no, you wouldn't.'

They stood together now at the back of the trap. She could just see his face. His eyes were so kindly, so full of tenderness and concern. She told herself yet again that she was very fond of Arnold, very fond; yet when he put his arms out and drew her gently into them she stiffened. It was only the slightest movement of resistance but he felt it and said reassuringly, 'It's all right, my dear, there is no one about.' He turned his head to look one way, then the other. 'All are going to their rest, animals, men and women alike. God made the night for rest and for . . . ' The word that jumped into her own mind was love, but when, after a slight pause he added peace, she wondered if in the future his stilted phraseology, his pedantic way of speaking might not get on her nerves. He had taught her to speak correctly, he had corrected her diction from when she was small, and later had tried to guide her thinking, but in the latter he had never succeeded, for her thoughts had always run wild.

When his lips touched hers they created no responsive feeling; his fingers caressing her wrists twanged the strings of passion in her more than his lips did; but he was Arnold, dear, dear Arnold, and the day after tomorrow she would be his wife.

Her books and two cases of clothes were all the personal possessions she was taking with her, although Amos had been surprisingly generous at the last. He was giving her the china cabinet from the drawing-room, and at least a third of the cutlery, besides the small silver tea service that had never been used, and also the furniture from her bedroom; all these would go to the Vicarage tomorrow on the farm cart.

Over the past few days Amos's manner towards her had been exemplary; she had never known him to be kinder, or more considerate. He was, she knew, trying to make up to her for the scene in the dining-room. As he had said last night, he had only one sister and he wanted her to go on loving him, no matter where she was. She had been very touched, and she told herself again that if only he had been like this over the past two years she could not have borne to leave him.

'Good-night my dear, dear Jane. Only one more parting and then we'll be together, always together.' He now took her face tenderly between his hands, adding, 'Don't be afraid, my dear, of anything. Your peace of mind will be my whole concern; you will know nothing but tenderness and consideration at my hands.'

'Oh Arnold! Arnold!' She was near to tears, and impulsively she clung to him, almost fiercely, until he laughed shakily and said, 'There now, there now, I must be away; even Betty is getting impatient.' His lips touched hers gently; and then he got up into the trap, and immediately Betty moved off.

She followed the trap until it passed through the farm gates into the road and there she called, 'Good-bye, Arnold. Good-bye.' And he answered her, 'Good-bye, my dear. Good-bye.' Then she stood watching the jogging lights disappear into the distance.

It was dawn the next morning when the trap and pony and parson were found at the bottom of the valley. The parson was lying beneath the pony; the trap had disintegrated into match-wood underneath the boulders that had come down in the land-slide from Shale Tor.

Three

'She's like someone demented.' Molly stared down at Davie. 'She's bent on getting up, but the doctor said she had to stay put for at least another week or so. An' she hardly opens her mouth, except to say "Yes, Molly. No, Molly. Thanks, Molly." She lies there, starin' ahead, for all the world as if she was seeing something that wasn't there. You know what I mean?'

Davie nodded, then absent-mindedly pushed away from him the head of the cow he was milking.

'And you know somethin' else? She's never opened her mouth to him, not once, leastways not when I've been there.'

Davie turned his head sharply towards her now as he asked, 'Has she said anything, I mean why she's not speakin' to him?'

'No, not a word. But I can say this, he's been different since the parson went. Give him his due, he's done everything in his power . . .'

'Aye, he's done everything in his power.'

'What did you say? What did you say, Davie?'

'I was just thinkin'.'

Molly continued to look at him for almost a full minute before she said quietly, 'Biddy's bein' married the day.'

Again his head jerked towards her. 'She is? Well, well. Now why didn't you go down? Why didn't you?'

'I was, I was for it, but I ask you, could I leave Miss Jane like this? She hasn't a soul to turn to; not even the old crabs who used to swarm round the parson come visitin' her ... But that's 'cos of him, they're feared of him. I've never seen anybody so lost lookin' as her, so I couldn't go off.'

Davie stared into her round hazel eyes. She had a heart for people's troubles; as he had said afore, he'd give her credit for that. But it wasn't right, she should have been at her lass's wedding, she should have had that much out of life. He checked his softened thinking with regards to her; he no longer held any animosity towards her yet he was still determined within himself that she wasn't getting any further than his outer skin. And so he said, 'I think the best thing would be if she did get up. Lying there, she'll just brood. The days are cuttin' in; she should get out in the air while the weather's fit. I would let her get up if I was you.'

'Aye, perhaps you're right.' She gazed at him as she nodded; then she turned slowly away.

Again he pushed at the cow's muzzling head. Then rising, he unloosened the chain that held her to the milking stall and slapped her rump as she backed out and followed the rest of the small herd into the fields. He then carried the last pail of milk into the dairy where Mickey, pausing in the business of filling a churn from surrounding buckets, remarked flatly, 'Don't know how much you've got there, Davie, but this's down again; soon not be worth the cartage into town.'

Davie was on the point of retorting sharply, 'Well, that's not your worry,' when he checked himself. Mickey was a good lad, and in a way he was concerned for the place, for he had been bred on it. It was his home, he had known no other, but the lass he was courting had no mind to start life here. Moreover, she was scared to death of Master Amos, so in a short time he'd likely follow Johnnie and start his married life elsewhere. What he said was, 'It's a problem I wish I could see the end of.'

Mickey asked now, 'Do you think there's any truth in this business of him sellin' the bottom fields?'

'I should say there's no smoke without fire, lad.'

'But how's he goin' to go on for hay and winter feed, he's not daft, he knows that if you can't grow it you've got to buy it?'

'You don't need winter feed if you haven't got any cattle.'

'You mean . . . you mean he'd do away with the lot? But, but how would he live?'

'Sheep and pigs he says. Sheep on the hills and just enough land to grow tatties, an' a cow or two for his own use. That's how he sees things.'

'God! the place'll be no better than a shanty plot.'

'You've said it, lad; no better than a shanty plot.'

'Eeh! it's a wonder the master doesn't turn in his grave.'

'It's my guess he's turned so often of late he's so dizzy he's havin' to hang on to the handles.'

Mickey's burst of laughter brought a slow chuckle from Davie, then he was laughing as loud as the young fellow.

'Eeh! that was funny, Davie.' Mickey wiped his eyes. 'It does you good to laugh.'

'Aye Mickey, it does you good to laugh.' He turned away thinking, 'tis strange how a man changes, for who would have thought I'd crack a joke over McBain.

A few minutes later when crossing the yard he stopped as he saw Molly come running from the house. 'What is it?' he asked.

'She's up an' gone, she's gone out. She's not in the house anywhere.'

'Well, don't frash yourself; she's done what we said she should do, she's gone for a walk, taken the air.'

'No, no.' She shook her head. 'I don't think she's put any clothes on, and she doesn't seem right in her mind. There's no knowin' what she might do.'

'No clothes on!' He screwed up his face, then said quickly, 'I'll go up on the ridge and look over the land from there, you go down by the burn.'

'But if she's not there . . . ?'

'Well, go and see, woman. How do you know she won't be there until you go and see?' His voice was harsh, and he saw her bridle for a moment before she turned sharply away.

He ran swiftly into the road now, across the fields, over the stone walls and up on to the ridge. The sky was high, the light was clear. It was silvery white light through which you could see for miles. He picked out the various paths and roads, and saw on one what could be the trap returning from Hexham bearing the 'Lord of The Manor' back to what remained of Cock Shield Farm. His thoughts were always tinged with sarcasm when they dwelt on Amos. Finally, he looked up towards the Tor, because that was the last place, he imagined, she would make for. But there, on the winding path, moving around the face was a figure. It could have been anyone from this distance, man, woman or child, but immediately he knew it was her.

He leaped down the slope, the impetus acting like springs to his feet, then raced across the fields, swung himself over three low stone walls, all the while descending into the valley to a spot just to the right of where he had helped to lift the body of the parson in the early morning of the day before he was to be married.

He was gasping for breath when he reached the Tor road. Then he was running up the winding path, and when he reached the summit he stopped, both from lack of breath and surprise, for there she was in her night attire standing in front of the rocking stone, her finger pointing down to it, as if she was accusing it personally.

He drew in a number of short breaths before he moved slowly towards her. He reached to within three yards of her and she didn't turn or move from her position. Very softly he said, 'Miss Jane!' Then again, more firmly now, 'Miss Jane!'

Her finger wavered, her eyes blinked. Slowly she turned her head and looked at him. Then like a child whimpering after receiving a fright, she said, 'Davie . . . oh, Davie.'

'It's all right, Miss Jane.' He moved another step towards her. Her arm dropped to her side now. Her body looked limp, slumped, she didn't seem aware that she was still in her night attire. Her nightdress was made of lawn with a small frilled collar; the sleeves came down to the wrists and ended in frills; the hem fell below her ankles and showed a faded pair of blue velvet slippers, dust covered now, as was the hem of the nightdress. He said gently, 'It's all right, Miss Jane, it's all right. There's nothing to worry about.'

'Oh yes – Davie – yes – there – is – something – something to worry about.' She was speaking like a child now, her words resting on her tongue before she delivered them. 'The stone . . . Davie.' She turned now and pointed again to the

212

stone. 'He could never move this . . . not this one.'

God Almighty! she knew; that's what it was, she knew. It had turned her brain because she knew. His granda was right and his smelling of rats. What was to be done?

'Davie.'

'Yes, Ja . . . Miss Jane.'

'Look.' She held out her hand and caught his, and now she led him across the top of the Tor to the raw jagged edge left by the fall. He had to check her from going too near. Her finger was again pointing stiffly, but downwards towards their feet now, as she said, 'He had them all lined up here. The boys from the village, he said the boys from the village had moved them, but I knew a long time ago he had done it himself, Davie.' Her voice was breaking now and her face, like a child's, was crumpling into tears. 'Da–vie, he killed Arnold. Amos ki–lled Arnold. I . . . I heard Betty scream. A horse screams when it's frightened, Davie. It screams louder than anything in the world a horse does. Davie . . . Davie, he killed Arnold. He said he wouldn't let me leave him; he was lonely, he wouldn't let me go, so he killed Arnold.'

The tears were dropping over her lower lids now, big, slow drops. They seemed to be falling into his own throat, swelling it. She still had hold of his hand. He put out his other and took her arm and drew her gently back from the edge. Now she was gulping her words out while she blinked up into his face. 'He . . . he was drinking when I went into the dining-room that night. He . . . he didn't expect me. Davie, he didn't expect to see me. He . . . he started, and, and he was . . . was drinking. Amos doesn't drink. He gambles but he doesn't drink. Whisky, a big glass of whisky. Gulping . . . gulping it.'

'There now. There now. Don't distress yourself!'

'Davie, Davie, I'm . . . I'm lost and I've nowhere to go. I can't . . . I can't get away from him, and I cannot tell the police because . . . because I still love him, Davie. He . . . he is my brother and I'm all he has, but . . . but I hate him, Davie. I love him and I hate him. I am distressed, Davie, I am very, very distressed.' Her voice had risen; her face was contorted; the tears were choking her, her sobs turning into wails. When she fell against him he put his arms about her and stroked her hair while he murmured, 'There, there, there now, cry it out. That's it, cry it out.' And all the while he was aware of her body near his, Miss Jane's body near his. No, not Miss Jane's body, Jane's body.

His face was resting in her hair and her wailing was subsiding when Molly's head and shoulders appeared over the edge of the Tor. He stared down at her but didn't move. She looked up at him and for a time she didn't move either.

When she came up to them his head was straight but he still had his arms around Jane, and he said, 'She cried it out, she'll be better now. Let's get her down.'

Between them they led her down the Tor and back into the house. Then Molly took her upstairs and put her to bed, and almost immediately she went to sleep.

Later, when Molly entered the kitchen she was surprised, and yet she wasn't, to see Davie waiting for her. He said, 'She knows that he killed the parson.'

'Who? You don't mean that he . . . that he did that an' all?' There was horror in her face and voice.

'Aye, this is the second notch on his stick.'

'Oh, dear God!'

'If I had gone up that night when me granda told me I could have prevented it.'

'You've known then?'

'Aye, sort of. The old 'un had spotted him going up the Tor a number of times when it was late. He must have been waiting for the parson going home. Still' – he turned slowly about – 'he would have got him some other way, he wouldn't have let it be. He's a devil, a devil from deep hell, that one.'

'What are you gona do about it?'

'What can I do? There's no proof; no one saw him do it, no more than they saw him kick his father downstairs.'

'I've still got the coat to prove that.'

'It's only your word against his, and who's going to believe that a legless man could climb that staircase post; it would take me all me time to reach that beam. No, you would come worse off out of that I'm afraid, as I would if I went to the polis about this, because I doubt if Miss Jane would speak against him.' He moved towards the door and, his voice thick, he muttered, 'There's only one thing I wish now, that I were away to hell out of this.'

She stood looking towards the closed door. She, too, wished he was away to hell out of this; but she knew that she was the only one who did wish it, because in his heart he himself didn't. Nor did Miss Jane.

There had been something niggling at her mind for a long time now, for two years in fact, ever since he came back on to the farm, and this was it; it had come to light when she saw them standing together up there.

Miss Jane might have been out of her wits but he wasn't, his face had been buried in her hair like that of a lover.

She couldn't stand this, not this; she couldn't bear any more, she was tired, weary. She began to cry, slow tears which rolled down her cheeks unheeded until, sitting down at the kitchen table, she dropped her head on to her folded arms and gave way to the pain inside her. As her tears, like a rising river, gushed down her face she cried out against her life and fate. She didn't deserve to be treated like this, she didn't, she didn't. She had paid for what she had done. People altered; she had just been a lass, he should understand that. Was he doing it to spite her? No, no, she didn't think that; it was one of those things that just happened. But it had happened between the two people she liked best in the world, loved best in the world. God, she wouldn't be able to witness it, she couldn't, she'd have to get away. Fred Bateman would have her. He had been knocking on for her since his wife died. He had five bairns and there was still time to have some of her own. God in heaven, what a prospect! But it was either that or stay here and watch them grow closer.

Slowly she raised her head and blinked rapidly as she stared at the fireplace framed in its gleaming copper pans and brass, and she said to herself, 'But . . . but they haven't started yet, the parson's been buried but a week. Don't meet trouble halfway, wait till they start, wait till it's in the open. And then there'll be nothing you or anybody else can do about it.'

On this last thought she suddenly exclaimed aloud, 'Oh my God!' There was one who'd do something about it if she knew anything. They said everything went in threes. Well, Davie Armstrong was no fool, so if anything would deter him from letting his ideas run wild with regards to Miss Jane, the knowledge that he could be Master Amos's third choice should do it. She was a fool, but she'd sit tight and wait.

Four

It was almost a year to the day before it came into the open. Molly had watched it gradually grow. She had watched them both fighting it, and in the process she had become sorry for them, and many a time she had wished to God they would get it over with and put her out of her misery.

Davie, too, wished it would come to a head, while at the same time fearing to speak. Not just because any alliance between the daughter of Angus McBain and himself would be derided from all quarters; for he was well aware that The Manor would, for a convenient time, forget that Cock Shield was not the place it once had been and that Jane was no longer the daughter of a gentleman farmer, they would consider only that, in stooping to him, she had broken a social code. The main deterrent was the fear of what Amos would do. What would be the outcome if he were to go to him and say, 'I want to marry your sister; and, what is more to the point, she wants to marry me'? Hadn't he already accounted for two people who had stood in his way? He could understand him doing for his father, but not the man who had been kind to him from birth, who had tutored him and been his friend, his only friend, other than Jane; if he could kill the parson in cold blood what value would the madman put on himself?

What Jane's thoughts were concerning Amos's reaction on this particular subject he did not know; he was sure of one thing, he had only to speak and she would be his.

Besides everything else his days were heavy with work and worry concerning the farm; also that his grandfather was slowly letting go of his vital grip on life. For the past few nights he had sat by the old man's bedside and each time that sleep had overcome him he had awakened to the thought, he's gone. But no, there he lay looking into the candlelight, his breathing scarcely audible. Yet sometimes the old man would speak in a strong clear voice as if twenty years had slipped from him. 'Are you there, lad?'

'Aye, Granda.'

'Now why can't you get yourself away to bed, you've got work facin' you in the mornin'?'

216

'I'm all right, Granda.'

'All right be damned! Look, lad, when my time's near I'll know, an' I'll tell you. An' don't you worry your head. Now I'm tellin' you, don't worry your head, 'cos we've all got to go. Feathers in the fire; that's all we are, lad, feathers in the fire.'

Feathers in the fire! Aye, that's all they were, feathers in the fire. Life slipped by. It was galloping by him, and what was he doing with it? What had he done with it? Nothing. He should have a wife and a family now, be a settled man, and here he was, neither flesh, fish, nor fowl.

Last night he'd had a full night's rest for the old man seemed so much better. It was as if he'd had a new lease of life. And now today, for his dinner he had drunk every drop of broth Molly had brought him up.

Davie took the basin from his hand, saying, 'Well, you made a clean sweep of that, old 'un?'

'Aye; never tasted better, lad. She's a good cook, is Molly.'

'Aye, she's a good cook, Granda.'

'And a good lass an' all.' The old man's pale blue eyes looked up at Davie, and he repeated, 'She's a good lass an' all, Davie.'

He was on his way to the door as he said, 'Yes, she's a good lass, Granda.' Then turning about he added, 'Now don't forget I'll be gone for a few hours; there's hardly a mouthful of hay for the animals. But whether Morton'll give us any more tick remains to be seen.'

'You say he's been gone since yesterday, lad?'

'Aye, Granda, our lord an' master has gone on his monthly spree. He must have got the money for the land some time last week. Well, it's to be hoped he cleared up Morton and Rymill; if not, it won't be only the horses that'll go without their feed.'

'He's a bad 'un that one, a real bad 'un. Lookin' back on things it's a pity Molly didn't do what she set out to do in the first place, that's what I say.'

'I'm with you there, old 'un.' And strangely, he was; the time was long past when he had stopped condemning Molly for attempting to drown the child, now he blamed himself for having interfered. That's what you got for doing the right thing. Playing God, as Molly had said.

'God help Miss Jane, that's all I say.'

Davie could have added, 'And I'm with you there an' all,' but instead he said, 'Now mind, behave yourself. I'll be back as

217

quick as I can; Molly will keep lookin' in. Ta-rah.'

'Ta-rah, lad. Don't hurry yourself; take it easy for once.'

He went across the narrow square of landing and into his room, and there he changed into his town clothes, which were the trousers of his seafaring days and a worsted coat of a lighter shade. He put on a clean blue striped shirt and a neckerchief; then he picked up his hard bowler and went downstairs.

He had already harnessed the horse to the wagon and when he reached the yard he was surprised to see Jane standing beside it. She, too, was dressed for the town, and she said to him, 'Will you drive me in, Davie, I have business in Hexham?'

'On the wagon . . . Miss?'

'Yes, Davie, I . . . I don't mind the wagon.'

'But look' – he jerked his head up towards the sky – 'there's a storm brewin'. We might be caught in it, and there's no shelter unless you get under the tarpaulin.'

'I'll . . . I'll risk that, Davie. But . . . but I must get into town.'

'Very well, Miss.'

As he held out his hand and assisted her up on to the high wooden seat Molly came to the kitchen door, and he was aware of her eyes tight on him as he walked around the horse's head to the other side of the wagon and pulled himself up. Before giving a command to the horse he paused and, looking across the yard at her, he asked quietly, 'Will you give an eye to him?' For answer she inclined her head but didn't speak. 'Gee-up! there,' he said. 'Gee-up!' And the cart rumbled out of the yard.

They had gone some distance in silence when Jane said, 'You don't mind taking me in, Davie?'

'Mind?' He turned his head quickly towards her. 'Why should I mind?' He could have said, 'That's a daft question, Jane; I'm in no position to mind, now am I?'

She dropped her gaze from his and looked down at her hands, then said softly, 'I'm . . . I'm going to the jewellers, I'm going to sell some trinkets.'

There was a pause before he asked, 'Didn't he give you anything out of the sale?'

'No.'

'It's a bloody shame. Excuse me . . . Miss.'

'It's all right, Davie. I . . . I can endorse what you say; I, too, feel like saying, it's a . . . bloody shame.'

They glanced at each other. It was a moment when they

218

should have smiled, laughed. She had sworn. Once she had repeated after him, 'God Almighty!' and that had tickled him, but now she had sworn, even if politely, but they didn't smile.

They were looking ahead again when she said, 'I don't know whether they're saleable or not, but Mr Pearson is a very fair man, he would not cheat me. There isn't much, two signet rings, a gold lever watch and chain, and a gold and ivory cameo of my grandmother. They all belonged to my grandfather, and I came across them in a separate drawer. If . . . if he had seen them first I wouldn't have them now, for he claimed all he could lay his hands on at the time. But . . . but I felt justified in keeping these.'

'You were that. Aw' – he moved his head slowly – 'words fail me. They do.'

There followed another silence before he asked quietly, 'Where's it all going to end?'

'I wish I knew, Davie.'

'You can't go on like this for ever you know.'

She made no answer but after a while she asked, 'Do you think you'll get the hay?'

'If he's paid something off to Morton I will; if not I can see me coming back the way I'm goin'.'

They had jogged on for almost a mile before he spoke again, and then he remarked, lightly, 'Well, it looks as if we might miss the storm.'

'Yes, yes, it does.' She turned her eyes towards the sky, and now, her voice little more than a whisper and as if talking to herself, she said, 'I used to think there was no place in the world like this. I know I haven't travelled but I have read a lot about other places and I always found them wanting in comparison. Now I want to run from it, lose myself in a town, a city, where everything is flat; I never want to see a hill again.'

He passed no comment, but his hands gripped the reins tightly and the horse shook its head, impatient at the pull on its bit; it knew its pace along this stretch of the road and it was going to go no faster or no slower than was usual.

After a moment she said, 'You have seen most of the world, Davie, how do you compare it with this?'

'Oh, well like you, I found every place wantin', but like you I've changed. You can't blame the place, can you? It's people who want to make you stay or go, after all's said an' done.'

'When old Sep dies there'll be nothing to keep you?' Her face was turned towards him, and he didn't look at her for as long as it took the horse to do twenty paces; and then, his eyes slowly turning to meet hers, he said quietly, 'That depends.'

'On what, Davie?'

He saw that her lips were trembling and that her hands were locked tightly over her beaded handbag.

If he said 'You' he could be signing his death warrant. Yet that didn't really worry him, for forewarned was forearmed; he could let that young maniac know that he was aware of his two exploits and had taken his knowledge a step further than Molly had. He could tell him that he had sent a letter to a solicitor in Newcastle which was to be opened if anything happened to him – he had read about that trick in a book when he was at sea, but he could apply it here all right, and it would put a stop to his gallop. So what was he hanging back for?

The answer he gave her was, 'Oh, a number of things,' and when he saw her turn her head slowly away he wanted to draw the horse up and pull her into his arms and say, 'Jane, Jane, let's stop playing games, let's go ahead with what we both want, and be damned to it.'

They spoke no more until they reached Hexham, and as he helped her down from the cart it began to rain.

'How long are you going to be?' she asked.

'Half-an-hour if I get the hay; if I don't, well then, just the time it'll take me to get to Morton's and back.'

She looked along the street now and said, 'The tea rooms; I'll go and have a cup of tea after I have finished the business at the jeweller's. I will see you from the window. But in any case I'll be here in this street.'

'Good enough.' He nodded at her, then added, 'Don't let him beat you down.'

'I won't.'

He watched her walk up the street towards the jeweller's shop. From behind she looked like a young girl, and she walked like one, quick and sprightly. But that was from the back. From the front she looked like a lost woman, a lost and lonely woman, a woman who had missed life. Even Molly didn't carry the look on her face that she did. But then, Molly hadn't missed life, had she? She'd had it to the full: 'No matter whose name I take, Master, there'll only ever be you. Always remember that, there'll only ever be you.' He had lived with those words for years. But lately he had scarcely recalled them, and so he didn't know why he was doing it now. Oh yes he did; it was a sort of comparison. The figure going along there hadn't been handled by any man; she was as a man expected a woman to be when he took her to his wife, whereas Mistress Molly had given her virginity away, first in a hay rick, then, while still a very young lass, had let an old man take her, slaver over her. Aw! to the devil! He should be worryin' about the hay; it was the animals' needs he must think about at the present moment, his own must wait . . .

To his surprise Mr Morton met his order without comment, which meant that Amos had settled the bill, or at least had paid something off it.

Within a few minutes of his drawing the cart up outside the tea shop Jane made her appearance at the door, and, without speaking, he helped her up into the seat. As they drove off it began to rain, and before they had left the town they were sitting under a downpour.

Urging the horse into a trot he said, 'I think we're in for it. Look over there.'

She turned her head and peered through the rain over the gooseberry fields and orchards and remarked briefly, 'Yes, it's black.' Then looking ahead again, she added, 'It doesn't matter.'

'You could sit under the cover at the back, that would save you some.'

'No, no, Davie; don't worry, I'll be all right. It won't be the first time I've been wet through.' She gave a little laugh.

'But this is going to be a bad 'un by the looks of it.'

By the time they came to the crossroads and were still four miles from home, the lightning was flashing and the thunder was rolling like an army of drums above their heads, and he shouted to her, 'I'll take the main road; it'll be longer but it won't be so bogged.'

She didn't answer for she had scarcely heard him, she had her head down and her shoulders hunched against the onslaught of the wind and rain.

When a terrific clap of thunder burst above them the horse stopped, tossed its head, then attempted to rear, and it took Davie all his time to hold it. Pushing the reins into her hand and shouting, 'Hold hard!' he jumped from the cart and went to the horse's head and led him further up the road to where a gap in the stone wall opened into a field. Tying the reins firmly to an iron spike that had once supported a gate he then reached up and almost pulled her down from the seat, and ran with her to the back of the cart. There he pushed her unceremoniously underneath the tarpaulin cover and in between the bales of hay; then he drew himself up and in beside her.

It was black dark under the cover. Their heads were touching it and the rain was beating on it and into their brains like so many hammers; they were half sitting, half reclining and close together. There was no lead up to the beginning. He put his arms about her and held her quietly for a moment to gauge her reaction, and when her face fell to the side of his and her lips moved over his ear he pressed her thin body into him. His hand made no fumbling movement as it went among her wet clothes, and she did not utter a word; no words at all passed between them. When she moaned it was more like the muffled lilt of a song . . .

Half-an-hour later he lifted her down from under the cover, and she stepped into another world. The storm had passed, the last rays of the setting sun were jewelling the whole world, her whole world; as far as she could see everything was sparkling. She brought her gaze to his face and she muttered on a cracked note, 'Oh, Davie . . . Davie.'

'Jane!' His arms went round her again, but gently now. 'Are you all right? You . . . you won't regret it?'

'I'm all right, Davie. And no, never. Whatever happens, never, never will I regret it.' There was no break in her voice now, her words were clear and strong, and she added, 'It's been a long time.'

'Too long. Aye, too long. Ten years too long.'

Her face widened into a smile, and she asked now, 'Did you care for me then?'

He blinked, trying to recall how he felt ten years ago, and he threaded his imagination with kindness as he said, 'I must have; anyway, I knew you should be married. And . . . and now I think the same, but what about it, how do we stand?'

'Oh! Davie, I'd marry you tomorrow, or now, now.'

'How's he going to take that?' He stared down into her face. 'We've got to be prepared for him trying to get rid of me.'

'Oh, no! he wouldn't.' Her voice was filled with horror. 'Not that; he'd never go that far. Besides, he . . . he likes you.'

'He liked the parson at one time. If he only killed where he hated like he did with your fath – ' He stopped. She was leaning

222

back from him, still within his hold but with her mouth dropping open. 'No . . . o!' She brought the word out slowly.

'Yes; swinging from the beam at the top of the stairs.'

'Oh, dear Lord!' She now put her hand over her mouth, and he said softly, 'I'm sorry. I'd have to let it come out now. I'm a fool, it's spoilt it.'

'No, no.' She forced her attention back to him. 'No, no, Davie; nothing could spoil this. It was just the shock. And yet . . . yet, you know it wasn't such a shock as it should have been, I feel I must have known all the time. All the things he did, then the way he went on, and the will. He looked for the will.' She shook her head. 'Davie' – she was clinging to him now – 'we could go away, we could work together. I got thirty-five pounds for the things. I . . . I think it was a fair price. We could go any time . . . ' She stopped, the words hanging on her lips; then she muttered, 'I forgot . . . I forgot . . . old Sep. But . . . but Davie, as soon as you are free we will go?' It was a question.

'We'll go. That is a promise. As soon as granda goes we'll go.'

'We mustn't tell anyone about . . . about us.' Her face was flushed and her eyes held a shyness. 'We must act as if nothing has happened; we must not even let Molly know.'

When his look altered just the slightest and a shadow seemed to pass over his face she said quietly, 'Molly . . . will this hurt her?' And he answered on a high note, 'Hurt Molly? No, no; why should it hurt Molly?'

She had not questioned his feelings with regards to Molly. It was herself he loved, had he not proved it, so he could not think anything of Molly.

'Come along, we must get back.'

She did not move immediately but stared at him for a moment, then with an impetuous gesture that she might have used when she was seventeen she flung her arms around his neck and, gazing up into his face, whispered, 'Oh I love you, Davie. I love you, I love you. I've always loved you. I cannot remember the time when I didn't love you. Oh darling, my darling.' When her mouth came on his he did not answer it for a moment; his whole body was still under a sense of wonder, the wonder of her voice, her words and what they were telling him. This would be a different kind of love altogether from that which he would have experienced if he had taken up with any one of his own standing, such as Molly Geary or her like. This was going to be not only a love of the body and its wants, but of

223

the other emotions, of words and tenderness. He was going to learn a lot from this love.

'Aw, Jane! Jane!' He held her from him and looked his wonder into her face. Then drawing her to him he kissed her, a gentle lingering kiss.

Five

Jane stood in front of the window peering out into the dark night; she was standing in blackness for she had quenched the light in her bedroom. She turned about and focused her gaze on the door, then groped her way towards it and stood listening. There was a strong wind blowing, and although it could not penetrate the thick walls it rattled the windows and created strange echoing sounds around the chimneys, but in her mind she separated these noises from those usually heard in the house, and the house appeared silent.

He had been up in his room for more than half-an-hour now but she must wait a little longer to make sure he was asleep. He had taken to drinking of late, not whisky like her father, nor yet wine, but beer, strong, thick stout. Stout was supposed to induce sleep and she was hoping that he had drunk enough of it to send him off quickly tonight. She would soon tell once she was outside his door for he snored in his sleep. He always had; it was, she thought, because of his short neck and deep chest.

Earlier in the evening she had felt like boldly saying, 'I am popping over to see old Sep; it may be for the last time.' But then, she had used that excuse before and old Sep hadn't died – she had never known anyone take so long in dying.

It was six weeks since the day Davie had driven her into Hexham; six weeks since she had been reborn, into joy, into ecstasy, but only once had they managed to be together since that night. She was being very careful, most circumspect, but it was so hard at times to control her feelings when she saw Davie. She had never paid so many daily visits to the cow byres as she had done these past few weeks for she felt impelled to see him often; at times she was driven to leave what she was doing and go into the yard on some pretext just to watch him at a distance. Sometimes she thought Molly had guessed her secret, for she would look at her with a strange look – she could not put a name to her expression.

She turned her back to the door and leaned against it and, clasping her joined hands to her mouth, she bit on the knuckles of her thumbs to prevent herself from hoping that old Sep would die tonight. Within a week of his going they could be away; the Gladstone bag was already packed in the bottom of the wardrobe; she required so little. The most important thing was money and the thirty-five pounds was safely hidden in the bottom of the bag.

It was strange, she considered, that Davie should have more money saved than her, she, who was the daughter of Angus McBain, at one time the richest farmer for miles around. If her father were to come back he would die a thousand deaths to see what had happened to his farm. Although towards the end of his days he himself had let it go somewhat, the place was now little more than a glorified smallholding with land hardly able to sustain a dozen cows, and that land so poor and deficient in the vital minerals that they had lost two cows during the last three weeks. Both had died with the shivers. The shivers had always been a warning that animals needed a change of pasture, but now there was nowhere for them to change to.

She turned and opened the door slightly and, putting her head on one side, listened. She thought she heard a movement from along the corridor. She knew that once he had the slightest suspicion of what was afoot he'd be quite capable of playing with her like a cat with a mouse. One thing she was certain of now, her brother was deformed not only in his body, but also in his mind, and that if she had to spend the winter with him, the spring would not find her sane. Last night he had looked at her across the dining table and with the smile that wasn't a smile on his face he had said, 'It's going to be a long winter, Sister.' He had never before called her sister. 'Soon there'll only be the two of us, now Mickey's gone, old Sep dying, and old Curran on his last legs. That only leaves Davie and Molly, and they'll likely go off together. I shouldn't be a bit surprised. What do you say?'

She hadn't been able to say anything; she had simply stared at him through the lamplight like a rabbit would at a stoat, until he added, 'Mind, I don't envy him that piece. But then there's been nobody else about to ease him, has there, and a

225

man has his needs.' Then she thought she'd be sick.

She had risen from the table, saying, 'If you have no other topic of conversation I'll bid you good-night.'

When she went to pass him he had put out his hand and held her, as he had done once before, and had said softly, 'You're an old maid, Jan; you'll go down to the grave an old maid. But I don't mind, I like you this way. As I said there'll soon be nobody else here but us, just we two, as it was in the beginning up in the attic. Yes, as it was in the beginning, is now, really, and ever shall be.'

Having wrenched herself from his hold she had to prevent herself from flying out of the room, flying out of the house yelling, 'Davie! Davie!' She was filled with panic at the thought that perhaps he knew and was playing with her. But then, in the quietness of her room, she reasoned that it was impossible for him to know anything. The second time that Davie and she had met privately had been on a black night, down by the burn, and at a time when Amos was away from home on one of his jaunts. So, she reasoned he could not know anything about them and that it was just the fear of what he might do to Davie were he to find out that was making her suspicious.

She tip-toed along the corridor, paused opposite his door, and when the rhythmic sound of his snoring came to her she went on and down the stairs and out of the house . . .

Amos heard her go. He rose from the bed fully clothed, donned a dark coat, pulled a dark cap on to his head, then on to the end of each crutch he tugged a lambswool stocking. When he went from the room his movements were not audible, not even to himself.

The play, he thought, was nearing its end. Jane was a fool. She had always been a fool, a soft-hearted fool, but he had given her the credit for more intelligence than she possessed.

If he hadn't ridden the main road on his way from Newcastle in the storm that day and seen his horse and wagon in the field and glimpsed the contortions under the tarpaulin, he would still have known there was something between them, for her every action when she returned to the farm had betrayed her. He hadn't known how much he loved her until he had watched her get down from the cart with her face aglow. It was then that his own body had been rent in two with a torment that was fresh to him.

The love that he'd had for Biddy had been that of a boy for a

226

girl; yet if it had been fulfilled it might have satisfied him, half-sister or no half-sister; but the love he now felt for his sister dimmed the feeling for Biddy, as a star would an oil lamp.

He had debated for some time what to do about Davie. The fact that he was the only man he had ever really liked had checked the suggestion of putting a quick finish to him, checked it, not actually dismissed it. In some strange way Davie represented life to him. He remembered that he first realised he was alive that day he jumped into the deep water in the burn, and it was ten to one he would have drowned if the sailor hadn't come down and got him. Moreover, hadn't he given him life in the first place? So he felt a certain reluctance about taking his life. He would be satisfied, he told himself, if he could put him somewhere where he would no longer be able to interfere.

He went noiselessly out into the yard, then in the direction of the cottages.

Molly was in the kitchen brewing some tea; her movements were slow as if she were carrying a weight on her body, and in her way she was, for her heart was like lead.

Things, she knew, were fast drawing to a head. Old Sep upstairs there; he'd surely go this time, then they'd go too. And what was left for her? What was she to do? Stay here and look after him? No! No, begod! Far better Fred Bateman and his squad than be here alone with that maniac, for who knew but he'd try and do her in next. She was no weakling but she'd have a job to fight off arms like his. He was a dirty fighter. She had seen him, supposedly in fun, in the yard there. He went for the legs and whipped them off the ground, then held on with a grip that was like no other man's!

She pulled a chair round to face the fire; she'd sit down a few minutes for she was tired to death. What was more, they could do without her going up there, oh aye, they could do without anybody going up there. For a moment bitterness like acid ran over her feelings for both of them, and she bowed her head and shook it slowly. Then it was brought sharply up and a startled exclamation came from her as she looked towards the back door and saw the muffled form of Will Curran standing there.

'In the name of God; what's up with you, sneakin' in . . . '

'Ssh! Ssh!' He held up a warning hand; then closing the door softly behind him, he came towards her saying, 'Are those curtains closed?'

'Curtains?' She turned her head sharply. 'Aye; what's up with you? You nearly scared the wits out of me.'

'The wits are nearly scared out of meself, never mind you.' He thrust his head towards her, muttering thickly, 'If he finds me here, he'll do for me, he's capable of it.'

'Who?'

'Who do you think? Look, I've left the trap tethered near the turnpike an' I had to practically crawl back in case he spotted me. I'm on me way into Hexham for the polis.'

'For the what!'

'That's what I said, for the polis. They're to come round at first light, he said, and 'vestigate; he's lost some things.'

'Name of God!'

'Aye, name of God. I said more than that when he got me out of me bed, me at my age. I told him I wasn't for goin' at first, an' then he put the screws on me. Near me time, he said, I wanted to finish me days in the cottage, didn't I? This night might be cold but the workhouse would be colder. That's what he said.'

'But who does he want the polis for?'

'Need you ask? There's only one he wants out of the way now, Davie. He's spotted what's been goin' on and found a way to put a stop to it. He's a cunnin' devil if ever there was one, by God! he is that. An' wicked. Aye!'

'How do you know what's going on?' She stared at him with her mouth slightly agape.

'I'm not blind.'

'What you going to do?'

'What can I do? I'll have to go, only I thought I'd put him wise, an' if he's got any sense he'll be out of it afore the mornin'.'

Molly stared at the old man standing before her, and Will Curran was an old man. She had never liked him and the thought of taking him for a husband had made her sick, yet in this moment she wanted to put out her hand and shake his; more so when he next said, 'I've got no love for Davie Armstrong for he stepped into the place that should rightly have been mine; comes back after fifteen years and just walks into it. It wasn't fair. But then, there's nowt fair in this life.' He stared at her. 'The luckiest one among us I guess is the old 'un upstairs; he's gettin' out of it.'

She said nothing, words were hard to come by in a situation

like this, but it was odd, she thought, that everyone had to suffer; even the ones you had no time for, ones you thought were too thick-skinned and dim-witted to feel, they too passed along a similar road to yourself, tripping over disappointments and heartbreaks all the way.

She stood staring at the door through which he had sidled out into the dark; then she turned about and rushed out of the room and up the stairs, remembering to tip-toe into the bedroom only at the last minute.

Old Sep was lying as he had been for the last twelve hours; he was in a coma and this time he wouldn't wake. She looked at Davie and Jane within a joined hand clasp from each other; she had no doubt but that their fingers had been linked a moment before. Beckoning them to come out on to the landing, she looked from one to the other in the dim light before she gabbled, 'Now listen, listen. He's on the war-path, he means business. Will Curran's just sneaked in by the back door to tell me he's on his way to Hexham for the polis. They'll be here by first light. It's . . . it's you he's after.' She pointed her finger at Davie. 'The message he's got to give is they must come and 'vestigate 'cos there's things missin'. He's . . . he's likely planted something in here.' She made a circular movement with her hand now. 'He's come in to see the old 'un when we've all been at work; he could easily have done it, planted somethin'.'

Neither of them had spoken while she was talking, but now Jane, turning and grasping Davie's hand, cried softly, 'Oh! Davie, Davie, I knew something like this would happen. You must get away; he'll . . . he'll have you imprisoned.' She stopped, and they both looked at Molly as she said, 'You'll both have to get yourselves away.' Her eyes came to rest on Davie's for a moment, and he gazed back at her. He was about to speak but changed his mind and, swinging around, he beat one fist into the palm of his other hand, saying, 'Who would believe it? I ask you, who would believe it?' Then he looked through the open door and to the bed and the heaving chest of his grandfather, and after a moment he said flatly, 'I'm not goin' till he goes, no matter what.'

'Don't be a blood . . . don't be a fool; the old 'un's already gone, he'll never wake again.'

'She's right. Molly's right, Davie. Molly's right; it's only a formality now. Please, please.' She had hold of his hands again. 'I'll stay until old Sep goes, and . . . and then I'll join you.'

He did not answer her for a minute. Then, his face screwing up, he said, 'God damn! if he's planted something in the house, then the thing to do is to find it. Look' – he touched Jane's arm – 'you sit by the bed and Molly and me here, we'll scour the place. It shouldn't take all that long; if there's anything to find we'll find it. We'll start downstairs. You take the scullery, Molly, I'll take the kitchen, an' we'll work our way up. And if there's any change' – he motioned his head towards the bed – 'give us a shout.'

Half-an-hour later the three of them were again standing on the landing looking at each other. They had scoured every crevice and cranny of the cottage. Davie had even turned out his old sailor bag, and remembering Amos's agility concerning beams, he had looked on the beam at the top of the stairs, but with no success.

'We don't even know what we're looking for,' he said thickly now.

'It'll . . . it'll be some form of jewellery,' Jane said; 'not money, you cannot identify money.'

'Perhaps he stuck it in the cow-shed somewhere,' said Molly. 'But then that would involve Will, wouldn't it?' She shook her head. 'No, whatever it is, it's in here. I feel it's in here.' She looked around for a moment; then fixing her gaze tight on Davie, she said, 'He'll have you, he means it. He must have been workin' up to this for some time, he doesn't do things by halves. Remember the other two. Look, I'll tell you what. As soon as it's light, have your things ready and go down to the malt house. If he thinks you've gone, he'll imagine you're far afield; he won't think you'd stick around here.'

Davie stared into Molly's face for a moment, but without seeing her. Then he said slowly as if having weighed everything up, 'I can't go while there's breath in him.'

'Do you think he would be happy knowing you were in prison?'

He turned and looked at Jane. Her face was white, her eyes large and filled with love and pain. 'Go to the malt house as Molly suggests, and . . . and I'll stay here with Sep until the end. Then I'll join you.'

Molly's tone was weary as she put it now, 'He's got you both taped. He's got us all taped. It'll be better, Miss Jane, if you go back to the house an' pretend to go to your bed. And you, Davie, do as we said, as soon as it's light go down to the malt house. An' if when the polis comes the idea that you might be down there enters into that maniac's head an' they make for there, I'll ring the bell good and hard. What do you say?'

There was silence among them for a moment, then Davie, nodding, said, 'You make sense, Molly; you've got to play him at his own game.' He turned to Jane. 'Go now, as Molly says, and try an' rest if you can, because there's a long day afore us, and God knows what's in it.' He did not touch her, nor she him, but they looked at each other deeply before he turned and went into the bedroom; then she went down the stairs and Molly followed her.

Six

Jane awoke from what appeared a nightmare. She was aching all over, particularly the back of her head and the bottom of her spine. She was lying on the bed in a dim light, candlelight, and there was a face above her and a voice was saying, 'Drink this.'

Where was she, and what had happened? The last she remembered was groping her way along the passage and entering her bedroom. This . . . this wasn't her bedroom, this was . . .

'Come along, drink this.'

She took a mouthful of the liquid, then gulped, as her taste registered laudanum. It was the medicine her mother used to take to soothe her nerves and put her to sleep. As she spluttered she knocked the glass flying. Then, her eyes wide, she went to pull herself up, but the hand on her chest prevented her, and Amos's voice said, 'It's no use, so you might as well give in gracefully. You're here and you're staying here, for the time being at any rate, until you learn to behave yourself. I'm surprised at you, Jane, letting yourself down to the level of a farm labourer.'

'Let me up!'

'You're not getting up. I'll give you a choice, you either drink more of this' – he moved his head towards the bottle standing on the side table – 'or I'll tie you up and gag you. You have your choice.'

'Amos! Amos!' She began to plead now. 'Please, I beg of

231

you, don't do this, let me go. I'll go eventually; you can't keep me.'

'Can't I? You'd be surprised what I can do.'

'No! no!' Now there was no pleading in her voice and she barked at him, 'I'd never be surprised at what you can do after ... after murdering Arnold.'

'Oh!' He raised his eyebrows. 'So you've known about that?'

'Yes, I've known about that.'

'And you didn't give me away ... Why didn't you give me away?' He waited for her answer, and when none came he said, 'I'll tell you why, because you loved me. And I'll tell you something else, I love you, and that's why I can't let you go ... You understand what I'm saying, Jane? I love you.'

She felt her body shrinking back into the bed in terror now. She had no need to look for a definition of his word love, she was well aware that the prefixes of motherly or sisterly wouldn't fit the love he was speaking of. The horror of the situation lent strength to her arms, and now she was struggling with him like someone demented, while she screamed, 'Davie! Davie! Molly! Davie! Davie!'

They were on the floor rolling together as they had done years ago on top of the Tor, and all the while his arms held her as if in a vice, and from time to time his body lay on hers. She had only one advantage over him, her knees, and she used them when she could. One vicious jab into his loins caused him to yell and release his hold on her for a moment, and, her hands groping wildly at the wall, she dragged herself to her feet and found she was near the window. She had just managed to open it when he was on her again; and now she screamed at the top of her lungs ...

They both heard it together, it came like a thin high voice on the wind. It brought Molly from a light doze by the fire and Davie to his feet in the bedroom; then they were both at the bottom of the stairs looking at each other.

'It was a scream; it sounded like a scream.'

Before Molly had finished speaking Davie was running out of the house and she after him.

When they burst into the kitchen and paused for a moment, the sound of the struggle came to them from above as some article of furniture overturned and crashed to the floor.

Davie took the stairs two at a time, but when he reached the first landing he stood looking upwards, unable to see the stairs that led to the attics. It was odd that he should have lived close to this house for the first nineteen years of his life and never got beyond the ground floor.

'Along here! Along here!' Molly was now running past him around the dark corner of the landing and up the four steps on to the old landing. But here he passed her and made for the dim narrow stairs that led to the attic.

When he thrust open the door he saw nothing for a moment, then at the sound of panting coming from the far side of the bed he rushed across the room, and there she was, spreadeagled on the floor, with Amos on top of her, his arms pinning her down.

He uttered no sound, but his hands flashed out and, gripping the back of Amos's collar, he hauled him upwards and flung him against the fireplace.

When he went to lift Jane from the floor Molly was already by her side, and between them they guided her to the door.

He had his back to the room as he said thickly, 'Get her downstairs,' and it was as he turned to see what the maniac was up to that the end of the poker hit his shin bone, and he cried out aloud as he leapt into the air.

Bending now and holding his leg tight against the excruciating pain he looked to where Amos was grabbing up a pair of tongs from inside the fender. With a lop-sided leap he flung himself on him, and again Amos was rolling on the floor, but with a difference this time, for now he was like a mad bull and with a mad bull's strength, and it wasn't until he sank his teeth into Davie's wrist and blood spurted that Davie became a match for him. Filled with rage, he fought as he had seen men fight on board ship, like savage animals; yet it took him all his time to free himself from Amos's hold, for his arms seemed to be everywhere. They were like the tentacles of an octopus; you released yourself from one and another caught you. Only when he used his knee as Jane had done did Amos go flying from him and straight through the open door on to the landing.

He lay still now, and Davie stood gasping while he watched him. The blood was pouring from his wrist, and he gripped it in an effort to stop the flow; his leg was paining damnably; his body felt bruised as if he had been tossed about in a bilge in a storm.

Slowly he moved towards the still figure and stood looking down on it for a second; and it could only have been a second before once again he found himself on his back. Amos having

233

swept his legs from under him, was in the act of jumping on him when Davie's hands came instinctively upwards and with a mighty effort he hurled the stunted body backwards over his head. Then he lay still, his arms outspread, listening to the repeated thumps and guttural cries.

In the silence that followed he slowly turned himself on to his hands and knees and peered down the dark stairway to the darker form lying at the bottom, then helping himself to his feet by pulling on the balustrade post he descended the stairs.

At the bottom he stood looking at the humped body, but this time did not stoop towards it. Not until he satisfied himself that there could be no more tricks did he bend over him; then his hand slowly dropped on to the high chest and he held it there, for a second, just long enough to feel the faint heart beat and to experience a strong emotion of fear and disappointment mixed.

He wasn't dead. Like his father, he could linger on for months; and what then?

He wasn't conscious of having knelt on the floor, only of the hesitation in his mind whether to put his thumb on the gullet or his hand tight across the mouth.

'Are you all right?'

When Molly's hand came on his shoulder he froze.

'Is he dead?'

'N . . . not quite.'

'Pray God he soon will be.'

'I second that.' He stumbled to his feet.

'You're, you're bleedin'. Look at your wrist.'

'I'm all right; it'll clot. How is she?'

'In an awful state; can't stop cryin'. She's in hysterics I think, on about him. Aw, if ever there was a swine on this earth he's one.' She progged the inert body with the toe of her boot, then said, 'I think you'd better come down. But . . . but what are we going to do with him?'

He hesitated, then said, 'Give me a hand with him; we'll put him in his bed and let the devil take care of the rest.'

When, after a struggle, for the stumped body was a dead weight, they had laid him on the bed, Molly asked, 'Hadn't you better lock the door in case he comes round?'

'I don't think it'll be necessary, but we'll do it nevertheless. If he does come round he won't do any hoppin' for some days I should imagine.'

As they went out and locked the door Jane's cries came to them, and he ran down the stairs and into the drawing-room and, taking her shivering body into his arms, he muttered, 'It's all right, it's all over. Quiet now, quiet. Don't cry like that.'

'Da . . . vie! Davie!'

'Yes, dear. Now, it's all right, don't worry.'

'He . . . 'll k . . . kill me. He'll kill me.'

'He'll kill nobody else.'

Gasping, her face contorted, the water running from her eyes, nose and mouth, she spluttered, 'Dead! . . . is he dead?'

Regretfully he shook his head and answered slowly, 'Not quite.' He now turned to Molly. 'Make some strong tea, will you?' he said, and when she replied, 'The kettle's on,' she also added, 'Shouldn't one of us be along the road?'

'Aye, yes.' He nodded at her. 'I'll slip along.'

But when he went to move away Jane clung to him and he said soothingly, 'There now, there now, I won't be a tick. I promise you. It's all right, he's locked in. Even if he could move, he can't get out.'

When she continued to cling to him he looked at Molly with a shamefaced look, and Molly, bustling, took her from his arms, saying tersely, 'Come on now, pull yourself together. It's all over, or soon will be.'

Hurrying out of the room and the house, he ran up the lane to the cottage. But as soon as he entered the room he knew that he was too late, his granda had gone.

He stood looking down on the old man's face. The eyes, which had been closed for days, were now open; the mouth too was open, as if he was about to speak, to say something pleasant, for his whole face looked at peace. At the very last moment he must have wanted to look on his own, and his own wasn't there.

A great bitterness flooded him and he had the desire to go back to the house and finish off that maniac with his own hands. He regretted not having done so when the urge was on him.

He went to cover the still head with the sheet, but halfway in the act he stopped and slowly he knelt down. He was no pray- ing man; he had never been on his knees in prayer, nor had he uttered a prayer since McBain had disillusioned him. He didn't pray now, but he took the bony blue-veined hand in his as he whispered aloud, 'Good-bye, Granda. If there's a God an' He's just you'll have a happy passage.' His bottom lip trembled and he pressed his teeth into it, but this did not stop the tears from raining down his face . . .

On his return to the farm he walked slowly. When he entered the sitting-room Jane was lying back on the couch. She was quiet. She looked towards him, as did Molly, and it was Molly who spoke. 'He's gone then?' she said; and to this he nodded.

'Did he wake at all, come round?'

'I don't know; he had gone before I got back.'

'Oh! Davie.' Jane was sitting up and holding her hand out towards him, and as he went to her they were all brought into a fixed stillness by a sound coming from the kitchen. Molly, her eyes flashing from one to the other, whispered, 'It can't be, we locked the door.'

'Stay there.' Lifting his feet and treading as softly as he could, Davie went from the room. Warily he glanced round the hall and up the stairs, then made his way to the kitchen, and when he burst open the door he drew in a long slow breath at the sight of Will Curran leaning against the table.

'What's up?'

Holding his hip and limping towards a chair, Will said, 'Bloody horse took fright at a rabbit or hare or summat goin' across the road, and side-stepped into a ditch.'

'Whereabouts?'

'Beyond turnpike.'

'Is he hurt?'

'No, just frightened. I managed to get him out of the shafts. I tried to get him to pull the trap out but the wheel had buckled. It's a good job he was on his feet lest I'd never have got him out.'

'You brought him back?'

'Aye, but he wouldn't let me get on him, I had to walk him. He's as skittish as a new foal. Bloody rabbits!'

'You didn't get to Hexham then.' It was a statement, not a question.

'Hexham? How could I?'

'That's all right, Will, that's all right.' Davie sighed within himself. That was one bit of trouble waived anyway. 'Help yourself to some tea,' he said, 'and I'll try to get you a drop of something.'

As he went towards the door Will Curran asked, 'What's up, anyway? I came 'cos I saw all the lamps on. What's happened that you're in here this time a night?'

Davie paused for a moment before he said, 'He had a go at Miss Jane, almost did for her. He fell down the attic stairs.'

'He's hurt?'

'Aye, I should say so.'

'Bad?'

'I hope so, Will. For everybody's sake I hope so.' Then he added, 'Thanks for tipping Molly off. It was good of you, knowin' how you feel about things. Oh' – he turned his head away and waved his hand in the air – 'I know, Will, I know. I would have felt the same in your place, worse in fact. But hang on, things might take a turn for the better from now on. When Miss Jane runs the place she'll see you're all right.'

'Aye, Davie, aye.' Will Curran's tone had changed, the look on his face had changed, and when Davie said, 'Soon as you drink your tea get to bed 'cos you'll have to go for the doctor when it's light,' Will again said, 'Aye, Davie, aye,' as if he was speaking to a friend, whereas he had never before shown anything in his manner towards Davie but envy and obstinacy.

When he entered the sitting-room again he said immediately, 'There's one trouble we haven't got to face, the polis won't be here in the mornin'. The trap went into the ditch, and Will's come back with the pony.'

Jane closed her eyes and put both hands over her mouth and spoke through her fingers as she said, 'Thank God! Oh, thank God!'

'Were they hurt, the horse or him?'

He looked at Molly and shook his head, saying, 'Will's limping a bit, that's all. He's for bed, and' – he turned his head towards Jane – 'that's where you're going.' When she began to protest he said, 'Now no more words, not tonight. Just go to bed, and me and Molly will see to things.'

Molly was standing apart now. It was right, she thought, that Miss Jane should go to bed, she had gone through something the night, but she herself was tired to death. She'd never had a full night's rest for weeks now, she could sleep standing on her feet, but he had no feeling for her. 'Me and Molly will see to things,' he had said. He hadn't a kindly thought in his whole body towards her. Oh, he was civil enough now, but that was all. She'd had hope while he slated and scorned her, but not since he had spoken civil to her; from then she had known that he had closed the door on any feeling he might have had for her. And he'd had feeling for her; oh aye, a man doesn't get angry

237

and shower his scorn on a woman he doesn't care for. But now he was civil spoken.

When Jane, looking at her, said, 'But Molly's worn out too. You should go to bed, Molly,' and he put in quickly, 'Don't you worry about Molly, she's as strong as a horse,' she felt that she was about to make a fool of herself and burst into tears.

That's how he would look on her for the rest of her life, as strong as a horse, a beast of burden. Could she stand it? Was she up to it? No, no, she wasn't.

The doctor came out of the bedroom, and Molly followed him. They walked to the top of the stairhead before he spoke. Then, his voice low, he said, 'You tell me he attacked his sister?'

'Aye, he did, sir.'

'I'm very surprised at that, I always understood that they were close. She was more like a mother to him than a sister. It is very surprising. Was there any reason for it?'

'She told him she was going to leave, sir. Things hadn't been going too well here, you might have heard?'

'Oh yes. Yes, you hear all kinds of rumours, and there's no getting away from the fact that the place has changed drastically since your master died. But to attack her. How did he do it?'

'It was in the dark, sir. He knocked her out, then must have dragged her up to the attic.'

The doctor's face was showing his disbelief as she put in quickly, 'Oh, he could, sir. He used to sit on his backside – well, I mean he used to sit on the stairs and hoist himself up backwards, and pull things up that way. It was amazing the things he took upstairs. He was only about five when he dragged his four-wheeled cart up there, and now he's as strong as a bull. Leastways, he was.'

'Yes, leastways, he was.' He wagged his head; then said, 'Miss Jane . . . where is she?'

'In the sitting-room, sir, she's got her feet up. She's still not herself.'

She led the way down the stairs and opened the sitting-room door for him, and he entered, saying, 'Well! well! Jane. Well! well!' When he took the seat by the side of the couch he looked down and added, 'This is distressing news, distressing.'

Jane said nothing. She was in a high state of nerves. She was feeling much worse than she had done in the middle of the night; moreover she was anxious to know his report on Amos; and when he said, 'I'm afraid your brother is in a very bad way, Jane,' she still made no comment, simply stared at him wide-eyed, waiting.

'Besides concussion and a dislocated shoulder he has, I'm afraid, seriously injured the bottom of his spine. I suspect it may have affected him internally for he is' – he hesitated on the word – 'incontinent at the present moment. This is a bad sign. It may be that he is paralysed from the waist; I cannot make a final examination until he's fully conscious. I will come back tomorrow and look at him again.'

'He is going to live?' She made the statement slowly, her eyes in a fixed stare.

'That, too, I cannot say with any certainty at this stage . . . Now, about you. How do you feel?'

'Not very well, Doctor.'

'No, you don't look well. Now what you must do is to rest for a few days. I understand from Molly that you've had something of a shock. If you can send into the town today I will make up a sedative for you, if not I will bring it tomorrow.'

'Thank you.'

'Now just rest; you need rest.' He got to his feet. 'Well, I must be on my way, but remember, Jane, you must rest.'

'Yes, Doctor.'

He stooped and patted her head as if she were a child; then straightening his creaking back he bade her good-day, and she answered, 'Good-day, Doctor.'

A few minutes later Molly came back into the room saying, 'Well, that part's over.'

'He didn't question about his falling?'

'No, I just told him what we said I should.'

'What will happen when he regains consciousness? He might tell the doctor it was Davie.'

'You leave that to Davie; let's meet the trouble as it comes.'

'If . . . if he lives he'll need nursing, Molly.'

'Aye, aye, he will.' Molly was replenishing the fire now, and she had her back to Jane as she spoke.

'It isn't fair to ask you to do it.'

Molly thrust the poker through the lower bars and raked vigorously. It was on the point of her tongue to retort, 'There's nothing fair in this world, Miss,' but she checked it and made

239

herself say, 'Don't worry your head about that.' She now dusted one hand against the other and picking up the empty scuttle and saying, 'Lie quiet,' she went out.

She did not go straight through the kitchen and into the yard to fill the scuttle but put it down by the side of the wide hearth and stood looking at the black pot on the fire, which held a meat pudding she had made an hour ago.

During the past few hours she had laid out old Sep, she had stripped the clothes from that one upstairs, cleaned the filth from him and changed his bed. She had cooked the breakfast, prepared the dinner, tried to get Miss Jane to eat something, but instead had to hold her head while she vomited. It was this last that hurt her most, for this wasn't the first time that Miss Jane had vomited in the morning. She wondered if she knew what was wrong with her. She wouldn't be surprised if she didn't. She was guileless. Living on a farm where conceiving and birth were as common as God bless you, she had somehow never been part of it.

She reached up and laid her forearms crossways on the mantelshelf and rested her head on them. It was a favourite position of hers when she wanted to think. But now she was past thinking, she was tired. Her body was crying out for sleep, and her heart was crying out for something she would never have in this world . . .

She let out a high squawk as the hand came on her shoulder, and Davie had to steady her or else she would have fallen into the fire.

'You . . . you were half asleep, didn't you hear me come in?' He still had hold of her and she gazed at him through her blinking lids while he looked down at her. They stood like this for a full minute, and some quality in the look in his eyes which she had never seen before made her weak, so much so that she put her hand back and grabbed at the chair. When she sat on it he still kept his hand on her shoulder. 'You're all in,' he said. 'It's too much to expect. You've been on your feet for weeks now, what with the old 'un an' one thing and another, and I'm . . . I'm not ungrateful, Molly, I'm not.'

Again they were staring at each other, when he said, 'Jane's just told me what the doctor had to say, but as long as he lives I'll help you tend him, you can't do it alone. One thing we mustn't do, and that's let her go near him. Not that she will want to, she's scared to death of him now. She won't say exactly

240

what happened, but I've got me own opinion on that, an' it makes me sick.'

Her head came forward; she pulled herself away from the chair and his hand; then going towards the side of the fireplace she picked up the empty scuttle and made for the door. The latch in her hand, she turned and looked at him and said quietly, 'Talkin' about being sick, did she tell you she's been sick in the mornings? It might only be a nervous stomach, but then it mightn't. But you should know.'

Book Five

One

Davie stood by the side of the bed, not too near it; he did not
want to grapple with the one good hand Amos had left. But he
let his glance rest on it for a moment. The fingers were plucking the bed cover as if they were thinning out tow. The left
shoulder was mending but the rest of him would never mend, so
the doctor said. He was now paralysed from the waist. It was
a terrible predicament for any human being to be in, yet he
couldn't pity him. He was but a young lad of nineteen, broken
in what body he had and twisted in mind. Forgetting all his
past deeds, even the one against himself, and that had been
mean, for to plant six pieces of jewellery under the mattress of
a dying man took some beating; even so, his present condition
should call on his compassion, but it didn't for he was still wary
of him, still suspicious of him and the power of his mind. The
power showed in his face when his eyes fixed you with that
dense stare; you had to use your will not to drop your gaze
away from them, not to allow the jerking in your stomach to
pass like a tremor through you.

He watched the strong white teeth come slowly apart, and
then Amos was asking slowly, 'Do you sleep in the house?'

'Yes, I sleep in the house, and have done for the past month.'

'You have no right, you will go back to your cottage.'

There was a short silence while they stared at each other.
Then Davie, his tone in levelness matching that of Amos's,
said, 'I have no intention of returnin' to the cottage, now or at
any other time. For the rest of me life I am stayin' in this house;
I am marrying Jane the morrow.'

The hand stopped plucking the eiderdown and formed itself
into a fist. 'You can't. You won't. You daren't. Do you hear me?
You daren't.' He raised the upper part of his body from the bed

243

by lifting one shoulder and resting on his elbow, and his head craned forward as he yelled, 'You can't do this, do you hear? You won't, and I can stop you. When Cargill comes I'll tell him how I got this. It was you, you threw me down the stairs.'

'Do that. You do that' – Davie nodded at him – 'and I'll tell him and . . . and the Judges an' all that I came in answer to your sister's screams when you were trying to rape her.'

'That's a lie.'

'Well, say it's a lie, say you intended that for future use, there's still the little matter of Parson Hedley conveniently put out of the way the night before he was going to marry your sister, and Jane would explain how you did it. Then there's the other matter of your father's end. Molly would have a lot to say about that. Anything you could say against me wouldn't help your case at all. Nor would the predicament that you're in now. There are prison hospitals where men end their days, an' I would see you taken there without blinking an eyelid, so . . . so think on it. You've got a choice, you can rest comfortable here until you die, or you can pay for what you've done, it's up to you.'

In one movement Amos fell back on his pillow while his hand went out and gripped the heavy glass water jug from the side table, and as quickly Davie's voice came barking at him, 'You do! Just you do and I'll punch your lugs for you until your face is twice the size it is now.'

They glared at each other for a long moment. Then Davie turned and made for the door; but stopped before he reached it and, glancing over his shoulder, said, 'One more thing. You be civil to Molly or I'll see you lie in your muck. And that's no idle threat.' And on this he went out. But once on the landing the stiffness went out of his shoulders and as he walked down the four steps on to the lower landing and to the room that was now his, his whole body slumped.

Seating himself in the high-backed leather chair near the window, he let out a long slow breath; then half-aloud he said, 'He can't do anything. Anyway what could he do? He won't tell the doctor, so what can he do?'

No answer came to his mind, yet no reassurance that nothing could happen before tomorrow when Jane would be his wife and together they would sleep in that bed.

His head actually nodded towards the bed, the bed in which McBain had slept; the bed in which the first night he had been in this room had refused him rest of any kind. He had thought at one time that McBain himself was in the mattress prodding him into wakefulness, trying to kick him out. In the end he had got up and dozed in this chair by the window.

He looked out of the window now down on to the paved court and the arch that led into the main yard, then over the garden towards where, in the far distance, was the cow path above the malt house. Tomorrow, by law through his wife, he should be master of all this, this house that had been like a star to him in his youth, and, like a star, just as unreachable. But as it was he'd be playing at master, for the owner was still alive, the mind alert in a mangled body, and, as things stood, he'd be quite capable of willing everything away from Jane, even though it was mortgaged up to the hilt and beyond.

At this point there came to him a clear understanding of the desire that had driven Amos to get rid of those who stood in his path. He rose abruptly from the chair and went downstairs.

Two

The morning was bright; there was a tang about that promised winter; the trees in the copse were tinged with brown, some leaves having already fallen; the sky was high and cloudless, and the air caught at the throat like a sharp wine.

Jane stood in the hall, with Molly beside her. They were both pale. Molly was wearing a clean holland apron, the side of which she crumpled in her hand one minute and smoothed down the next. After a while she said, 'You look bonny.' She did not add 'Miss Jane'.

'Thank you, Molly; but . . . but I don't feel bonny.'

'Well, you are. Blue's your colour, and corduroy always looks cosy. Mrs Bennett made a good job of that although her hands are not what they used to be.'

'Yes, I think she made it very well.'

Now Jane smoothed down the front of her three-quarter-length corduroy coat with its matching skirt and, her head lowered, she said, 'I'd feel much happier if I thought I wasn't going to lose you.'

'We can't have everything in this life.'

Jane's head was brought up sharply by the tone and she stared at Molly whose face was now suffused by a deep blush. 'What I mean is, Miss Jane, you'll be married an' you'll have Davie, and Will has promised to look after him.' She jerked her head upward. 'He said he won't mind doing that, 'specially with winter coming on, it'll keep him out of the weather. Will knows when he's on a good thing, an' Davie will get another man. We've been into it, haven't we?'

'Yes, Molly, we've been into it. When are you going to see Mr Bateman?'

'Oh well; this afternoon, maybe, I'll take a walk over.'

'You can't walk all that way; Davie'll take you in the trap.'

'He'll do no such thing.'

There was the tone again that brought them looking at each other in silence. Then Jane said apologetically, 'Well, I only thought, it being on six miles . . .'

'Aw, what's six miles?' Molly was looking down at her hands twisting her apron once more. 'Do me good to stretch me legs. I'll have to stretch them longer than that to keep running after that squad.' She gave a nervous laugh; then they both turned and looked at the stairs, which Davie was descending, a new-looking Davie, a slightly awkward-looking Davie.

And he felt awkward in his new clothes; he had never worn such a light colour before, nor yet such tight trousers. The suit was made of tweed and the clothier in Newcastle had promised him it would last a lifetime. That, he had remarked to himself, remained to be seen; a little more weight and he wouldn't be able to get into it.

As he looked down at Jane waiting for him at the bottom of the stairs he felt he should apologise, for things were in their wrong order; it was the man who should be waiting for the woman. But he had been up since first light this morning seeing to the cattle; afterwards he had taken a bath in the closet room. He had humped the hot water up from the kitchen and for the first time in his life he had been immersed all over at one go with warm water. He had stayed too long in it and had then to scurry.

'Well then, we're ready for off?' He screwed his chin upwards out of his shirt collar – he wasn't used to anything so tight round his neck – then he pulled his white shirt cuffs well below his grey coat sleeves, and Jane, looking at him with love-filled eyes, replied, 'Yes, Davie, we're ready for off.'

Molly said nothing.

They walked out of the hall, Jane going first, he following, and Molly coming up in the rear. They went on to the drive where the trap stood, Amos's trap, the seats altered, the low steps taken off the back. It was a gig to be proud of.

As he went to hand Jane up into the trap she turned impulsively to Molly and, catching her hands, said, 'I wish you were coming, Molly. I do. Oh, I do.'

Molly seemed to find difficulty in answering; then she said, 'I'm where I'm needed most, Miss; Mickey and his wife can both write and that's all that's needed, just to sign their names.'

Jane shook her head slowly before turning quickly and getting into the trap.

Davie, his foot on the step, paused and looked at Molly, and she at him. For one long moment they looked at each other and the years fell away and they were walking through the fields again, both chewing rose hips, and when their shoulders touched they bounced from each other like rubber balls and laughed.

Now he bounced up into the trap, and it rocked like a boat.

'Gee-up there! Gee-up there!'

The pony trotted smartly out of the yard and when, going through the gate, Jane turned to wave to Molly she saw that the yard was empty.

In the kitchen Molly stood with her back to the stout oak door. She had her thumb thrust deep into her mouth and was biting on it so hard that she could scarcely endure the pain. But it was either that or giving way, and that must wait, she didn't want to face them at their breakfast with red eyes. She wouldn't give him that satisfaction, and she wouldn't upset Miss Jane, or Mrs Armstrong as she'd be in an hour's time. What she must do, she told herself, was to go and clean that one up, and that would keep her occupied and her mind off herself; her mind couldn't wander when she was seeing to him.

As she opened the bedroom door he raised himself on his elbow and cried at her, 'You've taken your time. Didn't you hear me shout?'

'Aye, I heard you, but I've been busy.'

'Busy! I'm your first concern to be busy about.'

'Now you watch it!' She nodded her head at him as she

247

stripped off the top cover. 'Keep that up and I'll leave you lying in it.'

He sank back into the bed and lay gasping for a moment; then closing his eyes, he asked her in an entirely different tone, 'Have you any idea how I feel lying here?'

She glanced sharply at him, then said nonchalantly, 'No; how could I, not being you?'

'That's the point, not being me, you couldn't understand what it's like. Molly' – he put out his hand towards her – 'I . . . I want to see Jane. He won't listen to me.' It was odd that Davie had now become HE. 'I promised him I wouldn't upset her. I . . . I just want to see her, just to have a word. Look, Molly, I'm sorry if I've gone for you, I am, I really am.' He gazed at her, his slant eyes soft. 'Ask him, will you? Just for a minute. She needn't come near me, just so's . . . so's I can see her. I'll go mad, more mad than I am now. Yes, I will. I'll go stark raving mad lying here seeing only you and him. I loathe him, do you know that, Molly? I loathe and hate him, and I used to like him, almost love him. But now I hate him even more than I did my father. God! how I hate him!'

She stopped stripping the bed and stared at him, and for a second she felt so sorry for him she almost put her arms around him. He looked like a very young lad on the verge of tears. After all, as he said, it was terrible lying there, helpless, seeing only her and Davie and the doctor. He was at their mercy, so to speak, and it must go against the grain with a character like his that wanted to dominate everyone, that did dominate everybody, crippled as he was.

'I've got to see her, Molly, I must. We understand each other, her and I. I've got to explain to her why he wants to marry her. It's just to get this place. He doesn't love her. She's plain, she's got nothing about her to attract a man like him; his kind don't go in for character, and that's all Jane's got, character, a sweet, sweet character.' He shook his head. And now, again pulling himself up on his elbow, he appealed to her, 'Look, ask yourself what harm can I do from here. The only thing I've got left is my mind, such as it is, and I don't know how long I'll have that. Tell her I promise I won't raise my voice or say a word out of place, if she'll just come in for a moment . . . Where is he?'

'He's gone out.'

'Well go on, Molly, ask her now, please.'

'I can't.'

'Why? Why can't you? Are you aiming to get your own back? I know you never liked me, and that's my fault, but you have the better of me now, so I beg of you do this for me, just this once. Please, Molly.'

'I would if I could an' I mean that, but . . . but you see, she's gone with him, they're on their way to the church now, they're to be married at nine.'

He made no sound for a full minute; then swinging his head from side to side he cried, 'No! No! No! . . . No! No!' As his voice got louder she shouted at him, 'Now stop that, stop workin' yourself up. They had to be married, they just had to. If you'd been up it would have made no difference, they would have been married.'

'NEVER! NEVER!'

'You can say that' – she was yelling back at him – 'but I tell you she would have married him, unless she wanted to be like me and my Biddy . . . she's been carrying his bairn for two months.' The bitterness in her own voice brought her to stillness and there fell about them a silence in which they both seemed embalmed for a moment, the only live thing in the room was the smell of excrement emanating from the bed and his exposed stunted limbs.

When he slowly brought his fist up to his wide mouth and rammed his knuckles between his teeth she thought how she herself, a short time earlier, had tried to stem her own agony, and she went to him and put her hand on his head. But he moved away from her touch, not abruptly or harshly; he just turned his head round and buried what he could of it in the pillow.

There was a great swelling of pride in Davie as he sat at the head of the table. He had eaten at this table for some weeks now but he had never sat in this chair; at Jane's insistence, he had taken the seat at the top of the table.

To all intents and purposes he was master of Cock Shield, what was left of it, fifty acres at the most. Still, it was up to him now. And he intended to start the way he meant to go on, as if Amos was already dead and buried. The doctor had given him six months, perhaps less, it all depended; but Amos dead or alive, he would work as if the place was his. It would likely take

249

him the rest of his life to clear the debts on it, but he would do it.

He looked at Jane. Her face had picked up the white light of the morning. He had always thought she had just missed being beautiful, but when she had turned to him on the altar steps she seemed to have caught up with the beauty that had long evaded her. From now on, given the chance, she would blossom, her body would grow plump, her breasts would fill and remain full, she'd be a woman, not an old maid of thirty. He put out his hand to her and asked softly, 'How do you feel?'

'Oh! Davie, I can't tell you, I haven't words to explain. Wonderful, fulfilled, marvellous, yet . . . yet still a little fearful.'

'Now, now.' He raised his finger to her. 'Remember what we said, it's our life and we're going to live it; the past is past. There's just you and me.'

'That's . . . that's what I'm fearful of, it seems too good to be true . . . Davie.'

'Yes, me dear.'

'I love you. I love you so much. I' – she smiled faintly – 'I feel indecent at times because I love you so much.'

She had the pleasure of seeing him put his head back and laugh. Then bringing his face down close to hers, he said, softly, 'Go on being indecent; I like you being indecent.'

'Oh, Davie! Oh, Davie!' She lowered her eyes at him, then softly they laughed together.

A moment later she looked down the table and said, 'Molly has done everything so nicely. Why didn't she stay until we got back?'

He took a mouthful of cold pork and chewed on it before answering, 'Well now, she did tell you that she was going over to Bateman's, didn't she?'

'Yes, but I thought not until around noon.'

'It's a good stretch.'

'Well, I told her you would take her but she said she wanted to walk. And . . . and what's more, Davie, I don't fancy the sound of this Mr Bateman and his house full of children. She's had a hard enough life here.'

'She doesn't mind youngsters, she was brought up among a crowd.' He continued eating, then breaking off a crust of new bread, he covered it with butter before he ended, 'She's like everyone else, she wants to marry and have a place of her own. It's understandable.'

'Yes, yes, of course.' She smiled at him, then said thoughtfully, 'But . . . but she's had lots of chances over the years. You know, Davie' – her voice dropped – 'I used to envy her. She had a way with her and men seemed to gravitate towards her. Look . . . look at my father . . .'

He took a long mouthful of tea before he answered, 'That was in her young days, she's getting a bit long in the tooth now. I haven't seen anybody scampering around her. And what is she? Going on thirty-six. You're showing wear at thirty-six.'

'Oh! Davie, Molly showing wear! Don't be silly, she's bonny. She'll always be bonny; women like her don't seem to age. Anyway, age or not, I'm going to miss her . . . Davie.'

'Aye, I mean yes?' He poked his face playfully towards her, and she tapped his cheek with her finger, then shook her head at him before leaning forward and proffering him her lips. After he had kissed her he asked, 'What were you going to say?'

She was looking into his eyes as she answered, 'Oh just that at one time I . . . I was jealous of Molly. I thought when you came back you might . . . well you might pick up where you left off years ago, because what happened wasn't really her fault . . .'

He rose abruptly to his feet and half turned from her as he said, 'Now, now, none of that. What put that into your head? That was over and done with afore we finished Sunday School. And I told you, didn't I, the past is past, all of it. So no more goin' back. Well now.' He tapped each lapel of his grey suit as he ended, 'These togs must go in the drawer with the moth bags, and the Lord knows when they'll come out again.'

'They will not go into the drawer with any moth bags, you're to wear them when you go into the town.' Her voice was prim, and laughingly he answered in the same vein, 'Yes, Ma'am. Yes, Ma'am.'

'Oh! Davie.' She came round the table, running like a girl, and into his arms. 'I'm so happy. I'm, I'm almost perfectly happy. Almost.' As she cast her eyes towards the ceiling her face clouded and he said sharply, 'You are perfectly happy; don't let your mind dwell on that part of the house. As far as you're concerned it doesn't exist. Remember what Doctor Cargill said, you're not to go near him. Your system, your nervous system won't stand up to much more. He said that, now didn't he? So leave him to me and Will, we'll manage him atween us. And promise me, now promise me that on no account do you go up those stairs on to that landing.'

She stared into his eyes for a moment before she said ' . . . I promise you, Davie.'

'That's a good girl.' And when his lips touched hers again she felt like a girl. For the first time since she was twelve years old she felt like a girl . . .

Davie worked for the rest of the day, and he planned as he worked. He'd split the herd and try a few of them down on that patch near the malt house, the grass was lush there, and from the returns he got from the milk, now that Master Amos couldn't get his hands on it, he would put a little aside and so be able to engage some casual labour. Perhaps only for a day or two at a time, but that would be a help, and such hands generally worked like slaves in the hope of being kept on. And should he come across an exceptional one he'd make him an offer, his food and a cottage and a small regular wage until things looked up. A decent man would take a chance.

At three o'clock in the afternoon he had gone in to a dinner cooked by Jane. It wasn't up to the standard of Molly's cooking but he praised it. By five o'clock it was raining heavily and Molly hadn't returned.

'She'll be wet to the skin,' Jane said when she came yet again to the cow byres to have a word with him.

'Not her: she won't be making the journey back this night, that's certain. The top an' bottom of it is, once he got her there he wouldn't let her go, so stop worrying on her account; Molly can take care of herself, never fear.'

It was around eight o'clock and the rain had fallen to a steady drizzle as he made the last round of the day. He went from the cow shed to the stables, where he spoke to the horses and the pony; he went round the hen crees and the piggeries; he passed the open barn where the dogs were, but knowing his step they made no movement, only blinked in the lantern light; then he walked by the side of the big barn and into the road and towards the main gate. And it was then he saw her, in the swinging gleam of the lantern shambling slowly, like a drunken woman, towards him.

'That you, Molly?'

She didn't speak, and he came close to her and held the lantern above his head. And not even then did she say anything; her face, running with rain, was crumpled as if she were crying.

'What's happened to you?' he asked. 'You're wringing to the

skin.' He touched her shoulder and it was this that seemed to loosen her tongue, for now she began to gabble in such a way that it was difficult to distinguish whether she was talking through laughter or tears. 'So much for the bolt hole; I thought I just had to walk in. And that's what I did, just walked in, large as life, an' there she was settled, a trollop if ever I saw one, a dirty, lazy, fat trollop, the end part of a trollop at that for her best days were over. She'd lost most of what she'd had except her tongue.' She gulped now and her head wagged again before she ended, 'He didn't open his mouth, just stood there like a pie-can, an' 'twas only a month gone since he begged me to take him an' his brood on, just a month.'

'Come on inside,' he said gently, 'an' get your things off. You'll get your death, it's turned bitter. And there's one who'll be glad to see you; she's been worried about you.'

She became still now as she peered at him through the lantern light and the rain. Then, her voice low and her words slow, she said, 'Aye, she'll be glad, but not you. You wanted me out of the way, didn't you? . . . Well let me tell you somethin'. I wanted to get out of your way an' all, so there was a pair of us wantin' the same thing. But now you're stuck with me until I find a place. When I'm prickin' your skin like a holly leaf just remember you're doin' the same to me. But it won't be for long; a day or two, I'll get something. Aye, I will; I can work anywhere.'

'Don't be silly, woman, don't be daft.' His voice was harsh. 'You have no effect on me, good, bad or indifferent, so you can stay as long as it pleases you. It's up to you.'

Her face seemed to swing with the movement of the lantern. He saw her mouth open wide and her eyes close before she flung herself round and leaned against the gate post; her head buried in her hands, she cried uncontrollably like a child would who had fallen down and grazed its knees, and he stood gazing at her helplessly while he warned himself not to touch her.

Three

'Davie, please, please let me see him. It's like my father all over again, keeping him tied to the attic.'

'Jane' – he put his hand over his eyes – 'you know what Doctor Cargill said, an' just a day or two gone. "It would be advisable," he said, "if you didn't disturb yourself in any way." Those were his very words, weren't they?'

'But my nerves are all right now, I've never felt better in my life. And he keeps going for Molly, shouting at her. I'd have to be deaf not to hear him. I . . . I won't go any further than the foot of the bed. And Davie . . . Davie' – she took his hands in hers – 'it isn't that I really want to see him, but morally I think I should. I've . . . I've forgiven him. And he needs forgiveness, he's dying.'

'Is he? I'm beginnin' to have me doubts about that. Six months now he's been lying there. Doctor said that was his limit, but he shows no weakness to me. In fact he can use those arms of his as well as ever he could. And' – he paused and brought his head down to hers and, his voice low, he ended, 'that's what I'm afraid of, those arms of his, tentacles; let them get hold of you and you'd swear he was an octopus.'

'But I promise you I won't go any further . . .'

'No, Jane. Not now, not at this time. When the child is born and if he's still there then you can go in to him, but as you are now the very sight of you like this' – he tapped his finger against the dome of her stomach – 'this would drive him mad. I know him, I know him better than you. I told you a while back that he's lying there concocting mischief, I can see it in his eyes. And another thing you'd better know, Molly's got the idea that he can move more than he lets on; in fact she's sure of it 'cos she watched him through the keyhole and saw him humping himself up in the bed by his arms. The next thing we'll know he'll be pulling himself out of the bed.'

'He couldn't, Davie, he couldn't do that, it's too high. Anyway, once he was out he'd never be able to get back.'

'Jane' – he cupped her face between his hands and gazed at her for a moment before saying, 'it's only six weeks . . .'

'Nearly seven.'

'Well, nearly seven. You've stood out all this long time, keep it up a little longer, just for me, and . . . and I'll promise you one thing, if I suspect at all that he's near his end you'll see him. Now I give you me word on that, so will you give me your word again, you won't go into him on your own?'

She stared into his face, into his beloved face, into the face that had given her rebirth; for if ever a woman had been reborn she had. If it wasn't for the thought of Amos constantly niggling at her mind she'd be so happy it would be unbearable. Her love for him was almost like a pain in itself. And it was true what she had said, she'd never felt so well in her life. And this in spite of carrying a child and working as hard as any hired maid. She had completely taken over the dairy; she made butter and cheese as good as Molly now; she helped to milk the cows, feed the pigs and chickens, and groom the horses. During her thirty-one years on the farm she had never spent so much time outside the house. Her mother would have thought it beneath her to lift her hand to an outside chore, and the kind of farmer her father had been, he had not expected it of her, so she had not thought it odd when she herself had not been trained in the ways of butter and cheese making and the like. There had always been Molly, and Winnie, and, before they had gone out into service, the Geary girls. But now she was rarely in the house during the day. And this was fortunate, for outside she did not dwell so much on Amos and his plight. She felt that Davie had arranged things so, giving her tasks that would keep her away from the house.

'Very well.' Her voice was soft, and her arms went up and round his neck as she said, 'I can't say no to you in any way, my dearest.'

When he had kissed her firmly and squarely on the mouth he pushed her from him, saying on a laugh, 'What would they say if anyone saw us, husband and wife kissing at ten o'clock in the mornin' in the barn? They can't be married, they'd say. That's what they'd say, they can't be married.'

'Oh Davie, go on with you!'

'Aye, an' I'd better go. You see that sky.' He pointed out through the open door. 'That's been coming up from the north-west since late on yesterday; I know that sign, we're in for a bad 'un. I'd better get Will to help me tie down the ricks.'

'I'll help you.'

'You'll do nothing of the sort. Go on back to the dairy, woman, about your business.' When he slapped her buttocks she put both hands on the place and hurried away, glancing at him over her shoulder, her eyes alight as if he had just bestowed a gift on her.

As he went out of the main gate and across the road into the open meadow where the two ricks were he was still shaking his head and half smiling. She was like a young lass. He had never seen a change like it in his life; she seemed to have gone back to what she was all those years ago before that day in the malt house. And that's how he wanted to keep her. And he would keep her like that, as long as she didn't see that maniac.

The storm broke at noon. It followed a dark, dead calmness when nothing moved. The bare branches of the trees in the copse looked as if they were painted on the low sky. The washing that Molly was grabbing in from the lines was hanging limp. The animals too were affected by the stillness, for they made no sound. There was no grunting or cackling or mooing; they, together with all life on the land for miles around, seemed to have become paralysed with the stillness. Even Molly's bustling movements were checked once she got inside the kitchen, for having dropped the wash basket on to the floor, she went and stood near the window and peered out into the yard, across which she could now scarcely see.

The first drops of rain were spaced and the size of hailstones; then with the suddenness of lightning the sky unburdened itself and the water fell in sheets which blotted everything from sight.

She stepped back from the window, saying aloud, 'God in Heaven! we're in for it the day. Eeh! I can't see a stime; I'd better light the lamp.'

She lit not only the lamp in the kitchen but also those in the hall and the dining-room; then she went upstairs and lit the one that stood on top of the landing; and finally the lamp in HIS room.

When she brought it from the central table to the bedside table so that he could see to read, she had to raise her voice to make herself heard above the din on the roof. 'We're in for it! ... I said, we're in for it!'

And the answer he gave to this remark was, 'Did you do as I asked you?'

256

'Now don't start that again, not at this time. We'll have enough to think about, it strikes me, afore this one's over.'

'Did you do what I asked you?' He was shouting now, and she shouted back, 'No, I didn't, 'cos I've told you a hundred times afore, it's no use.'

She watched him drop back against the head of the bed in that desperate fashion that hurt her, and when he spoke again she said, 'What did you say?'

'It's inhuman.'

She stepped back and stared at him. Aye, she supposed it was inhuman. She had never thought Miss Jane would stand out this long; but she was like a child in Davie's hands. His word was law to her. She herself used to say that he played at God, and Miss Jane had, in a way, turned him into one. But the plight of this one here hurt her sorely at times. She never thought there'd come the day when she'd feel heart-sorry for him, but, dear God, you'd have to be made of stone not to be melted by his predicament.

At times she felt fearful over his constant demands to see Miss Jane, for then he worked himself up into a frenzy. She had thought, and more than once, it wouldn't have done Miss Jane any harm just to stand at the door and have a word with him from there. He wasn't long for the top, the doctor said, so what harm could he do? As long as he stayed put in bed that was.

'Now mind you don't knock the lamp over.' She was shouting again. 'There's your books an' your drink; you've got everythin' to your hand. I'll bring your dinner shortly.' She nodded at him, then went out.

After staring towards the door for a long moment he turned his head slowly and looked at the lamp.

By seven o'clock the storm had in no way abated, in fact its fury seemed to be getting worse every moment. An hour ago it had lifted the roof completely off the hen cree and the birds had been tossed about the field like bits of straw. It had taken Davie, Molly and Will Curran all their time to marshal them into the main yard and to the barn; and then their efforts had resulted in only half the birds being brought to safety.

The tall tree at the end of the copse had been torn up by the roots, and its top branches had just missed the last cottage by a few feet.

257

The yard itself was strewn with slates from the house, and Davie had continually yelled at Jane to keep indoors in case she should be struck by one.

Right up till the hens had scattered she had worked by his side, now she was sitting near the kitchen table panting and spent. She ached in every limb; her head was bursting with sound; she was so weary that she told herself she wanted to die, then contradicted the statement hurriedly as if her wish would be granted. No, she didn't want to die – ever. She put her hand on the side of her stomach, just below her ribs. The child was kicking furiously, annoyed, as it were, by so much activity. She looked down tenderly at the bulge and thought with an inward pride that when her time came she'd be so big she wouldn't be fit to be seen. Last night Davie had moved his hands over her stomach as he said, 'You're carrying so high, there's room for two underneath,' and at this they had smothered their laughter against each other. Oh, life would be so wonderful, if only . . .

She rose heavily to her feet. She must see to the broth; they were all frozen.

As she neared the fireplace a blast of smoke came down the wide chimney and almost choked her, and she turned, coughing, and leant against the table. Through the window she heard a distant sound of grating; then a crash outside the back door which told of more slates coming off the roof.

For twenty-five years back she could recall storms, terrible storms when the river flooded, and the burn from its source became a great waterfall. During one such storm two ponies in the malt house had only been saved because they had been washed on to the stairs and so had managed to climb to the gallery. Then there was that weird and strange storm when there was no rain and the lightning struck the ricks and set them on fire. But these storms seemed to have come and gone within a limited time, gradually mounting, then easing away. This one had been raging at the same pitch since noon, and showed no sign of abating.

The door burst open and the wind rattled the crockery hanging on the dresser, bringing from it a sound like that of cracked bells. Molly stumbled in, followed by Will Curran and Davie, and it took Davie all his time to force the door closed.

'God in Heaven! did you ever know anything like it?' Molly tore the hood from her head, then pulled off her sodden coat, adding, 'I'm wringin' to the skin.'

'Did you change?' Davie was not addressing Molly but Jane, and she answered, 'My cape had taken most of it, I changed my shoes.'

'You should've changed altogether, you can't help but be wet through.' He felt her shoulders which were dry, and she smiled at him and said, 'There! Satisfied?' then added, 'It's you who needs to change. And you, too, Will.' She turned her face kindly towards Will Curran, and he replied, 'Wet doesn't worry me, Miss Jane. So used to it I take scant notice, 'climatised sort of.' He smiled at her, and she smiled back at him. He wasn't such a bad sort after all, Will. She had never liked him because of his appearance and his perpetual drip, but of late she had found him kind and willing. There was good in everyone if you only looked. The thought brought a sadness to her and she turned sharply from him, saying, 'We must all have something to eat, the broth is ready.'

As she went to the fireplace to lift the pot, Davie came to her side, saying sharply, 'Now leave that alone. Haven't I told you? God in Heaven! you're like a child; I have to keep on at you.'

He was reprimanding her before the servants, but they took no notice, and she smiled as if he had paid her a compliment. And he had for he was showing concern for his wife, and like any wife she replied, 'Oh, don't be silly, I've lifted heavier than that.'

Five minutes later they were all sitting round the same table eating, and no one of them but thought that times had changed, but for the better.

Towards nine o'clock the rain stopped, but the wind seemed to gain in momentum. At half-past nine Davie and Will Curran made one more round of the place. Then Will went to his cottage.

It was close on ten o'clock when Molly went to hers. She had left Amos right for the night. She had seen Jane to bed, and she had stood for a moment in the kitchen alone with Davie and remarked, 'There'll be some clearin' up to do the morrow,' and he had replied, 'You've said it there but no matter what we've got to do I think we'll be lucky compared to those down the valley near the river. Bet your life there's been some cattle lost there the day. I shouldn't wonder if some of the bridges aren't down. A force like this pushing at water will test

259

the stoutest pillars. I don't think I've seen a worse, even at sea ... Look, will I walk along with you?'

'Walk along with me?' She cast a glance at him over her shoulder. 'No! No! I've kept me feet so far, so I'll trust to them to get me there ... It's me feet that's keepin' me down, they've always kept me down.'

He had never known her to joke with him, although he'd heard her joke with others, and he laughed now and said, 'Aye, some of us would be right upstarts if it wasn't for our feet.'

She stared at him for a moment longer. He could have been speaking against himself, but he wasn't, for since he had taken on the mastership of the farm he hadn't played the big boss or cracked the whip, all he had done was to work harder, if that was possible. His efforts were paying off at that, for things were better than they had been for years; the place was beginning to look like it used to. Of course, it would never be as it was; there wasn't the land, or the cattle, or the people to run both, but nevertheless a change had come over the farm in the last few months. She fancied at times he forgot, like they all did, that the real master of the place was still upstairs.

'Have a good night,' he said.

'A good night!' She raised her eyebrows. 'I can't see anybody havin' a good night in this!'

'Well, here's one that's going to.' He nodded at her. 'Let me head get on the pillow and I won't have any say in it.' He smiled at her, but she didn't smile back. She knew what would happen when he got his head on the pillow; she had gone over it every night for months past. She couldn't break herself of the habit. She no sooner got into bed than the picture of them rose before her. At first she had thought it wasn't right. Apart from everything else it wasn't right, him havin' Miss Jane; until she remembered herself and the master. And she didn't like remembering that now. Anyway, this was different, she supposed, because they were married. He had put a ring on her finger; the ring made everything right.

Marriage was a funny thing, when you came to think about it. The parson said a few words, the man put a ring on your finger, and you could run around bare-arsed between sunset and dawn and it was all right, because it was done in the eyes of God. Odd, how much stock God laid on a ring. He classed the same thing bad without a ring, but good with it. She'd never laid much stock on God herself, and she laid less as time went on. She wished now she'd had some book learning, it might have cleared things up for her.

When he held the door open for her she went out into the tearing wind, her head down against it . . .

But it was as Davie had said, he'd hardly put his head on the pillow before he was asleep. And Jane too. She had kept awake until he had come to bed, but after he had taken her in his arms and kissed her, her lids closed and she was away.

She didn't know what time it was later when she awoke and realised that he was no longer by her side but moving about the room. She pulled herself up in agitation, saying, 'Davie! Davie! what is it? surely it isn't time yet; I don't feel I've been asleep . . .'

'It's all right, it's all right. Lie down. Wait till I light the lamp.'

'What time is it?'

'I don't know yet, but it's early on I think. Listen to that.'

She listened, but for a moment could only hear the howling of the wind. Then, as if from a far place, there came to her ears in between the gusts of high thin neighing, the unmistakable cry of a frightened horse. 'It sounds like Benny,' she said.

'Aye, it's him all right. And I put him in a stall by himself in case he started his antrimartins. He's likely kicking hell out of his box, and he'll set the others on.'

The lamp lit, he peered at his watch. 'Quarter-past twelve,' he said, 'Oh Lord! I hoped it might be near morning. Now you stay put and go to sleep, there's nothing you can do, not tonight anyway. There'll be more than enough for you tomorrow.'

'Be careful, Davie.'

As he went towards the door there came the sound of a crash from somewhere in the house, and he stopped for a moment. Then wrenching the door open, he ran on to the landing, and there at the end where the steps led up to the old part of the house a window had blown open. When he reached it she was behind him, and as he forced it closed he shouted at her, 'Now look! it's all right. Get back into bed.'

'The glass is broken, mind your hands!' she was shouting back at him.

'Well, we can do nothing about it now, we'll see to it tomorrow. Now get back into bed, I won't be long.' He pushed her across the landing and into the bedroom, then closed the door on her. And at the head of the stairs he paused a moment

261

and turned up the lamp that had been glimmering low, then ran down the stairs and out into the night . . .

Amos, resting on his elbows, strained his ears to distinguish the sounds not caused by the wind, and he knew when Davie had reached the bottom of the stairs.

Patience was a virtue. Old Hedley used to quote that ceaselessly to him. 'Patience is a virtue, my boy.' He had been patient for months, knowing that sometime, somehow, a solution would present itself to him. If she had relented and come and had a word with him, perhaps he might have seen things differently. Yet no; he knew that he would never have looked upon this situation differently. The only solution to the situation was to give it an end, a final end.

They had been waiting for his end, and not patiently. His clinging to life was disturbing them. He could see it in Armstrong's face; he even detected it behind Molly's sympathetic attitude towards him. Well, now they would get their wish, he'd bring it to a head. But he'd want company on the journey, he wasn't going alone. No, by Christ! he wasn't going alone. 'Go back to bed!' he had cried at her. 'Go back to bed!'

There was a great rattling above his head and he looked upwards, the slates were rolling off the attic roof. The wind would be rushing in, the cleansing wind; the wind from the hills would be sweeping his prison. Although he had lain there for months past in the room in which he had been born, his mind had been back in the attic reliving the experience of his childhood again. But soon the attic would be cleansed of thoughts and memories and he would be free. Putting out his arm, he leant over the side of the bed and when his fingers touched the floor he heaved with his shoulders and his useless body slid with a heavy plomp on to the carpet. He rested for a moment, as he discovered he was weaker than he thought; then raising himself on his elbow, he stretched out one hand and gently tipped towards the bed the side table on which the lamp was standing. It was a second before the flames burst upwards, and then the feather mattress and the pillows crackled into a furious blaze.

He didn't stop to see the progress, but, clutching at the carpet, he drew himself hand over hand towards the door, and it was a simple thing to reach up and turn the knob. Once out on the landing, he pulled himself towards the short flight of stairs. Here he found difficulty in descending for he had to try to prevent his useless stunted limbs from slewing sidewards and bringing him rolling to the main landing.

There was a wind blowing along the landing from the broken window, and it covered the sounds of his gasping breath. Instinct led him, not to the room that had previously been Jane's, but to the one that his father had occupied; and he knew his instinct had led him aright when he saw the thin stream of light coming from under the door. Softly now he reached up and turned the handle, and softly he pressed the door open. If the movement of the door made any sound it too was obliterated by the noise of the storm. He looked upwards towards the bed. It appeared a long way from the door. He could not see whether she was asleep or awake because of the draperies; in any case she was apparently not aware that the door had opened.

Slowly he drew himself over the carpet to the side of the bed, where stood the table with the lamp on it; and then he saw her. She was lying well up on her pillows as if she was patiently waiting. His two hands gently clutched the side of the bed and with an effort he pulled himself upwards until his head came just above the mattress, and there he held himself still while he looked at her.

He had no intention of speaking before he had done what had to be done, but his concentrated gaze must have penetrated her light dozing, for her eyes sprang wide as if she had received a shock or heard a loud noise. And then she was gaping at him. Every muscle of her face stretching, she tried to speak, but only her lips moved. When a strangled gasp came from her throat, her hands went instinctively to it as if to stop herself choking.

'Hello, Jan.'

Her terror increased.

'It's a long time since we've seen each other. You've changed, Jan.' His gaze moved down to her hands which were now gripping the bedclothes above her stomach, then back to her face again, and he asked, 'Why wouldn't you come and see me? Was it because you were afraid of him? You were always afraid of someone or something, weren't you, Jan?'

As he waited for her to speak, his hands began to lose their grip on the mattress, which he took as a sign that his strength was going. He knew he must get her into his arms before he

263

overturned the lamp. Once there, he'd have sufficient strength to hold her until the end.

It was the combination of the look on his face, his clutching hands, and a sudden awareness of a smell of burning permeating from the landing, that triggered off the scream that had been whirling upwards through her since she opened her eyes and saw his head like a disembodied thing sticking to the mattress. It spiralled out of her as she sprang to the other side of the bed in a frantic effort to get out. At the same moment he tipped the lamp, as he had done the other, but more sharply on to the bed. And then he was scrambling round the foot towards where she had just risen from her knees. Within a split second she was on the floor again, her body hitting it with a sickening thud as he brought her down by clutching her legs, and although she fought him it was in a dazed way, without much effort . . .

It was as Davie battered on Will Curran's door, shouting, 'Will! open up! I want a hand. The stable roof's caved in, they're pinned, two of them. Will! do you hear me? Wi – ll!' It was at this point that he turned his head in the direction of the house. The wind was blowing full on him and it brought to him a strong smell of burning. He lifted the lantern high and swung it, but could see nothing, the house was too far away. 'Will! Will!' he bawled now. 'Come on, man! Come on!' But he was running back down the road as he shouted.

When he reached the yard he saw the flames leaping red through the bedroom window to the side of the house, Amos's room, and he thought he was imagining things when, looking along the front towards the window of his own room, there was a reflection of the flames. He raced to the front door, through the hall and up the stairs, and although when he pushed the door wide, he couldn't credit what he was seeing, he knew that he had feared and expected something like this for months past.

'Jane! Jane!' He screamed her name as his arms wafted wildly at the smoke. The whole bed was alight, not only the mattress and the draperies, but also the posts which, being old and brittle dry, were burning like oiled paper.

'Da – vie! Da – vie!' It was more like a moan than his name but he rushed to the far side of the bed, and there through the smoke and flames he saw them. They were lying locked together near the wall.

Falling on to his hands and knees he tore at them both in an effort to separate them, but Amos's fist lashed out at him while with his other arm he clung on to Jane.

He was choking with the smoke, they were all choking with the smoke and he knew for a certainty that they would all die joined together here in the next few minutes. When his groping hand found Amos's windpipe he pressed hard, relaxing his hold only when he felt the body sagging. But when he grasped Jane's shoulders intending to drag her from the room he was again brought to the floor by Amos's last effort.

As he measured his length almost on top of Jane a madness seized him, and, coughing and spluttering, he hurtled himself upwards, then kicked out at the demoniacal face lit now by the flames not only from the bed but also from Amos's nightshirt.

As the body fell backwards he swung round and, again grabbing Jane, he dragged her limp body out of the door and well on to the landing, and there, coughing as if his lungs would burst, he beat at the bottom of her burning nightdress with his hands.

'Oh my God!' He wasn't aware of Molly's presence until she shouted, 'Is she all right? Is she all right? The whole place is afire . . . both ends. Oh my God! My God! Come on, get out of it.' She, too, began to cough and choke now with the smoke.

Unable to speak, he gesticulated wildly towards Jane's legs and between them they carried her down the stairs. As they were crossing the hall Will Curran burst in from the kitchen, but stopped at the corner of the passage for a moment and gaped at them before crying, 'The old part, Davie, the old part's alight. It's alight!'

Davie made no answer to this; instead, still coughing, he said between gasps, 'Give's a hand . . . with her, to . . . to the cottage.'

As Will Curran took Jane's legs he shouted, 'She'd be better on the trundler.' And at this Molly ran along the front of the house and into the yard and, picking up the shafts of the wooden-wheeled hand-cart, she dashed with it back to the house and held it while they laid Jane on it.

As Davie began to push the cart away, Will called to him, 'What's to be done?' and Davie shouted back, 'See to the horses first. There's one pinned under a beam. The roof's caved in. Give him a hand, Molly.'

'What about this?' she screamed and waved her hand back at

the house as she ran by his side. 'We should get some of the things out; it'll be like a bonfire in no time,' and he yelled back at her, 'See to the animals first, then do what you can. I'll be back as soon as she comes round . . . If she comes round.' The last he added to himself as he ran the cart towards the gate. Before he went through it Molly was by his side again, shouting, 'Go into my place, your beds will be damp, sodden.'

He nodded, then guided the barrow through the gate and on to the road, and then he began to run.

Perhaps it was the jogging of the cart or the pain of the burn on her leg that brought Jane back to consciousness, for she put out her hand and groped at the air.

When he faintly discerned her moving hand he stopped the cart and, peering down at her through the darkness, he said, 'It's all right, it's all right. Don't worry, you're all right. Just lie still until we get to the cottage.'

When he reached Molly's door he pushed it wide; then returning to the cart, he put his arms under Jane and carried her bodily inside.

It was strange but he had never been in this cottage since he was a young lad; he had no memory of what it was like, except that it was muddled and not over clean; not like his own home, which was spanking.

There was no light, but a dull glow from the fire showed up a wooden settle with a high back standing at right angles to the fireplace, and on this he laid her, saying softly as he did so, 'Are you all right, Jane? Are you all right?'

'Yes, Davie, I'm all right.'

'Are you burnt? Let me look.'

'No, no.' She put her hand on her knee. 'I'm all right. It's . . . it's only shock. Go back; please go back and . . . and try to put it out.'

'I couldn't, I couldn't put that out, Jane; it's at both ends.'

'Try . . . try to save something from the bottom floor, the small pieces, the silver. Go on, Davie, please, please try to save something otherwise – ' she stopped and shook her head.

'You'll be all right then?'

'Yes, I'll be all right. I'll . . . I'll lie quiet.'

'Promise?'

'I promise.'

He looked around the room. There were two of Molly's coats hanging on the back of the door. These he brought, and put them over her; then touched her tousled hair for a moment before hurrying out.

Once on the road, he raced along it. The whole place was illuminated now with the flames. The glass in the window of the side room had burst and the crackling of the fire and the raging of the wind appeared to him like hell gone mad. Smoke was pouring out of the front door in billowing waves and the deep red glow from his bedroom window showed the furnace within. If there had been any thought in his mind of going up there and trying to drag that one free, now that his rage had subsided somewhat he dismissed it; but perhaps there was still time to save the furniture from the bottom floors.

He dashed along the yard and towards the stables, and there saw Molly and Will struggling to lift the beams that were shutting in the two terrified horses. He noted instantly and with relief that the animals, although very frightened, were both unharmed. Stooping down and getting in between Molly and Will he put his shoulder to the beam, but immediately it began to move he saw the danger. The end of it was supporting another beam which was balancing precariously within a few feet of yet another one, and were that to slip it would break the animals' backs.

'Hold your hand! Hold your hand a minute!' He took his support from the beam, crying, 'Keep her steady till I get that down.' He pointed upwards; then climbing on to the partition between the boxes, he leant against the wall for support and, putting up both arms, he took the weight of the beam and slowly eased it sideways and down towards the floor. He did the same with the second beam. When he jumped to the ground again he put his shoulder to the main beam and between them they eased it from where it was jammed across the front of the box.

The animals freed, they now had their work cut out to hang on to them, and when they led them into the yard the smell of the fire so increased their fear that it was almost impossible to hold them.

Once they were in the field Davie yelled, 'They'll be all right, let them go.' Then shouting, 'Come on!' he turned and raced back to the yard. But at the entrance he stopped. Whatever hope he'd had of saving anything was gone. Although the flames hadn't reached the bottom floor the smoke was finding every outlet.

When Will Curran said, 'We'd never be able to get in there, we'd choke to death,' he made no response.

'Perhaps the kitchen, pans and things.' Molly looked at him and he at her. His eyes were red-rimmed and running water, his face looked grey like that of an old man. Like someone coming out of a dream, he repeated, 'Pans and things.' Then on a high note he cried, 'My God! where's me wits. The money, all there is! It's in the office desk.'

'Well it'll have to stay there 'cos you'll never get beyond the passage.'

'I've got to take that chance, it's all we've got.' He was running towards the house, she hanging on to him, crying, 'Don't be mad. Davie! Davie! Oh my God! Don't do it.' She had one arm around his neck, and he paused, but just for a second and looked at her; then thrust her aside, saying, 'Don't be so damned stupid, woman.'

The kitchen being separated from the hall by a passage was not yet impenetrable, but when he opened the door into the passage the smoke came billowing into the kitchen. Molly put her hands over her mouth, then closed the door and stood with her back to it.

Minutes passed, then she saw Will Curran through the smoke. He was shouting, 'The wind's changed. A spark could catch the byres. We'd better start pumping . . . Where's he? He's not gone in there! There's no chance Master Amos's still alive. Anyway, I'd let the young devil go – better that way.'

Molly turned from him now and with a frantic movement pulled open the door and, her head down, she ran into the passage.

It was at the bottom of the stairs that she felt him. He was crawling on his hands and knees, and after the shock of her touch he pulled her down with him and almost dragged her back along the passage. When they got into the kitchen he stumbled to his feet, still holding her, and coughing and choking they rolled like two drunks out into the yard. And there he thrust her from him saying in between gasps, 'Bloody – silly – thing to do. More – bother – than you're worth. Could . . . could have missed you. What then?'

She was standing up now drawing great draughts of air down into her breast, and after a moment she shouted back at him, ' 'Twas a bloody silly thing for you to do, wasn't it? Clever

268

bugger, as always, you are. Always playing God Almighty. Always have, always will.'

He passed his hands over his streaming eyes, then peered at her, and suddenly his body seeming to go limp, his head bowed and he muttered, 'I'm sorry. I'm sorry.'

She did not speak for a moment, and when she did her voice too was quiet. 'Did you get it?' she asked.

He nodded once and tapped his pocket, then said, 'Where's Will?'

'Pumping. The wind's changed. Look.' She pointed. 'It could take the dairy an' the cow sheds.'

'My God! My God!' He was running again, and she by his side. And it was there she stayed until well on into the night, carrying bucket after bucket, after bucket of water while their world grew into a great red waving mass of flame.

Towards dawn the house roof fell in and they stood, bodies slumped and weary, looking at it, and Molly said quietly, 'Well, that's put the lid on his coffin.'

Four

The house smouldered for a week until there was nothing left but the blackened window-gaping stone walls and pieces of charred wood.

The Justice of the Peace together with an official of the Police Force came from Hexham ... a man had been burned to death, how had it happened? A lamp had been blown over in the storm and the wind had caught it – they had all agreed that this was how it should be told ... Will Curran knew no other but that it was so.

A gentleman, sombrely dressed in a high stiff collar and a three-quarter-length coat, came from the bank in Newcastle. He had a clerk with him, and they arrived in a hansom cab. The gentleman talked to Jane of the mortgage and reparation through insurance, reparation to the bank, but not to her. It appeared that her brother had been warned several times that if he did not meet his commitments on the mortgage the bank would be forced to foreclose. Had she been aware of this matter?

269

No, she had not been aware of this matter. Nor had she found any letters from the bank concerning it.

He said he was very sorry and he would do the best he could for her. He hoped when the matter was settled there would be no need for them to distrain on the cattle and land.

The third dignitary who visited them was Sir Alfred Tuppin's younger son, and he began by asking Molly if he could see Miss McBain. He was standing at the cottage door, and it was Davie who answered him. Coming from the scullery, he crossed the room quickly, saying, 'There's no Miss McBain here; if you wish to see Mrs Armstrong you can come in.'

The young man had stared insolently at Davie for a moment before looking beyond him and Molly to where Jane sat on the settle near the fire. And he had gone towards her, saying, 'My father wishes to know if you're in need of anything.'

When she replied, it was like an actress on the stage saying her lines.

'Thank your father for me. Tell him I'm obliged to him, but I have everything I need.'

He had become nonplussed for a moment; then with a slight smile he had bowed slightly towards her, saying, 'I shall give him your message. He'll be glad to know that you're well provided for. Good-day to you.'

Jane did not answer him, but when he walked out she bowed her head and bit tightly on her lip. Davie had gone over to the fire, and with his jaws clenched he had stood gazing into it. Molly, after looking from one to the other, went into the scullery and left them alone.

The days that followed were days of grinding labour from morning till night, at least for Davie and Molly. Jane could do very little. Apart from her time drawing near, she had a burn on her leg which refused to heal and caused her intense pain at times, and she was forced to rest more than she would have done under ordinary circumstances.

Although Will Curran did his best, and with a good heart, ten hours' work was as much as he could achieve, and then, during the second half of the day, he slowed up considerably.

Davie sawed up the tree that had fallen near the cottage and kept the fire going day and night to air his old home. Molly scrubbed it down from top to bottom and washed the bedding, and for the last two weeks they had been installed there.

Davie was back where he had started.

The first night he lay with Jane by his side in the bed that his parents had shared for years, in the bed in which he himself had been conceived and born, he had thought: everything goes full circle. He had worked like two men all his life, and what had he to show for it? Well, he had Jane and the child that was coming, and he had a piece of land and a few cattle. But hold your hand! Don't count your chickens, he had warned himself, these last weren't sure. He was waiting to hear about them; he wouldn't be surprised if the next thing they would say would be that they were going to take the land. He'd be surprised at nothing any more.

Three weeks before her time, Jane started her pains. She had felt ill for days, but she put that down to her leg. There was a hole in it now. When the bandages were taken off the matter poured out. Doctor Cargill said she must keep it well covered up, but it was so painful she could hardly bear the linen strips near the flesh. Molly had put goose grease on to prevent the cloth sticking, but that hadn't helped.

She was woken from her sleep by a searing pain circling her middle. When she clutched at Davie he roused himself, saying, 'What is it? What is it?'

'I've got a pain.'

'Pain? But . . . but it's not due . . .'

'I know, I know, but . . . but it's a definite pain.'

'I'll . . . I'll get Molly.'

'No, no, it may be nothing, it might go away. Perhaps it's just a cramp . . . flatulence.' She never said wind.

The pain hadn't gone away by dawn, but increased, and he went into his old bedroom and knocked sharply on the wall, and a few minutes later Molly came running in, fastening on her clothes as she did so. Her teeth were chattering with the cold as she asked, 'Wh – at is it? What's up?'

He was standing at the top of the narrow stairs as he said softly, 'She's started her pains.'

'But it's not . . .'

'I know, I know. But it's them all right.'

'Not a fluke?'

'No; I should say not. I'm going to ride in for the doctor.'

'But she might be hours, a day or so.'

'I doubt not; not the way they're comin'.' And he promised

271

her he'd be here at the time, with her leg the way it is and the state she's in with one thing and another.'

As she passed him she said, 'He won't thank you for goin' at this hour.'

'I can't help that. Anyway, it'll be on light when I get there.'

She passed him and went into the room and bent over Jane, and they stared at each other both wide-eyed.

'You think it's them?'

'Yes, Molly.'

'Now don't you worry, everything will be all right. Davie's goin' for the doctor. He's good is Doctor Cargill with bairns. Not that I can't bring it meself, I've had nearly as much experience as him.' She smiled, but received no answering smile from Jane.

'I'm worried, Molly.'

'What've you got to be worried about? First 'un's always come days afore or days after. Me ma always said our Lena was so long in coming she thought she was goin' to go the full eighteen months an' have twins.' Her smile was wide now and she laughed. And Jane laughed with her, a short weary laugh. But the next minute she was hanging on to Molly while she gritted her teeth and the sweat ran down her face.

When it was over Molly drew in a deep breath and said, 'You made no mistake, it's them all right, short and sharp. Lie still now, I won't be a minute.'

When she reached the kitchen Davie was brewing tea and she said abruptly, 'You'd better leave that and get a move on if you want him to be here when it comes.'

'Eh!' He dropped the teapot on the table. 'As near as that you think?'

'Nearer. I wouldn't take the trap, I'd just ride Benny, he's fresh, you could be there in less than an hour.'

Before she finished speaking he had grabbed up his coat from the door; but as he went to go out he looked towards the stairs. But she said abruptly, 'There's no time for that,' and he turned and faced her for a moment, his face red and angry looking. Then he went out; but the next minute she was calling to him as she ran after him, 'Look here, put these gloves on, the reins will sear your hands. They're bad enough as it is.'

He grabbed the gloves from her without thanks, and she stood for a second in the dark listening to his feet pounding the road as he ran towards the stables.

An hour and a half later the child was born and Molly delivered it and cried joyfully as she saw the perfectly shaped feet slip out of the womb. 'God in Heaven! I've never seen anything so quick in me life. Well! Well! would you believe it. Aw, lass, lass.'

'Molly.' Jane's voice was a faint whisper.

'Aye, lass. Aye, Miss Jane.'

'Is . . . is it all right?'

'All right? Why, it's perfect. A little lass and it's perfect. Hair on its head an' all. Now lie still, lie still, don't move, I've got me work cut out. An' listen 'er, just listen 'er, she's lettin' you know she's here.'

She severed the cord and knotted it before wrapping the child in a warm sheet; then she attended to Jane, saying, 'Lie still, lie still, the afterbirth will be comin' away any time now. There, let's wipe your face. By! you look bonny. Aye you do, white but bonny.'

'Oh, Molly! Molly!' Slow tears ran down Jane's face. 'Oh, Molly! Molly!'

'There now! There now! Don't start me on else I'll flood us out.'

'Molly.'

'Aye, Miss Jane.'

'I . . . I don't know what I would have done without you, ever. Thank you, Molly.'

Tears gushing from her eyes, Molly turned away abruptly, saying, 'I told you, didn't I? I told you, an' as soon as he comes in the house he'll go for me. Bubbling your eyes out, he'll say, and upsettin' her. That's what he'll say, he always blames me. Aw!' Her tone changed as she bent over the white bundle. 'Aw! but she's lovely.' She lifted it up and carried it to the bed, saying between sniffs, 'Look. Look at her. Now just take her in your arms a minute, just a minute, 'cos I've got to get her cleaned up, she's in a mess.'

It was at this point that the door opened and Davie came in, and he stood stock still for a moment looking in amazement towards the two women and the child. Then he moved swiftly to the bed, and Molly stepped aside and went out of the room.

Slowly now he dropped on to his knees and stared at the little wrinkled face peering out from the white sheet. Then looking at her he murmured, 'Jane . . . Jane,' and he kissed her gently and stroked her face while she gazed up at him, unable to speak.

Slowly now he undid the wrapping round the child and looked down on its perfect limbs.

'A girl,' he said softly.

'You don't mind?'

'Mind? I wouldn't mind if it was a heifer.'

'Oh! Davie.' Her face crumpled into a broken smile. 'Don't. You're as bad as Molly. I . . . I don't want to laugh, I feel so tired.'

'Aw, my dear.' As he took the child and laid it on the bottom of the bed there was a bustle outside the door as Molly announced her entry, and she came in, saying, 'I'd better have it afore it needs a pick and shovel to get it clean.'

He looked at her as she picked up the baby and bustled out again. He wanted to say, 'Thanks Molly, thanks.' And he would, later. He knelt again by the side of the bed and stroked the wet hair back from Jane's forehead. 'Go to sleep,' he said. 'Go to sleep, my dear, my very dear.'

'Yes, Davie, I'll go to sleep, I'm very tired, so tired. But the afterbirth hasn't come yet.'

'Don't worry about that, it'll come in its own good time, and Doctor Cargill will be here shortly. By! he'll get a gliff just like I did.'

He watched her eyes close and her breathing get deeper. Then slowly she half opened her lids again and said in a thin, thin whisper, as if her thoughts were escaping in spite of herself, 'You have never said you loved me, Davie, do you know that, not once. You have never said you love me.'

The muscles of his face dropped as he stared down at her. Had he never said he loved her? But hadn't he proved it in a hundred and one ways? Yet had he never said he loved her? No, he hadn't, he hadn't said it in so many words . . . Oh Jane! Jane! He went to put his lips on hers, but realised she was fast asleep, and slowly he rose from his knees and stood looking at her.

He wasn't given to soft words but he must try to put this thing into words to please her, for she herself put it into words every day. Women were queer cattle; all of them were queer cattle.

The afterbirth didn't come away. When Doctor Cargill arrived at nine o'clock that morning it showed no sign of coming. Two hours later when he left it still hadn't come, and Davie returned

274

to Hexham with him to collect some medicine that would help it on its way.

By evening Jane was in a high fever and Davie sat by her side wiping her brow with a cold cloth.

At six o'clock Will Curran took the trap into Hexham, and at half-past eight Doctor Cargill was again in the house, and everything was bustle. Sprinkling chloroform on a pad of cotton wool he held it above her face for a moment as he said, 'Just breathe deeply and when you wake up everything will be all right.'

But when she woke up everything wasn't all right, for she was bleeding heavily. She held tightly on to Davie's hands while she retched against the sickly sweet smell of the chloroform and Molly, under the direction of the doctor, wrung out cold cloths from a bucket of well water and placed them on her stomach in an effort to stop the flow of blood.

Just before midnight before losing consciousness she whispered, 'Davie! Davie!' and, his face close to hers, he said, 'Yes, my dear; yes, my dear.' And her last words to him were, 'Name her Delia. My mother would have liked that . . . '

She died as the dawn was breaking, and he could not believe it, he would not believe it. He held her to him and rocked her and moaned, 'No! No! Jane. No! No!' and the doctor, worn out with his efforts, and Molly near to collapse, left them alone.

After a time he laid her back on the bed. Her face was white and smooth and beautiful; the beauty that had always just evaded her, except on her wedding day, had been permanently released by death.

Feathers in the fire. That's what his granda had said they all were, nothing but feathers in the fire. But why did the burning of a feather leave so much pain in the beholder?

Five

The summer had gone. It was October again and the winter loomed ahead. The child was six months old. It was a fat, bouncing, gurgling baby; strangely it had not suffered a day's illness since its premature birth. It laughed a great deal, and only cried when it was hungry; and when it was hungry it wouldn't be put off with a dum-tit.

Molly cared for the child. She washed, dressed and fed it, carried it in a wash basket and laid it in the yard outside the dairy whenever it was fine; when it wasn't she left it in the dairy. She never left it alone in either of the cottages, for fires were burning there night and day, and now she had a horror of fire.

She missed Jane as she would have a dearly beloved sister, yet at the same time she felt relieved at her going, but suffered for this failing with self-recrimination.

She had given him three months to get over the worst of his grief, but when the three months had passed, during which it had been difficult to get a word out of him, and he still showed no interest in her, and at times appeared barely civil, she experienced a new despair, a final despair, for if working along-side him from morning till night like a galley slave, if tending his child as if it were her own, and it could have been, judged on the feelings she bore towards it, if cooking for him and keep-ing his house clean could not draw from him a kind word, let alone a glance from his eyes that told her she was still a woman, then nothing could.

Her past, she felt, was as alive for him today as when it had happened all those years ago, a long lifetime ago. He had been a stubborn, block-headed youth then, and was now grown into a hard, unforgiving man.

She had made allowances when, following the fire and Jane's death, she would watch him at odd times, mostly in the late evening looking at the great shell of the house. She had only realised of late that Davie Armstrong had been an ambitious man, and the knowledge had created the thought that this could have been the reason why he had married Miss Jane; but she had dismissed it. She wouldn't give him the bad credit for being

276

so mean. But nevertheless he'd had a feeling for the house and the land more than was usual in a worker.

Then to cap it all, today she'd had a shock, and it had released a frightening prospect. They'd had a visitor. Into the yard, around three o'clock, had ridden Miss Agnes Reed. She had said she was thirsty and could she have a glass of milk, and while she drank it she had sat looking at the blackened house; then she had said, 'Mr Armstrong . . . is he about?'

'In the fields.' Her answer had been short and sharp. She had watched her ride down the road and through the gap in the stone wall.

The Reed girl had never shown her face at the farm after the master had died; what was she after now? Need she ask? She knew what she was after. She had a name, that one, a clothes prop with trousers on would do her, as long as it acted like a man. But Davie was no prop with trousers on, he was well set up, attractive, handsome; although his face was grim, he was still a handsome man, and what was more he had sense. But did any man have sense when a woman threw herself at him, and from the height of Agnes Reed's station? It was enough to turn any man's head.

Fifteen minutes later when she returned to the gate and saw him walking up the field by the side of the horse and rider all she could say to herself was, 'My God!'

Davie, too, said the same words, but to himself as he looked up into the smiling face of Miss Reed. But he added, 'What they'll stoop to!' And that Miss Reed was stooping he had no doubt. It wasn't the first time he had seen her since Jane had died; he had encountered her a number of times in Hexham, and although she hadn't acknowledged him with a movement of her head, her eyes had remained fixed on him much longer that was seeming in a woman of her standing. But what standing? From what he could gather she was nothing but an upper class unregistered whore.

'It seems strange,' she was saying as she looked down into his eyes, 'but if things had taken their course I would have been mistress of that dead pile. However, the course took a turn, and now you are master of it.'

'That's so.' He jerked his head, his face unsmiling.

'What do you intend to do with it? It's an eyesore as it stands.'

'Yes, you could say it's an eyesore, but . . . but I have me plans for it.'

'Really! I'm pleased to hear that. You must tell me of them sometime.'

He made no answer to this, just stared back into her pale grey eyes, eyes that strangely reminded him of McBain's. They had reached the gap in the wall, and he stood aside and said, 'Good-day to you,' and after a pause she said, 'And good-day to you, Mr Armstrong.' Then digging her heels sharply into the horse's flanks she cantered off, while he stood looking not after her, but down on to the top of the wall. The end sandstone brick had been worn smooth with the hands that had grasped it over the years as they went in and out of the field, and now he grasped it tight as he thought, slut! And the nerve of her, thinking he would jump on to her hook. Clients must be getting scarce in her quarter.

He was filled with a sudden wave of indignation as if he had just suffered an insult. He watched his fingers moving backwards and forwards rubbing the stone, and there returned to him her words, 'If things had taken their course I would have been mistress of that dead pile. However, the course took a turn and now you are master of it. What do you intend to do with it?'

What did he intend to do with it? He had thought once or twice lately that he would gradually knock it down and with the stone build a wall on the north boundary that would show old Tuppin he wasn't coming any further.

When it had become known that the land, and what was left on it, was legally his, Sir Alfred's solicitor had written him a letter offering to buy the place and had stated a sum he wouldn't have taken for the cow sheds. In his best writing, and his best manner, he had written back and said he had no intention of selling the farm now or at any time in the future. He had heard nothing since.

He was well aware that everybody was giving him the cold shoulder; he was out of favour in both camps, that of his own kind and that of those in power. He had been condemned by the former because he had gone to Jane's funeral in his wedding suit; true he had a black band on his arm but who had ever heard of a man going to his wife's funeral in a light grey suit? Jane had loved him in that suit, she had been proud of him

278

when he wore it. And he hadn't cared a damn what anyone thought.

And he had worn it again when he had been summoned to the bank in Newcastle, and there he had met the manager's condescension with arrogance, and had the last word in the interview, saying, 'I am not thanking you for letting me keep what I consider me own through me wife.'

No; no one had come to his aid, for he was, on all sides, considered an upstart, and they had left him alone. Except for the visitor today. He turned now and looked along the road; then gave a short mirthless laugh before walking briskly back to the farm.

Crossing the yard, he approached the house. He had never been in it from the day they had unearthed from among the charred beams what remained of Amos. Now he went through what had been the front door and, his feet crunching into the burnt wood, he stood where the stairs had been and looked upwards and into the high clear blue sky.

He remained standing in the hall for almost ten minutes, ten minutes idling, doing nothing, but think.

When he came out Molly was passing down the middle of the yard with the basket on her hip, the child in it, and he called to her, 'Molly!' When she didn't stop, just turned her head towards him, saying, 'I'm goin' to make the meal,' he looked after her puzzled for a moment. She seemed upset about something.

He hurried after her, shouting, 'Molly! Here, wait a moment.' When he caught up with her, she said, 'What is it? What do you want?'

'What do you mean, what do I want?' He stared into her face. She was in a temper. She had shown him nothing but kindness and consideration for months past; he felt he would have gone mad without her; but now she was fuming. 'Is something wrong?' he asked.

'Now what could be wrong? I ask you, what could be wrong?'

'All right.' He nodded at her. 'As you say, what could be wrong. You'll tell me in your own time I suppose, but ... but listen, I've got an idea.' He pointed back towards the house. 'I'm going to rebuild it.'

'What!' She jerked the basket on her hip and the child gurgled.

'Aye, I was for pullin' it down, but I'm goin' to rebuild it.

279

Not the old part, that'll go. It's had its day anyway. Look, give her to me. Here.' He grabbed the basket from her. 'Come on, I'll show you.'

She did not now walk by his side but remained a couple of paces behind him. In front of the house he placed the basket on the ground, then pointed to the front door, saying, 'I'm going to clear it all out. That's the first thing, clear it all out. Then brush the stone. The stone's all right except for a crack here and there, and that's easily remedied. Then I'll lay the floors, an' fix in the beams.'

Her voice came at him, derisive, saying, 'It'll take a lifetime. An' where are you goin' to get the wood, beams an' all that?'

He turned to her. 'Five years. I could have it up in five years. As for the wood, I'll buy a bit at a time for the floors. The beams, why' – he pointed out towards the road – 'there's all those trees in the copse. That's the first thing I'll do after clearing it out, get them down so they can be seasoned. I'm going to build, Molly.' His shoulders were bent, his head thrust towards her. 'The old house meant something to me, but it'll be nothing to the one I'll build. That'll be mine. Are you with me? Will you help me?'

She stared at him while the muscles of her face sagged. 'Help you?' she said.

'Aye, help me.'

'Well' – her shoulders jerked – 'you pay me, don't you, so I don't suppose it matters which way I earn me money?'

He stared hard at her for a moment. Then his gaze dropped away from hers, and he stooped and picked up the basket and, holding it out to her, said, 'I'll manage, I want no forced labour.'

Her mouth was tight as she turned away.

It was pitch dark and he hadn't come in. She looked at the child sleeping peacefully in the basket by the side of the fire. Will Curran had been finished this past hour.

The usual procedure that ended her day was that she cooked the meal in her own oven and between times washed the child and got her ready for the night; then when she heard Davie come in she gave him time to get his wash before taking both the meal and the child next door.

They had eaten together for months past now, but they were cheerless meals. Sometimes he didn't bother to speak. When he did it was on some aspect of the work. He always took the child upstairs with him at night.

When another half hour passed and there was still no sound of him, she pulled the basket well away from the fire; then, putting a coat around her, she ran out and down the road and into the farmyard.

The gleam of the lantern showed him bringing an armful of charred wood into the yard and placing it on the barrow. She called to him from the distance, 'Are you going to stay out all night?'

'Just comin',' he answered back.

'The meal's spoilin'.'

She was walking towards him as she spoke, and when she was near enough to see him she exclaimed, 'My God! you're a sight. You'd think you'd been down the pit.'

'Aye.' He knocked one hand against the other. 'I'll have to go to the burn to get this off.'

'What! the night? It's freezin'.'

'Well, I can't go inside like this, can I?'

She stared at him for a moment, then said, 'Another ten minutes; then come on home an' I'll have some hot water an' you can have a wash down in the scullery.'

'Oh, ta. Thanks.' He nodded at her, and she saw his blackened face move into a smile. It was the first time she had seen him smile since the child was born.

She turned away and hurried out of the yard and up the road. In the cottage she ground a kettle full of water on the fire, then went next door and put a full kettle on his fire. Taking a zinc bath from the nail on the outside wall, she placed it just inside the scullery door and scooped rain water into it from a barrel in the yard. Following this she took the kettle from her own cottage and stood it on the hob against the other one; then she went back and waited . . .

It was almost three-quarters of an hour later when he knocked on the wall, and at this she lifted the basket and took the sleeping child in to him, then returned and took the meat pie from the oven.

When she set the pie on the table he was standing with his back to the fire, and he looked down on it and said, 'By, I'm ready for that. That wash was a god-send, I feel I could start all over again, night shift. I'm going to get up an hour earlier in the mornings an' do two hours extra every night. That's the least I'll do because in the winter there won't be so much goin' outside, and there'll be time enough to spare. I'd like to bet if I stick at it I'll have the kitchen and hall roofed by spring. What do you say to that?'

She had just put three-quarters of the pie on to his plate and she only prevented herself from banging it on the table and saying, 'What do I say? I'd say you've found your tongue all of a sudden. Strange what a visitor will do for you.' But what she said was, 'It'll take you to be going.'

'I'll go all right.' He pulled a chair up to the table and sat down. 'And right from rock bottom, starting practically from scratch. An' what I make from now on will be me own. After all, fifty acres is fifty acres. There's many a man made a small fortune on less . . . This is good.' He chewed a mouthful of pie, swallowed, and then looked at her.

She had her eyes cast down; she was eating slowly, quietly.

The urge came into him, as it had done over the past few weeks, to put out his hand and touch her. It wouldn't have been disrespect to Jane; Jane would have understood. As for anybody else's opinion he didn't care a damn. Anyway, who was around here? Only Will, so what was stopping him? The old picture of her wantonness? No, no; that had faded into the past, years ago. No; he knew what was stopping him; and until he faced up to it and admitted it to himself he would never be able to make a move towards her.

For years he had denied that she meant anything to him. Inside himself he had scorned her, yet all the while he had known he was hiding something, feeling that if he let it see the light he'd be less of a man, for men, real men, didn't love trollops; they used them for their needs but they didn't love them.

For years he had thought of her as a trollop, but today, when that real trollop had come on the scene she had, in some strange way, wiped Molly's slate clean; she had certainly made him face the truth that had been buried for so long, and part of that truth was that he had even used Jane to help smother the undying feeling. Yet he had cared for Jane. Oh yes, yes, he had cared for Jane. But had he loved her? For long after she died the words that were almost her last had burnt him. 'You've never said you love me, Davie.' If only by way of thanks for all she had done for him, all she had given him, he should have

282

made the effort and said those words to her without being prompted. But he never had.

'You're not eating,' he said.

'I'm not very hungry.'

'You're tired,' he said.

'Aye.' She looked at him. 'I think that's it, I'm tired.'

'I've worked you too hard; I haven't been thinking.'

She lifted her head and looked at him. The kindness, the consideration, even the tenderness in his tone was too much. For twenty years she had longed for it. She had not supplemented the want of his tenderness with another man, or men; yet it wasn't for want of the chance. Over the years she had scourged her body into submission; from where had come the strength she couldn't tell, for she knew herself to be of a loving nature, wanting to give everything, aye everything. During his long absence at sea she had asked herself what was she waiting for, was she barmy, for even when he came back he wouldn't look the side she was on. But she reckoned that it would be just her luck that if she committed some indiscretion he would turn up, and then her chance with him would be gone for ever. She had seen him looking at her with those eyes of his, and they would say, 'You trollop.'

She tried to quell the flood of emotion that was rising in her. She looked into his eyes through a haze of tears, and with the contradictoriness of human nature proving itself to her, she cried inwardly, 'It's come too late, too late. I can't stand no more, I'm finished.' On top of this thought tumbled another that brought her fighting instincts to the fore again. Was he just soft-soaping her because he had his eye on the rider this afternoon, and knowing that that piece wouldn't want to soil her hands he would still want someone to do the donkey work?

He was saying to her, 'I don't expect you to help with the house, I'll see to that meself. And you were saying that Mickey would like to come back when I get on me feet. Well, I see no reason ...'

The storm broke. Twenty years of agony of both body and mind erupted; the pain of all the nights she had lain in her bed with her hands on the wall that divided them. Even during these past months she had lain like that. If there was no wind and the night was still she could hear the creaking of his bed springs, and their movement mangled her heart.

She had reckoned on a certain time for him to recover completely from Jane's loss, six months, but a year perhaps would be more decent; she didn't mind as long as he gave her a sign. She had waited so long, what were a few more months? But then today the arrival of the horse and rider and the knowledge that he could, and would, take a wife was more than she could endure.

'What is it? What is it? Don't cry like that.' He was standing over her, his hand on her shoulder. He recognised that she had reached the end of her tether; something had happened today that had been too much. He looked back to the only difference in this day from any other, the visit from that Reed trollop . . . THAT WAS IT. She must have thought . . . God! She couldn't have thought him capable of doing that to her? He had been a bit of a swine to her over the years; more than a bit at that. He had made her pay a whole lifetime for something that could happen to any lass, that did happen to half the young lasses in her position; human nature being what it was, how could they resist the advances of the master who had power over their very livelihood, their right to eat?

There might have been an excuse for his retaliation in the early days; he was hot-headed, hurt, the power of his own manhood had received an insult. But there had been no excuse when he had come back, well, perhaps still a bit, on his first visit; but not when he had taken up the job on the farm, for he had seen then she was different. She had changed; and yet she hadn't she was still the Molly he had known, the girl who had bothered him. Yet not even the fact that she had been respected by all those who had been against her, his own family in particular, had carried any weight with him. And why? Because deep inside him he had known that she held him in the hollow of her hand, and even as a grown man he wasn't big enough to admit it.

His hand went under her oxters and he lifted her from the table and turned her towards him. Her head was hanging, her whole body was shaking with her emotion.

'Molly!'

She took no heed. She was consumed with an anguish that had to flow out of her.

'Molly! look at me. Give over.' He became concerned and shook her by the shoulders, saying sternly now, 'Come on, come on. Enough is enough.' He had never seen anyone give way like this; even Jane's crying on the night Amos had first gone for her

284

had been nothing like this; and Jane with her finer calibre was the more likely to give way to hysteria . . . At this point he bludgeoned himself mentally for his thick-skulled thinking. This woman here had suffered through him as Jane had never done through Amos, for he had deprived her of bodily satisfaction for years while mentally attacking her. He knew in this moment that he wouldn't live long enough to make it up to her.

When he drew her into his arms her emotions shook his body; and now he made no effort to check it, but stroked her hair.

The fire crackled and fell in with a plomp. The lamp flickered, the child stirred in its sleep, and still they stood in the middle of the kitchen until, her sobbing easing, she lay against him spent.

Still he stood quiet, uttering no word.

When at last she raised her head from his breast and looked at him he pressed her slightly from him and, stooping and taking the bottom of her apron, a clean one, which from habit she donned before serving the meal, he passed it gently round her face; then turning her about he pressed her into a chair, saying thickly, 'Stay put.' Then swiftly he lifted up the basket and the child and took them upstairs. He was down within a minute and, standing before her, he held out his hand to her and, looking into her eyes, he said, 'Come on, Molly love.' And as Jane had once said to him, he added, 'It's been a long time.'

Through still streaming eyes she gazed up at him; then slowly she placed her hand in his and as he led her to the stairs he put out his other hand and shot the bolt home. It stuck at first for it was many a day since it had been used.

They had to go up the stairs in single file but he still held on to her hand, and each step took her from her mundane, work-weary, body-scourged life, right back to the beginning when Davie Armstrong had filled her sky from one end of the moors to the other. Yet there was no ecstatic feeling swamping her, she was numb, twenty years numb. The thawing would take time. Life was funny, crazy.

'Come on, Molly love; it's been a long time.'

THE END

285

HAMILTON
by Catherine Cookson

Maisie could never be quite sure when she met up with Hamilton; most likely, it was when she started talking to herslf as an often lonely seven-year-old. Hamilton, an imaginary horse, had to remain a secret for many years, for what would people think of Maisie if she revealed that the only friend she had was a horse who acted as her guide, philosopher and confidant? Life was difficult enough for Maisie without that, and increasingly so as she grew to womanhood and became a wife. But if she could not talk about Hamilton, she could at least write about him. And write she did, with results that would broaden her horizons far beyond her native Tyneside.

Catherine Cookson's novel is her most unusual and beguiling to date. It is a story in which she blends humour and pathos to irresistible effect.

0 552 12451 6

THE BLACK VELVET GOWN
by Catherine Cookson

There would be times when Riah Millican came to regret that her miner husband had learned to read and write, and then shared that knowledge with her and their children. For this was Durham in the 1830s, when employers tended to regard the spread of education with suspicion. But now Seth Millican was dead and she a widow with the pressing need to find a home and a living for herself and her children.

The chance of becoming a housekeeper didn't work out, but it led to Moor House and a scholarly recluse obsessed with that very book learning that could open so many doors and yet create so many problems; especially with her daughter, Biddy, who was not only bright but wilful . . .

The Black Velvet Gown is the story of a mother and a daughter, often at odds with each other, facing the need to challenge and light the prejudice of an age – a narrative of great power and diversity that is one of Catherine Cookson's major achievements.

0 552 12473 7

A DINNER OF HERBS
by Catherine Cookson

A legacy of hatred can be a terrible force in life, over which not even an enduring love and all the fruits of material success may prevail. Catherine Cookson explores this theme in a major novel that will absorb and enthrall her readers as irresistibly as any she has written.

Roddy Greenbank was brought by his father to the remote Northumberland community of Langley in the autumn of 1807. Within hours of their arrival, however, the father had met a violent death, and the boy left with all memory gone of his past life.

Adopted and raised by old Kate Makepeace, Roddy found his closest compainions in Hal Roystan and Mary Ellen Lee. These three stand at the heart of a richly eventful narrative that spans the first half of the nineteenth century, their lives lastingly intertwined by the inexorable demands of a strange and somewhat cruel destiny.

A DINNER OF HERBS is Catherine Cookson's most stunning achievement to date — a work that displays outstandingly the true storyteller's gift.

0 552 12551 2